ZEBRA BOOKS
KENSINGTON PUBLISHING CORP.

ZEBRA BOOKS

are published by

Kensington Publishing Corp.
475 Park Avenue South
New York, NY 10016

First printing: June 1986

Printed in the United States of America

This book is dedicated to two very special ladies:

My new little daughter, Caitlin Hannah Creel, who reminds me of life's miracles each and every day

My editor, Leslie Gelbman, whose assistance and encouragement are very *much appreciated.*

PROLOGUE

Wyoming Territory, 1877

Amidst a great flurry of steam and the high-pitched squeal of metal against metal, the massive black locomotive eased to a halt before the Rock Creek station. It was a typical summer day in the bustling frontier town, the late afternoon skies dotted with a profusion of clouds that settled varying shadows upon the rolling, grass-covered plains as well as the two mountains standing guard on opposite sides of the horizon. The air was warm, the slight breeze accented with an intriguing, not-too-unpleasant combination of horses, cooking, woodsmoke, and the heavy cloaking of aromatic black smoke which momentarily shrouded those waiting on the platform of the depot.

Micah Parker impatiently tugged the well-worn Stetson from his head, the breeze ruffling his graying black hair while his lips tightened into a thin line of renewed displeasure. His slate gray eyes narrowed to become mere slits as he squinted against the glare of the sun's rays in an effort to discern the faces of the passengers who made their way down the steps of the train and through the cloud of smoke. Micah's wife of thirty-five years turned to him in visible distraction once more, her own gaze wide and full of growing apprehension.

"Oh, dear, what if they didn't make it after all? What if those poor girls—"

"There's no use in borrowing trouble, Jane," Micah quietly ordained, his lined and clean-shaven features so darkened by years spent beneath the blazing Western sun that his eyes appeared almost opaque. The silver, star-shaped badge pinned to his cowhide vest glinted as the sun caught it, as if to underscore his well-deserved reputation as a tough, hard-as-nails lawman. It was this undeniable toughness that prevented him from returning the usually infectious grin flashed at him from the younger of two girls now stepping down from the train. In fact, the frown marring his face deepened into an outright scowl as his gaze swept up and down the pair of disembarking females.

"It's them! Oh, Micah, that's got to be them!" Jane Parker gasped out, her brown eyes shimmering with sudden tears as her hand tightly gripped her husband's arm. Her plump features relaxed into a smile of such genuine warmth and welcome that the youngest girl, an impish, red-haired child of seven, broke away from her sister's restraining hand and darted excitedly across the platform.

"You are our grandmother, aren't you? You look just as Papa always said you would!" She impulsively threw her slender little arms about Jane's ample waist as the pleasantly startled woman laughed and confirmed her identity.

"Elizabeth!" the other girl sternly admonished as she moved forward with an unconscious grace and self-assurance that was unusual in one so young. "You must not forget your manners," she added more softly, fixing her sister with a gently quelling look from eyes that were of an exquisite shade of pale blue. Twelve years of age, the girl possessed long, honey-blond tresses that were capped by a white, beribboned straw bonnet, and her slight form, displaying only a hint of her blossoming womanhood, was encased in a becoming, albeit dusty, concoction of rich emerald velvet and expensive French lace. Her sister was dressed in a similar fashion, both their unabashedly frilly attire of noticeable quality and expense.

"You might as well know right from the start that I don't hold with any of those damned useless furbelows such as you're wearing," Micah Parker gruffly asserted, his steely gaze narrowing again as his oldest granddaughter finally raised her eyes to his. Though the expression on her delicate, heart-shaped visage remained outwardly impassive, Micah could glimpse an answering spark within the opal depths of her eyes, a certain, unquenchable spirit shining forth. Jane, finding it difficult to speak as a lump rose in her throat, lifted Elizabeth in her arms and proclaimed a bit shakily, "I . . . I'm so glad you arrived safely, Rachel. I know the two of you must be worn to the bone with all the traveling you've done." She could feel the tears burning against her eyelids as she looked upon Ethan's daughters for the first time. They were so much a part of her already, a part of her she'd been forced to deny for twelve long years. She murmured something unintelligible and finally gathered Rachel close.

"Yes," Rachel responded simply, a tentative smile curving her lips upward as she drew away a few moments later and faced her grandmother. It took only the fraction of a second for her to decide that she liked the tall, sandy-haired woman who was so vastly different from her husband. There was a discernible kindness in Jane Parker's tear-filled gaze, an unmistakable sweetness of character which Rachel sensed would always help to make things more bearable.

"I beg your pardon, Grandmother, but I'm so very hungry!" Elizabeth piped up, then twisted about to grin down into Micah's unsmiling countenance in the next instant. "Aren't you going to kiss us, Grandfather?" Without waiting for a reply, she suddenly frowned and demanded, "What's that for?" Exhibiting her natural curiosity, she reached out to finger Micah's badge. He refused to acknowledge, even to himself, the powerful surge of emotion welling up deep within his breast.

"Come on. I've got work to do," he muttered, wasting no further time in collecting the girls' baggage and depositing it in the waiting buckboard. Jane lowered Elizabeth to her feet, but kept a maternal arm about the child's shoulders. Pausing to link her other arm through Rachel's, she ushered the sisters across the dust-caked planks of the perpetually busy depot.

"You mustn't mind your grandfather, my dear," insisted Jane, smiling affectionately down into the youthful beauty of Rachel's solemn countenance. "It's just that he . . . he hasn't quite gotten used to the notion of—"

"It's all right, Grandmother," Rachel assured her with a sad little half-smile. "I know this cannot be easy for him.

You see, our father explained a good many things to both Elizabeth and myself before he . . . before he died." There was a noticeable catch in her voice, and she was grateful for the comforting touch of her grandmother, a woman who had become familiar to her only through her late father's rare but treasured reminiscences.

"Papa said our grandfather was a stubborn, mule-headed man," Elizabeth was only too happy to elaborate, earning her a sharp reprimand from her sister.

"Elizabeth!"

"Well, he did!" the seven-year-old feelingly asserted. "And what's more," she added a bit haughtily, casting Rachel a look of childish defiance, "he said he was exactly like him!"

They had reached the buckboard by now. Micah sat staring stonily ahead, waiting with obvious impatience as his wife and granddaughters climbed up into the weathered, slightly ramshackle conveyance. Jane kept Elizabeth at her side, the child wedged rather tightly between the elder Parkers while Rachel settled her skirts about her on the hard, narrow seat behind them. She stole one last glance over her shoulder at the train, realizing that it was the last link with San Francisco and all she had known there. By the time Micah snapped the reins together above the horses' backs, however, his oldest granddaughter sat rigidly erect, her opal gaze fixed resolutely upon the town just ahead.

Almost unwittingly, her eyes were drawn in growing fascination to the curious collection of wooden buildings lining the wide main street. Situated in the middle of a virtual sea of grass, the town was a far cry from any she had ever seen. But, Rachel reminded herself with an inward sigh, she had never been outside of San Francisco before, had never been forced to leave the security of her fine home on Nob Hill for a new life with people who were little more than strangers to her. Everything was so vastly different . . . and more than a trifle frightening.

Micah and Jane were hailed by several of the townspeople as the buckboard rolled past, and Rachel stared curiously at the men in their boots and hats, the women in their simple dresses of homespun and calico and their matching sunbonnets. It seemed that there were horses everywhere, and she was startled to see a herd of cattle being driven boldly down the street in their direction. There was a profusion of noise and motion as folks went about their business in the small but prosperous shipping terminal with its crowded stockyards, saloons, hotels, and a wide array of other establishments. Rachel's head swam with the impact of it all, and she leaned forward a bit to see that Elizabeth was equally enthralled.

It wasn't long before they reached the single-story frame house on the outskirts of town. The neat, whitewashed building had been home to Jane and Micah for more than five years, and it was with an unconscious note of pride in her voice that Jane announced, "Rachel, Elizabeth, this is your new home."

"It is?" Elizabeth responded in disbelief, scampering down from the buckboard after both of her grandparents had alighted. Her wide brown eyes made a quick sweep of the clapboard house and outlying grounds, and she turned to her sister to remark in an embarrassingly audible whisper, "Oh, Rachel, is this truly where we're to live from now on?"

"Shhh!" cautioned Rachel, taking note of the momentarily unconcealed look of disappointment on their grandmother's face, and the undeniable look of displeasure on their grandfather's.

"Like it or not, things are different now. The sooner you get used to the fact that you're no longer living in pampered luxury, the better for us all," Micah ground out, then spun about on his booted heel and strode about to the rear of the buckboard to begin unloading the bags. Rachel said nothing in response, and even Elizabeth remained wisely silent. It was left to Jane to break the tension by declaring with determined cheerfulness, "You know, we've fixed it up so each of you will have your own room! Now let's get the two of you on inside. The first thing we're going to do is see to it that you get a good hearty meal! If the food on the train was as bad as I've heard tell, you'll be needing some of my cooking to perk you up!" She wrapped an arm about both of the girls and led them through the picket gate and down the narrow walkway, chattering all the while. In spite of her grandmother's attempts at lifting her spirits, Rachel was still painfully aware of the way Micah's eyes, eyes that were like her father's and yet different at the same time, followed her before she escaped into the sanctuary of the house.

It was long after nightfall before the elder Parkers got the chance to talk in private. Jane had lovingly tucked both Rachel and Elizabeth into their respective beds before taking her seat before the fire, her husband's lean frame already bent into his customary chair by the time she sank into the rocker beside his.

"Oh, Micah, it's like a dream come true to have them here," she murmured with a long sigh, then said in a voice suddenly choked with emotion, "If only Ethan—"

"No amount of wishing's going to bring him back,

Jane." Though his tone sounded a bit harsh and unfeeling, his wife knew better.

"I know that. But it's brought back all the memories to have his girls here. I've given my all to keep those memories from my mind these past twelve years." The tears came unbidden to her eyes once more, prompting Micah's features to tighten even further.

"What's done is done." His wife offered no response, and there was only the sound of the blazing logs popping and crackling for the space of numerous seconds, seconds during which the atmosphere in the firelit room was charged with unspoken yet painfully stirring memories. Finally, Jane's bosom rose and fell as she heaved a sigh and declared a bit tremulously, "The oldest one's so like Ethan . . . so like you, Micah."

"No," dissented Micah with a curt shake of his head and a deepening frown, his gaze never straying from the dancing flames. "She's not like Ethan at all, Jane. Neither of them are. It's plain to see they took after that mother of theirs," he bitterly concluded, his eyes narrowing in noticeably distasteful remembrance of the woman who shouldered a good deal of the blame in his mind, blame for the heartbreaking rift between Micah Parker and his only son.

"While Elizabeth undoubtedly favors Charlotte, there's no way you can sit there and deny how much Rachel looks like both you and Ethan!" his wife quietly but firmly insisted, folding her arms across her chest and leaning closer to the warmth of the fire. An expression of mingled sorrow and nostalgia crossed her face, closely followed by a soft smile of more joyful remembrance. "Why, her eyes are the same light shade of blue as Ethan's, her hair almost the very color of his as a boy . . . but it's the way she carries herself that reminds me of you, Micah. It's much more than the way she looks—it's a certain air about her, something I can't quite put my finger on but is there just the same."

"You're dead wrong," Micah replied in tight, clipped tones, abruptly rising from his chair to take a rigid stance before the fireplace. He gripped the rough-hewn mantel with both hands, his lined, chiseled features darkening with renewed anger. "How the devil can you compare either of those . . . those spoiled, frilled-up little brats to either me or Ethan? Hell, it would've been bad enough having to raise girls instead of boys, but to find out that they're just as pampered and useless as that mother of theirs—"

"That's not fair!" Jane vehemently protested, rising to her feet as well, her hand closing about his hard-muscled arm to force him about to face her. Her brown eyes were flashing with the spirit she displayed only when driven to the limit. "You're not even giving them a chance, Micah Parker! They're young, and they've just been through a terrible time. It was bad enough losing their mother two years ago, but now to lose their father as well . . ." A look of heartfelt appeal appeared in her gaze as her words trailed away. Micah found himself at a loss for words, and it was a moment before Jane continued with, "It means the world to me that Ethan wanted them to come to us. Don't you see, Micah? No matter what happened, he still believed they'd be better off with us than anyone else."

"Maybe so. But I can't help thinking they should have stayed where they belonged. There must have been some kin of that woman's who wanted to take them."

"Her name was Charlotte. In the name of heaven, Micah, the poor woman's dead! Isn't it about time you brought yourself to at least call her by her Christian name?"

"It makes no difference," he decreed in a low, dispassionate tone. "Her girls are just like her. They haven't got enough backbone to make it out here. They'll never adapt to the hardships, never get used to a way of life that's completely foreign to them. No, Jane, Ethan was wrong to send them to us. And dead or not, I'll never forgive his wife for bringing this on us all."

Although Jane did her best to try and convince him that it was indeed for the best that Ethan's daughters had come to them, it soon became apparent that Micah's opinion could not be altered, at least not by mere words. Neither of them was aware of the blond-haired girl who watched them from her vantage point just beyond one of the inner doorways, her ears catching every disparaging remark and accompanying defense. Her beautiful young countenance wore a stricken look, her pale blue eyes glistening with hot tears.

On her way to make certain Elizabeth was resting peacefully, Rachel had become an unintentional eavesdropper. Her first instinct had been to return to her room at the end of the narrow hallway and close the door against the distressing conversation taking place, but her hasty steps had been arrested upon hearing her mother's name mentioned.

All of the pain and resentment and bitterness in her heart came flooding to the surface, and before she had taken the time to contemplate the wisdom of her actions, she burst into the outer room to confront her grandfather. Her shining, unbound hair framed the pale, delicate oval of her face, and her slight curves trembled almost violently beneath the protection of her white, high-necked nightgown. Looking much like some youthful, avenging tigress, she did not hesitate before positioning herself between the startled adults and fiercely demanding of Micah, "How can you say such awful things? How dare you presume to judge either of my parents when it is you yourself who are to blame? My mother was one of the kindest, gentlest people in all the world, and my father was . . . was nothing at all like you! He was thoughtful and caring and full of laughter—qualities you could never understand! You . . . you are . . . are mean and hateful and . . . and I . . . I . . ." She could scarcely speak now, the tears coursing freely down her flushed cheeks and the sobs welling up in her throat threatening to choke her.

"Oh, Rachel!" murmured Jane through her own tears, trying to put her arms about the girl and pull her close. Rachel, however, resisted her grandmother's comfort, choosing instead to vent even more of her wrath upon her strangely silently grandfather. His narrowing eyes and tightly compressing lips were the only outward evidence that he had even heard her.

"Elizabeth and I would rather be anywhere but here with you!" Rachel lashed out, dashing impatiently at the tears. "My father told me the reason you refused to have anything to do with us after my birth! He told me all about your . . . your 'disappointment' in him, in the fact that he wanted to make a life of his own with the woman he loved instead of remaining in your shadow! And simply because you couldn't accept his independence, the very independence you had instilled in him, you . . . you—"

"He made his choice and I made mine," Micah interrupted to declare in an oddly distant, barely audible voice. His eyes never wavered from Rachel's face as he towered above her, the firelight playing across the rugged lines of his own countenance.

"Please, Rachel, don't," earnestly pleaded Jane, finally succeeding in placing an arm about the girl's quaking shoulders. "You don't understand."

"I understand all too well! I know you didn't want us here! I know you were already prepared to hate Elizabeth and me just as you had come to hate our father!" Rachel accused Micah, her voice breaking on a sob at the last. She buried her face in her hands and would have crumpled to the floor if not for the support of Jane's arms about her. Jane paused to send her husband a helpless, plaintively bewildered look before gently leading the emotionally drained girl from the room.

It was some time later before Jane emerged from Rachel's room. She found Micah seated before the fire again, his eyes glancing up briefly to meet her gaze as she sank into her rocking chair once more.

"Thank the Lord she's asleep now," murmured Jane, her kindly features looking weary and drawn. "Oh Micah, I'll never forget the pain in that poor girl's eyes when she came in here tonight. I'll never forget the way she rushed in to defend Charlotte and Ethan. Poor girl. Poor, poor girl." She sighed heavily and dabbed at her eyes with her handkerchief, then sat quiet and motionless. Nearly a full minute passed before Micah surprised her by declaring in a low, even tone, "I was wrong about that one, at least. Seems she's got some backbone after all. You were right, Jane. She's her father's daughter." While his wife could only sit and stare at him in astonishment, a ghost of a smile played about his lips. "She's a Parker."

The transition was difficult, but no obstacles proved totally insurmountable. It was almost as if Micah and Jane had been given a second chance at life, or at least at parenthood, and though it took a good deal of time and patience, all four Parkers benefited from the adjustments and compromises made. Love between the hardened lawman and his granddaughters took seed and grew as the two girls from San Francisco soon willingly embraced life in the wild West, learning to ride, to handle a gun, and to cope with the dangers and perils of their new home in a land that was still virtually untamed. As the years passed, the painful memories of that disastrous beginning blurred and were eventually all but forgotten . . .

I

Montana Territory, 1884

Rachel Parker, peering outward through the streaked windowpane at the buff-colored, sandstone rimrocks which rose like a wall about the frontier city of Billings, lifted a hand to the feathered bonnet perched atop her golden curls in an effort to prevent its displacement as the engine took a sudden lurch forward before coming to a screeching halt before the station. Lizzie, who had been seated immediately to her sister's right, had become so engrossed in her own sightseeing that she was caught totally unprepared for the abrupt motion of the train. Muttering a very unladylike curse, the red-haired adolescent hastily regained her balance.

"Can't one of these confounded things ever ease to a stop?"

"Don't say 'confounded', Lizzie," her grandmother dutifully admonished, though her soft tone was noticeably lacking in conviction. Micah Parker stood beside his wife and briefly winced at the stiffness in his joints, then stepped aside to begin ushering his womenfolk out of the crowded passenger car.

"I reckon this is it now. Let's get going," directed Micah, his voice edged with impatience. Having already halted momentarily back down the line at the empty structure which was actually the year-old Northern Pacific depot but had never been used as such, the train had arrived at its final destination none too soon for the weary and travel-worn passengers.

The Parkers soon found themselves standing before a very large, two-story building situated close beside the tracks. A number of people thronged on the upper and lower verandas of the whitewashed structure to greet those disembarking at the railroad-spawned community. Brimming with constant and ever-increasing activity, Billings had sprouted almost overnight when the Northern Pacific Railroad had first snaked through the Yellowstone Valley two years earlier. Gazing curiously about, a fascinated Rachel concluded that the town, or at least what she had glimpsed of it so far, was not at all what she had expected. Although young and still in a chaotic state of growth, it nonetheless possessed a certain, inexplicable appeal, and her beautiful features relaxed into a smile as she told herself, with a mixture of satisfaction and relief, that it was a place that was vibrantly alive—precisely the opposite of what she had been unhappily anticipating since her grandfather first announced his intention of moving his family to Montana.

"Jane, you and the girls take what you'll need for the night and go on inside the hotel. I'd best see to it the rest of our things are put in storage till tomorrow," declared Micah, nodding downward to indicate the bags he had just fetched and placed on the stained and dusty boards forming the platform above the tracks.

"All right," Jane agreed with a faint sigh, lifting one of the valises as Rachel and Lizzie did the same. "We'll go ahead and see about getting a room. Don't be long now," she affectionately exhorted, then turned and sailed into the building with her granddaughters following silently in her wake.

The interior of the Headquarters Hotel, known as such because it had once housed workers putting the railroad through, was surprisingly luxurious, its widely varied guests including millionaires from back East, trail herd riders from Texas, tilted nobility from all over Europe, local vigilantes and other "colorful" characters, as well as more than a few mysterious personages who declined to list any occupation or even their true surnames. Rachel, who had never ventured outside of Rock Creek for the past seven years, was reminded of San Francisco again, of the opulent, decidedly well-heeled type of life to which she had once been accustomed. Though she experienced a sharp pang of remembrance for the pleasures, the happiness she had known so long ago, she realized that it was a different but deeply satisfying life she lived now.

"Rachel! Rachel!" Lizzie suddenly whispered, drawing her sister out of her silent reverie as they paused a short distance behind their calico-clad grandmother, who was in the process of speaking to the clerk at the massive, polished oak counter situated along the far wall of the plush, red-and-gold-decorated lobby.

"What is it?" she asked, favoring a mischievously grinning Lizzie with a slight frown.

"Look at the way those men over there are staring at

you! Land's sake, I doubt if you'd attract any more attention if you were standing here without a stitch on!" her younger sibling bluntly decreed. Rachel was dismayed to feel herself blushing as her gaze involuntarily strayed to where a group of cattlemen, some barely out of their teens and some much older, were virtually devouring her with their eyes. "You'd think they'd never seen a woman before!" added Lizzie with a snort of youthful disgust.

"Oh Lizzie, hush!" Rachel stridently whispered, resolutely turning her back on the avid spectators. Dressed in a ruffle-trimmed gown of white sprigged cotton which buttoned down the front, its square neckline allowing only a hint of a full, creamy bosom and its fashionable bustle ornamented with tiny ribbons of pale blue satin, Rachel had no idea how fresh and eminently alluring she appeared to the men, men who were treated to only a cherished, occasional glimpse of such a desirable specimen of ripe yet innocent young womanhood. She could not know that it was often several long, hard months at a time before the cowpunchers drinking in the sight of her were afforded the opportunity to admire any females at all. They spared only a passing glance for the noticeably less mature, still-blossoming redhead beside her, their piercing gazes fixed unwaveringly upon the nineteen-year-old Rachel.

Grateful for the reprieve from their discomfiting attentions a few short moments later, Rachel smiled warmly up at a returning Micah and accompanied her relatives up the narrow, carpeted staircase leading to the second floor. Assigned to a room which adjoined their grandparents', the Parker sisters were soon settling in. There was a wood-burning fireplace in each room of the hotel, and Lizzie was only too happy to perform the honors of lighting a fire. Nightfall was fast approaching, a lingering chill already permeating the small but cheerfully furnished interior of the bedchamber.

Rachel took a seat on the edge of the gleaming brass bed and removed her bonnet, then unpinned her bright tresses and gently shook her head. A soft sigh escaped her lips, prompting a perceptive Lizzie to query, "What's the matter?"

"I'm tired, that's all," Rachel hastened to assure her, turning to begin searching through her bag for her wrapper and clean undergarments.

"You aren't by any chance still upset about our leaving Rock Creek, are you? Because, if you are, Rachel Parker, then it's about time you accepted the fact that we'll never be going back there again! This is what Micah wanted, what Grandmother wanted, and it's what I wanted as well," she decisively proclaimed, her brown eyes shining with a sense of accomplishment as the fire blazed to life. She climbed to her feet and moved across the room to her sister's side, her starched petticoats and slightly too-short yellow gingham skirts rustling as she walked. "Aren't you the least bit excited about our adventure?" she demanded, giving an expressive toss of her head so that her coppery curls danced about her round, faintly freckled face.

"Adventure?" echoed Rachel, meeting Lizzie's questioning gaze. She sighed again before answering, "Oh, Lizzie, you simply don't understand. This isn't an adventure—it's yet another new way of life for us. And it's one I'm not at all certain we should have undertaken!"

"But it's still an adventure!" insisted the opinionated

fourteen-year-old, whirling about and flouncing away to take a stance at the single, multi-paned window. Absently fingering the white lace curtains as she peered outward into the deepening twilight, she seemed hardly aware of her sister when Rachel rose to her feet and announced, "I'm going down the hall to take a bath before supper. If either Grandmother or Micah asks for me, please tell them I'll return shortly." Frowning to herself when she received no response, she took up her bundle of clothing and set off for the room, readily identified by a hand-lettered sign, located at the opposite end of the dimly lit hallway.

Satisfied to find that the bathroom was both spacious and well equipped, Rachel closed the door and began disrobing. She had already slipped out of her dress when she discovered a pair of men's boots resting beneath the huge, claw-foot bathtub. The dark tan leather had been polished to perfection and the shanks embellished with undeniably skillful stitching. It was immediately apparent to Rachel that the boots were of very high quality, and also that their owner had been quite remiss in leaving them behind. She temporarily dismissed them from her mind, however, and bent over to twist the ornate brass handles which controlled the flow of water into the glistening porcelain tub.

Within a few short minutes, she was stepping cautiously into the steaming water, her clothing arranged neatly upon the small velvet chaise against one papered wall, her hair pulled upward into a thick, single golden mass atop her head and negligently secured with a blue ribbon. The twin frosted-glass lamps burned brightly above her, their steady flames casting a comforting golden glow across her pale, silken flesh as she leaned gratefully back against the curved, water-warmed porcelain and reveled in the soothing liquid engulfing her fatigued body.

It had been a long and wearisome journey, for they had traveled all the way from Rock Creek to Billings without once leaving the almost stifling confines of the train. The seats of the old-fashioned "emigrant cars" used by the Northern Pacific were merely wooden slats, and there had been no upholstery to make them even passably comfortable. At night, the slats were pulled out to make an upper and lower row of sleeping berths, and each family was assigned a narrow section of the "beds". A large coal stove in one corner of the car heated the interior and also served as the cooking area for those families traveling with their own hampers of food.

Rachel, languidly reflecting that she had never been so glad in her life to see a real bed once again, took up the cake of soap she had brought with her and began lathering her gleaming satiny curves. Her thoughts drifted back to that day, less than two weeks earlier, when Micah had come home with the news that he had purchased a small ranch in Montana . . .

"Montana?" Jane and Lizzie echoed in unison, the two of them quickly setting aside their duties at the supper table and facing Micah with expressions of startled disbelief. Rachel paused only briefly before resuming her own task of removing the bread from the oven and placing it to cool beside the huge cast-iron stove. When she turned to meet her grandfather's gaze, she was disconcerted to find that his gray eyes were alight with an unusually conspicuous excitement, and it wasn't long before she discovered that she alone remained unwaveringly skeptical of his decision.

"But, you . . . you don't know anything about ranching," she dazedly pointed out, feeling a tightening knot of dread in the very pit of her stomach. Montana! she mentally repeated, immediately envisioning a vast, untamed wilderness populated by nothing more than bloodthirsty savages, wild animals, and—from what she'd heard—even wilder cowboys.

"Then it's high time I learned," replied Micah, a ghost of a smile tugging at the corners of his mouth as he casually took his seat at the head of the table. "Just maybe it's time I gave up this profession and took life a little easier, tried something I've never tried before." Lizzie suddenly recovered voice enough to exclaim, "A ranch? In Montana? Jumping Jehoshaphat, wait till I tell that snake-eyed Johnny Stinson and all the others!" She didn't seem in the least bit affected by the quelling glance her older sister shot her.

"Oh, Micah!" breathed Jane, sinking into the chair beside his. "Are you sure about this? I had no idea you were getting restless again. Why didn't you tell me you were wanting to leave Rock Creek?" She had followed her husband all over the West for more than thirty years, was used to the way he had of announcing out of the blue that he had decided to move on and seek employment elsewhere. There had always been plenty of towns in need of a sheriff, and Micah's well-earned reputation as an honest, at times perilously dauntless, peace-keeper had usually preceded him wherever they went.

"I wasn't planning on pulling out just yet. But then I wasn't figuring on having such an irresistible deal thrown my way either." He stood and gripped the top of the ladder-back chair, his tanned, leathered features taking on a certain glow as his gaze swiftly traveled from his wife to each of his granddaughters, then back. He could literally feel the anticipation emanating from them before he finally explained, "I arrested a man over at the Sagebrush Saloon today, a four-flusher who got caught cheating at poker and decided to shoot his way out of the argument. He's a stranger in these parts. But the man he killed worked for Alfred Flannagan's outfit down in Laramie. And it just so happened that I'd bought the ranch from him less than an hour before he died. Turns out that he'd won it last night from the very man who killed him."

"Merciful heavens!" murmured Jane, her eyes filling with horror at the thought of the murdered man, as well as the realization that Micah had been in danger yet again. It was something she'd been forced to endure, to learn to live with, but there were times when the knowledge that her beloved husband was in the midst of jeopardy prompted her to fervently wish he had followed another calling entirely.

"So you purchased a ranch that belongs to some man who will no doubt very shortly find himself hanged?" Rachel asked, an involuntary shiver running the length of her spine.

"Not 'belongs'—'belonged'," Micah corrected her, a faint scowl crossing his face. "The cowpuncher I bought it from won it fair and square, Rachel. And no, there's little doubt at all that his murderer will soon be swinging at the end of a rope."

"Where is this ranch?" Jane calmly inquired, rising to her feet as well and moving to the stove to help Rachel carry the food to the table. As her grandmother paused to give her an encouraging smile, Rachel was afforded a brief glimpse of what appeared to be a sort of weary resignation in the older woman's eyes.

"Near a place called Miles City. We'll have to take the train to Billings first, then eastward," supplied Micah, sitting down again as his countenance took on a guarded expression.

"Why in tarnation is everyone acting so down in the mouth about all this?" Lizzie vigorously demanded. It was quite apparent that she, for one, considered the announcement to be a cause for celebration. "Imagine how exciting it's going to be to live up there with all those buffalo and Indians and—"

"No buffalo, I'm afraid," Micah broke in to amend, the merest hint of a smile touching his lips. "And all the tribes are on reservations now." He glanced up, his steely gaze meeting and locking with his eldest granddaughter's once more. Their relationship had grown into something far deeper than either could have ever imagined possible, and it was as if Micah was silently pleading with the golden-haired young beauty for approval. Rachel forced herself to smile across at him.

"Well, if we're to be heading off to Montana soon, we'd best finish our supper and start making plans," Jane asserted with a note of determined brightness in her voice. The three Parker women took their places about the lone male at the table, the meal they had worked so hard to prepare receiving very little attention as they plied Micah with questions and discussed a myriad of details regarding the upcoming move. Only Rachel said little, though she was acutely aware of the frequent, searching looks her grandfather cast in her direction.

In the end, she knew there was very little to be gained

by maintaining any resistance. She told Elizabeth of her persisting reluctance, but no one else. For Micah's sake, she pretended an enthusiasm she was far from feeling. Inwardly, however, she couldn't seem to shake the disturbing sensation that trouble awaited them in Montana. And she continued to be plagued by an unsettling sense of destiny . . .

Releasing a long sigh, Rachel splashed the cooling water across her full, rose-tipped breasts and mentally chided herself for her uncharacteristic melancholy. Reflecting that she was no longer a child and should therefore endeavor to accept and make the best of things—just as Elizabeth had decreed—she rinsed the last of the lavender-scented foam from her body and gripped the edges of the tub for support in order to rise.

Just as she came fully upright, however, the bathroom door swung open without warning to disclose a tall, undeniably masculine stranger. The intruder stopped dead in his tracks at the gloriously revealed sight of the naked, dripping wet goddess before him, and it was an excruciatingly long moment before Rachel's body obeyed the impulses from her brain and dipped back downward into the scant protection of the soap-clouded water as a tiny shriek escaped her lips.

"How . . . how dare you!" she indignantly sputtered in the next instant, crossing her arms tightly across her bosom in an absurdly inadequate effort to shield her womanly charms from his piercing, sea-green gaze. She could feel herself blushing fierily, was painfully conscious of the fact that the devastatingly handsome man's eyes raked over her trembling, outraged softness with an immensely distressing boldness. "Get out of here at once!" she commanded with all the imperious bravado she could muster under the humiliating circumstances.

"Didn't anyone ever tell you about squatter's rights?" he sardonically retorted in a deep, resonant voice, a tiny glimmer of amusement visible in his gaze as he nonchalantly leaned against the door frame and kept his eyes fastened unrepentantly upon a stormy-faced Rachel. "I had already staked my claim on the tub," he supplied, nodding briefly to indicate the pair of boots still resting alongside one clawed foot of the bathtub. Rachel's flashing blue gaze followed his before hastily returning to the chiseled perfection of his sun-bronzed countenance.

"Would you be so kind as to leave me to my privacy?" she fairly hissed at him, more furious than she had been in quite some time. "For heaven's sake, take your boots and go!" She huddled stiffly against one side of the tub, her knees drawn up and her arms tightening across the swelling curve of her breasts as she shot the dark-haired stranger a venomous glare.

"I have no intention of leaving before I get what I came for," the tall stranger, whom Rachel numbly surmised to be a year or two shy of thirty, proclaimed with a faint, mocking smile. Lean and muscular, he was attired in nothing more than a pair of fitted denim trousers and an unbuttoned white linen shirt.

"You may take your boots and go!" Rachel angrily repeated. A loud gasp escaped her lips when he merely pushed the door quietly to behind him, then took a seat on the edge of the chaise. "Wha . . . what are you doing?" she breathlessly demanded, her eyes growing round as saucers as she watched him reach up and start drawing off his shirt.

"I told you. I'm not leaving until I get what I came for—a bath." His chest was completely bared now, its magnificently broad expanse covered with a softly curling mat of dark brown hair that narrowed and tapered intriguingly downward to disappear beneath the waistband of his faded, comfortably worn trousers. Rachel gasped again and choked out, "I . . . I'll scream!" This couldn't be happening! she dazedly reasoned with herself. The man was undoubtedly some kind of lunatic! "I mean exactly what I say. If you don't get out of here this very instant—"

"Go ahead and scream. You'll succeed in bringing a highly appreciative audience of at least another three dozen or so. They'll be only too happy to avenge your 'outraged modesty' while taking advantage of the opportunity to do a little bit of 'sightseeing' of their own." While Rachel could only stare up at him in shocked, debilitating confusion, he muttered a curse beneath his breath and said, "Damn it, woman, you can rest assured that your virtue is entirely free from danger at this moment. I've had the devil of a day, and I'm sure as hell not in the mood to do any ravishing of innocent young virgins who don't even have the courtesy to respect a man's privacy!"

"A man's privacy?" Rachel echoed in stunned disbelief. Feeling as if lost in some never-ending, perturbably nonsensical dream, she suppressed a shiver as the water cooled yet another degree. "Are you completely and utterly daft? You, sir, are invading *my* privacy and if you don't remove yourself from my presence at once, I'll . . . I'll—"

"I'm warning you now that you'd best see about

'removing yourself' from that blasted tub without further delay or you'll find things a bit too crowded for your maidenly discriminate tastes!" His narrowing eyes now glowed with a purposeful light, boring relentlessly into hers as she blanched beneath the dangerous look crossing his ruggedly handsome features.

"Oh!" Rachel uttered wrathfully, her own eyes blazing opal fire and her temper flaring almost entirely out of control. Faced with the choice of either screaming for assistance and thereby bringing upon herself further humiliation, or climbing out of the tub while the insolent stranger was in the same room, she reluctantly chose the latter.

"Well?" he impatiently queried, towering ominously above her while she shot him a contemptuous look which effectively bespoke the extent of her resentment and fury toward him.

"You might at least have the decency to turn your back while I get up!"

"Not a shred," he caustically parried, but nonetheless growled deep in his throat in thoroughly masculine exasperation and followed her wishes with a noticeably ill grace.

Rachel, waiting until she was certain he intended to remain standing with his back to her, rose slowly and quite cautiously to her feet, her eyes never leaving the ill-mannered invader's hard, lithe-muscled form. She was blissfully ignorant of the fact that the arrogant man was afforded a clear view of her exquisite feminine curves as a result of a gilt-framed mirror hanging in a most strategic position upon the wall to his left. His eyes lingered upon the reflection of her entrancing nakedness with deceptive nonchalance, for he was in actuality hungrily devouring the sight of her delightfully trim yet well-rounded young body while a rapidly increasing fire raged within his blood.

Damn, but she's beautiful, the rakish stranger mused to himself, his virescent eyes gleaming with fierce desire as he noted the glowing, satiny perfection of her long, shapely limbs . . . the silken enchantment of her unmistakably feminine derriere . . . the graceful curve of her back and shoulders . . . and her breasts. The twin pale, delectably rounded globes were the most irresistibly alluring he had ever seen, and he found himself reflecting that they seemed to invite a man's touch, the beguiling rosy peaks of her nipples to beg for the warm caress of a man's lips.

But it was a small, intriguingly shaped patch of silken flesh on the upper portion of her right hip which ultimately drew his intense, burning gaze. Apparently a birthmark, it unmistakably resembled a four-leaf clover, and it was of a deep golden hue that contrasted strikingly with the more ivory tinge of the beauty's flawless skin.

His fascinated gaze narrowing imperceptibly as it swept back up to the young woman's breasts, the handsome intruder mused that it had been a long time since he had experienced such an all-encompassing stirring of his senses, and he was none too dismayed to realize that the decidedly rampant passion flaring to life within him was even more powerful than any he had ever felt before. What the devil was it about the girl that prompted such a reaction? he irascibly wondered, a dark scowl turning the corners of his mouth downward.

He was denied the opportunity to ponder the question any further at the moment, for Rachel, who had just finished donning her wrapper and was now in the process of drawing the edges of the ribbon sash tight about her slender waist, suddenly wheeled about and caught him boldly observing her reflection in the mirror she had belatedly spied.

"Why, of all the despicable— You . . . you unscrupulous . . ." she stammered in profound indignation, unable to find the appropriately disobliging terms with which to vent her outrage as hot color flooded her face. Snatching up the rest of her things, she drew herself rigidly erect and took a step toward him, her chin tilting upward in a gesture of mingled pride and defiance, her beautiful eyes sparkling with easily discernible spirit. He slowly turned to face her, his expression inscrutable but his gaze narrowing almost imperceptibly in begrudging admiration. Rachel was once again unavoidably reminded of the fact that he was standing half-naked before her, and she was equally discomfited by the knowledge that she herself was clothed only in a thin cotton wrapper.

"I haven't a shred of decency, remember?" he noted wryly, a slight huskiness to his voice. Rachel bridled beneath what she perceived to be his taunting, knowing gaze, and she was further infuriated when he folded his arms across his chest and lazily observed, "You know, there's a gal here in Billings with a rose tattooed in about the same spot as that little clover on your backside. But, I have to admit," he added with a mocking grin, "yours is a hell of a lot prettier."

Rachel, provoked well beyond reason now, hesitated only the fraction of an instant before raising her hand and bringing it quite forcefully against his handsome, sun-kissed cheek. The stinging contact was painful to them both, the tall rogue's skin marked by a fiery red imprint identical to Rachel's burning palm.

Drawing in her breath upon a sharp gasp, she was appalled at her own actions, her mind in a tumultuous whirl as she waited in growing apprehension for the bare-chested scoundrel towering above her to react. Astounded that she had dared to slap him, she who had never struck out at another person in the entirety of her young life, Rachel was thrown into confusion by the fact that he had neither moved nor spoken, indeed had not acknowledged the blow in the least. But, swiftly raising her eyes to his again, she took note of the barely controlled violence contained within their smoldering sea-green depths.

Anguished embarrassment, coupled with more than a twinge of outright alarm, washed over Rachel once more. A strangled, scarcely audible cry escaped her lips as she spun about and attempted to wrench open the door. She succeeded only in opening it little more than an inch before one bronzed arm shot out and clamped like a band of steel about her slender waist, eliciting a highly audible intake of breath from Rachel.

"Let go of me!" she desperately commanded, her voice rising on a note of hysteria. Another loud gasp was forthcoming as her captor merely yanked her closer without ceremony, so that her soft, supple curves were pressed with shocking intimacy against the length of his sinewy hardness. A dull flush of anger had risen to his tight-lipped, previously impassive face, and his eyes darkened to a deep jade, glittering with something Rachel dared not name as he lowered his head so that his face was mere inches from hers.

"No one, man or woman, strikes me without paying a forfeit. A man would more than likely pay with his life, but from you," he told her, his voice quite low and laced with simmering fury, an inordinate fury aimed at himself as well as Rachel, "from you, my fiery young beauty, I will exact a far different price, and you can damn well count yourself fortunate I did not see fit to retaliate in a like manner!" Rachel struggled feverishly within his grasp, but to no avail, her resistance entirely futile against his superior strength. No sooner had she opened her mouth to scream when he silenced her with the ruthless pressure of his lips crashing down upon hers.

Rachel was at first too overwhelmed to do anything more than remain temporarily subdued and pliant against him, only vaguely aware of the moment his other powerful arm came up to wrap possessively about her stunned, faintly quivering form. Her mind spun at an alarmingly turbulent pace, and she was thoroughly dazed by the warm feeling of vibrancy, of the heretofore unfamiliar yearning blazing to life within her. His skillful lips, at first hard and punishing, soon became more gentle, more seductively persuasive as they moved upon hers, his arms tightening about her body to draw her even closer.

A soft moan welled up deep in Rachel's throat as her ripe young breasts, covered only by the flimsy protection of her wrapper, swept against the hard-muscled breadth of her captor's chest. It seemed as if the highly sensitive peaks were being seared by the warmth of his undeniably virile form, and the wild, abandoned impulses his impassioned embrace provoked within her finally compelled her to renew her struggles to escape.

Bringing both of her hands up in a frantic effort to pry herself from the rogue's startlingly evocative grasp, Rachel was unprepared for the abruptness of her sudden release. Her head reeling dizzily, she would have fallen if not for the steadying hand which still gripped her arm. She stared up at him in breathless, open-mouthed amazement, unable as yet to form any rational thought, unable to do anything more than remain as if rooted to the spot.

"The next time you're tempted to slap a man, sweetheart," her darkly handsome, green-eyed subduer remarked with a faint, crooked smile which belied the dangerous gleam of simmering anger and heated desire in his eyes, "you'd do well to make sure he's enough of a gentleman to refrain from—"

"It's plain to see you're no gentleman!" cried Rachel, jerking her arm from his grasp as her eyes, though sparkling with tears, flashed scathingly up at him. "As a matter of fact, I'd say you were about the least gentlemanly person I've ever had the misfortune to encounter!" She was unprepared for the way he reached out and drew her roughly back to him, his chiseled lips curving upward into a decidedly wicked grin.

"And I'd say it's just as plain to see you're the least gentlemanly person I've met either," he proclaimed in a deep voice brimming with unholy amusement, his searing gaze once again raking boldly up and down her outraged curves.

Before a gasping, newly indignant Rachel could respond, her devilishly handsome tormentor spun her unceremoniously about and quickly leaned over to open the door. In the next moment, his hand delivered a hard, familiar smack to Rachel's unsuspecting bottom.

"On your way, 'Clover'," the impudently dashing cowboy directed. "I'd consider letting you stay, but I doubt very seriously you're much in the mood to scrub my back!"

"Why, you . . . you . . ." Rachel sputtered once more, her opal gaze virtually shooting daggers at his head before she drew herself up with all the proud dignity she could muster and beat a hasty, long-overdue retreat from the bathroom. She was almost certain she heard the sound of a low chuckle behind her, but she did not look back as her furious steps carried her back down the hallway to the sanctuary of her bedchamber.

II

Rachel was still plagued by embarrassingly vivid memories of the previous night's incident when she accompanied her family from the hotel and boarded the train the following morning, but she had resolutely pushed images of a rakishly handsome, woefully arrogant stranger to the back of her mind by the time she took her seat beside her sister. Gracefully settling her skirts about her, she tucked a stray tendril of honey-blond hair beneath her black felt hat and turned her gaze upon the sun-drenched landscape outside the window.

Although not yet nine o'clock, the late June day was already quite warm, and Rachel soon found herself regretting her decision to wear the tailored suit of gray faille. The white lawn blouse visible beneath the form-fitting jacket was fashionably high-necked, the accordion-pleated underskirt equally impressive, and yet she silently lamented that the entire ensemble was far less suitable for the weather than Lizzie's simple blue cotton.

Oh, to be as childish and carefree as Lizzie! she mused

with an inward sigh. Lizzie was not yet bound by the same rules of convention, did not have to concern herself with her appearance to the same degree as her older sister. Even if Rachel had remembered nothing else of her mother's strict, long-ago lessons in ladylike comportment, she would never have forgotten the proper way to dress. Upon leaving San Francisco to make her home with Jane and Micah these past several years, she had of necessity become quite adept at dressmaking, the result being that she was without a doubt always the most fashionably attired young lady in Rock Creek.

You were far from being fashionably attired when that tall rogue's green eyes roamed over you with such shocking intimacy and utter shamelessness last night! an inner voice gleefully reminded her. Rachel's cheeks flamed anew at the recollection of his disturbingly intense gaze fastened so . . . so *hotly* upon her nakedness. And the burning, impassioned kiss he had forced upon her, the way his powerful arms had swept her against his searing hardness with such steely purposefulness . . . even now, she experienced such a perplexing mixture of outrage, humiliation, and irrestrainable excitement that it made her head spin quite alarmingly.

"Looks like we're going to have a full load today." Micah spoke behind her, his hand briefly gripping the back of Rachel's seat and thereby prompting her complete return to the present. He tugged the hat from his head and used a large white handkerchief to wipe the perspiration from his brow. "No doubt it's going to be another scorcher today," he decreed in a low voice that provided more than a hint of his displeasure with the uncooperative Montana weather. Rachel was tempted to remind him that it had frequently been a good deal warmer in Rock Creek.

"At least we've only a day's travel left," noted Jane, unbuttoning her light serge jacket and easing it off, then giving an instinctive pat to her securely pinned hair.

"But we won't get to see our new ranch till tomorrow!" complained Lizzie, once again making known her impatience. She released a heavy sigh and crossed her arms against her chest. It wasn't long before she became absorbed in watching the last of the passengers file past and take their seats, while Rachel and her grandparents turned their attention back to the scenery opposite the platform.

A burst of steam and a blast of the train whistle signaled their departure. The locomotive slowly chugged away from the hotel, soon gathering speed and leaving behind the bustling frontier community which had only two years earlier been nothing more than a city of tents. Billings was already well on its way to prosperity, and Rachel told herself that it would be interesting to return someday and measure its progress.

Reflecting that she was glad Lizzie had so generously allowed her the seat next to the window, she quickly became engrossed in watching the countryside rolling past. She lost all track of time, impervious to the talk and activity about her as she viewed the unfamiliar landscape that was only vaguely similar to what she had seen in Wyoming.

Although the land was dominated by grasslands, there were numerous clusters of trees, mostly cottonwoods, along the river and streams. The vast plains, carpeted with short grass and sagebrush and dotted with a colorful array of summer wildflowers, swept all the way to the intensely blue horizon. The monotony of the green-tinged prairie's horizontal dimension was effectively broken by a succession of gently rolling hills, fertile river valleys, narrow gullies snaking through both the flats and the rises, and an increasing number of tall, steep-sided hills which Rachel would soon learn were called buttes.

Making a mental note of the fact that the train's route closely followed the sinuous course of the Yellowstone River, Rachel found herself wondering if the ranch her grandfather had purchased was perhaps situated anywhere near the historic waterway. They had in their possession only a rather indistinct description of the property's location.

She released a faint sigh and squirmed a bit in an effort to find a more comfortable spot on the hard wooden slats of the seat. Finally taking a moment to gaze about the crowded railroad car, she turned to see that there were only a few women included among the occupants, and even fewer children. The wives seemed subdued and a trifle ill-at-ease in their surroundings, while the husbands took a more active role in initiating conversation with their fellow passengers.

The men were as widely varied a group as she had seen in the hotel the day before, though the majority of them were dressed in the perpetual denim trousers and colorless cotton shirts, with leather boots and low-crowned hats completing the typical cowpuncher's costume. To Rachel, they looked very much the same as the men back in Rock Creek.

Except for one.

She inhaled sharply as she caught sight of him. Distressingly certain that her face had just drained of all color, Rachel could not seem to tear her stunned and widening gaze from him. He was standing near the rear door, evidently having just entered the car from another one behind. And he was at that moment gifting her with a slow, insolent grin and a slight, albeit undeniably meaningful, narrowing of his magnificent sea-green eyes.

"Oh no!" breathed Rachel in horror. She abruptly twisted back around upon the seat, clenching her hands tightly together in her lap and prompting her younger sister to cast her a look of noticeable displeasure.

"For heaven's sake, Rachel, please be still!" demanded Lizzie. "I was almost certain I'd just seen a red-tailed hawk over there!" she provided, nodding toward the window. Swiftly abandoning her annoyance at finding her view blocked by Rachel's stylish felt hat, the petite redhead leaned forward a bit to gaze speculatively at her sister's curiously flushed countenance. "What is it? What's wrong?"

"Nothing!" Rachel whispered with suspicious anxiety, feverishly wondering if the handsome scoundrel would have the audacity to approach her. Dear Lord, she silently beseeched, please don't let him come near me! She knew without a shadow of a doubt that Micah would not hesitate to kill any man who dared to insult one of his womenfolk. That was the reason she had told no one, not even Lizzie, about what had taken place between the unprincipled stranger and herself.

"There *is* something, isn't there?" the other girl persisted.

"No!" Rachel choked out, then hastily turned to her sister with a desperately pleading look on her beautiful face. "Please, Lizzie, just don't say anymore!"

"Rachel? Lizzie? Is something wrong?" their grandmother interjected, apparently having caught a word or two of their odd conversation. "What are you two whispering about up there?" Lizzie subjected Rachel to another long, searching stare before loudly replying, "Nothing. Everything's fine." She did not fail to miss the mixture of relief and gratitude shining forth from her sister's light blue eyes, and she made certain Jane and Micah were preoccupied with their own discussion once more before lowering her voice to proclaim, "Either you tell me what it is that's got you so nervous and upset, or I'll take it upon myself to—"

"I . . . I can't explain it to you now, Lizzie!" murmured Rachel, suddenly feeling a trifle weak and shaky. The rocking motion of the train didn't help matters any.

"Why not?"

She was attempting to formulate some sort of rationalization for her sister's benefit when she became acutely aware of a man's long legs moving nonchalantly into her line of vision beside Lizzie. A pair of taut, lean-muscled thighs were molded to perfection by the blue denim of his trousers, and Rachel could feel her face burning as her eyes were irrevocably drawn upward . . . past a pair of trim, manly hips to an admirably broad, linen-covered chest . . . to a ruggedly masculine, sun-bronzed visage that wore a mocking smile of pure devilment.

His eyes were full of the same sort of sardonic amusement she had glimpsed within their gleaming jade depths the night before. He paused in the narrow aisle beside them, withdrew the hat from his head with studied unhaste, and nodded down at an inexplicably mesmerized Rachel.

A startled Lizzie tilted her chin back to stare up at him at the same moment her blushing sister awakened from her momentary trance and tore her sparkling opal gaze away from his silently taunting one. The red-haired girl's lightly freckled countenance wore a puzzled frown as she transferred her closely scrutinizing gaze to Rachel, then back to the stranger. She watched as he replaced the hat atop his neatly trimmed, thick brown hair and sauntered forward to an empty seat in the very front of the car.

"Do you know that man, Rachel?" Micah suddenly questioned behind her. He had spared only a passing glance for the man who had momentarily paused in the aisle and looked down at Rachel a few seconds earlier, but he scowled darkly as it now occurred to him that the tall stranger might actually have been paying more than proper attention to his beautiful young granddaughter. Micah was well accustomed to the masculine admiration Rachel drew with such disturbing frequency.

"No, Micah," Rachel managed to say, giving a swift shake of her golden head. She did not turn to face him, realizing that if she did so, he would immediately notice something amiss. "I have no earthly idea who the gentleman is," she added for emphasis, telling herself with an inward snort of disgust that she should have truthfully referred to him as anything other than a "gentleman!"

Her cheeks blushed rosily once more as she recalled with disquieting clarity the feel of the rogue's hand on the thinly covered roundness of her derriere, the insulting laughter in his resonant voice as he called her "Clover." *Clover.* A new wave of humiliation washed over her at the thought that he had seen what no other man had!

"He acted a damned sight too familiar to suit me," Micah finally muttered, but obviously dismissed the matter from his mind as he and Jane resumed their discussion of the family's dwindling finances. It was going to take practically every cent remaining to purchase the needed supplies and stock once they arrived in Miles City.

Rachel, meanwhile, sank even lower into her seat and refused to so much as glance forward, fearful of encountering a certain pair of taunting green eyes. The ever-perspicacious Lizzie, suffering no such qualms, only added to her sister's discomfort by subjecting the man in question, who was now lithely bending his tall frame into the seat several rows ahead, to a bold, calculating look. She then made known her conclusions in a rather offhanded manner.

"I'll grant you he's a fine specimen, sister dear, but he behaves a bit too self-assured. To tell the truth, I wouldn't have thought he was at all the type of man you'd find so fascinating. It's plain to see that you do, you know. Where did you meet him?"

"I didn't meet . . . I don't know who he is!" Rachel denied in a strident whisper, too perturbed to take much notice of the sizable herd of pronghorn antelope roaming across the plains outside her window. She reached up and almost tore the hat from her head, jabbing the hatpin into the unresisting fabric and pretending an icy composure she was far from feeling as she smoothed a wayward golden curl from her silken brow. Why oh why did he have to be on the same train? she fervently bemoaned.

"Well, he sure as thunder seems to know you," Lizzie opined. It was with seldom displayed prudence that she finally dropped the subject, at least for the time being, and settled back against the seat in an effort to relax and perhaps catch a few extra winks of sleep.

Sleep, however, was the last thing on Rachel's mind.

As the morning wore on, she began to feel increasingly stiff from sitting in one position so long, and her neck had begun to ache as a result of the time she had spent staring out the window. It was not at all the way she had envisioned the day's journey.

The train pulled into the next station a little before noon, affording the passengers a much-appreciated opportunity to stretch their legs and get a bite to eat. Jane, like the few other women on board, had packed a goodly supply of food in a large woven hamper, and the Parkers were only too happy to take advantage of the brief respite in travel as they stepped down from the train and made their way to a tree-shaded spot near the small, tin-roofed depot.

Rachel's eyes seemed to have a will of their own, for no matter how much she endeavored to keep them from straying about the area, they were persistent in an attempt to catch sight of the irrepressible knave who was responsible for the topsy-turvy condition of her stomach. But he was nowhere to be seen. Soon, everyone boarded the train again and settled back for the second half of the journey.

"I don't see your cowboy anywhere," Lizzie confided to her sister as the two of them resumed their seats.

"He's not 'my cowboy'!" firmly corrected Rachel, straightening her jacket with a no-nonsense tug and repinning a portion of her skillfully arranged chignon. Inwardly, she was quite dismayed, and more than a little confused, by the strange sense of disappointment she felt. He had not reentered the car by the time the engine jerked the train forward again, and Rachel told herself that the midway depot must have been his destination. He was more than likely on his way home now . . . perhaps to his wife.

Pity the woman who must endure such a wayward scoundrel, that inner voice of Rachel's expounded with mischievous sarcasm.

The corners of her mouth turned down into a severe, self-reproaching frown, and she released a heavy sigh before turning her attention upon the passing landscape once more. She was staunchly determined not to waste another moment's thought on a highly unsavory incident that was best forgotten!

"Miles City!"

The conductor bellowed the name one last time for the benefit of any passenger who might possibly be a bit hard-of-hearing. His voice rang out above the din inside the car, now brimming with activity, the passengers eager to disembark as they hurried to gather their things and throng toward the doorways. As usual, the Parkers were the last to leave, Jane having professed in the very beginning of their travels a profound reluctance at fighting her way through crowds.

When Rachel finally stepped down beside her sister and grandparents, she was momentarily stunned by the sight which met her eyes. She was unprepared for both the size and civilization of the Montana cow town.

Situated on the south bank of the Tongue River, only a short distance from where the Tongue empties into the mighty Yellowstone, Miles City was built on two sides of a large square. The buildings, most of them two-storied and ranging from substantial, neatly painted frame structures to the more contemporary brick, were of an impressive number. Practically every kind of business appeared to be in evidence—hotels, saloons, restaurants, dance halls, general stores, a theater, a sawmill, and even a brewery. A sprawling livestock yard, complete with loading chutes for the cattle, was located near the spacious Northern Pacific depot where Rachel and her family stood gazing curiously about.

A neat row of street lamps ran down both sides of the crowded main thoroughfare, and newly strung telephone lines could be seen atop the narrow, rough-hewn poles towering above the wooden sidewalks and unpaved streets. A profusion of horses and mules were hitched to the splintered rails bordering the store fronts of the major supply center which had been founded in 1879 but had enjoyed a spiraling boom since the coming of the railroad some three years earlier. Miles City was now the very heart of a vast kingdom of cattle, and the city teemed with men who were involved in the business of raising the bovine stock.

But, as Rachel noted, the people filling the streets were not all cattlemen. There were gamblers, doctors, lawyers, merchants, saloon keepers, common laboring men, and even soldiers in blue uniforms who were enjoying a day's leave from the nearby cavalry post called Fort Keogh.

The female population, however, was the most easily classified—it was not at all difficult to discern which women were employed by the saloons, dance halls, and "sporting houses." The other women were either wives and daughters, teachers, cooks and waitresses, seamstresses, or other such "honorably employed" ladies.

Rachel was aware of the fact that the country for hundreds of miles about was still virtually wilderness, a wide-open prairie where thousands of buffalo had flourished only a few years previously. She had glimpsed enough of the surrounding landscape to know that it was one of sharp contrasts, and she now somewhat dazedly reflected that the city before her wasn't at all what she had expected.

"It's time we got moving," pronounced Micah at last, raising his voice to be heard above the noise that was a combination of people, horses, wagons, dogs, cattle, and the faint strains of piano music which drifted on the warm afternoon breeze. He was a trifle overwhelmed by the size of the place, having envisioned a much smaller settlement along the lines of a few towns they had passed along the way.

"Where to first?" asked Jane, her own kindly features reflecting a certain bemusement at all the noise and hustle-bustle.

"The livery stable ought to be a good place to start."

There were a surprising number of such establishments from which to choose, but Micah finally settled upon one he spied across the street with a large, hand-painted sign bearing the names of its proprietors—Farrell and Johnson's. The Parkers then discovered that crossing the flurry of activity that was Main Street was easier said than done, but they managed to dodge several careening wagons and buggies as they headed into the place where they would purchase horses and a conveyance of their own.

Once they had seen to making all the necessary arrangements for supplies, they procured rooms at what was apparently the most popular hostelry in town, The Macqueen House. Headquarters for cattlemen, as well as those hoping to become cattlemen, the lobby of the wooden structure was filled with a great number of rather boisterous patrons, making it imperative that Rachel,

Elizabeth, and Jane remain close together as they followed Micah's instructions and went upstairs while he took himself off to see to a last bit of business elsewhere. It was no easy task for the three Parker women to reach the welcome privacy of their rooms without being rudely jostled by some of the more rambunctious guests stomping up and down the crowded stairway.

A short distance away, Micah entered the Custer County courthouse, a large brick structure boasting decidedly gothic architecture, and presented one of the clerks with the handwritten bill of sale to his newly acquired property. When he returned to the hotel and his patiently waiting family less than half an hour later, it was with the news that he now possessed an exact description of where the ranch was situated.

Rachel, sitting beside her grandfather in the hotel's restaurant later that evening, seized the opportunity provided when Jane and Elizabeth momentarily absented themselves from the table. She turned to Micah with a slight frown of concern knitting her brows and gently probed. "There's something else, isn't there? You learned something else about the ranch when you were at the courthouse, didn't you, Micah?"

"What makes you say that?" he evasively countered, looking unusually discomfited as he averted his eyes from hers.

"You might as well tell me," Rachel insisted with a soft smile, "because you know better than anyone how capable I am of badgering you until you give in!" Micah gave a low chuckle, then grew solemn again and shifted in his chair before reluctantly conceding, "All right. But don't breathe a word of this to the other two. I don't want them worrying." Rachel nodded in silent agreement, and his gray eyes clouded with angry remembrance as he quietly divulged, "Just as soon as I gave the fellow over at the courthouse that bill of sale, he started acting mighty peculiar. He wanted to know how I'd come by the property."

"Did you tell him?" She had known from the very beginning that Micah's impulsive purchase of a murderer's ranch would lead to nothing but trouble!

"No. I told him it was none of his damned business. Then I told him to go ahead and see to transferring the deed, but he mumbled something about having to make certain the bill of sale wasn't a forgery. Said 'no MacBride would willingly part with his land'." He paused a moment, his weathered features darkening, his flinty gaze narrowing. "The fact that the bastard was near to calling me a thief was bad enough, but he had the gall to tell me he wouldn't transfer the deed till he'd got hold of a man by the name of Logan MacBride."

"Oh, Micah!" sighed Rachel, the expression on her beautiful young face growing quite troubled. "What are we going to do now?"

"We're going to go on out to our ranch tomorrow and take possession, just like we planned." There was an obstinate set to his face, and the uneasy feeling within Rachel increased. She wanted to question him to an even greater extent, but her sister and grandmother returned at that point, thereby making further discussion of the matter impossible. She told herself that she would have to find a way to be alone with Micah later.

But a way never presented itself, and Rachel was forced to curb her impatience to speak with her grandfather as the long summer evening deepened into a cool, moonlit night. Elizabeth had already drifted off to sleep by the time Rachel finished readying herself for bed. There were no baths on the top floor; the only one was located downstairs just off a barber shop, so she had bathed herself as thoroughly as possible in a wash basin in the tiny room she shared with her sister. The walls of the hotel were so thin that the guests were able to catch every sound from one end to the other, resulting in more than one embarrassed gasp from the minority of female patrons in the building.

Rachel drew the nightgown over her head and took up a silver-handled hairbrush to begin tugging it carefully through the mass of gleaming blond tresses cascading freely about her face and shoulders. She had just turned away from the oval, gilt-edged mirror hanging on the papered wall above the washstand when her ears detected a sudden commotion on the upstairs landing just outside her room.

She heard the slurred voices of two men raised in anger, swiftly followed by a muffled oath and what sounded suspiciously like bare, hard-boned flesh connecting with more of the same. As she stood listening with wide-eyed intensity in the pale lamplight filling the sparse confines of her room, there was a strangled cry of pain, almost as if some wild animal had just been mortally wounded.

Rachel could stand no more. Pausing to fling her wrapper about her shoulders, she crept to the doorway and silently drew the bolt. Intending to do nothing more than peer cautiously outward and make certain no one had been seriously injured, or perhaps killed, she was totally unprepared for what happened next.

She had eased the door open only a fraction of an inch when a body came smashing violently against its hard bulk. Rachel was sent hurtling backward into the room, a sharp gasp torn from her lips as she came into forceful contact with the opposite wall. It was due to an admirable sense of balance that she managed to keep from stumbling forward and falling to her knees, and she hastily shook the riotously tumbling hair from her face as she endeavored to pinpoint the cause of her abrupt misfortune.

Stunned and breathless, she clapped a hand to her open mouth as her horror-stricken gaze fell upon the unconscious form of a man lying in the open doorway of her room. She had time to do nothing more than steal a quick, anxious glance over at the slumbering form of Elizabeth, who merely stirred a bit and rolled onto her side, before another man, this one upright but swaying unsteadily, appeared in the dimly lit doorway.

Of quite a bit more than medium height, he appeared to be a rather young fellow, though it was difficult to tell when given the bruised and bloodied condition of his face. His bleary, red-rimmed eyes focused on a temporarily dumbfounded Rachel with some difficulty, but his grip was surprisingly firm as he suddenly reached out and seized her hand.

"Hot damn! Come on, honey!" he rasped out with a crooked yet unmistakably lecherous grin in her direction. "Now that I've taken care of that snake-eyed son of a bitch, let's you'n me see about havin' ourselves a little celebration!" Yanking her forward before she could force a scream from her dry throat, he lifted her bodily and slung her over his shoulder as if she were nothing more than a sack of meal, then spun about and headed back out into the deserted hallway.

"No!" Rachel finally managed to gasp out, struggling in frantic protest now. "Let go of me! Put me down!" Her breathless cries were further muted by the thick curtain of hair streaming about her as she was bent upside-down over her slightly inebriated captor's shoulder. She was shocked into renewed speechlessness as she felt his hand sliding up her lower body to her hips, his fingers probing the soft flesh through the thin covering of her white cotton nightgown as her wrapper was easily tugged away.

"You ain't nearly as well padded as some of them other gals, but I don't aim to complain!" he pronounced, chuckling evilly. Rachel kicked and writhed with increasing vigor, and she had just opened her mouth to emit an ear-piercing scream for help when her captor, suddenly finding his path blocked, growled menacingly, "Get out of my way!" Rachel's struggles abruptly ceased, and she nearly fainted with relief. Trying in vain to catch a glimpse of the man who had just reached the top step and positioned himself between her tormentor and the stairway, she could see only a pair of long, denim-covered legs and dark tan leather boots. The boots looked vaguely familiar to Rachel—their owner's voice even more so.

"You're drunk, you stupid bastard," the tall, broad-shouldered man drawled. His countenance wore a faint, inoffensive grin, and his low tone was good-naturedly mocking. Rachel could see the way he negligently looped his thumbs into his belt loops and leaned unconcernedly against the top bannister of the narrow staircase. "If I'm not mistaken, your little friend there doesn't seem too happy about being treated like a side of beef. Why don't you let her go?" His words, though quietly and amiably spoken, were nevertheless more of a command than a request.

"I am *not* his friend!" protested Rachel, still trying in vain to twist about to face her questionable rescuer.

"What business is it of yours?" her dangerously intoxicated captor sneered at the other man. "Now get out of my way, damn it!" He clamped a rough hand to his prisoner's futilely squirming backside and tried to push his way past.

The next thing Rachel knew, she was watching the rug-strewn wooden floor of the landing come up to meet her. A soft, strangled cry escaped her lips as she felt herself falling. Before she could be crushed beneath the heavy weight of her suddenly crumpling abductor, however, a strong arm snaked about her waist and pulled her upward to safety.

"The blasted fool must have been drunker than I thought. I barely hit him," her liberator remarked in a deep, resonant voice laced with amusement. His sinewy arm was still fastened tightly about Rachel's waist, her back pressed against the length of his hard-muscled body. She jerked her awestruck gaze away from the limp, unconscious form of the man lying only a few feet away from his equally misguided companion and turned it upon her heretofore unknown champion.

It was obvious that he recognized her at the same moment she gasped in acknowledgment of his identity.

"You!" proclaimed Rachel in stunned astonishment, her sparkling blue eyes growing round as saucers.

"Well, well, if it isn't 'Clover'," he murmured, the irony of the situation bringing a slow smile to his handsome face. "Tell me," he said, holding her close as he peered speculatively down at her upturned face in the semidarkness of the hotel passageway, "do you always go about getting yourself in these 'peculiar' situations? Or is this perhaps something you staged for my benefit?"

"For your—" she started to echo in disbelief, then broke off as she bristled beneath his well-remembered, taunting sea-green gaze. "Let go of me!" she furiously snapped, attempting to pry his arm loose.

"How can I be sure you won't get into any more trouble?" he retorted with a low, mocking laugh, ignoring her determined but ineffectual efforts to free herself. "You know, I feel somewhat responsible for you now, seeing as how I've already had the pleasure of—"

"Are you going to release me, or am I going to be forced to summon assistance?"

"Haven't we been through this before?"

Rachel was, once again, quite pointedly aware of the feel of his lean and muscular body against her struggling softness. The nameless rogue was equally conscious of the repetitive intimacy of their position, for he was battling a powerful surge of reawakened desire for her as he watched the delectable curve of her full breasts rise and fall above his arm as her thinly clad, delightfully feminine hips fanned across his responsive masculinity.

"Shouldn't you be expressing your undying gratitude to me instead of shooting sparks at me with those beautiful cat's eyes of yours?" he taunted, his warm breath stirring the golden curls near her ear.

"Cat's eyes?" Rachel indignantly repeated, twisting back around to confront him again. Her lovely young face was quite stormy, the opal fire in her gaze promising him dire retribution. "Unhand me this instant, or I shall see to it that you are arrested for your . . . your impertinent manhandling!" This has to be a nightmare—this can't be happening again! she reasoned with herself in silent desperation, her distress fueled by the undeniable stirring of her blood at his touch. Good heavens, was she no better than the sort of woman her former captor had assumed her to be? What was there about the green-eyed scoundrel that caused her to experience such a disturbing array of emotions?

"It's no crime to rescue a fair maiden and then request an appropriate reward," he retorted. A strange light glowed in his eyes in the next instant, the same purposeful light Rachel had viewed within those deepening jade orbs once before. All traces of humor had disappeared from his ruggedly handsome countenance by now, and it was without warning that he gripped her arm and spun her about. "And by damn, reward I'm going to have!" he huskily decreed, his voice edged with what sounded like devil-may-care defiance as he yanked Rachel close.

She was unaware of how wild and disheveled—and innocently seductive—she looked, what with her thick golden tresses streaming unrestrainedly about her and her supple curves shielded from his burning gaze only by the scant protection of her thin cotton nightgown. She suddenly found herself struck speechless, able to utter nothing more than a soft gasp in protest as she was swept away from the staircase to the darkness of one corner of the landing.

Her feet scarcely touching the floor, Rachel was imprisoned by two powerful arms tightening about her trembling softness like bands of steel. Before she could finally vocalize her objections, she was silenced by a warm, imminently skillful mouth descending upon her parted lips. A low, helpless moan rose in her throat as she tried in vain to push away. A firm hand moved up to the back of her head to ensure her submission, his fingers entwining within the fragrant golden curls as his lips tutored hers in a deep, sensuously persuasive kiss.

He explored the sweet nectar of her mouth, his tongue teasing and caressing at hers while an overwhelmed and disoriented Rachel felt all coherent thought temporarily slipping away. She was aware only of the tall stranger's hard, muscular body pressing against her pliant softness from head to toe, of the provocative, impassioned way his lips claimed hers.

She drew in her breath upon another gasp when his hand left her head and followed a bold, searing path down her spine to the faintly quivering roundness of her buttocks. His fingers curled possessively about the twin, womanly spheres as he drew her even closer against him, and Rachel's eyelids fluttered open in startlement when her lower body came into contact with the unmistakable evidence of his virility.

But her momentary return to reason was abruptly ended as his other hand moved to the beckoning fullness of her breasts, the breasts he vividly recalled as being so perfectly formed and tipped with pert, enchanting rosiness. Rachel moaned quietly at the exquisite assault of his hands and mouth, her entire body filled with a bewildering but undeniably beguiling warmth. She gasped once more as his hand closed gently about one of her breasts, his palm rubbing with tantalizing slowness across the sensitive peak. With only the delicate fabric of her nightdress serving as a barrier, she was well able to feel the heat of his passion-fevered flesh against hers.

His other hand suddenly relinquished the silken curve of her hips and stole insistently upward to the row of tiny pearl buttons on the front of her high-necked gown. With surprising deftness, he unfastened the prim garment as far down as possible, exposing the shadowed valley between Rachel's breasts.

Her head tilted backward as her senses reeled, and an involuntary tremor shook her when his lips roamed urgently across the tops of her breasts, his hot mouth searing the pale, swelling flesh of the satiny globes. In a benumbed state of consciousness, Rachel told herself that what she was doing was sheer madness, that it was beyond belief for her to be allowing a man who was little more than a total stranger to touch and kiss her with such wild abandon. Dear Lord, what was happening to her?

"And I say let's go on up and get some shut-eye. We ain't gonna be no use at all it we can't stay astride tomorrow!" a man wearily told a group of young, bleary-eyed cowboys who were at that moment climbing the stairs with an accompanying scuffling of boots and creaking of strained wood.

Rachel's eyes popped wide open, the realization that someone was approaching serving the same purpose as a dash of cold water upon her face. Tearing her lips from the irresistible rogue with a muffled cry of heartfelt shame, she would have darted away from him and toward the sanctuary of her room, but his hands held her fast, the two of them remaining unobserved in the darkened corner.

"Hey, ain't that ole Stan and J.T. over there?" a second member of the ascending group remarked, reaching the top step only to take note of the unavoidable sight of the two drunken cowpunchers still lying exactly where they had fallen.

"Come on. Let's get 'em to bed," decreed one of his cohorts. It wasn't long before they had managed to lift the men known only as Stan and J.T., their efforts punctuated by several ear-stinging curses, and carried their now loudly snoring friends down the long, narrow hallway to rooms at the opposite end.

Rachel, once more left alone with the devastatingly handsome knave who had provoked such a perplexing wealth of sensations and unfamiliar yearnings deep within her, took action as soon as she heard a succession of doors slamming. She was surprised when he did not attempt to stop her as she pushed abruptly past him and headed for what she had earlier believed to be the safety of her room she shared with her sister.

Giving a silent prayer of thanksgiving for the fact that her grandparents had been assigned a room farther down the hall, for it would have been unthinkably disastrous if Micah had witnessed her shame, she could not prevent her eyes from straying back to the man who stood watching her belated flight.

He had stepped from the secluded darkness of the corner into the dim light of the landing again, and Rachel was certain she glimpsed a mocking smile lurking about his mouth, though there was no accompanying chuckle this time. She paused in the doorway, unaware of the fact that as she did so, the lamplight streaming forth from the interior of the room behind her revealed a highly shocking display of the perfect figure beneath the flimsy material of her nightgown.

"If I never see you again, it will be too soon!" she stridently whispered, her hand clutching at the unfastened neckline of her gown. Her eyes were blazing magnificently, and there was a most becoming rosiness to her cheeks. She would have been further chagrined to know how much her indignation only added fuel to the man's raging desire for her.

"Fate seems determined to throw us together," he drawled, a deceptively impassive expression on his sun-bronzed face. There was an unfathomable gleam in his eyes as he told her in a low, even tone, "I think you'd better take my advice and run the other way if you ever see me coming, for I'll be damned if I can make sense of what keeps happening between us!"

Rachel's eyes widened in alarm. She whirled about and finally took refuge in her room, closing the door with a bit more force than was necessary. She then stood leaning breathlessly against it, startled when she heard the just-awakened redhead in the big iron bed irritably demand, "How's a body supposed to sleep with all the confounded noise you're making?" Rolling to face her sister, Lizzie squinted across at a visibly shaken Rachel. "What in tarnation happened to you?"

"Just . . . just go back to sleep, Lizzie!"

"What happened to your hair?" asked the increasingly curious girl as she sat up in the bed and subjected her sister to a closely scrutinizing look.

"My hair?" echoed Rachel, her hands moving from her burning cheeks to her wildly disheveled locks.

"It looks as though you pitched it up in the air and then stepped under it," Lizzie happily supplied.

"Oh, I . . . please, Lizzie, I just want to get some sleep!" She hurried across to the small table beside the bed and blew out the lamp. But even the prevailing darkness could not conceal her lingering distress as she climbed into bed beside her sister and desperately sought the blissful unconsciousness that would not come.

III

Telltale shadows underscored the luminescence of Rachel's eyes the following morning, and there was a faint but noticeable pallor to her usually glowing features, but none of her family remarked upon it as they set about loading their things into the new wagon and headed out to take possession of their ranch. The vehicle they had purchased was open, its long body surrounded by shelboards to increase its hauling capacity. Their baggage was piled high in the bed of the wagon, along with the provisions they had deemed necessary for setting up housekeeping in their new home.

Leaving the commotion and flurry of Miles City, they drove south along the Tongue River, often referred to as the "crookedest stream in Montana," but whose name was more than likely derived from the tonguelike, tree-dotted outcrop of rock near the confluence of the Tongue and Little Tongue Rivers. The warm June day had dawned bright and clear, with only an occasional patch of puffy white clouds to cast shadows upon the plains. The heavy carpeting of "short grass," a surprisingly verdant pasturage that served to keep thousands of grazing cattle in excellent condition, rolled in the never-ceasing wind much like a sea. As far as the eye could see, there was the vast, sagebrush-mantled prairie, with sporadically situated buttes and thick groves of cottonwoods providing welcome contrast.

Rachel sat beside her sister in the wagonbed, the two of them exchanging comments about the countryside as their grandparents on the seat above them did the same. There were few signs of civilization in evidence as they traveled farther away from Miles City, and they passed no one as the wagon wheels bounced over the uneven, rutted surface of the road. Most of the morning had passed before either Rachel or Elizabeth realized it, but they were nonetheless exceedingly grateful for the brief time of rest Micah proclaimed when the sun was positioned almost directly overhead. After stretching their legs and partaking of the lunch Jane had packed, they were anxious to be on their way again.

Their interest was caught a brief time later when they spied a collection of tiny mounds rising from the ground. A black-tailed prairie dog assumed an alert stance as the wagon neared, and he quickly began emitting a series of high-pitched barks to announce the approaching danger to the colony. Within moments, there was an incessant din of shrill chatter that swelled in intensity before the animals dashed into the safety of their burrows.

Shortly thereafter, Rachel spied a vulture gliding and circling in the air currents overhead. Her imperceptibly narrowing gaze was drawn downward, and for the first time since she and her family had arrived in Montana, she was afforded a close view of a herd of the short-horned cattle she had already heard so much about.

Although thousands of Texas longhorns shared the range, it was generally acknowledged that the fat shorthorn stock from Idaho and Oregon were the best cattle to run on the Montana prairie, and thoroughbred shorthorn bulls were frequently purchased by the local cattlemen to upgrade the existing herds. With any luck, mused Rachel, they would soon find that a shorthorn or two belonged to them now.

By the time they finally arrived at the property whose location had been reluctantly disclosed to Micah by the clerk at the courthouse, it was already well into the afternoon. The size of the ranch awaiting them proved to be more than a trifle astonishing, especially considering the bargain price Micah had paid for it. Aside from the main house, which was a single-story structure built of logs in the shape of an L, there was a log stable for horses, a small bunkhouse for the hands, a large stock barn, and even a tin-roofed shed which served as a blacksmith shop and which, along with the bunkhouse, formed two sides of the split-rail corral. There was a wide, tree-flanked stream flowing near the impressive array of buildings that were nestled amongst a gentle, sloping rise in the land.

"It's a hell of a lot more than I thought it'd be," decreed Micah with a slight, expressive nod.

"Oh, Micah!" breathed an awestruck Jane as she allowed him to help her down from the wagon. "Are you sure this is our place?"

"This is it right enough. The directions were clear. The road runs right past the place, just like the man said." He strode forward a bit and pointed toward the house. "See that? The name 'MacBride' is carved there above the door." A rare smile of pure pleasure lit his weathered, harsh-lined face as he pulled the hat from his head. The warm summer wind, blowing with remarkable uniformity, tugged at his graying black hair. "This is it. This is our new home, Jane." He took his wife's hand and drew her along with him as he set off to inspect the house.

"I . . . I can't believe it," murmured Rachel, watching her grandparents and wondering how such a prosperous-looking place could have belonged to a cold-blooded murderer, a murderer who had only a week ago paid for his crime at the end of a rope.

"Thunderation! How in the world was Micah able to afford a place like this?" Lizzie marveled aloud. She gathered up her dusty calico skirts and climbed down beside her sister. Scanning their surroundings with more than a touch of youthful wonder, she frowned thoughtfully and remarked, "We all know he was never paid a decent wage as a sheriff. How do you suppose he got enough to—"

"I think the seller was willing to take whatever he was offered for it. If you'll recall, the man who sold it to Micah had never seen it." Rachel felt another sharp twinge of uneasiness at the recollection of the way their grandfather had acquired ownership of the property, but she staunchly told herself that there was no use in dwelling on what was already past. The ranch belonged to Micah now. And she, for one, was going to do everything she could to help him make a go of it.

But, as Rachel and her family soon discovered, ranching required a great deal more work than any of them had anticipated. It took the first several days for them to set the house to rights and make all the necessary repairs about the place, and only then were they able to turn their attention to the actual business of raising stock. Micah had already arranged for the delivery, within a week's time, of a hundred head of longhorns and three good saddle horses, all of which he had purchased from a man at the livery stable on that first day in Miles City.

They still had no way of knowing how many head of cattle might have belonged to the ranch's previous owner, although Elizabeth had eagerly suggested they set aside all the more domestic endeavors and head on out to the open range without further delay. Her suggestion had been reluctantly waved aside by her grandfather, who judged it wisest to wait until they could be mounted on the properly trained cow horses due to arrive any day. They had as yet to become familiar with the lay of the land, he had gone on to insist, and he didn't want to find himself and Lizzie stranded out in the middle of nowhere on a pair of "good-for-nothing buggy nags."

Throughout those first days at the ranch, the unbidden image of a certain mocking, green-eyed rogue flared persistently to the forefront of Rachel's thoughts. No matter how determined she was to forget him, to forget the mortifying details of their two brief, albeit impassioned, encounters, she could not erase the memory of his masterful embraces from her troubled mind.

She buried herself in her chores, endeavoring to toil so long and so hard that she would have neither the time nor the inclination to think of him . . . but to no avail. Even when she succeeded in blocking all thought of the tall, devilishly handsome stranger from her mind for a brief period of time, he invaded her dreams at night, causing her to toss restlessly and awaken far from refreshed. And though she constantly berated herself for her weakness, she could not seem to help experiencing a tremor of renewed excitement whenever she recalled the feel of his hard, demanding lips upon hers . . .

It was on the fourth day of the Parkers' habitation of the ranch that Rachel spied a group of horsemen approaching. Having just finished sweeping the long, narrow front porch of the cabin, she was staring thoughtfully toward the early morning horizon, her chin resting on her crossed hands atop the broomstick. An appreciative smile lit her face as she noted the way the cloudless sky was ablaze with the last yellow-orange streaks of the dawn, but the smile quickly faded when her gaze fell upon the riders who had within moments thundered directly up to the house.

Rachel scarcely had time to set aside the broom and call for her grandfather before the men abruptly drew rein before her. There were half a dozen of them, their faces disturbingly solemn and tight-lipped.

"You the Parkers?" asked one of the riders, his narrowed, gold-flecked brown eyes raking insolently up and down Rachel's well-proportioned form. She was uncomfortably aware of the boldly admiring gazes of the others upon her as well, and she suddenly found herself wishing she was wearing something a bit more concealing than the worn and faded gray cotton gown she reserved for housecleaning. But she lifted her chin proudly and confronted the young, raven-haired leader of the group squarely.

"Yes. We just moved in a few days ago," she answered calmly. Her silken, honey-colored tresses, swept away from the delicate oval of her face with a black velvet ribbon, caught the sunlight as she took a step forward, and she found herself the recipient of a strangely unsettling look from the apparent leader's dark, piercing eyes. Possessed of a swarthy complexion and ruggedly aristocratic features, he was undeniably striking, though a trifle hawkish-looking, and Rachel surmised that he was only five or six years older than herself. There was something about him, however, something in the way his lips curled upward into the beginning of a slow, arrogantly mocking smile, that seemed vaguely familiar to her.

"I hadn't counted on finding someone like you out here," he told her in a voice full of hidden meaning as he negligently tipped his hat farther back upon his head. His eyes gleamed with undisguised covetousness, and he was momentarily tempted to waver from the course of action he himself had set.

Rachel stared wordlessly up at him, her breath catching on a silent gasp and a dull flush rising to stain her cheeks as she glimpsed the obvious lust in his eyes. The other riders, most of them as young as Rachel, remained watchful and silent, making her feel increasingly discomfited as she was subjected to another long, lingering perusal by the man who sat astride an impatiently snorting, chestnut-colored stallion.

"Mornin'," Rachel was relieved to hear Micah quietly proclaim as he finally rounded the corner of the porch and moved to stand beside her. He had been in the stock barn with Jane and Elizabeth when Rachel had called him, and his hand still lightly gripped the pitchfork he had been using. As always, his gun rested in a tooled leather holster buckled low upon his hips. He nodded curtly toward the horsemen before asking with only the merest hint of a polite smile, "What can I do for you?"

"You've got that backwards, mister," the lead rider

drawled with derisive sarcasm. "We've come to tell you what *we're* gonna do for *you.*" For the first time, there were signs of shared, sinister amusement on the faces of his companions.

"Who are you? And what do you want?" demanded Micah brusquely. Rachel moved closer to him, her blue eyes clouding with apprehension.

"The name's MacBride—Vance MacBride. And it so happens that you're trespassing on MacBride property."

"It's Parker property now," Micah tersely corrected. A deep frown creased his weathered brow as his slate gray eyes narrowed up at his accuser. "I've got a bill of sale." The younger man leaned forward a bit, his hands curling tensely about the horn of his saddle at the same time his lips curled up into an unmistakable sneer.

"I know all about that. Heard about the way you tried to get clear deed to the place over at the courthouse the other day. I'm telling you here and now that the 'bill of sale' you're so damned proud of is nothing more than a worthless piece of paper as far as I'm concerned!" There was a menacing light in his dark eyes now, a dangerously grim set to his jaw. "This is MacBride land. I don't know what the hell made you think you could come in here and—"

"I own this ranch," Micah reiterated in a low, deceptively even tone, his fingers tightening upon the handle of the pitchfork, "and I'll be damned if I'll let you sit there and call me a liar! Now get off my land!"

Rachel's eyes widened in growing alarm as they flew up to encounter the look of malevolent intent upon Vance MacBride's swarthy, fury-darkening features. Her worried gaze moved hastily back to her grandfather, and she could literally feel the explosive tension in the cool morning air.

"It's MacBride land, damn you—always has been and always will be!" snarled Vance MacBride, then demanded in a tone seething with barely controlled violence, "This place belongs to my cousin Tate. And Tate would sooner die before selling off any of the MacBride spread!"

"I told you to get off my land!" responded Micah, his own words spoken between tightly clenched teeth. His right hand dropped to his side, positioned in readiness for his gun. Vance MacBride's fingers inched slowly downward toward the weapon sheathed within a leather scabbard on one side of his saddle.

Inhaling sharply as she viewed Micah's defensive stance and the corresponding intent in the other man's eyes, Rachel hastened to intervene. She placed a gently restraining hand upon her grandfather's arm as her voice rang out clearly in the charged silence.

"My grandfather purchased this property from a man back in Wyoming. It so happens that he won it from your cousin during the course of a game of poker." She felt a sharp quiver of fear when MacBride, who obviously did not believe the simple explanation, turned an expression of blazing fury upon her.

"Tate never would've wagered his ranch!"

"But he did!" insisted Rachel earnestly. "What's more, he—"

"That's enough!" Micah tersely cut her off. There was a silent warning in his dully glowing eyes as he spared her a quick look before meeting the smoldering gaze of the younger man. "It makes no difference how I came to own this ranch. The point is, I *do* own it, and I'm telling you for the last time to get the hell off my land!"

The man known as Vance MacBride visibly hesitated.

Wavering between the desire to have it out with the old man then and there, and the realization that if he killed Parker he'd have hell to pay as a result, he begrudgingly accepted the fact that it was best to wait. After he'd done some checking up on Tate, after he'd had some time to investigate the validity of the girl's story, *then* he'd make certain these no-account "honyockers" were sent running with their tails between their legs!

The girl was the only regret he'd have about what was going to happen, Vance told himself, acutely aware of a new surge of pure animal lust as his dark gaze lit briefly upon her once more. Given the time, he'd like nothing more than to—

"Get going!" growled Micah.

Vance, his eyes narrowing into mere slits of rage, battled the temptation to make the old man pay for his insolence. Finally, he signaled to his obediently silent companions and tugged curtly on the reins of his mount, pausing only to issue one last threat to Micah.

"We'll be back, you old bastard. And don't count on winning so easily next time. Next time," he promised with another contemptuous curl of his lip, "you'll find out what happens when you cross a MacBride!" He shot Rachel a frighteningly carnal look before reining about and riding away, his men following in his dust-stirring wake.

The incident left Micah thoroughly incensed, while Rachel was more than a trifle shaken. She gripped his arm as the two of them watched the unexpectedly hostile group of riders growing smaller in the distance.

"Oh, Micah! What will we do when they return?" she anxiously queried, fearful that he would eventually allow his temper to get the better of him and thereby seal his own disastrous fate. The former lawman's hardened features softened a bit as he slowly turned to face her.

"We'll stand our ground," he quietly decreed, his eyes staring deeply into hers. "No one's going to make me give up what's rightfully mine."

"But you heard what he said!"

"I heard. But what he said doesn't mean a blessed thing, Rachel." His steely gaze shifted back toward the now tiny spot of movement disappearing into the deepening gold of the horizon. Muttering a vicious curse beneath his breath, he remarked, half to himself, "I don't give a damn who he is! Just because the young fool seems so confident that the mere mention of his name is guaranteed to strike fear in the hearts of anyone who's got gumption enough to stand up to him . . ." His voice trailed away as Rachel suddenly peered closely up at him, a noticeably dubious light in her opal eyes.

"You know more about the name than you've let on, don't you, Micah? I seem to recall your telling me that the clerk at the courthouse brought up the name of MacBride, too. The name *is* an important one, isn't it? Why?" she demanded, folding her arms across her chest and fixing him with a look that bespoke her determination to know the truth. "Why did that man come here? Why did he behave as if we have no right to be here?"

"Because, as it was my ill-timed luck to learn the first day we set foot in Miles City, the MacBrides own just about the whole damned eastern third of Montana!" he startled her by disclosing with an accompanying grimace of disgust. "And this place is right smack-dab in the middle of their range!" Then, as if he had said too much, Micah's face became an all-too-familiar mask of inscrutability, and he strode wordlessly past Rachel with the pitchfork still clasped in one hand.

Rachel's eyes grew very wide, and an expression of dawning consternation crossed the flawless beauty of her countenance. Gathering up her full skirts, she spun about and hurried after Micah, her mind awhirl with questions.

"I don't understand! How can we possibly hope to make our home here if we are surrounded by relatives of the murderer you arrested and hanged?" She was forced to come to an abrupt halt when Micah unexpectedly stopped and wheeled to face her.

"This is our land now!" he ground out, his eyes taking on the look of cold steel. "No one, I don't give a damn who they are or what they threaten, is going to run us off! We can't turn tail and run, girl. I've never backed down from a fight in my whole life, and I sure as hell don't aim to back down now!"

"But what if he—"

"He was bluffing, Rachel. He knows there's really nothing he can do. I bought this property. I've got a bill of sale to prove it. And even if I do end up having to fight off every damned one of Tate MacBride's kinfolk, I mean to hold what's mine!" Once again, his lips compressed into a tight, thin line of simmering fury as he turned away and headed toward the barn.

Staring after her grandfather in helpless exasperation, Rachel wanted nothing more than to run after him and plead with him to see reason. But she prudently battled the urge, heaving a sigh and smoothing a stray lock of hair from her forehead as the corners of her mouth turned down into a troubled frown.

If Vance MacBride's display of antagonism was any indication of things to come, how could she and her family hope to live there in peace? How could they hope to make a success of the ranch if all of their neighbors were against them? And what if the man's threats turned out to be more than a bluff?

Another long sigh escaped her lips as she raised her eyes to see her grandmother and sister walking purposefully toward Micah. Jane and Lizzie had become unbearably curious about Micah's prolonged absence, and Rachel could hear them demanding to know why he had not as yet returned to help them with the cleaning of the stalls. It seemed the two of them had been so busy chattering to one another in the barn that they had overheard nothing of the unpleasant events of only a few minutes prior.

"MacBride." Rachel murmured the name aloud, her eyes clouding with renewed disquiet. Fervently wishing Micah had never crossed paths with a certain unfortunate member of the mysterious clan, she stood and watched as her family disappeared inside the log-sided barn. The persistent, inexplicable feeling of uneasiness increased, but she resolutely ignored it and marched off to complete her chores.

A brilliant, fiery sunset was just deepening into a star-filled night when a lone horseman guided his magnificent thoroughbred ebony stallion toward the beckoning fire of the roundup camp. Riding with an easy, masculine grace, it appeared as if he had been born to the saddle, his lean yet powerfully muscled thighs maintaining a negligent grip about the animal's sleek midsection as his hands kept an equally casual hold upon the reins.

The rider's trappings were those of an experienced

cowpuncher—a fine, hand-tooled saddle with a rope coiled about the horn, a silver mounted bridle and silver spurs, a pearl-handled six-shooter and cartridge belt with a silver buckle, a fancy quirt with silver mountings, leather chaps buckled on over his form-molding denim trousers, and a bright red kerchief knotted carelessly about his neck. From his stiff-brimmed felt hat sporting a band of diamond-backed rattlesnake skin to his exquisitely fitted, dark tan riding boots, he was the epitome of the Montana range rider, save for the fact that he was a few years older than the men he had hired to work the roundup. The crowd gathered about the fire near the chuckwagon was made up mostly of punchers who were barely out of their teens, the majority of them having followed the trail drives up from Texas.

Whatever they might lack in chronological maturity, the tall rider mused to himself with an inward grin, they sure as hell compensate for in ability. He drew up beside the wagon and agilely dismounted, looping the reins of his mount across the rope spanning one side of the old military conveyance for that purpose.

"Hey, Logan, you comin' on in to stay?" called out one of the participants squatting on one knee before the men-ringed blaze. Some of the company were sitting on the ground, while others were enthroned on their bedrolls. In their hands were tin plates piled high with potatoes, baked beans, beefsteak, and canned tomatoes.

"I need a word with you, Brodie," the other man insisted with quiet authority, already tugging the hat from his head and sauntering toward an unoccupied spot of moon-kissed prairie a short distance from the others.

Brodie MacBride, his youthful, golden features displaying only the merest hint of a frown for the scarcely discernible note of annoyance in Logan's deep voice, lost no time in unbending his slender frame and following his older cousin. The two of them soon faced each other in the silvery glow of the night, Brodie's raven hair shimmering beneath the lunar rays and his startlingly blue eyes narrowing a bit as he raised them to study his cousin's momentarily inscrutable visage. Although considered quite tall by the standards of his mother's people, the Crow, the younger man stood half a head shorter than Logan.

"Something bothering you?" queried Brodie in a low tone, then silently cursed himself for being a jackass and asking the obvious.

"I've got to head on out at first light," supplied Logan, a grim set to his mouth.

"But you just got back a couple of days ago! I thought you were planning to stay until—"

"I was. My plans have changed." Logan MacBride spun about on his booted heel and ground out a savage curse, leaving Brodie to stare in astonishment at his cousin's unusual display of temper. "I got word this morning that Vance is stirring up some new trouble." Vance and trouble, his mind repeated . . . it seemed that the two were synonymous.

"What kind of trouble?" Brodie was well aware of the fact that Vance, a cousin to both himself and Logan, had earned a certain notoriety as the family's "black sheep" these past several years. It was always falling to Logan, as the patriarch of the MacBrides, to make amends for Vance's misdeeds. Until recently, it had been Logan's father who ruled the clan, but now the unwanted task had fallen to Dugan MacBride's only son.

"Stuart rode out to tell me. Seems there's a family by

the name of Parker claiming to have a deed to Tate's ranch."

"That can't be true! Why, you know as well as I do that Tate would never sell his ranch. He might not be too good at working it the way he should, but, damn it, Logan, he'd never sell off any of the MacBride land!"

"Maybe. Maybe not," his cousin murmured thoughtfully, raising a hand to untie the red kerchief and slip it from his neck. He clenched the bandanna in one hand, his eyes gleaming with intense displeasure. "Right now, it's not the authenticity of this Parker fellow's claim that concerns me—it's Vance. Stuart said Vance and some of his men were planning to pay a call on the newcomers. And you and I both know what sort of 'call' Vance is—" He broke off and swore fiercely once more. "Hell, the last thing we need is to have some damned 'honyocker' go screaming to the law about having his rights violated!"

"Maybe they won't turn out to be farmers," remarked Brodie, a faint yet hopeful smile on his handsome young face.

"It won't make any difference. It's MacBride land they're claiming. And in case you don't remember, Tate's place bisects the rest." Heaving a sigh of pure irritation, Logan replaced the hat atop his head and angrily stuffed the kerchief into a back pocket of his trousers. "You're in charge again, Brodie." He hated like anything having to miss the remainder of the spring roundup, which was mainly for the purpose of branding calves, and it galled him mightily to think that no sooner had he been able to rejoin the long-anticipated effort when, because of some thieving bastard taking it into his mind to seize control of a strategic portion of the MacBride spread, he was being forced to leave again.

"Sure, Logan. At the rate we're going, I expect we'll be through by the end of the week." Brodie flashed his cousin a consoling, endearingly lopsided grin. "Ever find yourself wishing you'd been born on the wrong side of the blanket like me?"

"Old Dugan MacBride would no doubt turn over in his grave if I answered you truthfully," Logan sardonically quipped, unable to keep the corners of his mouth from turning up into a responsive smile of appreciative irony. Clapping the younger man on the back, he moved with long, easy strides back toward the fire and the special comradeship of the roundup camp, temporarily dismissing all unpleasantness from his mind as his eyes swept across the huge, softly lowing body of cattle milling restlessly about upon the vast, moonlit range in the distance.

Would *she* be there when he got back to Miles City? Logan suddenly found himself wondering. He had firmly resisted the temptation to try and discover her name, but there was still a damnably tenacious urge within him to find out more about the golden-haired wildcat who possessed the disturbing ability to set his blood afire at every turn. No matter how hard he tried, no matter how much he cursed himself for the peculiar, highly unsettling weakness that had taken hold of him and refused to let go, he couldn't prevent a riotous leaping of his pulses at the mere thought of holding her in his arms once more, of kissing her until she begged for mercy . . .

Muttering a self-deprecating malediction, he was unaware that he had spoken it aloud until his cousin's voice cut in on his thoughts.

"What?" questioned Brodie, casting the taller man a

puzzled frown as he wondered who or what had earned Logan MacBride's fearsome displeasure now.

Logan forced a half-smile to his lips and wordlessly shook his head, then took his place with the others at the fire. Although his handsome face remained inscrutable, there was a telltale gleam smoldering within his sea-green gaze.

Rachel blew out the lamp and scrambled across the bare wooden floor, shivering a bit at the unexpected chill filling the room. Snuggling hastily beneath the patchwork quilt in the bed she shared with her sister, she released a soft, contented sigh as her fatigued body found warmth at last.

"Hell's bells, Rachel, your toes are like icicles!" wailed Lizzie, annoyed at having her own comfort disturbed.

"Oh, Lizzie," Rachel wearily admonished, "you know how it upsets Grandmother to hear you use such unladylike phrases!" She flung one of her long, honey-colored braids over her shoulder and drew the quilt up to her chin as she turned upon her side.

"Grandmother may as well realize once and for all that any hopes she might cherish of my turning out to be like *you* are entirely in vain!" the petite redhead retorted saucily, rolling as far away as possible to the opposite edge of the feather mattress. A heavy sigh filled the night-cloaked silence of their room, which was situated in a back corner of the log house, and Lizzie's youthful features grew unusually solemn a moment later. "You know, I'm beginning to wonder if our coming here was such a good deal after all." There was a discernible note of plaintiveness in her voice, and Rachel's momentary exasperation with her sister quickly evaporated. Easing upright against the brass and iron headboard, she peered solicitously down at the girl beside her, able to make out only the outline of Lizzie's form beneath the mountain of covers.

"Why, Lizzie! I thought you—"

"I know. I was the one who backed Micah's decision the most. But something's troubling him, Rachel. Haven't you noticed? He just doesn't seem to have as much enthusiasm for this place as he did at first. Now that I think about it, it wasn't really until today that he started acting so . . . well, so worried about something."

Rachel bit at her lower lip, her light blue eyes darkening as she wavered between the impulse to tell Elizabeth about the situation with the MacBrides, and the desire to keep from causing her sister undue concern should nothing come of Vance MacBride's threats. Drawing up her knees and clasping her arms about her slender limbs, she chose her words very carefully.

"Micah has a great deal on his mind right now, Lizzie. I'm sure he'll regain his enthusiasm once we're settled in right and proper. It may simply take a few more days." She was startled when Lizzie swiftly rounded on her.

"You know what's troubling him, don't you?" accused the youngest Parker, her brown eyes narrowing up at her sister in a futile attempt to scrutinize her face in the darkness. "You know and you haven't seen fit to tell me!" Before Rachel could answer, Lizzie bounced to her knees upon the bed, her bright red locks tumbling about her shoulders in their usual disorderly fashion. "This place has already come to mean the world to Micah! If there's something going on, something that's standing in the way of our whole family's happiness, then I have a right to know!" she dramatically asserted.

Hesitating for several long moments, Rachel finally concluded that Lizzie's words held undeniable merit. Although Micah might vehemently protest, she would gain an ally by telling Lizzie—a much-needed ally who would help her in trying to caution their grandfather against any possible dangers he faced by refusing to heed Vance MacBride's warning.

"Very well," she quietly acquiesced. She waited until Lizzie scrambled to take a seat beside her, then placed an arm about the girl's shoulders and settled back again with a sigh. "To tell the truth, Lizzie, I don't know if what happened deserves the importance I've attached to it. But the whole thing has to do with where this property is located, as well as with its former owner. You see, the—"

She got no further with her explanation, for a gunshot abruptly shattered the stillness of the night air outside their window. The echoing report was soon followed by another, then another.

"Dear God!" gasped Rachel, scrambling from the bed and flying instinctively to the window. Tearing back the curtains, she gazed in dawning horror at the strengthening flames which snaked about the perimeter of the stock barn.

"What is it?" Lizzie excitedly queried, reaching her sister's side a brief instant later. She clapped a hand to her open mouth, her own eyes widening in alarm at the sight of the engulfing conflagration bursting to life as a result of a few well-placed torches. "Merciful heavens, someone's burning our barn!"

"Whatever you do, Lizzie, don't leave this room!" commanded Rachel, wasting no time before flinging her wrapper about her nightgown-draped shoulders and wrenching open the bedroom door. She raced toward the front doorway, possessed of no clear notion as to what she was going to do once she reached the porch, yet driven by an instinctive force within her to try and put a stop to the destruction. Hampered by the darkness, she nearly collided with Micah, who had just emerged from his and Jane's room in an opposite corner of the house and stood in his nightshirt and trousers, clasping his rifle in protective readiness.

"Stay inside!" he tersely instructed, punctuating his words with a curt nod of his head at Rachel. She had no more than opened her mouth to plead with him against venturing outside alone, when he flung open the front door and stormed vengefully across the rough-hewn planks of the porch. Jane appeared beside Rachel in the next instant, the two of them exchanging brief looks of mutual apprehension before scurrying out into the flame-brightened night after Micah.

"Micah, please!" his wife desperately implored, her words nearly drowned out by the din that was a terrifying combination of gunshots, the roaring of the blaze that was well on its way to consuming the barn, the frightened whinnying of the horses as they galloped away into the night, and the sound of men's voices raised in ill-begotten revelry.

"No, Micah, don't!" cried Rachel. She and her grandmother gathered up the generous folds of their nightgowns and wrappers and sped across the porch. Micah had already rounded the side of the house before they could climb down the steps and give chase.

The moonlight had been obscured by a dense blanket of clouds by this time, but the fire's red-gold glow, its devastating flames reaching up toward the heavens with deadly grace, provided more than ample illumination as Rachel quickly outdistanced her grandmother and darted around the corner after Micah.

She drew up sharply, a ragged gasp escaping her lips at the sight which met her horrified gaze. Micah had just raised his rifle to take aim at one of the mounted aggressors when another member of the drunkenly rampaging group, all of whom had tied their kerchiefs up about the lower half of their faces in order to conceal their identities, threw a looped rope about the proud old lawman and yanked it tight. The other end of the imprisoning rope was secured to the horseman's saddle-horn, and his companions laughed in shared, malevolent amusement while Micah, his rifle clattering to the ground at his feet, struggled in vain against his bonds.

Everything happened with such dizzying swiftness that Rachel could at first only stand and watch in numbed horror as the masked rider spurred his horse forward, dragging her grandfather along the rough ground behind him. She drew a long, shuddering breath as she saw Micah grip the rope and grimace in pain.

"No! Oh, please God, no!" she breathed, her fingers tightening about the edges of her wrapper as she now raced toward the riders gathered near the burning barn, her long golden braids streaming down her back and her thin cotton nightgown flapping about her trim ankles. "Stop it! Let him go!" shouted Rachel, her voice ringing out in sharp, clear tones as she made a frantic attempt to help her grandfather.

She could feel the blood draining from her face as half a dozen masked faces turned to her in the firelight, their attention effectively transferred from a scratched and bruised but otherwise unharmed Micah to his beautiful, half-dressed granddaughter. Jane immediately hastened to her husband's side and knelt beside him. Rachel had no time to contemplate her growing terror as one of the men suddenly reined about and headed straight for her.

She lifted her chin proudly and stood her ground, but the man reached down and swooped her up before him in one quick, seemingly effortless motion, positioning her across his lap. Both of her grandparents cried out at her rough treatment, but no one paid them any mind.

"Look what I got me!" the man crowed in triumphant exuberance to his appreciative cohorts. He kept one hand on the reins while the other began insolently tugging up the hem of her nightgown, prompting Rachel to strike furiously out at him.

"Let go of me!" she demanded hotly, kicking and twisting in an effort to escape as her captor merely snickered. His mirth was quieted in the next moment, however, for Rachel's frenetic movements caused his horse to snort loudly in protest and rear backward. The man cursed and was forced to release his prize in order to control the skittish animal.

While the other men hooted and shouted taunts at their companion's misfortune, Rachel seized the opportunity and hastily pushed herself downward. She was relieved when her bare feet made contact with the cool hardness of the ground, but she was unprepared when the man retaliated by backhanding her across the face. Sent sprawling in the dirt by the blow, she could hear Micah hoarsely proclaiming, "Damn you! I'll kill you for that!" His brave words were met by even more derisive laughter.

"Clear out, Parker!" one of the masked riders

suddenly rasped out, his voice stilling the others. Although he had taken no noticeably active part in the treachery, it was obvious that he was in command. "This is only a taste of what's to come if you don't get off MacBride land and stay off!"

His threats were muffled by the kerchief across his mouth, but Rachel was almost certain she recognized something in his voice. There was little doubt left in her mind when he rode leisurely forward to where she was scrambling hastily to her feet and turned his dark, piercing gaze upon her. He spoke not a word—he didn't have to, for his eyes said it all. Rachel suffered a sharp intake of breath at the pure, unbridled lust in his boldly assessing gaze, and she knew then that it was none other than Vance MacBride who had initiated the night's villainy.

Before she knew what was happening, Rachel saw Lizzie come flying past her to launch herself at the dark-eyed leader. The girl seemed totally oblivious to the danger of her actions as she feverishly pummeled the horseman about the legs and back with her small, clenched fists.

"You blasted coward!" shrieked Lizzie. "You yellow-hearted bastard!"

"No, Lizzie, no!" Rachel desperately cried. She sought to pull her sister away, but was unable to subdue the little spitfire long enough to prevent the man from bringing his hand down across Lizzie's shoulder with punishing force.

"Stupid little bitch!" he growled. A strangled cry broke from Rachel's lips as her sister suddenly lost her footing and toppled beneath the horse's hooves. There was an accompanying scream from Jane, while Micah found his constricted throat to dry to utter a sound. Only

Vance MacBride's skillful handling of his mount kept the girl from being trampled to death, but one of the hooves made painful contact with Lizzie's chin before Rachel could pull her to safety.

"Lizzie!" Rachel brokenly gasped out, cradling the unconscious redhead in her arms as she knelt upon the firelit ground. Nearly blinded by the rush of tears in her eyes, she turned a look of sheer hatred upon Vance MacBride.

The leader of the masked band spared only a passing glance for Rachel and the injured girl before signaling to his men to be off. The rope securing Micah was cut loose, and he staggered to his feet as Jane hurried to see to Elizabeth.

The riders had soon disappeared into the darkness of the Montana prairie once more, satisfied that they had left behind a trail of destruction that would serve to convince Micah Parker they meant business. The fire they had set raged for nearly an hour longer, and the stock barn was finally nothing more than a pile of smoldering ashes by the time the first rosy rays of the dawn met the last bluish gray streaks of the night.

IV

Logan MacBride slowed his horse to a walk as he approached the ranch that had until recently belonged to his cousin Tate. Before it had been Tate's, it had been his father's. Of the four MacBride brothers who had left Scotland all those years ago to build an empire for themselves in the vast, untamed wilderness called Montana, only Tate's father, Andrew, had proven to have no stomach for the cattle business. And his son had turned out just like him, Logan mused with a faint scowl.

There was no longer any doubt about the validity of Parker's claim. Logan had retrieved a telegraphed message intended for Vance earlier that morning in Miles City—a message from Rock Creek that not only confirmed Micah Parker's purchase of the ranch, but revealed something else as well . . .

It was the "something else" that bothered him. There was no telling how Vance and some of the others would react when they learned that Micah Parker not only bought the ranch from some four-flusher who had won it from Tate, but that Parker was also responsible for Tate's being arrested and hanged for murder. Reflecting that he had always known Tate would come to no good end, Logan swept the hat from his head, ran a negligent hand through his thick brown locks, then donned the stiff-brimmed Stetson once more.

"Easy, Vulcan," he murmured to the impatiently prancing stallion beneath him. His mouth tightened into a thin line as his sea-green eyes darkened to a glowing jade. "Let's go have a look." And let's get this damned thing settled once and for all, he silently added with an expression of obvious distaste crossing his handsome features. Telling himself that he sure as hell knew of better ways in which to occupy his time, Logan cursed inwardly and lightly touched his silver spurs to the horse's sleek flanks.

It wasn't long before he was afforded a glimpse of the still-smoking rubble that had once been Tate's barn. The warm afternoon sunshine beat down upon his shoulders as he drew up before the smoldering ashes, an almost imperceptible clenching of his jaw the only outward indication of the fury boiling up deep inside him.

Vance! he thought, muttering a savage oath beneath his breath. He hadn't believed his cousin would take action so quickly, at least not before gathering all the facts first. But there was no doubt in his mind that Vance MacBride had left his calling card on the Parkers last night. It was Vance's way.

"Damn you, Vance, I'll make you answer for this!" he vowed in a tone scarcely above a harsh whisper.

It was at that precise moment that Rachel emerged from the back door of the house, her hands gripping a washtub that she intended to empty near the ruins of the barn. She did not immediately catch sight of the lone rider who sat astride the magnificent black stallion only a short distance away, nor did she see the look of utter incredulity on the man's rugged, smoothly bronzed countenance.

A thunderstruck Logan MacBride couldn't believe his eyes. Of all places to find her again, why the devil did it have to be here? he inwardly raged. Why did the one woman who haunted his every waking moment as well as his dreams have to turn out to be a damned Parker?

His unwavering gaze darkened even further as he watched her move away from the house. Her gleaming honey tresses, secured with a blue satin ribbon at the nape of her neck, fell in a glorious cascade down the graceful curve of her back. Her slender, shapely form was encased in a fitted gown of rosebud-printed, pale cream cotton, its stylishly pleated and bustled folds protected by a starched, ruffled white apron. If anything, she looked even younger and more lovely than the last time he had seen her—save for the fact that there was most assuredly nothing childish about the delectable swell of her breasts and naturally seductive sway of her rounded hips that even the layers of clothing could not hide.

Once again, Logan found himself recalling with inflaming vividness the feel of that soft body against his, the way her entrancing curves, so pale and perfect, had glistened beneath the lamplight the first time he had seen her . . .

Finally, Rachel became aware of a nagging sensation that she was being watched. She turned slowly about, her fingers tightening convulsively about the metal handles of the washtub before relaxing their grip entirely as her eyes fell upon Logan. The washtub slid unheeded to the dirt at her feet, its soapy contents spilling everywhere.

"You!" she breathed in stunned disbelief. A fiery blush rose to her beautiful face, and she instinctively raised a hand to the place where her full bosom swelled above the square neckline of her snug, corseted bodice as she sought to regain control of her suddenly sporadic breathing.

Logan, his searing gaze displaying a certain, unquenchable envy as they followed the fingers which spread almost protectively across the top of Rachel's silken, deliciously curved bosom, smiled faintly and swung lithely down from the saddle. Maintaining a negligent hold upon the reins of his horse, he advanced upon Rachel with tantalizing unhaste, sweeping the hat from his head with mocking gallantry as he approached the spot where she stood shocked into speechless immobility.

"You might as well know. My name's MacBride—Logan MacBride," he stated in a low, almost caressing tone, his voice deep and resonant and slightly husky with something she dared not name.

"MacBride?" Rachel echoed shakily, finding her own voice at last. "Logan MacBride?" It took a moment for the significance of his words to sink in. He paused to stand towering above her, mere inches away from where she stared mutely up at him, her eyes alight with momentary confusion and expectation. "You . . . you're a MacBride?" she finally murmured, her words more of a statement than a question. Her eyes then became suffused with a fierce, vengeful blaze as her expression grew quite stormy. "How dare you show your face here! How dare you set foot on our land after last night!"

"Last night was none of my doing," he quietly insisted, his handsome brow furrowing into a slight frown. "I didn't even know anything had happened until I rode up just now."

"I don't believe you!" She was dismayed to feel hot, angry tears burning against her eyelids, and she wanted nothing more at the moment than to escape the unsettling presence of the tall, perplexingly virile man who had caused her nothing but shame and embarrassment, the man whose very name had already come to mean villainy and destruction for her beloved family. "Go away, Mr. MacBride! Your kinsman has done enough harm for the time being! Have you perhaps come to do more?" she lashed out at him, bewildered at the dull ache deep in her heart.

"Suppose you tell me exactly what happened last night," Logan evenly directed, his eyes never leaving her face.

"Very well! If you're going to pretend ignorance, then I shall be more than happy to inform you of another MacBride's treachery!" There was a noticeable tremor in her voice, and Logan found his fury with Vance increasing tenfold. "Not only did Vance MacBride and his band of masked cowards destroy our barn, they also saw fit to rope and drag my grandfather! And my sister, who is little more than a child, lies inside at this very moment recovering from the effects of having been very nearly killed when Vance MacBride knocked her to the ground!"

"Your sister?" he repeated, then sharply queried, "Is she going to be all right?"

"Yes, no thanks to you!" she retorted with bitter sarcasm. Turbulently reflecting that she could bear no more of the insolent, green-eyed rogue she now knew to be called Logan MacBride, Rachel whirled to flee inside the house. Logan's hand shot out and closed firmly about her wrist before she could escape.

"You're not going anywhere until you've heard what I have to say!" he masterfully decreed, tugging her back toward him and spinning her effortlessly about. Her eyes flashed resentfully up at him, her lips compressing into a tight, thin line of stubborn defiance, but he seemed impervious to the venomous looks she cast at him as he told her in a voice that made it clear he would brook no interference until he had finished. "First off, I was out on the range when I got word there might be trouble here. I rode back to Miles City first thing this morning. Secondly, if Vance MacBride was indeed responsible for what happened last night, then you can rest assured I'll see he makes amends."

"What do you mean 'if'?" Rachel indignantly demanded, attempting to jerk her wrist free. "There is no doubt that it was your kinsman who led the gang of blackguards here last night!"

"I thought you said they were wearing masks."

"They were, but there was no mistaking the leader's identity! He had already paid my grandfather a visit earlier in the day, had already made threats. And though I had anticipated the possibility of his threats becoming reality, I held the belief that he would at least trouble himself to make certain about the authenticity of the bill of sale my grandfather holds!" She finally succeeded in jerking away from him, and her chin tilted upward as she feelingly stated, "He and his men deserve to be thrown into jail for what they did!"

"Without absolute proof that it was my cousin who was here last night, the law won't interfere," Logan quietly declared. Rachel was forced to acknowledge the truth of his words, for her grandfather had told her the same thing—as long as they could produce no tangible evidence of Vance MacBride's involvement, nothing could be done. Because of his many years of experience as a lawman, Micah was well aware of how abruptly the wheels of justice would grind to a halt without witnesses or inarguable proof.

"Even if we had proof, would the sheriff dare go against the MacBrides?" Rachel caustically parried, hating herself for the weakness assailing her as her eyes roamed with a will of their own across Logan's devastatingly irresistible features. His fitted, pale blue cotton shirt only accentuated the healthy glow of his skin, the broad expanse of his chest, and the deep, striking green of his eyes. Swallowing a sudden lump in her throat, she angrily ventured, "We've been in Montana less than a week now, but my family and I have already become familiar with the deplorable, thoroughly barbaric tactics employed by a supposedly powerful clan of scoundrels named MacBride in order to get whatever it is they want!"

"Is it fair to judge all of us by the actions of one?" he countered with another frown, his gaze burning into hers.

"You forget, Mr. MacBride—I've had the misfortune to cross paths with you before, and it is from those particular 'demonstrations' of your arrogance and . . . and impertinence that I formed the opinion you are much like your cousin! I daresay the two of you are in no doubt representative of the other members of your family!"

"On the contrary, 'Clover'," retorted Logan, a sardonic grin tugging at the corners of his mouth, "I've not forgotten the 'demonstrations' to which you refer. As for my being like my cousin Vance—in that you are very much mistaken. And I don't think the rest of my family would take kindly to being compared to him, either," he remarked, setting her pulses racing as he flashed her a disarmingly crooked grin.

"Why did you come here today?" Rachel unexpectedly demanded, painfully conscious of the hot color staining her cheeks at his reference to their first disastrously humiliating encounter. "Was it merely to taunt me, to add insult to injury?"

"I'd no idea you were here," Logan revealed with a brief shake of his head. "I came to speak with your grandfather."

"You mean you came to offer your own threats!"

"Are you always so damned unreasonable, or is this latest display of feminine bullheadedness for my benefit alone?"

"Why, you . . . you . . ." sputtered Rachel, so incensed she could not speak. A slow, lazily seductive smile spread across Logan MacBride's handsome visage, and Rachel was nonplussed by the way his eyes trailed slowly downward to rest suggestively upon the rapid rise and fall of her breasts.

A sudden tendency toward violence caught her in its grip, but she was saved from doing something she would no doubt have been given cause to regret when Micah Parker appeared upon the scene. He came out of the back door of the house, initially too preoccupied with his own thoughts to take notice of the tall stranger looming so ominously above his granddaughter. But when he finally raised his eyes and saw Rachel standing just ahead with a man who could easily be described as eye-catching, he ground to a halt and curtly demanded, "Who are you? And what are you doing here?" Several long strides carried him to Rachel's side before Logan could answer. Micah subjected the tall stranger to a narrow, harshly speculative look from his flinty gaze as he pulled Rachel protectively behind him and clasped his rifle in both hands. "What do you want?"

"Are you Micah Parker?" asked Logan, absently wondering how such a hard, granite-faced man could be related to the exquisitely fashioned young beauty peering over his shoulder. It occurred to him that he still didn't know her name . . .

"I am," the older man confirmed in a tone edged with noticeable suspicion.

"I'm Logan MacBride." It was a simple, almost offhanded statement of fact, but Micah received it with something far more than equal nonchalance.

"I'll give you thirty seconds to get the hell off my land, MacBride!" he snarled with barely concealed fury. "Thirty seconds—then I start shooting!" His fingers gripped the rifle so tightly that his knuckles turned white, and he hoisted the weapon with a no-nonsense clarity of intention.

"You and I have no quarrel, Parker," Logan asserted coolly, betraying not even the slightest hint of fear at the older man's threat. His deep green eyes, however, sparked with a faintly discernible wariness.

"Go inside the house, Rachel," Micah gruffly commanded, his raw gaze fastened unwaveringly upon Logan's deceptively impassive features.

Rachel. So that's her name, thought Logan. A recollection of the old Bible story, the one where Jacob labored for so long to win Rachel, flashed across his mind, prompting him to muse that the golden-haired wildcat before him was aptly named.

"No," she defied, her voice little more than a whisper before gathering strength. "I'm staying right here!"

"I said get inside!" snapped Micah, reaching hastily behind him with one hand and giving her a none-too-gentle shove. He looked both angry and slightly embarrassed when she still refused to do his bidding. Folding her arms against her chest, she remained where she stood, the fire in her eyes a perfect match for the spirited look of obstinacy on her becomingly flushed countenance. Logan suppressed an appreciative grin as he told Micah, "She might as well hear the reason I've come."

"Your thirty seconds are just about up!" the older man shot back. Logan's face grew solemn.

"I'm sorry about last night's trouble, but I had nothing to do with it. I rode out here with the intention of offering you a good price for your ranch, Parker."

"My ranch isn't for sale!"

"I think there are a few things you ought to be aware of. This property has been in my family for several years. The range for miles around is MacBride territory."

"I don't give a damn who my neighbors are! This is free range country, MacBride. You don't own all of it!"

"We own enough of it to make it ours," insisted Logan, a slight narrowing of his eyes giving evidence of his own intense displeasure with the situation. "That's why you'd do well to consider the offer I'm prepared to make you. There's no way I can promise that what happened here last night won't happen again." His gaze was drawn irrevocably to Rachel's, affording him a glimpse of the mingled shock and trepidation therein. Damnation! he swore inwardly, experiencing a sudden, near murderous rage toward his cousin Vance for causing her grief.

"I'll not turn tail and run because of those bastards!" Micah ground out.

"Then there's something else you ought to know," said Logan, tearing his eyes away from Rachel and fixing Micah with a long, intense stare. A dark scowl marred the rugged perfection of his sun-bronzed features. "I know all about your role in Tate MacBride's death, Parker. And while I'm trying to be reasonable about the matter, telling myself that you were only doing your duty as sheriff, I can almost guarantee that some of the other MacBrides won't tend to be so understanding when they find out you were the one who arrested and hanged one of their own. No, they won't be as reasonable as me—they'll think only of revenge."

"Revenge is on my mind, too, MacBride," declared Micah through tightly clenched teeth. "Revenge for burning a man's barn, for raising a hand to two innocent girls, for—"

"Two?" Logan abruptly broke in, his eyes straying back to Rachel and taking note of the way the flush tinging her beautiful face grew even more heightened as she hastily looked away.

"One of those snake-bellied sons of bitches subjected my oldest granddaughter to rough treatment, while the leader of the bastards nearly killed the younger girl! So when it comes to any talk of scores to settle," Micah finished with another fierce scowl and tightening of his grip upon the rifle, "you make damned sure those other

MacBrides know I'm planning to settle one of my own! Now get the hell off my land and stay off!" he harshly commanded.

There was a dangerously savage gleam in Logan's sea-green gaze as it locked in silent combat with Micah's. The savagery was more on account of Vance than the stubborn old man facing him with such obvious belligerence, but Logan found himself furious with Micah Parker for allowing his own damnable pride to endanger the lives of his womenfolk—particularly the life of the young woman now determinedly avoiding his gaze, the one who aroused in him such an inexplicable, overwhelming protectiveness . . .

"You don't have any idea what you're getting into, what a hornet's nest you're stirring up. It's hard enough running cattle in this wilderness and trying to turn a profit without having everyone for miles around against you. If you won't think of yourself, think of your family. For their sake, Parker, sell out and go back where you belong," Logan advised him in a low, even tone that belied the sharp twisting of his heart at the thought of never seeing Rachel again.

"You're wasting your time. Get going!" Micah emphasized his words with a curt gesture of the rifle, and Logan knew there was no use in trying to talk any sense into him, at least not for the moment.

Rachel finally raised her eyes to his again, and she could literally feel the vibrant, invisible current passing between them. A powerful ripple of disturbingly pleasant sensation ran the length of her spine, provoking a sharp rise of something akin to panic within her as she looked hastily downward again.

Micah was a bit puzzled by the strange half-smile

playing about the other man's lips, but he seemed aware of nothing amiss as Logan donned his hat once more and turned away to mount up. The tall, youthful patriarch of the MacBrides settled easily into the saddle, gathered the reins loosely in one hand, and drawled amiably, "Think it over, Parker. I'll be back in a few days' time to see how you're getting on."

"Save yourself the trouble, MacBride," grunted Micah.

Logan merely touched a finger to the front brim of his hat, shooting Rachel one last penetrating glance before a simple movement of his knee prompted the huge black stallion beneath him to spin about and start forward at a slow, measured pace. Once past the spot where waves of heat could still be seen rising from the ashes of the barn, the sleek animal gradually quickened its pace to a gallop and raced across the green-carpeted prairie like the wind.

Rachel was well prepared for the grim expression of parental disapproval Micah turned upon her. He was still so incensed by his favorite granddaughter's show of disobedience in front of another man, especially one who had turned out to be an adversary, that he positively glowered at her.

"I know what's on your mind, but it doesn't matter!" she defiantly asserted before he had even said a word. "There was never even the remotest possibility that I would leave you alone with that man. I'm all too familiar with your temper, Micah Parker, and if you think for one moment I would have allowed you—"

"Damn it, girl, it's not up to you to 'allow' me anything!" He muttered something unintelligible and strode furiously away. Rachel clutched at her apron and went after him, her long hair bouncing and sweeping riotously across her back as the warm, smoke-scented breeze whipped playfully at her skirts.

"Oh, Micah, I know you don't want to admit defeat, but perhaps you should consider what Logan MacBride said!" she earnestly implored, forced to hurry in order to keep up with him. "How can we hope to make this our home if we are surrounded by hostile neighbors? After last night, I should think it would be clear to you that any man bearing the name MacBride will stop at nothing to drive us away!" Suddenly recalling what Logan had said about judging them all by the actions of one, Rachel felt a sharp twinge of conscience.

"The decision's mine, Rachel—not yours!"

"That's not true! Grandmother, Lizzie, and I are involved in this every bit as much as you! Has it occurred to you to consider the danger to us?" She immediately regretted the remark, and could have bitten her tongue when Micah abruptly halted and turned to her with a noticeably stricken look in his gray eyes.

"I've considered it. It's never left my mind. Whatever else you may think of me—" he told her in a flat, distant voice, then broke off and sighed heavily. "It isn't just because of what I want that I'm aiming to stay here, Rachel—it's because of you and Lizzie and your grandmother as well. We can have a good life out here if we don't quit before we've even started." Rachel blinked back sudden tears as he lowered his gun and drew her to him in a rare display of physical affection. "We can make it if we hold strong," he stubbornly assured her. When he released her a moment later, she was startled to hear him confess, "I did take some of what MacBride said to heart. First thing in the morning, I'm taking you and the others into Miles City."

"To Miles City? But, why?"

"We've got a little money left. I'm going to put the three of you up at the Macqueen House for a few days, hire on a couple of hands and build a new barn, then see about making this place into a working ranch once more. I don't want you in the middle of this blasted war those MacBrides have declared on me."

"No, Micah," she responded with a firm shake of her head. "I know both Grandmother and Lizzie feel the same way I do, and we're not about to leave you! We belong here with you!"

"I'll have my hands full without having to worry about my family," Micah declared in a low, slightly hoarse tone. "You'll do as I say and stay in Miles City until I think it's safe enough to come home." With that, he lifted the rifle again and headed toward the stream. "Tell your grandmother to get things ready."

Rachel's eyes were clouded with renewed anxiety as she watched him go. Realizing the futility of arguing with her incredibly headstrong grandfather any further, she turned slowly about and started back for the house. She hadn't gone far before Logan MacBride seized control of her thoughts.

Shock was too mild a word for what she had experienced upon seeing him again! And then, to discover that he was none other than a relative of both the detestable Vance MacBride and the late, murderous Tate MacBride . . .

It was far more than the matter of his kinship which bothered her, mused Rachel with a strangely restless sigh. Every time he turned that disturbing green gaze in her direction, it was as if he were mentally undressing her, remembering the way he had first seen her—stark naked. Her cheeks flamed anew, and a returning blaze sparked within the brilliant opal depths of her eyes.

"Logan MacBride, you can go straight to—" she breathed aloud, then broke off in startlement at both the vehemence and unsuitability of her intended directive. Groaning inwardly, she pressed her lips tightly together, gathered up her skirts, and raced inside the house.

"It took some doing, but I found a couple of young cowpokes who are willing to work for room and board until the ranch starts to pay," announced Micah, sweeping the hat from his head as he stepped inside the hotel room to say his good-byes. He had also paid a visit to the man with whom he had contracted for the delivery of the horses and cattle, had been assured that the stock would finally be driven on out the following day, and was now ready to head back to the ranch.

"I don't suppose there's any use in trying to talk you out of this," Jane sighed unhappily. Just as Rachel had expected, both Jane and a fully recovered Lizzie had loudly protested the separation from Micah. They had, however, capitulated in the face of his unwavering obstinacy. Jane, of course, was well accustomed to Micah Parker's high-handed ways, but that didn't prevent her from casting him a wifely frown of disagreement as he stepped forward to embrace her.

"It's only for a few days, Jane," he reiterated, quickly brushing her cheek with his lips. "You know as well as I do that I stand a better chance with two able-bodied men at my side instead of you and the girls."

"I've been at your side for most of my life, Micah Parker, and I should be there now!" she retorted, holding him close with a sort of quiet desperation visible in her glistening brown eyes. "I thought you were through getting yourself in such danger when you decided to quit the law and become a rancher. I'd no idea you'd only end up jumping from the frying pan into the fire!" When he kissed her once more and drew away to bid farewell to Lizzie and Rachel, Jane wheeled about so that he wouldn't see the tears spilling over from her lashes and coursing down her face.

After charging a bravely unweeping Rachel with sending word to him should the need arise, Micah took his leave. It was only then that his eldest granddaughter allowed herself the luxury of tears.

The next two days passed with excruciating slowness for Rachel. She and Lizzie spent a good deal of the time exploring the town, while Jane managed to while away the hours by catching up on her sewing. They were as frugal as possible with the dwindling funds Micah had left them, ordering simple meals in the restaurant downstairs twice a day, but sharing only a loaf of bread and a bit of cheese in their room at noon. The tiny room was a trifle cramped with the three of them occupying quarters meant for two, but they cared little about the inconvenience, concerned only with thoughts of Micah and what was happening back at the ranch.

It was on the third day of their stay in Miles City that they learned a dance was to be held that same evening in the dining room of the Macqueen House. Jane had heard the clerk at the front desk make mention of the fact that all hotel guests were invited to the gala affair that was a traditional celebration of the end of spring roundup. Believing the dance would provide some much-needed socialization for Rachel and Lizzie, Jane had insisted upon their attendance. The two girls had reluctantly agreed, mainly to please their grandmother.

"Micah would be so proud if he could see the two of you right now," declared Jane with a beaming smile of maternal satisfaction as she surveyed the results of very nearly an entire afternoon spent in preparation.

Lizzie tugged uncomfortably at the high, lace-trimmed neckline of her best gown and gave her head a toss that sent her fiery curls bouncing. Fashioned of palest buttercup velvet, the dress's uncorseted bodice molded Lizzie's blossoming figure a little too snugly. The short, puffed sleeves and gathered skirts were undeniably feminine, prompting the spirited young redhead to voice a self-disparaging remark about trying to make a silk purse out of a sow's ear.

An indulgent smile curved Rachel's lips as she glanced away from her sister to critically inspect her own appearance in the gilt-edged mirror hanging above the washstand. Her gown of deep blue watered silk was sleeveless, its draped, unornamented neckline revealing a modest but tantalizing glimpse of the creamy, rounded flesh swelling above her corset. The tight waist accentuated her trim shapeliness, and the bustle of matching, frilled satin provided her with the fashionably horizontal projection at the back. Her full, ruffle-flounced skirts fell in graceful folds all the way to the floor, where embroidered kid slippers peeked out from under fine, lace-edged white muslin petticoats.

Giving a last pat to her dark golden tresses, which were swept high upon her head and allowed to descend in a gleaming cascade of curls, Rachel smiled softly at her reflection in approval and drew on her elbow-length white gloves. An exquisite cameo which had once been her mother's hung from a black velvet ribbon spanning the slender column of her neck and nestled in the satiny hollow of her throat.

Jane, who was going along in order to properly chaperone her granddaughters, looked quite attractive in a less elaborate but nonetheless stylish concoction of emerald satin. She ushered the young women from the room and down the stairs toward the music which had already begun to drift upward from the dining room.

Canvas had been spread over the beautiful rugs gracing the polished wooden floor, and the room was filled with a dazzling array of color. The ladies, many of whom were Rachel's age or even younger, were attired in magnificent gowns they saved for just such occasions, and some even wore diamonds which sparkled at their smooth white throats. A number of young officers from Fort Keogh were in attendance, looking resplendent in their full dress uniforms of blue. The cowpunchers, who made up the biggest part of the crowd, had bought new outfits for the dance, their boots gleaming and their bright-colored silk kerchiefs knotted with appropriate carelessness about their necks.

The Fifth Infantry orchestra from the fort was playing a popular Highland waltz when Rachel and Elizabeth, closely followed by their grandmother, reached the large open doorway to the spacious, high-ceilinged dining room, already filled near to bursting with eager participants.

"We never had anything like this back in Rock Creek!" proclaimed a suitably impressed Lizzie, her reluctance to attend all but forgotten.

"You girls go on inside and have fun!" Jane cheerfully instructed. "I think I'll just find someplace to sit and watch for a spell!"

"Come with us, Grandmother," entreated Rachel. "Why, you're every bit as good a dancer as anyone else!"

"Bless you for the compliment, my dear, but I'd truly prefer to watch, and perhaps even make a few friends amongst the other 'old women' lining the walls! Now, go on!" She laughed, giving the two of them a gentle, affectionate shove forward.

Within seconds after joining in the festivities, Rachel and Lizzie found themselves surrounded by young men, and a veritable deluge of requests to dance caused their heads to spin. They soon lost count of how many enthusiastic partners, officers as well as civilians, had whirled them about the canvas dance floor. The usually tomboyish Lizzie found it exhilarating to be the object of so much attention, and she joined in the laughter and flirtations with gusto, while a more subdued Rachel, who was well aware of the unspoken code which made it a deadly insult for a girl to refuse to dance with a cowboy at such a celebration, found herself quite out of breath within a short amount of time.

Finally persuading a particularly gallant young captain that she was in dire need of refreshment, Rachel was relieved to be led from the dance floor and over to a long table spread with an impressive assortment of sandwiches and pastries, as well as a huge crystal bowl containing fruit punch that someone would no doubt manage to spike before the evening grew much older. She accepted a cup of the as-yet-untainted punch and turned a warm smile of gratitude upon the slender, fair-haired young officer.

"How long will you and your family be staying in Miles City?" he asked, making no secret of his admiration as he took note of the soft, rosy glow upon her lovely young face and the enchanting way her blue eyes sparkled.

"I'm not at all certain," she answered evasively, realizing that she spoke the truth.

"I would consider it an honor if you would grant me permission to call upon you, Miss Parker." Glancing up to meet his flatteringly worshipful gaze, Rachel heaved an inward sigh. He seemed a very nice young man, one of whom she was certain her grandparents would approve, and yet she hesitated. A sharp, unbidden image of a devilishly handsome, green-eyed rogue once again insinuated itself into her mind, and she found herself unable to prevent a silent comparison between Logan MacBride and the boyishly attractive young captain before her . . .

Rachel suffered an uncomfortable speechlessness as the man anxiously awaited her reply. She was spared the difficult task of following her instincts and denying his request when an exuberantly promenading cowboy and his partner, apparently a bit carried away by the music, suddenly propelled themselves into Rachel's admirer. The contents of his half-empty cup of punch went flying directly onto the front of Rachel's blue silk gown.

"Oh, Miss Parker! Please forgive me! How clumsy of me!" The poor captain spoke in an agitated rush, his eyes filled with horror at the dark stain spreading across her skirts.

"It wasn't your fault," Rachel hastened to assure him, flashing him a compassionate smile before glancing back at her dress and announcing, "If you'll please excuse me, I think I should see what I can do about this before it dries." Without waiting for a response, she made her way through the crowd and toward the spot where she had earlier glimpsed Jane talking with a group of matronly townswomen. Her grandmother, however, was nowhere to be seen at the moment, so Rachel exited the room alone, sweeping hurriedly to the doorway and up the stairs.

There was a soft, accompanying rustle of her silken skirts as she turned the key in the lock and entered the moonlit darkness of her room. After lighting the lamp and turning it up so its single flame bathed the confines of the room in a soft golden glow, she tugged down the shade at the window and unfastened her gown, slipping it off and spreading it carefully upon the bed.

Clad only in her undergarments, consisting of a fine white cotton chemise tucked into frilled, open-leg drawers, a stiff taffeta evening petticoat and embroidered gray coutil corset, and a tied-on bustle of dull red cotton, Rachel turned to the washstand and quickly poured water from the large porcelain pitcher into the matching bowl. Taking up a towel, she plunged it into the water, wrung it tightly, then set to work blotting the punch stain from her dress.

Bent to her task, she could not see the doorknob behind her slowly turning. The door flung open in the next instant, and Rachel whirled about in wide-eyed alarm, her breath catching on a loud gasp.

Logan MacBride's tall, lean-muscled frame filled the doorway.

V

As had been the rule governing her previous encounters with the rakishly handsome scoundrel before her, Rachel was shocked into speechless immobility by his unexpected appearance. His smoldering, sea-green gaze made a swift, encompassing sweep of the room before he stepped inside and closed the door behind him, then abruptly shot the bolt.

Rachel finally parted her lips to scream, but Logan was across the room before she could make a sound. Seizing hold of her with one sinewy arm, he clamped his other hand across her open mouth and cautioned in a low, unmistakably menacing tone, "Don't even think about it."

Her eyes grew even rounder when they viewed the dangerous gleam of intent in his. His face was mere inches from her own, and she felt a rush of lightheadedness at his close proximity, his arm clutching her so tightly about her slender, corset-cinched waist that she found it difficult to breathe. Acutely conscious of the disconcerting state of undress in which he had found her yet again, Rachel felt a fiery blush rising to her face. She began to struggle, her hands pushing mightily at the broad, immovable hardness of his chest and her slippered feet kicking at his booted shins.

"I've only come to talk, damn it!" he declared tightly, his deep voice edged with an inordinate amount of displeasure. Rachel, obviously doubting the sincerity of his words, merely doubled her highly physical efforts to inflict bodily harm upon him and thereby secure her release, her hands clenching into fists as they beat at the bronzed, corded muscles beneath the snowy whiteness of his shirt. Legs flailing wildly and petticoat rustling, she managed to place a well-aimed kick to the unprotected area of his left, denim-trousered shin just above his boot, prompting him to mutter a savage oath and topple her unceremoniously backward onto the bed. The entire length of his hard, undeniably masculine body was pressed atop her outraged softness as he quickly followed, quite effectively imprisoning her as his superior weight pushed her deep into the feather mattress.

"If you'll hold still and promise not to continue behaving like a damned fool female, I'll let you salvage some of your dignity, Miss Parker," he remarked with biting sarcasm. His eyes, though still reflecting an inexplicable anger, were brimming with noticeable amusement at her expense, and Rachel cast him a murderous glare. "Well, what's it to be?" demanded Logan, his hand across her mouth still forcing her silence as his handsome face took on a particularly dark and intimidating look in the lamplight. "I'm warning you—my patience is already worn thin!"

An increasingly alarmed Rachel, dazedly wondering

what could have caused his thunderous mood, hesitated only a brief moment longer before finally nodding in reluctant capitulation. She despised herself for surrendering so easily, but there was something about the grim-faced man atop her, something within his disturbingly raw gaze that sent an involuntary shiver running down her spine . . .

Logan released her with unexpected abruptness and stood up, all six feet four inches of him towering above Rachel as she came bolt upright, snatched her dress from where it lay crumpled beside her, and held it against her trembling body like a shield. Opal eyes blazing up at him, she challenged in a voice that was not quite steady, "Couldn't you have asked to speak to me in a more . . . a more civilized manner? It was hardly necessary to so rudely invade the privacy of my room in order to say that you wished to talk! And how dare you—"

"Let's get this over with," he impatiently broke in, his voice whipcord sharp and his brow creasing with another menacing scowl.

"Better yet, Mr. MacBride, let's dispense with this latest unpleasant episode altogether!" retorted Rachel with a flash of spirit, forgetting her earlier fear of him. "Now, will you kindly leave my room?" she went on to frostily decree, her chin lifting proudly. Her manner might have appeared impressively regal if not for the fact that she was clad only in her lacy undergarments. Her elegant coiffure had been disturbed by Logan's rough treatment—a goodly portion of her thick tresses had escaped the restraint of their pins and now streamed with riotous abandon about the pale rosiness of her face and shoulders. To Logan, she had never looked more damnably desirable, and he mentally ground out a curse before summoning every ounce of will to maintain his own outward composure.

"Listen to me, Rachel," he commanded in a quiet, oddly vibrant tone, his piercing, sea-green gaze darkening to jade. Rachel, experiencing a sudden, perplexing tremor at the sound of her name upon his lips, fell silent as her fingers tightened within the silken folds of her dress. "Since your grandfather refuses to listen to me, I thought you might be able to convince him to see reason. He's got to sell out before it's too late."

"Has something else happened?" she questioned sharply, rising hastily to her feet before him. "Micah's all right, isn't he? There hasn't been—"

"Nothing else has happened—yet," Logan solemnly assured her. "So far, I've managed to suppress the knowledge of your grandfather's involvement in Tate's death, but Vance or one of the others is going to get wind of it sooner or later. And heaven help Micah Parker when they do. They won't stop at barn-burning next time," he warned, his eyes staring deeply into hers. He'd done all he could these past few days to make certain Micah Parker was left alone, but he knew he couldn't control the other members of his family indefinitely. No, he mused, even though the death of Dugan MacBride had left him in charge, there was no way on God's green earth he could police the actions of all the MacBrides. And he realized that he couldn't bear to think of Rachel getting caught in the middle . . .

"Did you come all the way to town just to tell me this?" Rachel indignantly countered, feeling an irrational surge of fury toward him. She knew his words to be true, was well aware of the danger in which Micah's continuing defiance of the MacBrides had placed himself and his family, and yet she felt compelled to lash out at the arrogant, infuriatingly self-assured rogue who had done nothing but taunt and willfully provoke her from the very first.

"Of course not," he easily lied, a puzzling note of rising temper in his resonant voice. Damnation! he silently raged. He wasn't even sure himself why he had come all this way to talk to her. When he'd discovered that she was staying in town, he had suddenly changed his mind about attending the dance. And then, to stroll inside the Macqueen House and see her dancing and laughing with such carefree enjoyment, to see all those blasted men swarming about her like flies drawn to honey . . . the mere recollection of it made his blood boil.

"I see. You came to attend the dance and thought now to be the perfect opportunity to try and enlist my aid in getting some of your precious MacBride land back, is that it?" she bitterly charged.

"No, damn it! I came to try and talk some sense into you, to try and make at least one of you Parkers understand that the situation is far more hazardous than you seem to believe!"

"Am I supposed to be grateful to you for your so-called assistance? Forgive me for questioning your motives, Mr. MacBride, but isn't it quite possible that your professed concern for my grandfather is prompted by nothing more than . . . than the desire to avoid public condemnation for your family's treachery?" Her eyes were virtually shooting sparks, and her bosom rose and fell rapidly beneath the folds of shimmering blue silk she still clutched against her. "I've heard a great deal about the powerful MacBrides these past few days, and what I've heard has only served to further convince me that all of you are entirely without conscience or principles! You allow no one to question or defy you—they dare not try, for you own very nearly the entire county! Well, Mr. MacBride, you do *not* own me or my family, nor the ranch which now legally belongs to my grandfather!"

"You little fool!" growled Logan, his hands closing with almost bruising force upon her bare arms. His answering wrath was fueled by a lingering jealousy over what he had observed at the dance below as well as a nearly uncontrollable desire to crush the beautiful young spitfire against him and kiss her into submission. "Forget about your feelings toward me for the moment and think about your grandfather! He'll only end up losing this fight, and losing everything he owns in the bargain. Can't you get it through that thick skull of yours that what he's trying to do is hopeless? Hell, he'd still have no cattle to run if I hadn't finally given permission for the stock to be delivered!"

"Permission?" echoed Rachel, her resentment visibly increasing as she twisted beneath his iron grip. "We certainly don't require your 'permission' to take up residence on our own property, nor to conduct business with anyone else!" She inhaled sharply, biting at her lower lip to suppress a cry as his fingers dug ruthlessly into the soft flesh of her arms. In the next instant, he released her as if he had been scorched by the contact.

"Confound it, woman, don't you realize that you yourself could be dragged into this, that your own welfare might be endangered?" Logan bit out, his handsome countenance becoming a mask of smoldering rage at the thought.

"And why should that be any concern of yours?" defiantly queried Rachel, the fire in her stormy blue gaze well-matched by the fierce blaze in Logan's glittering jade orbs as they flickered briefly over her faintly trembling softness. She did not allow him time to answer, however, before her flaring temper took control and she rashly directed in a perilously rising voice, "Get out of here, Mr. MacBride. Even if I were able to persuade my grandfather to leave, my efforts would be purely for the sake of his well-being, and not in the slightest bit influenced by your false, underhanded declarations of concern! Now get out of here before I have you thrown out!" Lifting a hand to gesture pointedly toward the doorway, she was stunned by the sheer violence of Logan's reaction.

"Like hell you will!" He took advantage of her unsuspecting pose, reaching up to jerk the silk gown from her startled grasp. Not even to himself would he admit the true provocation for what followed—that it was the turbulence of his feelings for Rachel making him want to both punish and arouse her, making him want to put his brand on her as no other man ever had or ever would. He knew only that he had been burning to possess her since their first, searingly memorable "meeting," and he'd be damned if he'd wait any longer! She was his . . . for whatever reasons, she belonged to him. Of that he was certain.

"No!" breathed Rachel in dawning horror, tugging frantically at the ballgown in Logan's hand before he sent it sailing across the room to land in a discarded heap near the washstand. "I will scream if you don't get out of here this instant!" she vowed, her voice quaking with a combination of fear and indignation . . . and a bewilderingly chaotic leaping of her pulses.

"Scream all you like," Logan replied in a dangerously low and level tone, his eyes gleaming with a purposeful light as he advanced upon her. Feeling strangely weak-kneed, she backed away from him and took a deep, steadying breath before warning, "Stay away from me! If you dare to lay a hand on me, my grandfather will kill you!" It was immediately clear to her that he had absolutely no intention of heeding her warning. "I . . . I despise you, Logan MacBride! If you so much as touch me—" Acting out of a growing desperation, she finally gathered courage enough to open her mouth and emit an ear-piercing shriek.

The soft strains of music drifting upward from the dining room swelled to a crescendo just as Rachel screamed. But even if the orchestra had not strengthened the waltzing tune at that precise moment, her shrill cry for assistance would have gone unnoticed, for Logan wasted no time in seizing hold of her and yanking her close, his mouth crashing down upon her parted lips with relentless fury.

Moaning in futile, panic-stricken remonstration, Rachel exhibited all the fierce defiance she had displayed only a few short minutes earlier, beating and kicking and squirming within Logan's forceful grasp as he sought to bend her to his will. His arms were like bands of steel about her, his lips hard and bruising upon hers. To no avail she tried to jerk her head away, to escape the invasion of his tongue as it ruthlessly plundered the softness of her mouth. Feeling much like a trapped animal, she blinked at the hot tears scalding her eyelids, her head reeling dizzily as Logan bore her backward upon the bed once more.

She screamed low in her throat when her back made contact with the quilt-covered mattress, and her slippers fell to the floor as her slender, stockinged limbs flailed with unbridled vehemence in an effort to displace the hard-muscled form of the man pressing her into the mattress. Her fists drummed with desperate abandon upon his broad, linen-clad back. He seemed impervious to her struggles, his arms locking tightly about her as he suddenly rolled so that she was imprisoned atop him.

Certain that his intentions were to savagely conquer instead of lovingly initiate, Rachel was startled when his hard, bruising lips grew unexpectedly tender in the next instant. His punishing kiss became warmly persuasive, his tongue dancing sensuously with hers and causing her to experience an altogether different sort of faintness. His skillful, gently seductive mouth demanded a response, and she was shocked to realize that her lips were beginning to move beneath his with an answering passion. As his arms loosened a bit and allowed her lungs to draw air more easily, she found herself slowly relaxing, found all her inclinations to resist abruptly subsiding. Her arms, which had been trapped beneath him, now curled of their own accord about his neck as her trembling body became more pliant, its soft curves molding with perfection atop the lithely muscled planes of Logan's magnificent hardness.

She could do little more than breathe a halfhearted protest when his lips left hers to trail a searing path across the silken smoothness of her softly flushed face. Her eyes swept closed as his mouth teased and nibbled provocatively at the sensitive flesh of her earlobe before scorching a trail downward along the graceful column of her neck, to the hollow in her throat where her pulse beat with such alarming rapidity, then lower to where her full breasts, covered only by the thin fabric of her lace-edged chemise, swelled above her corset.

Passions flared and spiraled so rapidly that Rachel was caught up in a dizzying vortex of emotion and rapturous sensation, unable to form any coherent thought or offer any belated resistance. There was only Logan . . . only Logan MacBride and the enchanting, oh-so-sensual magic he performed upon her senses and her body.

Her eyelids fluttered open, her breath catching upon a gasp when she felt Logan's hand possessively cupping one of her breasts before moving urgently to the beribboned neckline of her white undergarment. Before she could voice any maidenly objections which might have risen to her lips, he had rendered her speechless again by masterfully tugging the chemise downward, ripping the delicate cotton in his impatience to expose the satiny, rose-tipped globes of her breasts in all their delectable glory.

His hands closed about her waist and lifted her slightly upward as his warm lips roamed hungrily across the naked, perfectly formed flesh positioned so conveniently for his moist caress. Rachel stifled a moan as his mouth fastened greedily about one of the sensitive peaks, his tongue teasing erotically at the taut, rosy nipple. She gasped again and again as his lips gently suckled at her ripe young breast, eliciting such a blaze of tempestuous desire within her that her slender fingers, threaded within the gleaming thickness of his hair, clutched almost convulsively at his head. And when his lips followed an imaginary line across her burning skin to console her other, temporarily neglected breast with a like caress, her hands moved to his shoulders and held on for dear life, as if she were drowning and Logan was the only means by which she could be saved . . .

"Rachel. Sweet, beautiful Rachel," he whispered

huskily, tugging her back down so that his lips could claim hers once more. She trembled as her naked breasts rubbed against the soft linen of his shirt, then gasped anew as his hands closed intimately about the twin spheres of her firm, womanly bosom before moving lower to curl about the entrancing roundness of her buttocks. Even through the layers of her petticoat and drawers, she could feel the undeniable evidence of his masculine arousal against her, and it was only then that a silent warning sounded in her brain.

Suddenly, Logan rolled again, stretching the length of his hard body over her as before, his lips never leaving hers. Rachel had just begun to awaken from her trance and renew her struggles when, almost before she knew what was happening, she felt his hand purposefully drawing up her taffeta petticoat.

"No!" she gasped out, tearing her lips away from the impassioned mastery of his. "No!" But it was too late. His mouth silenced her breathless protests as he captured both of her wrists in one of his hands and held them above her head. His other hand moved with an ever-increasing urgency as it quickly drew the flounced hemline of her petticoat higher and higher, pausing only when the lower half of her softly curved body, now beginning to push and writhe in earnest once more, was clad in nothing but her frilly, open-leg drawers and black silk stockings.

Rachel's eyes flew wide in alarm, their sparkling opal depths filling with something akin to sheer, debilitating panic when Logan's warm, nimble fingers delved within the unfastened edges of her drawers along her inner thighs and trailed upward across the trembling smoothness of her creamy flesh. His hand appreciatively explored the bare, tensing firmness of one temptingly rounded hip before moving with unwavering resolve toward the velvety treasure between her thighs.

A scream welled up deep within Rachel's throat when he touched the downy, honey-colored curls protecting the sweet bud of femininity upon which his skillful fingers sought to bestow their beguilingly gentle yet demandingly seductive caress. She arched violently upward, successfully freeing her lips long enough to choke out, "No, Logan! No, damn you, no!"

"You're mine, Rachel!" Logan hoarsely murmured, his eyes glowing with the brilliant fire of his raging passion. His lips descended forcibly upon hers again, and she began to feel as if all was lost, as if her final, humiliating defeat was unavoidable . . . for she knew that she would have to fight against herself as well as Logan in order to prevent the ultimate, irresistibly pleasurable disaster beckoning her onward . . .

"Rachel? Rachel, are you in there? It's Lizzie. Let me in!"

Good heavens—Lizzie! Rachel's mind cried, her movements abruptly stilling. She had forgotten all about both her sister and her grandmother, had become oblivious to the fact that she would naturally be expected back at the dance. With Lizzie's voice calling her and a loud, accompanying knock sounding at the door, reality returned.

"Damn!" swore Logan beneath his breath. He raised himself upward and peered intently down into Rachel's wide, visibly thunderstruck gaze for what seemed like an eternity. She caught her wildly erratic breath, waiting in anxious expectation for him to speak, but he said nothing. The next thing she knew, he had left her alone on the bed and crossed to the window. The pounding at the door resumed, and Lizzie's voice grew sharp with impatience.

"Rachel! Doggone it, Rachel, open the door!"

Logan, his handsome features appearing quite grim, paused to send Rachel one last burning look. His eyes raked over her as she pushed herself unsteadily upright and clutched dazedly at the torn edges of her chemise, and he uttered in a deep, vibrant undertone that sent yet another chill down her spine, "Though I'd like nothing more than to stay and show you just how much you 'despise' me, Miss Parker, I'd hate like the devil having to kill your grandfather because of his thirst for revenge over your 'damaged' reputation. But, heed me well—" he commanded softly, his sea-green gaze clouding with still-smoldering passion, "you *will* be mine."

Hot color flooded Rachel's beautiful face again, but she could not offer him a suitably defiant retort, could merely watch as Logan effortlessly flung open the window and disappeared. Within the numb recesses of her brain, it occurred to her that he seemed to be quite adept at beating a hasty retreat through second-story bedroom windows . . .

"Rachel, are you all right? If you don't open this confounded door this very instant, I'm going to get someone to break it down!" vowed Lizzie. Her fist was poised to strike the door again when her sister finally complied with her highly vocal demands and eased the door open several long seconds later.

Rachel's face was still brightly flushed, but there was no other telltale evidence to indicate the tumultuous events of the past several minutes. She had hastily donned her blue silk dress and dragged the few remaining pins from her hair, but now pretended to be in the process of rearranging her coiffure and exchanging her stained gown for another.

"I'm sorry, Lizzie, but I was occupied!" she snapped, feigning displeasure at the intrusion. She avoided Lizzie's narrowed, searching gaze and spun about to snatch her hairbrush from the small oak table beside the rumpled bed before explaining in a rush, "There was an accident, and I've got punch all over my gown, and I've been trying to decide what to wear in its place!" She was perilously close to tears, which fortunately served to aid the credibility of her story.

"Well, why didn't you answer me? Land's sake, why get all bothered over a little punch?" Lizzie demanded with a frown of sisterly exasperation. "Grandmother was beginning to get a bit worried when she couldn't find you, so I told her I'd check up here." Stepping inside the room, she was immediately aware of a rush of cold air, and her gaze traveled to where the curtains billowed at the open window. "Is it your intention to catch pneumonia?" she queried wryly, titian curls bobbing saucily as she swept across to put an end to the draft. Turning back to a strangely silent Rachel, she said, "You'd better hurry and come down before a certain member of the Fifth Infantry perishes of a broken heart. I caught a glimpse of the way his eyes were devouring you while the two of you danced." She had reached the door again and stood staring expectantly at her sister. "Well? Are you coming or not?"

"I'll be down shortly," murmured Rachel, still facing away from Lizzie. She was vastly relieved when the petite redhead finally heaved a sigh and took herself off, remembering to close the door on her way out.

True to her word, Rachel rejoined the festivities

downstairs within a quarter of an hour. She forced a bright smile to her lips and was once again immediately besieged by a throng of admirers, foremost among them the attractive young officer who had been the indirect cause of her humiliation at the hands of Logan MacBride. But she was determined to obliterate all thoughts of her roguish, devastatingly seductive tormentor from her mind, and so she danced and flirted and laughed with more abandon than ever before, the uncharacteristic gaity of her behavior bringing a puzzled frown to her grandmother's kindly visage.

Rachel was blissfully unaware of the savage glow in a pair of sea-green eyes that watched her through one of the dining room's lace-curtained windows. She did not see the way her tall, ruggedly handsome observer's lips tightened into a thin line of jealous fury as he paused before the hotel on the moonlit boardwalk outside, nor the particularly murderous glare he directed at the fair-haired young captain who smiled adoringly down at her as he whirled her about.

It was only after she and her family had retired for the night that Rachel surrendered to the temptation to think of Logan again, to dwell upon what had occurred between them. In all actuality, she had never been entirely successful in her endeavors to block his image from her mind. And once she was huddled beneath the covers on the same bed where Logan had earlier subjected her to his exquisitely torturous assault, the vivid recollection of his captivating embrace prompted her to experience a powerful current of newly awakened desire. It coursed through her like wildfire, leaving her body weak and uncomfortably flushed. She thought of the words he had spoken before disappearing, and her eyes kindled as she remembered his provokingly self-confident prophecy that she would belong to him.

"Never!" she vowed in a fierce whisper.

Feeling exceedingly distraught as a result of her own shameful yearnings for such an arrogant rake, Rachel mentally consigned Logan MacBride to the devil and prayed at the same time that she would never see him again!

A few short hours later, Rachel was forcibly reminded of the fact that prayers are not always answered in the affirmative.

Not long after breakfast, Jane and Lizzie ventured out into the unseasonably hot and humid morning intent upon browsing through several of the well-stocked general stores. Rachel had begged off with an all too authentic headache, promising to join them later for the special treat of a light luncheon in the hotel's dining room.

It was scarcely eleven o'clock when, nearly bored to distraction with the normally fascinating book she had been attempting to read, Rachel fastened a small white straw bonnet atop her upswept golden curls, marched resolutely out of the hotel, and set off down the crowded, dirt-laden boardwalk to find her sister and grandmother. She had not traveled far before noticing that there seemed to be an unusually large number of people in town that day, and it wasn't long until her curious gaze was met with the reason—a horse race was about to take place.

Main Street had been cleared for a considerable distance, from the courthouse to as far westward as the area's top "horse flesh" were to run in one of Miles City's frequent, well-attended equine competitions. A great deal of money changed hands as literally hundreds of cowpunchers, still celebrating the end of a tough but prosperous roundup, swelled the town's ranks and brought with them their own unique brand of revelry.

Rachel, encountering no little difficulty in seeing over the heads of a tightly packed group lining the boardwalk, caught a glimpse of one of the mounted cowhands who were stationed at all intersections of the streets in order to hold the festive crowd off the race course. Inhaling sharply, her blue eyes filled with startled dismay as they fell upon Vance MacBride.

A cynical half-smile marked his darkly attractive yet sinister countenace as he sat astride a powerfully built bay gelding. His eyes, negligently perusing the crowd of onlookers, made a broad sweep of his surroundings, and Rachel felt an intense dread for the moment when his piercing golden gaze would almost certainly find her.

Not tarrying long enough to see if Vance had indeed taken note of her presence, she hastily wheeled about and began maneuvering her way along the boardwalk in the opposite direction. Holding fast to her bonnet as she was rudely jostled by more than one slightly intoxicated celebrant, she quickened her steps past a large, newly constructed building which housed a rink for the increasingly voguish pastime of roller skating, past the furniture store which had been the first brick structure in Miles City, and past an entire row of saloons and dance halls which were at the moment almost totally deserted as the usual frequenters were outside waiting for the race to begin.

When she finally slowed to a walk once more, Rachel

found herself in front of the Cosmopolitan Theater. By no means considered to be a legitimate playhouse, it had gained a reputation as the most popular establishment amongst the area's cattlemen for presenting a "hurdy-gurdy" type of entertainment. It was also equipped with a very convenient dance floor, where men could pay their money and purchase the undivided attention of a comely and willing partner for a few minutes. Rachel had heard talk pertaining to the many disturbances of the peace occurring within the theater, and she couldn't resist pausing a moment to stare in curiosity at the bright red double doors and gaily decorated sign hanging above.

The noise pervading Main Street rose to an almost deafening roar as a hat was finally waved to signal the start of the race. Rachel had just turned her head to catch a glimpse of the horses thundering past, spectators cheering them on as choking clouds of dust rose from their hooves, when she felt a hand close in an iron grip about her arm. Before she could utter a sound in startled protest, she was pulled forcibly inside the theater.

VI

Rachel gasped in heart-stopping alarm as the powerful arm clamping about her waist bodily lifted her through the doorway and into the cool semidarkness of the Cosmopolitan's deserted entrance foyer. Once her feet met the floor and she could twist about to confront her assailant, she raised sparkling opal eyes that reflected a conflicting mixture of profound relief and righteous indignation as they discerned his identity.

"Take your hands off me!" she scathingly directed, struggling with an anger born of her resentment at not only this latest display of his proclivity toward man-handling, but also several previous demonstrations as well—last night's "demonstration" in particular.

"Shut up and stand still!" commanded Logan, his deep voice edged with unexpected harshness. Rachel blinked up at him in bewildered surprise as he roughly set her away from him. His handsome face wore a dangerously purposeful look, and a fierce, disturbingly unfathomable glow lit his green eyes. "You can rant and rave all you like once I've had my say. But, for now, you're going to keep quiet and hear me out!"

"I'll do nothing of the kind!" she retorted with as much bravado as she could muster in the face of his formidably intimidating disposition. Her eyes grew very round and she caught her breath on an involuntary gasp at the darkly menacing scowl he cast her. She took a sudden step backward as he moved to tower ominously above her, his narrowed gaze boring relentlessly into her wide, more than slightly apprehensive one.

"Listen to me, damn it!" His hands shot out to close upon her arms, and Rachel suddenly found herself unwilling, at least for the moment, to defy him. "I've given it a lot of thought, Rachel Parker, and I've come to a decision," he informed her in a low, resonant tone, his bronzed features visibly tightening. "The only way your grandfather might come out of this blasted mess alive is if you marry me."

"Wha . . . what?" Rachel breathlessly faltered, her eyes appearing even more enormous as a look of open-mouthed astonishment crossed the flawless beauty of her face. Surely he hadn't said what she thought she'd heard!

"If you were my wife, I don't think any MacBride would raise a hand against your grandfather. You'd be a MacBride, and Micah would be a kinsman through benefit of our marriage. The way I see it, you have little choice but to agree."

"The way you see it?" she echoed, feeling quite dazed by his unbelievably preposterous declaration. Why, she numbly reflected, the man was . . . was absolutely insane!

"Well, are you going to be reasonable about this or not?" demanded Logan, his hard grip on her arms becoming almost painful.

"Reasonable?"

"Yes, damn it, are you going to marry me or not?"

"I most certainly am not!" Rachel asserted vehemently, finally regaining control of her senses. Her cheeks flamed as she brought her hands up to push at Logan's broad chest. "Let go of me! I would never, never even consider marrying—"

"Hell, it won't be a real marriage!" Logan shot back, holding fast and disregarding her indignant struggles to escape. "You can even get an annulment after a few months' time. After this ruckus about Tate and your grandfather dies down, we can go our separate ways. Which won't be too soon as far as I'm concerned!" he ground out, knowing damn good and well that his last words were a lie. A combination of fury and jealousy such as he had never known raged within him whenever he thought of any other man touching Rachel, even looking at her. Damn it all to hell, she was his!

"I don't believe you!" she furiously retorted. "You're nothing but a scheming, arrogant, overbearing, underhanded scoundrel, Logan MacBride! Do you really think me naive enough not to recognize the true reasons behind your . . . your loathsome proposition?" Her eyes flashed and her face burned anew as she sputtered, "After . . . after what you tried to . . . after last night—"

"Don't flatter yourself, 'Clover'!" he quipped with biting sarcasm as he abruptly released her. She stumbled backward against the rosebud-papered wall near the doorway. "If I wanted to take you, I'd damn sure do it without feeling obligated to shackle myself to you for the rest of my life! The devil with your wounded pride and outraged virtue! I'm talking about saving a man's life—more specifically, your grandfather's life!"

"Why should you care whether my grandfather lives or dies? What concern is it of yours if your cousin murders him? After all, isn't that the MacBride way?" Rachel bitterly charged, hot tears shimmering within the blazing depths of her eyes as she raised her chin and faced him squarely.

"You don't know what the hell you're talking about," Logan replied in a quiet, seething tone. His eyes gleamed with barely concealed fury, and Rachel's trembling fingers tightened within the folds of her gathered muslin skirts. She opened her mouth to speak, but her throat had suddenly gone dry.

Logan took a step closer, his smoldering gaze moving over her with insulting boldness. She blanched inwardly at the underlying note of savagery in his deep voice, and a warning bell went off in her brain as he stated with deceptive calm, "I'm not the kind of man who takes an insult lightly, Rachel, particularly when it's unfounded. You know nothing about me. You're so all-fired determined to make me into a villain, and I think I know why. You're afraid that if you let down your guard for one brief moment, you'll find out you don't hate me at all." He paused and edged even closer, provoking a veritable floodtide of sensation to course through Rachel's body as she stared mutely up at him. She was only dimly aware of the fact that the commotion outside had diminished, that an intriguing array of shadows danced silently upon the opposite wall as people drifted past the theater's front windows.

"You're going to marry me, Rachel. The two of us are going to do what we can to prevent useless bloodshed on either side," Logan softly decreed. In the next instant, one sinewy arm snaked out and yanked her close, while his other hand firmly cupped her proud chin and forced her to meet his fiery, sea-green gaze. "Like I said, our union will be only temporary—no union at all in the literal sense. But I think maybe I ought to remind you of what you'll be missing as my 'kissless' bride!"

"No!" Rachel gasped in panic-stricken protest as she read the intent in his eyes. Trying desperately to twist her head and thereby free her chin from his grasp, she feelingly cried, "I'll never marry you, Logan MacBride! I'll never—"

His lips descended upon hers with lightning-quick speed, his strong fingers soon moving from the delicate planes of her chin to curl possessively about the enticing fullness of her breast. Even though protected by several layers of clothing, Rachel's soft flesh tingled beneath the onslaught of Logan's demanding caress, and she could not prevent a moan from welling up deep in her throat as his arm easily held her captive and his warm, sensuous mouth conquered hers.

The embrace ended almost as quickly as it had begun. Rachel struggled to catch her breath while Logan, forced to summon every ounce of will in order to let her go, stepped aside and flung open the door.

"I'll call on you at the hotel tonight. You can have your grandmother and sister with you if it will make you feel any safer," he remarked as a faint, mocking smile curved his lips. "Either way, I'll have your answer. And it had better be the right one." With that one last subtle warning, he was gone.

Initially able to do nothing more than raise a hand that was not quite steady to her kiss-reddened lips, Rachel made a valiant attempt to recover her composure. Swallowing the lump in her throat, she withdrew a lace-edged silk handkerchief from the small brocade reticule dangling from her wrist and dabbed impatiently at the tears glistening upon her lashes. She straightened her absurdly tilting bonnet and smoothed down the disheveled bodice of her pale blue muslin gown, then proudly squared her shoulders and sailed through the doorway with an outward air of self-possession. Inwardly, however, she was a mass of strained nerves and warring emotions.

Dazedly musing that it must have been a dream, that Logan MacBride couldn't possibly have proposed marriage to her, she heaved a long, ragged sigh at the undeniable certainty of this latest confrontation's reality. There was no escaping the truth of the matter. The rogue had actually submitted the outrageous notion that the two of them enter into the bonds of holy matrimony! Only it wouldn't be holy at all, she reminded herself, oblivious to the men and women passing her on the boardwalk as she headed instinctively back toward the hotel—it would be nothing more than a deception, a temporary arrangement calculated to help her grandfather . . .

But if such were the case, then why had Logan kissed her? And why did she feel certain that there was more to his proposal than a desire to serve as peacemaker in the difficulty between Micah and Vance MacBride?

You know nothing about me, Logan had said. It was true. He was still almost a complete stranger to her, in spite of their several, ultimately humiliating encounters. But perhaps she had indeed jumped to all the wrong conclusions. Perhaps she was being unforgivably selfish in her refusal to consider his proposal. After all, wasn't her grandfather's welfare truly more important than anything else? If Logan's warning about Vance MacBride's quest for revenge came to pass, would she ever be able to forgive herself for not doing all she could to save Micah?

"No," she truthfully acknowledged, unaware that she had spoken aloud. She was also unaware that she had finally reached the corner of the Macqueen House, and that a man who had caught sight of her seconds earlier was striding forward with the purpose of blocking her path.

"Well, well, if it isn't one of my new neighbors," Vance MacBride tauntingly drawled, his voice drawing her forcefully out of her silent reverie. He flashed her an insolent grin as she halted just in time to prevent a collision between them.

"You!" breathed Rachel, raising her widened eyes to his hawkish face. Although his close proximity prompted a sudden, involuntary tremor of fear within her, she was determined not to offer him so much as a hint of her disquiet. "Please get out of my way, Mr. MacBride," she coolly requested, subjecting him to an icy stare that had discouraged many an overzealous admirer.

"Now is that any way to greet a neighbor?" he mockingly reproached. A group of men had gathered nearby, and Rachel was certain she recognized at least some of them as Vance's companions. Saucy amusement played over their faces as they watched their leader purposefully bait the golden-haired young beauty. Rachel sought to ignore them, instead turning her attention to making her way around Vance. Each time she attempted to sweep past him, however, he maneuvered himself in front of her again.

"Get out of my way or I shall call for assistance!" she

bravely avowed, her eyes kindling with rapidly increasing anger.

"Hell, honey, there's no one in this town who'll stand against a MacBride!" he proclaimed with a short, scornful laugh. "Seems to me like you ought to know that by now." Tipping his hat farther back upon his head, a meaningful smirk touched his lips as he hooked his thumbs through the front belt loops of his trousers and rocked lightly back upon his heels. "Yes sir, Miss Parker, ma'am, you should know better by now than to think you can stand against me. Why, if I wanted to—"

"The only thing I know about you, Mr. MacBride, is that you are a coward—a contemptible, ruthless, spineless blackguard who lacks the courage to face a man without an entire band of mercenaries to back you up!" Goaded beyond reason as she recalled the pain and destruction the man had brought upon her family, Rachel was fairly quaking with the force of her wrath. "You see, Mr. MacBride, I'm well aware of the fact that you were the one to instigate the attack on our ranch the other night! I don't expect you to be pleased to hear that both my grandfather and my sister have recovered, at least from the physical wounds inflicted upon them. Nor do I expect you to be pleased to learn that your treachery failed to achieve the desired results!"

A soft cry broke from her lips as Vance's hands shot out, his punishing fingers curling like talons about her arms. He yanked her close, his dark features twisting into a malevolent sneer as the glint in his narrowed golden eyes became undeniably feral. Fighting against a rising tide of panic as well as against the man who held her captive, Rachel looked frantically about for help, but no one came to her aid.

"You're a feisty one, aren't you? Yes sir, a right pretty little hellcat of a female—just the way I like my women! But I can see I'm going to have to teach you a few manners, honey. You're in need of a bit of taming, and it looks like I'll have to be the one to do it!" Before Rachel could guess his intent, he enveloped her in a brutal embrace and brought his lips crashing forcibly down upon hers. A powerful shiver of revulsion ran the length of her spine as his cruel mouth ravaged hers, and a wave of nausea washed over her at the hot invasion of his tongue. Although nearly overcome by faintness, she continued battling fiercely to escape, while Vance's men merely laughed appreciatively at their leader's domination of her.

A scream welled up deep in her throat as she felt one of Vance's hands moving lower to her buttocks, his fingers boldly exploring and painfully gripping the futilely squirming roundness of her derriere before clutching her so tightly against him that she was made acutely aware of the lust surging through his manhood. Tears of mingled rage and terror stinging her eyes, she struck out at him again and again, but it was as if she were locked in a vise, as if the very worst of her nightmares was coming true . . .

Suddenly, there was freedom. Rachel found herself stumbling backward against the building at the same time Vance MacBride found himself literally dragged away from her and spun about to receive a grueling blow to his chin, the force of which sent him reeling to land on the hard, dirty planks of the boardwalk.

"I ought to shoot you down like the dog you are, MacBride!" roared Micah, standing poised for action above him. The gun in his hand, aimed directly at

Rachel's stunned persecutor, left little doubt as to the sincerity of his threat.

Caught off guard by the attack, for none of them had noticed Micah Parker's approach until it was too late, Vance's companions could only stand and stare in helpless frustration as they watched the former lawman battle with the temptation to pull the trigger. Rachel shook off her numbness and flew toward the spot where her grandfather stood pointing his cocked pistol at an uncharacteristically speechless Vance MacBride.

"No, Micah, don't!" she cried, a desperately imploring look on her beautiful, tear-streaked countenance as she reached his side. "Whatever he's done, you can't kill him!"

"I'd like to know why the hell not!" growled Micah. His eyes, their glittering depths looking much like molten steel, never left Vance's tight, stoic features, and only the younger man's sharply vigilant gaze provided an indication of his underlying fear. "No man's going to lay hands on you and walk away—"

"You pull that trigger, Parker, and we'll send you to hell before your gun's through smoking!" rasped out one of Vance's men, his tone seething with vengeful rancor.

"No!" Rachel's horror-stricken gaze shifted hastily back and forth between her grandfather and the coarse-faced man who had made the threat. "Please, Micah! I . . . I'm all right! Leave it be!"

"Make your choice, old man," Vance MacBride finally spoke up. Rising to his feet with studied unhaste, he shot Micah a narrow, unmistakably challenging look from his hawk's eyes. There was an accompanying curl of his lip as he stared mordantly back at the other man and waited, knowing full well that Micah had little choice. Several long moments passed, during which time Rachel held her breath and prayed fervently that her grandfather's sense of honor would not be his final undoing. She felt weak with relief when he ground out, "You come near her again and it won't make any difference how many trained curs you've got backing you up, MacBride. We'll make the trip to hell together." He now backed slowly, cautiously away from the group, his gun still cocked and ready to fire should the need arise.

Engrossed with the danger in which her unexpected rescuer had been plunged, Rachel was surprised to see that a crowd had gathered a short distance away. But still, no one had offered assistance. She shuddered at the realization that her grandfather could have been killed in cold blood, that there would have been no interference other than her own . . .

Moving to keep pace with Micah as he signaled her with a curt nod of his head, she knew that she would never forget the white-hot fury in Vance MacBride's savage gaze as he watched the two of them disappear inside the hotel.

Vance muttered a particularly vile obscenity, and his hand closed purposefully about the gun in his holster just as Micah backed through the doorway of the Macqueen House. He had taken no more than a single menacing step forward when his men rushed to stop him.

"No, Vance! Now ain't the time!" one of them anxiously protested.

"Now's as good a time as any!" viciously snarled Vance, struggling wildly in an attempt to break free of their restraining hold upon him. "I'll kill that old bastard, I'll kill him! Then I'll show that granddaughter of his—"

"Now ain't the time!" another man reiterated, knowing full well how difficult it was to reason with his employer whenever his damnable temper exploded. Vance's temper had frequently gotten them all into trouble, and he didn't want yet another tangle with the do-gooders of the town if it could be avoided. "You can't go waltzing in there and shoot a man in cold blood! You got to wait, Vance. You got to wait till the old man's back out at his ranch!"

"Tate's ranch!" Vance furiously amended. "It's MacBride property, damn it, and always will be!" His struggles finally diminished as a plan began to take shape in his head. "Let go of me, damn you! I'm not going to kill him—yet!" They obeyed, relieved to see the maliciously pensive expression on his swarthy face.

"What you plannin' to do, Vance?" the lanky young cowhand to his immediate left ventured to ask.

"We're going to have ourselves a little party tonight," he revealed, a malevolent light glowing in his strange golden eyes, "and I think it's about time someone demonstrated a certain 'rope trick' for Micah Parker's benefit!"

"But what about Logan?" the youngest of the group was foolish enough to ask. "Logan ain't gonna—" His words were abruptly cut off by virtue of his raven-haired boss's hands gripping and ferociously twisting the neckline of his brand-new, store-bought shirt.

"Logan's got nothing to do with this! You'll do as *I* say, understand?" Vance spat at him, his eyes gleaming with an unspoken promise of retribution should the other man decline. The suitably intimidated fellow, however, did not decline—he quickly nodded his assent and released a heavy sigh as his shirt was released. "Anyone else got any questions?" challenged Vance. Satisfied that he had the unspoken loyalty of his men, he led the way back down the boardwalk toward the row of saloons, his long strides carrying him directly beneath the window of Rachel's hotel room.

Watching until Vance and the others were out of sight, Rachel allowed the curtains to fall back into place and turned back toward her family.

She and her grandfather had remained downstairs for several minutes, during which time they spoke of Vance MacBride's attack upon her and his subsequent confrontation with Micah, who had thankfully been pulling up in front of the hotel just as Vance grabbed her. After composing herself and assuring Micah that she was indeed unharmed, Rachel had climbed the stairs with him in shared, thoughtful silence.

Jane and Lizzie were blissfully unaware of the latest danger to Micah, and Rachel had reluctantly consented to keep it that way. Only recently returned from the morning's excursion, the two women were in the room freshening up for the planned luncheon with Rachel when Micah's appearance in the doorway brought mutual exclamations of surprised pleasure to their lips. There followed a great deal of hugging and kissing, which Micah endured quite admirably, and it was only after answering numerous questions that he was given the chance to explain his presence in town.

"You're all coming back with me. The hands I hired have worked out even better than I expected, and we've already got most of the barn finished. There's been no new signs of trouble with the MacBrides," he told them, pausing momentarily to exchange a sharp, conspiratorial glance with Rachel, "so maybe they've finally realized that we aim to stay. Whatever the case, I'm sick and tired of my own cooking and I want you all home," he finished, his mouth curving into a faint smile.

"Micah Parker, tonight I'm going to cook you the best meal you ever tasted!" Jane laughingly declared, hugging him again.

"Hallelujah!" offered Lizzie, obviously delighted with the prospect of returning to the ranch. "I can't wait to get out of these confounded dresses and into some pants!" she asserted, knowing full well that her grandmother would never permit such a thing. "It's about time we got around to doing what we came to Montana for!"

Rachel's blue eyes lit with momentary amusement at her sister's enthusiasm, but any smile which might have risen to her lips was quelled by returning thoughts of Vance MacBride, closely followed by a startlingly vivid image of his handsome older cousin. How could two men be related to one another and yet be so vastly different? she wondered, then staunchly told herself that she was being foolish, that there wasn't much difference between the two men at all. Granted, there were the obvious physical contrasts, but there were also disturbing similarities—foremost in her mind was the recollection of the ill treatment both of them had subjected her to that morning, and all within the space of a few minutes. It was still almost beyond belief that fate could have been so merciless as to have thrown both MacBrides in her path on the same misbegotten day!

But Logan's kiss set you on fire, the tiny voice at the back of her mind mischievously expounded. And he had suggested—no, *ordained,* that the two of them marry. A marriage in name only. A temporary arrangement that would mean nothing in the personal sense.

Rachel was quite dismayed to feel a sharp twinge of something distressingly akin to disappointment. Firmly telling herself in the next instant that it didn't matter what Logan MacBride had decreed, that there was absolutely no way she could ever consider binding herself to him in marriage, however insubstantial the bonds, she was once again plagued by the memory of Vance MacBride's hate-filled eyes . . .

The trip back out to the ranch was pleasant and uneventful, the faint, fresh scent of rain carried on the warm breeze promising a welcome respite from the heat. Once home, Jane immediately headed for the kitchen, while both Rachel and Elizabeth accompanied their grandfather to the new barn. The two young men Micah had hired were hard at work up on the partially finished roof, but they were only too happy to climb down and make the acquaintance of their employer's granddaughters—particularly Rachel.

"Jace, Culpepper," Micah solemnly made the introductions, "these are my granddaughters, Rachel and Lizzie."

"Right pleased to make your acquaintance, ma'am," Jace eagerly declared to Rachel, his fingers sadly crushing the hat in his hands as he inclined his head briefly toward Elizabeth and added, "You too, ma'am," before turning his rapt attention back to her sister. Although a year older than Rachel, he looked even younger, his round-cheeked face generously sprinkled with freckles and his head covered by an unruly mass of thick, straw-colored hair. Of little more than medium height, he was quite slender and obviously not accustomed to spending his days outside beneath the hot Montana sun, given the way his fair skin was sporting a newly acquired redness.

"Likewise, ma'am," Culpepper told Rachel more shyly, following his friend's lead and nodding politely in Lizzie's direction with, "and ma'am." He was both taller and heavier than Jace, but certainly no older. His features were ruddier and more weathered than the other man's, and his tightly curling hair was a sun-streaked brown.

Rachel responded to the two young men with a warm smile, Lizzie with a knowing grin, and Micah with a heavy sigh of impatience.

"You planning to stand around and stare all day?" he grumbled. "We've got work to do, remember?" He frowned as Jace and Culpepper took the time to gallantly murmur their good-byes to the young ladies before taking themselves off to finish their chores. Once they had gone, Micah nodded at Rachel and Lizzie. "The two of you go on inside and help your grandmother. Tell her I'll be bringing the hands to supper tonight."

"I'm sure they'll appreciate both the meal *and* the opportunity to undress Rachel with their eyes some more," Lizzie opined with an irrepressible twinkle in her brown eyes.

"Lizzie Parker!" Rachel sharply reprimanded, flushing to the roots of her hair. "They did no such thing!" The redhead was about to offer further audacious comment upon the subject when Micah tersely directed, "Get inside!" Rachel, all too familiar with the expression of intense annoyance on his hard-lined face, took her sister's arm in an unrelenting grip and marched her into the house. As usual, however, her anger with Lizzie quickly evaporated. By the time Micah came to the supper table with the young ranch hands, the spirits of all three women were high, and Jane literally beamed with satisfaction as everyone set about devouring the culinary results of hours spent in the kitchen.

Thunder rumbled in the near distance, and the gathering twilight was further deepened by the clouds, dark and laden with life-giving moisture, roiling overhead. The air was heavy with the coming rain, and charged with the impending promise of a storm.

"Anyone for more coffee?" asked Jane, bustling happily about the table with coffeepot in hand.

"Thank you, Miz Parker, don't mind if I do," confirmed Jace, a broad grin spreading across his boyish, freckled countenance as he held his cup aloft. "That's just about the best dam . . . er, best coffee I've tasted in a coon's age," he remarked, hastily amending the compliment at a sharp, quelling glance from Micah's steely eyes. Rachel, seated next to him, suppressed a smile and turned to Culpepper, who occupied the chair opposite hers.

"Does everyone always address you by your last name, Mr. Culpepper?" she wondered aloud, her eyes sparkling warmly in an effort to help ease his obvious nervousness.

"Yes, ma'am."

"But, why?" probed Lizzie, her curiosity aroused. "Seeing as how you're working for Micah, it seems too formal for us to be calling you 'Culpepper' all the time. Don't you have a first name?"

"Yes, ma'am." He shifted uncomfortably in his chair and appeared to have developed a sudden fascination for the dwindling contents of his plate.

"Well, what is it?" Lizzie demanded to know. A dull, telltale flush rose to the hapless young man's face, and he visibly hesitated. Finally, Jace chuckled and cast his friend an openly teasing look.

"He doesn't want to tell you, 'cause he'd probably die of embarrassment if you found out his name is—"

"Jace Owens, you shut your blasted mouth!" Culpepper ground out with unexpected vehemence, coming out of his chair like a shot and reaching across the narrow breadth of the table to lay hands upon an unrepentantly grinning Jace. Rachel, Elizabeth, and Jace stared at them in open-mouthed amazement, while Micah directed in a harsh, no-nonsense tone, "Damn it, Culpepper, you and Jace stop acting like savages and sit down!"

They were never given the chance to prove obedience to Micah's sternly reproving command, for it was in the next moment that the back door of the house was flung open and more than a dozen masked men came bursting into the room.

"Micah!" His name was a strangled cry upon Jane's lips as her wide, horror-stricken eyes watched her husband set upon by several of the men. She gasped in terrified disbelief as she herself was seized and held. Curses and shouts of defiance filled the room, but everything happened so quickly that there was very little to be done in the way of resistance.

"Dear God!" Rachel choked out. Lizzie clutched frantically at her as both Jace and Culpepper were easily overpowered and dispatched to unconsciousness with a single blow each from a pearl-inlaid pistol butt. Then, Rachel and her sister were imprisoned by two of the masked intruders, their arms yanked behind their backs and a hand clamped across their mouths. They struggled fiercely, but to no avail, hot tears blinding them both as Micah was dragged outside. Only three of the men remained in the house with the women.

"No! Please, I beg of you, don't!" screamed Jane, twisting so violently within her captor's grasp that she managed to temporarily free herself. She had no more than reached the doorway before she was caught and borne forcibly backward. "Micah! Micah!" she sobbed in frenzied despair. The burly, black-haired man assigned to hold her apparently grew weary of her struggles, for he raised his fist and sent it crashing downward against Jane's chin. She crumpled to the floor beside Jace and Culpepper.

"The boss said we wasn't to hurt none of the women!" the man restraining Rachel chided tensely, encountering no little difficulty of his own in trying to subdue the golden-haired wildcat who kicked and twisted beneath his increasingly rough hands. Lizzie also made it quite clear that she would not meekly surrender, and it was mere seconds later that Rachel, taking advantage of the timely diversion created when her sister delivered a particularly well-placed kick to her own restrainer's kneecap and raced around to the opposite end of the table, jabbed her elbow into her captor's unprotected mid-section and sped outside before any of the men could give chase.

A rope had already been thrown over the massive limb of a cottonwood towering beside the barn. Micah's hands were bound behind his back, and a black hood had already been placed over his head. Rachel emerged from the house just as her grandfather was being lifted up to the bed of a wagon, and her horrified gaze quickly moved to where a pair of horses, hitched to the wagon, were straining nervously against the harness.

Several torches had been lit, their flames whipped by the strengthening wind and casting an ominously irregular glow upon the deadly proceedings. Another clap of thunder rumbled through the heavens, closely followed by an answering flash of lightning as the storm prepared to break.

Rachel did not hesitate before dashing forward, her hastily searching gaze drawn almost immediately to the man who stood apart from the group alongside the wagon. His raven hair was visible beneath his hat, and his golden eyes glittered with malevolent satisfaction as he watched the perpetration of his orders. She knew that it was Vance MacBride.

"Stop her!" yelled one of the two men who darted out of the house in hot pursuit after her.

The leader of the bloodthirsty mob turned, his lips curving up into a predatory smile beneath the kerchief covering the lower half of his face as he caught sight of Rachel. Holding up a hand to signal away any interference, he moved in a few long strides to intercept her as she made a hopelessly desperate attempt to reach her grandfather.

"Micah!" cried Rachel, her voice breaking on a sob. Vance chuckled evilly, his arms enveloping her with such cruel tautness that she could scarcely breathe.

"Rachel! For God's sake, Rachel, go back in the house!" Micah Parker's muffled, pain-filled voice rang out. "Leave her alone, you bastards! I'm the one you want! Leave her be!"

"Hold it right there, honey!" jeered Vance, ignoring Micah's frantic pleas on Rachel's behalf. "We can't have you spooking the horses before it's time, now, can we?"

"You can't do this!" cried Rachel, wincing involuntarily as his arms bruised her squirming softness. "Please, he's done nothing to deserve this! You've got to let him go!" Her honey-colored tresses streamed wildly about her face and shoulders, and her brightly flushed cheeks glistened with the tears spilling from her lashes and coursing freely downward.

"He was warned. Now he'll get what's coming to him!" Vance bit out, a renewed burst of fury surging upward as he recalled his humiliation at Micah Parker's hands earlier that same day.

"No!" She strained wildly against him, freeing one of her hands long enough to reach up and jerk his mask downward. "It won't do you any good to hide behind a mask, Vance MacBride! You and the others will still be every bit as guilty of murder if you hang my grandfather!"

"Are you willing to do anything to save him?" he unexpectedly propositioned, his swarthy face lowering so that it was suffocatingly close to hers. "*Anything?*" His eyes glowed with a dark, foreboding light, and Rachel abruptly stilled, inhaling sharply at his undeniable meaning.

"No, damn you! Leave her be!" Micah bellowed, his furious struggles growing so intense that it was nearly impossible for Vance's men to hold him.

Rachel's eyes were full of agonizing indecision as she choked back another sob and looked to where her grandfather was being so brutally and inevitably defeated. Another cry broke from her lips as she watched a man swing his fist with grueling force into Micah's midsection, sending the bound and hooded prisoner, gasping painfully for breath, to his knees.

"Yes! Yes, I'll . . . I'll do whatever you say!" she finally consented, her voice hoarse and quavering with despair. "I'll do anything you want if you'll only let him go!" Vance's eyes lit with malicious triumph, and his lips curled up into a slow, particularly disdainful smile as his dark, penetrating gaze bored down at the helplessly trembling woman in his arms. He stood silent and still for a number of agonizingly long moments, until one of his men obviously grew impatient and curtly demanded, "What's it to be, boss?"

"Hang him. Hang the bastard high!" Vance MacBride's voice rang out above the rain-scented wind. His malefic amusement only deepened as Rachel, her opal eyes stricken with renewed horror, gasped and cried in a voice choked with emotion, "No! I told you I'd do whatever you wanted!"

"And you will, honey. You will," he drawled lazily, then merely laughed at the expression of stunned disbelief crossing her beautiful, tear-streaked face. Momentarily paralyzed with both fear and a numbing sense of unreality, Rachel could only stare mutely up at Vance as he gave a curt nod of his head toward the spot where her barely conscious grandfather was being hauled to his feet again in the wagonbed. The rope dangling from the tree was yanked downward and the already prepared noose looped over Micah's hood-shrouded head.

"No!" shrieked Rachel, coming to life again when she saw the noose being tightened about Micah's neck. She battled against Vance's imprisoning embrace once more, sparing no thought to her own safety as all impulses from the terror-filled recesses of her brain prompted her to react with more unbridled violence than ever before. Screaming and kicking wildly, she succeeded in raking her nails down one side of her captor's swarthy face, and was rewarded by a blow which sent her sprawling in the dirt at his feet.

Two of Vance's men rushed forward to take control of Rachel as their leader muttered a curse and put a hand to his burning cheek, blood oozing from several deep furrows in his sun-darkened skin. For a moment, it appeared that Vance MacBride would surrender to the murderous impulses reflected in the smoldering glare he turned upon the young woman whose strength was rapidly waning. Instead, he spun about on his booted heel and roared, "Get on with the hanging, damn it!"

The first, chilling drops of rain began to fall as dust swirled about the group in a choking whirlwind. Rachel's heart-wrenching sobs were scarcely audible above the explosive rumble of thunder. Micah Parker made no sound as the rope's tautness was double-checked by the masked henchmen.

Vance MacBride raised his arm in purposeful readiness. His narrowed eyes were suffused with an almost fanatical light, his dark features contorted with the force of his bloodthirsty lust for vengeance. His hand clenched into a white-knuckled fist as his arm lowered in a silent command.

Micah Parker's entire body tensed as the horses, snorting and whickering loudly, were urged abruptly forward by the sharp crack of a whip above their heads. One last shrill scream broke from Rachel's lips as her grandfather's boots scraped noisily against the moving bed of the wagon . . .

Without warning, the blast of a rifle pierced the storm-charged air.

VII

"What the—" muttered Vance, watching in stunned disbelief as Micah slumped into the wagonbed. The noose was still fastened tightly about his neck, but the rifle's bullet had neatly severed the rope at the point where it stretched over the high limb of the cottonwood. The horses were roughly jerked to a halt by the wagon's astonished driver, and more than a dozen pairs of eyes flew to encounter the grim faces of the impressively substantial number of armed horsemen who rode forward to form an intimidating semicircle about the masked assailants. The riders were led by none other than the patriarch of the MacBrides.

"We MacBrides don't settle our disputes this way, Vance," Logan declared in a deep, resonant voice edged with unmistakable authority, "and you damn well know it!" With a deceptive air of nonchalance, he settled the stock of his rifle on his lean-muscled thigh, his other hand maintaining a steady grip on the reins of his mount. An excellent marksman, he was the one who had fired the shot to prevent Micah's death.

A spellbound Rachel was unable either to move or speak. Still held by Vance's men, she seemed oblivious to everything but Logan. There was a tight wariness to his handsome face, a certain, unfathomable light glowing within the darkening green depths of his eyes as his gaze never wavered from Vance's rage-flushed features.

A flash of lightning sent another crackle of thunder, and the slow yet intensifying barrage of raindrops stung against any unprotected skin. Logan's men, far outnumbering Vance's corresponding band, remained perfectly still and vigilant astride their horses, their guns drawn and resting across their saddlehorns.

"This is none of your affair, Logan!" snarled Vance. "This is a personal matter between me and Parker!"

"It goes beyond 'personal' when it comes to this," Logan harshly dissented. "I'm not going to let you string a man up simply because of—"

"Damn you, stay out of this! The son of a bitch has asked for everything he's got coming to him!"

"You and your men mount up and get going," Logan tersely directed.

"You planning to shoot us if we don't?" Vance parried with contemptuous sarcasm.

"Don't tempt me," warned Logan, the merest hint of a smile tugging at the corners of his mouth. "Now do as I say and get the hell out of here, all of you!"

For a moment it appeared that Vance was going to defy him. He even went so far as to drop his hand to the gun holstered low upon his hip. But something in Logan's eyes apparently prompted him to reconsider. Firing his cousin a savagely venomous glare, Vance MacBride accepted the inevitable with an ill grace and flung about to stalk across the rapidly dampening ground, joining the men gathering in silence to retrieve the horses they had left tied near the newly erected stock barn. Logan turned a dangerously intense look upon the men who still restrained Rachel.

"Let her go and get over there with the others." They wisely chose to follow his orders, leaving Rachel to shake off her numbness at last and hasten across the yard to her grandfather. Micah, staggering upright in the wagon, was helped down by some of Logan's men. The hood was quickly pulled from his head and his hands untied, and it was all Rachel could do to keep from breaking down again as she threw her arms about him. Though still a trifle unsteady on his feet, he returned her embrace and murmured words of comfort close to her ear.

"You sure that's all your men?" Logan demanded of Vance, whose only response was to scowl murderously across at the other man.

"There was another one inside the house!" supplied Rachel, drawing away from Micah to face their rescuer. The fiery gleam in his eyes sent a strange, powerful current running through her. "My grandmother and sister are still in there, along with the two ranch hands!" she told him in a tremulous voice, forcing herself to meet his disturbing gaze as he swung down from the saddle.

Micah breathed a curse and headed for the house, with Rachel, Logan, and several of Logan's men following closely after him, but another shot rang out before they had reached the door. Vance, meanwhile, wasted no time before jerking on the reins and riding off into the stormy night, sparing no thought to the man he and the others were leaving behind.

Logan, his gun clenched tightly in his hands as he quickly overtook both Rachel and her grandfather, was the first to storm through the doorway. He drew up short at the startling, albeit profoundly relieving sight which met his eyes.

The last of Vance's mercenaries lay sprawled across the table where he had fallen after being knocked senseless by the capable fists of Brodie MacBride. Jace and Culpepper were just beginning to regain consciousness, the two of them groaning as they struggled into a sitting position on the polished wooden floor. Jane, who had come to several minutes earlier, flew across the room to hurl herself upon Micah's chest as he burst inside. And Lizzie, her youthful features wearing an oddly worshipful expression, pressed a raggedly liberated piece of her petticoat to the spot on Brodie's forehead where a bullet had thankfully only grazed his smooth golden skin. Brodie impatiently waved away the girl's tender ministrations as he quietly, almost casually, informed Logan, "Thought I'd come on inside and have a look. It's a good thing I did, since that bastard there heard what was going on outside and apparently got it into his head to use the women to make good his escape."

"He almost got himself killed while saving us!" added Lizzie, tilting her head back to cast him another look of unabashed adoration.

"Oh, Lizzie, thank God you're all right!" murmured Rachel, moving to embrace her younger sister. She smiled tearfully up at the handsome, dark-haired young man beside Elizabeth, her shining eyes full of immense gratitude. "Thank you," she said simply. Her eyes were irrevocably drawn to Logan's somber countenance, but Micah and Jane hurried across to join their granddaughters in an emotion-charged reunion, while Brodie and the rest of Logan's men began to file back outside into the rain-filled darkness to join their companions.

"No, wait!" protested Jane, drying her eyes and hastily smoothing several wayward locks of gray-streaked sandy hair away from her bruised and swollen face. "I want everyone to come on inside and have some coffee and something to eat. It's the least I can do . . . I don't know how we can ever repay you for what you've done for us tonight . . ." Her voice trailed away as the tears sprang to her eyes again, and her husband's arm tightened about her trembling shoulders.

"We'd take it kindly if you'd accept our hospitality," Micah declared a bit stiffly, obviously uncomfortable at being indebted to Logan MacBride. His steely eyes met the younger man's, and a look of silent understanding passed between them, though the gazes of both lacked warmth. "You saved my life, MacBride. I don't know why, but the fact is, you *did*. I want you to know I'll think of some way to repay you. We Parkers always pay our debts."

"I want no repayment from you," Logan asserted in a low, even tone, his eyes imperceptibly narrowing. "But I'll accept your offer of hospitality for my men. The barn will do just fine." At that, he turned and was gone, but not before directing a long, speaking look at Rachel. She caught her breath on a soft gasp, thrown into confusion by the silent message he had been conveying to her. Brodie and the others followed silently in Logan's wake.

"What happened?" Jace suddenly piped up, having curbed his impatience almost beyond tolerance. He and Culpepper stood leaning against the wall for support, their heads still aching terribly. "The last thing I remember—"

"Sit down, the both of you!" Jane briskly cut him off,

softening her words with a faint, motherly smile. "You can hear all about it while I see to those wounds of yours." Resolutely setting aside the horror of the recent ordeal, she motioned Micah into a chair as well and set to work. A warm but weary smile touched Rachel's lips before she left the room to change into dry clothing, with Lizzie hurrying after her.

It was only a short time later that the two sisters, accompanied by the still light-headed but determinedly helpful Jace and Culpepper, carried trays bearing mugs of hot, steaming coffee across the yard and into the lamplit barn. It was certainly no easy task, for the Montana thunderstorm had unleashed its full fury by now, turning the ground into a perilously slick river of mud and sending dense, wind-whipped sheets of rain slamming against the earth. Even though some of the coffee had spilled during the difficult trip from the house and was cooled somewhat by the combined effects of wind and rain, it was received with heartfelt expressions of gratitude by the men settling down for the night within the dry interior of the barn that had been completed earlier that same day.

While Jace and Culpepper were drawn into a conversation with some of the cowpunchers whose acquaintance they had made a time or two previously, Lizzie stayed close to Brodie, subjecting him to a vast array of questions pertaining to the country and the cattle business there. He and those around him couldn't help but be amused by the petite young redhead's lively spirit, as well as by her obvious enthusiasm for their way of life, and Brodie even began to feel a bit flattered by Elizabeth's wide-eyed attentiveness to his every word.

Rachel had already pulled her grandfather's slicker up

over her head again and was preparing to return to the house when a firm hand on her arm stopped her. Turning slowly about to face the tall man who seemed to suddenly materialize in the doorway beside her, she was not at all surprised to discover that it was Logan. Just the same, she felt a perplexing leap of her pulses as she forced herself to confront him squarely. Her gaze traveled upward, from his mud-splattered boots and damp clothing that molded his wholly masculine form to perfection, to the ruggedly handsome, unsmiling face that haunted her dreams. She was inordinately alarmed by the glow emanating from his clear, strikingly virescent gaze.

"I had a feeling Vance might pull something like this tonight," he remarked in an undertone, his eyes locking with hers. "I heard about what happened at the hotel. As soon as I found out you had left town, I rounded up some of my men and rode on out. We made it as quickly as we could," he concluded grimly, his deep voice edged with still-smoldering fury over the nightmarish ordeal she and her family had endured. His hands shot out to take her shoulders in a firm but gentle grip as he studied her face closely. "By damn, I could have—" he muttered with a barely controlled violence, breaking off and forcing himself to release her. "You're all right, aren't you?" he asked in a tight voice, mentally cursing the fact that their conversation was so public.

Rachel did not immediately respond. She glanced briefly downward to where her breasts rose and fell rapidly beneath the tucked bodice of her pale lavender gown, then toward the group of men a short distance away. Her unbound locks were tumbling softly about her face and shoulders, and her blue eyes clouded with an emotion Logan could not name as her gaze finally met his again.

"You said I was to give you my answer tonight, Mr. MacBride." Her voice was scarcely audible, and she could feel her cheeks flaming as she nonetheless proudly lifted her head and declared, "Very well. I agree to the arrangement you proposed—a marriage in name only. For the sake of my grandfather, I will marry you."

"When?" Logan quietly demanded, displaying no surprise at all as he towered above her. It was as if he had been confident of her acquiescence all along. "The sooner we tie the knot, the sooner—"

"Whenever you say!" she told him in a ragged whisper, then immediately sought to regain her composure. "In spite of what you did for us tonight, I am quite certain my grandfather would never consent to our marriage. I . . . I will therefore have to leave the house without his knowledge."

"I'll come for you at first light," he vowed in a low, vibrant tone, his sea-green eyes darkening to jade.

Rachel swallowed a sudden lump in her throat as she looked away again. Acutely conscious of Logan's penetrating gaze upon her, she could not seem to face him any longer. Without another word, she tugged the canvas slicker upward and sped breathlessly out into the storm, forgetting all about her sister until she had reached the sanctuary of her bedroom.

Rachel reluctantly told Lizzie of her plans when the girl finally climbed into bed beside her that night. In truth, the last thing she wanted was for any of her loved ones to know of what she perceived to be her impending dishonor, even if it was only a symbolic disgrace, but she knew that her grandparents would be worried sick about her once they discovered her gone. She was hoping that Lizzie could explain things in such a way as to spare them as much pain as possible. What she had not counted on, however, was Lizzie's adamant objections to her older sister's intended manner of sacrifice.

"Rachel Parker, that's the most harebrained idea you've ever had! Why, you don't even know the man! Oh, don't think I didn't recognize him as the cowboy who got your dander up on the train from Billings . . . but then to find out that he's a MacBride and that you're going to sell yourself to him—"

"I am *not* selling myself!" Rachel hotly dissented, her eyes flashing in the darkness. The storm continued to rage outside, and a steady volley of raindrops could be heard pelting against the glass of the bedroom window and drumming on the roof above.

"That's exactly what you're doing! You're giving yourself to one MacBride in the ill-placed hope that it's going to prevent another MacBride from being what he is—an evil, heartless bastard who's no doubt in league with the devil himself! Vance MacBride is bound and determined to run us off this land, Rachel, and it's quite obvious that he'll stop at nothing. Do you really think that—"

"Oh, Lizzie, I don't know what to think! But you've got to try and understand! It's the only way. What other choice do I have, do *we* have? After what happened tonight . . ." Experiencing a sudden, violent shudder of remembrance, she blinked against the fresh onslaught of tears which sprang to her eyes. "You'd do the same thing in my place, Lizzie. Though Logan MacBride is little more than a stranger, he is offering me the chance to save

Micah. And, heaven help me, I've got to go through with it!" Another tremor assailed her, but it was provoked by unbidden images of a tall, rakishly handsome scoundrel bending over her with the fire of passion in his eyes . . .

No! Rachel cried in silence, her head spinning and her pulses racing. If she dared allow such thoughts to enter the turbulence which—until Logan MacBride had come into her life—was once the peaceful orderliness of her mind, she'd never be able to endure what was to come!

"When is this disaster supposed to take place?" Lizzie demanded, her flame-colored eyebrows knitting into a severe frown.

"He said he'd come for me at first light," her sister answered in a voice that was far from steady. "I . . . I thought I'd try to get a few hours of sleep before . . ." The sentence was left unfinished as a thunderbolt split the heavens and another unnerving vision of Logan burned itself into Rachel's brain.

"You realize that it's going to break Micah's heart, don't you?"

"But at least he'll stay alive. And that's all that truly matters, Lizzie."

"What am I supposed to tell him and Grandmother?" Lizzie then queried, apparently having conceded defeat as she released a long sigh and abruptly drew the covers farther upward.

"I think it's best if they believe I'm marrying him of my own free will—which I am, in a way. But I don't want them to suspect the true reasons."

"You want me to tell them it's a love match, is that it?" the redhead asked, her youthful voice tinged with appreciative irony in spite of the gravity of the situation. She grew quite solemn in the next instant, casting the blonde beside her a sharp, speculative look. "It *isn't,* is it, Rachel? I mean, you don't really—"

"Of course not!" Rachel broke in to deny most ardently. Dismayed to feel her cheeks flaming, she went on to fervently expound, "Why, Logan MacBride is the most arrogant, overbearing, unscrupulous rogue it has ever been my misfortune to encounter!"

"Only a moment ago, you told me the man was little more than a stranger. How is it you seem to know so much about him then?" probed Lizzie, her brown eyes narrowing in sisterly suspicion. "Are you sure there's not something else you'd care to tell me about your relationship with your future 'husband'?"

"It's a long story, Lizzie, and one that I'm not at all certain I'd care to repeat, even to you," disclosed Rachel, perilously close to tears once more. Her nerves were strained to the limit by the night's terrible events, as well as by the prospect facing her with the dawn. "I don't want to talk about it anymore. What's done is done. I've made my decision and I'm going to stick by it. Please, let's just try and get some sleep. I'm afraid I'm going to need all the strength I can muster to prevent my courage from deserting me entirely when Logan comes for me!"

When Logan comes for you, an inner voice of hers took perverse delight in reiterating. This same time tomorrow, she would be Mrs. Logan MacBride. The thought gave her quite the opposite of comfort as her fingers tightly clenched the bedcovers and her sparkling opal gaze reflected the intense disquiet within her. She knew that the night would seem agonizingly endless . . . as well as much too short.

* * *

Rachel awoke with a start. Drowsy surprise turned to dawning alarm as her gaze flew to the window. She had not intended to fall asleep again, and her breath caught in her throat when she noted the way the glistening drops of moisture still clinging to the glass were turned to liquid gold by the first pale rays of the rising sun.

She had no sooner leapt from the bed when a faint but insistent knock sounded against the window frame. Shooting an anxious glance toward Lizzie, who lay peacefully slumbering beneath the mound of covers, she battled the temptation to wake her, for she felt in dire need of another dose of moral support before facing Logan. Reluctantly acknowledging to herself that it was best not to risk disturbing her grandparents' sleep, Rachel snatched up her hooded blue merino cloak and flung it about her shoulders.

Her simple, gathered skirt, sadly wrinkled as a result of her unanticipated doze, was fashioned out of a heavy brown cotton, and underneath it she wore a plain white petticoat and drawers. Topping the skirt was a tucked but untrimmed shirtwaist of cream-colored linen, its high neckline and severe design adding to the overall austerity of her attire. Realizing that the day's plans would no doubt include a great deal of riding, she had wisely scorned the use of a corset, instead wearing only a simple cotton chemise beneath her blouse. Thick stockings and low-heeled riding boots completed the serviceable but not particularly attractive ensemble, and she had fastened her shimmering, honey-blond tresses into a tight chignon at the nape of her neck.

Rachel's troubled gaze swept the room one last time before she moved stealthily across to the window and eased it open. Logan stood waiting with typically masculine impatience, one hand clasping the reins of two mounts while his other hand lightly slapped his hat against his thigh. Rachel took a deep breath of determination when her eyes took in the sight of his chiseled, faintly scowling profile.

"You'll have to help me out," she whispered as she leaned outward to catch his attention.

"My pleasure," Logan quipped in a low, sardonic tone. Almost before Rachel knew it, he had donned his hat and reached inside to encircle her waist with one powerful arm, then lifted her effortlessly through the window and set her on her feet before him. His eyes raked swiftly over her, and he frowned before offering by way of complaint, "Looks like you're going to a funeral."

"I find the occasion almost as grim!" she retorted, bristling beneath the censure she read in his gaze. "Shall we go? My grandparents will be up soon!" she fairly hissed at him, already whirling away and stiffly marching to one of the horses. She had no more than grasped the saddlehorn and lifted her booted foot to the stirrup when she felt Logan's hands closing about her waist. Unceremoniously tossing her into the saddle, he then spun wordlessly about and mounted up beside her.

Rachel stole one last, helplessly yearning look at the house before urging her mount after Logan's as he led the way toward town. Wondering just how intense her grandfather's reaction to her marriage would be, she whispered another prayer and tried not to think of Micah or Jane. She had made her choice and would have to stick by it. For better or worse, she would be wed to Logan MacBride before the day was out. And no matter how desperately she tried to convince herself that everything would turn out all right, she could not shake the persistent feeling of uneasiness which settled upon her—a feeling she knew had nothing whatsoever to do with anyone other than the disturbingly virile rogue ahead of her. Her eyes widened with involuntary appreciation of the way he rode with such a wholly masculine grace, and she blushed to the roots of her honey-blond hair when she realized that her gaze had fastened upon the gently rocking motion of his lean hips in the saddle. It was only moments later when he urged his midnight black stallion into an easy gallop, and Rachel was forced to concentrate solely on controlling her own mount as she hastened to keep pace.

The trip to Miles City, passed in rarely unbroken silence, seemed of thankfully short duration to Rachel. Almost before she realized it, she found herself standing beside Logan in a small, cluttered office inside the Custer County courthouse. It had initially perturbed her that her "bridegroom" had not offered her the option of being married by a minister, but she had then reflected with a touch of bitter irony that it would have been a sacrilege for the two of them to become bound together as man and wife in a house of God when neither of them had any intention of honoring their vows. And so it was that she and Logan were being married by the local justice of the peace, with only two court clerks to serve as witnesses to the "happy event."

Inwardly wavering more than once before forcing herself to participate in the nuptials, Rachel hesitated for an uncomfortably long interval when the moment came for her to enunciate the two simple words which would legally bind her, supposedly forever, to Logan MacBride. She was acutely conscious of the three pairs of eyes fixed expectantly upon her as she swallowed hard and sought to master the feeling of panic welling up deep within her. A silent warning signal went off in her brain, but she determinedly ignored it. Finally, she lifted her head and met Logan's steady gaze. Reading the unmistakable challenge reflected within those piercing, dark green orbs, she dazedly wondered what his look meant, but the firm, insistent pressure of his hand upon her arm prompted her to murmur somewhat tremulously, "I . . . I do." Dear Lord, what have I done? she silently bemoaned. Only dimly aware of the gruff, white-haired justice of the peace declaring her and Logan to be husband and wife, she was nonetheless painfully cognizant of his admonition that "no man put asunder what God hath joined together." The next thing she knew, Logan was pulling her toward him for the traditional kiss.

The passionate embrace which followed, however, was far more than the usual brief sealing of the marital vows. Logan swept an unsuspecting Rachel masterfully against him, his powerful arms tightening almost fiercely about her shocked and outraged softness as his warm, demanding lips claimed hers. She was left pale and shaken when he abruptly released her a few seconds later, and she numbly allowed him to keep a supportive arm about her waist as he turned to the bespectacled older man who had performed the ceremony.

"Thanks, Sam." Logan shook his hand, the two of them exchanging curt nods.

"My sincere congratulations to you both." If he was a bit startled by the fact that he had been called upon to marry Logan MacBride and the obviously overwhelmed young woman standing before him, Sam Lexington kept it to himself. He was well accustomed to the impulsiveness of the MacBrides, though he had always believed Logan to be different. But, he mused to himself with an inner scowl, who the devil was he to question the actions of a man as powerful as Logan MacBride? Surmising that the newlyweds had been overcome by a youthful passion he was long past feeling, he watched solemnly as Logan led his new bride from the room. News of the wedding would be all over town before the day was out, and he had no doubt that it would cause quite a stir. Yes sir, he thought as a faint smile played about his lips, many a female heart would be broken when news of Logan MacBride's marriage hit the fire.

The newlyweds, meanwhile, had emerged into the dazzling sunlight outside the ornate building once more. Rachel, no longer caring if she created a scene, wrenched her arm from Logan's possessive grasp and rounded on him with belated indignation.

"How dare you manhandle me that way!" Her eyes blazed resentfully up at him, and her entire body trembled with the force of her anger. "Our agreement—"

"—is that our marriage be in name only," Logan finished for her, favoring her with a perplexingly unfathomable look as he tossed her up into the saddle. She could have sworn his low voice contained more than a trace of caustic amusement as he paused beside her long enough to reiterate, "We've got to make it look authentic, Rachel. And that includes behaving like the loving couple we're supposed to be, especially after we've just been joined together in 'wedded bliss'." He swung agilely up into his own saddle and gathered the reins in a loose, practiced grip. Rachel flushed angrily as he cast her a brief, mocking smile. "Shall we go home, *Mrs. MacBride?*"

"Don't call me that!"

"It's your name now. You'd better get used to it," he dispassionately asserted, reining about as he once again led the way through town. He negligently touched a finger to his hat as they passed several of his acquaintances, while Rachel rode stonily a few paces behind him and sent invisible daggers hurtling at the broad, hard-muscled expanse of his back.

They had traveled only a mile or so from Miles City when it suddenly dawned on Rachel that she hadn't the vaguest notion of what to do now that she had carried through with her supreme sacrifice for her grandfather's sake. Tugging sharply on the reins, she glanced ahead to where Logan's black-as-midnight horse was swiftly putting considerable distance between them.

"Mr. MacBride! Mr. MacBride, will you please stop!" she called at the top of her voice. The animal beneath her pranced impatiently, but she held the reins firmly and waited while Logan pulled his own mount to a halt and headed back toward her. His handsome face wore an expression of undeniable displeasure as he demanded in a deep voice edged with impatience, "What is it?"

Rachel took a deep breath and staunchly proclaimed, "We have to talk."

"There'll be plenty of time for talk later. Right now, we've got to get back," he tersely decreed.

"That's precisely what I wish to speak to you about. I would like to know—"

"I told you—we'll talk later." Logan autocratically cut her off. While she sat gazing after him with open-mouthed astonishment, he guided his horse about and began galloping across the sun-drenched prairie landscape once more. Rachel, though sorely tempted to remain exactly where she was and thereby force him to come back, realized that she really had very little choice but to follow suit. Angrily reflecting that it would be just like the ungallant scoundrel to leave her stranded alone in the middle of nowhere, she touched her heels to the horse's flanks and set off after her new husband.

It was almost noon when they reached Micah Parker's ranch. As the two of them wordlessly dismounted in front of the house, Lizzie suddenly came flying outside with her grandmother in her wake. Jane had obviously been crying, for there were telltale streaks marring her plump, kindly visage.

"Oh, Rachel! Oh, honey, why did you do it?" she brokenly queried, clasping her granddaughter to her in a rib-crushing embrace.

"Micah's taking it even worse than we feared!" Lizzie breathlessly informed Rachel. Glancing worriedly up at a silent, outwardly impassive Logan, the petite redhead hastened to caution him, "You'd better get the hell out of here, MacBride!"

"Wha . . . what's happened?" Rachel stammered in anxious bewilderment, drawing away from a newly tearful Jane. Seizing her younger sister's shoulders, she stared closely down into Lizzie's unmistakably apprehensive features. "What do you mean, 'he's taking it even worse than we feared'?"

"He says he's going to kill him! He says he doesn't for one minute believe you weren't forced into this!" Lizzie supplied in a rush.

"Oh, dear God, no!" whispered Rachel in growing horror.

"You'd best be on your way, Mr. MacBride!" Jane now fearfully warned, dabbing at her swollen, red-rimmed eyes with a handkerchief. There was a heart-wrenching note of appeal in her voice as her hand closed upon his arm and she pleaded, "Please, please get out of here before Micah returns!"

"Returns?" echoed Rachel, moving to her grandmother's side as she looked up to encounter Logan's inscrutable gaze. He had not spoken a single word as yet, and she wondered what thoughts were running through his mind upon hearing of this unexpected danger.

"He rode off after you!" disclosed Lizzie. "It wasn't long past sunup when he came into our room looking for you. He said he wanted to talk to you about something, but he didn't say what it was. When he discovered you gone, I . . . I told him what you and I had agreed to tell him. But he didn't buy it, Rachel. He wouldn't believe you had willingly eloped with a man you barely knew!"

"I don't believe it, either," added Jane more steadily, placing an arm protectively about Rachel's shoulders as she met Logan's gaze squarely, "but the most important thing right now is to do what we can to avoid trouble until Micah calms down. You see, Rachel and he are very close, Mr. MacBride, and he has a habit of listening to his heart instead of his head when it comes to those he loves."

"All the more reason for me to remain, Mrs. Parker," Logan finally responded in a low, resonant tone. His eyes, their sea-green depths darkening to jade, briefly touched Rachel's face before he continued. "There's only one thing for us to do. My wife and I will simply have to convince your husband that our elopement was prompted by nothing more than our mutual regard for one another."

Rachel blanched inwardly at hearing herself referred to as his wife, but she understood all too well the reasoning of his statement. Unless Micah believed she had indeed married Logan MacBride of her own free will, her sacrifice would have been for naught. She would have to lie to her beloved grandparents—something she had never done before. But she would do it. She would tell them anything if it would save Micah's life.

"Is that true, Rachel?" Jane Parker quietly probed, fixing her granddaughter with a lengthy, scrutinizing stare. "Did you marry this man because you wanted to and for no other reason? Micah seems to think you did it because of what happened last night. Did you? Did you marry Mr. MacBride for love . . . or to save Micah?"

Rachel could feel the hot color flooding her face, and her eyes involuntarily dropped before the older woman's searching gaze. She could hear her sister catching her breath beside her, could feel Logan's eyes burning down upon her as he waited for her answer. It proved to be one of the most difficult things she had ever done, but she forced herself to look directly at Jane while she uttered the falsehood that would seal her fate.

"For love, Grandmother. Only for love." Rachel was aware of the way Lizzie released a long, pent-up sigh, and she was nearly faint with relief when she glimpsed the acceptance in her grandmother's glistening brown eyes. She wasn't at all certain, but a quick glimpse in Logan's direction provided her with what she thought to be unspoken evidence of his approval, for it seemed that his tall, lean-muscled form relaxed a bit.

"Then that's that," pronounced Jane, resolutely drying her eyes and managing a weak smile up at Logan. "I apologize for doubting you, Mr. MacBride, and I want you to know that, once my husband hears the truth, he'll be just as sorry for flying off the handle."

"I only hope he'll take the time to listen!" remarked Lizzie. Shading her eyes against the sun, she hastily scanned the horizon as a sudden movement caught her attention. "And unless I'm not mistaken, it looks like we'll get the chance to find out just how reasonable Micah's going to be in about sixty more seconds!"

The three women tensed as Micah Parker approached the ranch house. Logan, however, maintained his devil-may-care pose beside them, only an imperceptible narrowing of his eyes giving a clue to his instinctive wariness. Although it was not immediately apparent, he was poised in defensive readiness by the time the older man drew to a halt and dismounted to stalk belligerently forward. Without pausing to question either the wisdom or justice of his actions, Micah raised his rifle to aim it directly at Logan as he snarled, "Damn you, you worthless, black-hearted son of a bitch! You no-account bastard, I ought to shoot you down—"

"Micah, no!" cried Rachel, her frantic plea ringing out in unison with Jane's and Lizzie's. Acting solely on impulse, she darted in front of Logan and announced in a voice quaking with emotion. "We're married now! Logan MacBride is my husband!" She inhaled sharply as she felt her arms being seized in an almost bruising grasp. Setting her toughly away from him, Logan glowered fiercely down at her as he ground out, "I'll not hide behind your skirts, Rachel!"

"Touch her again and you're a dead man, MacBride!"

growled Micah, his eyes glittering savagely and his harsh, lined features twisted into a menacing scowl. "It makes no difference to me if she bears your name or not—no granddaughter of mine is going to be forced into marriage with the likes of you!"

"I wasn't forced!" Rachel vehemently denied, rapidly crossing the distance between them now. "Oh, Micah, it wasn't that way at all! No one forced me into doing anything!"

"They love one another, Micah!" interjected Jane, edging closer to Logan. "We've got to accept it."

"You did it because of me, didn't you?" Rachel's grandfather challenged, his steely eyes boring into her tear-brightened ones as he disregarded his wife's words. "What did he promise you, Rachel? Did he trick you into thinking there'd be no more trouble if you gave yourself to him? That's why you did it, isn't it? Tell me the truth!"

"I *am* telling you the truth!" she desperately asserted. "I went with him because I . . . because I wanted to marry him. There was no other reason. We're married now, Micah. I'm his wife," she finished, placing a gently restraining hand upon her grandfather's forearm. "Please, you've got to try and understand."

"Understand what?" he bitterly retorted, his gaze slicing into hers. "That you ran off with a man whose kinfolk tried to hang me? That you were so madly in love with him that you'd forsake your own family? I don't believe it, Rachel. I can't believe we mean so little to you!" He glared past her to where Logan stood a few feet away. "And unless you felt you had no choice, I know damn good and well you'd never marry a man you don't even know!"

"But I *do* know him!" Rachel insisted. She felt her

cheeks flaming as she reluctantly divulged, "I . . . I met him in Billings. We've seen each other on several occasions since then."

Her startling confession was met with greatly varied reactions. Lizzie gaped at her in speechless amazement, Jane turned a crestfallen look of mingled hurt and disappointment upon her, and Micah's face became a mask of unbridled, vengeful fury at the thought that Logan MacBride had played loose with his innocent and naive granddaughter. Rachel's troubled gaze shifted between them all, until finally becoming transfixed upon Logan.

Meeting her look of painful confusion, his eyes took on a strangely intense glow. Without a word, he began moving toward her, his strides long and easy as his boots made nary a sound upon the damp, hard-packed earth. He seemed oblivious to the fact that Micah had not lowered the gun.

"It's time we were getting home, Rachel," Logan calmly decreed.

"Home?" she echoed, a blank look crossing her beautiful face. Then, as realization set in, she told herself that it couldn't be true—he certainly couldn't expect her to actually *live* with him, could he? Good heavens, she had never even contemplated such a possibility!

"She's not going anywhere with you!" Micah rasped out, his hand closing upon Rachel's wrist to pull her close beside him. "Now you get the hell out of here and don't ever come back! I'm warning you, MacBride—I'm liable to forget the fact that you saved my life last night if you so much as—"

"You're my wife, Rachel, and you're coming with me," Logan commandingly declared, his handsome visage revealing nothing more than an unwavering determination. His eyes were now suffused with a fiery gleam that caused Rachel's breath to catch upon a soft gasp. There was a highly charged feeling of anticipation in the warm, breeze-stirred air as she gazed mutely up at him. Lizzie and Jane both remained silent and expectantly watchful, while Micah turned to stare down at her with another dark frown creasing his weathered brow.

"Tell him, Rachel," he tersely directed. "Tell this bastard you won't be going anywhere with him!"

Rachel felt as if her heart was being torn asunder. The last thing on earth she wanted to do was hurt Micah. And yet, what else could she do? In order for her plan to be successful, she would have to make her grandfather believe her marriage was genuine. Once the danger to him was past, then she could tell him the truth. Then she could dissolve her marriage to Logan MacBride and never see her arrogant, overbearing "husband" again! But until such a time came that Vance, as well as the other MacBrides, no longer posed a threat to her family, she could not allow her personal feelings to interfere. She would have to go with Logan, even though every fiber of her being rebelled at the thought and warned against it!

"I'm sorry, Micah," she murmured, battling the tears as she forced herself to proclaim, "I . . . I must go with my husband. I love you, but I must do what is right." She nearly lost the strength to carry through when she observed the undeniable pain clouding his gray eyes. The expression on his face became rigidly guarded in the next instant, however, and Rachel choked back a sob as she allowed Logan to draw her arm through his and lead her back toward their horses.

"I'll send someone over for her things tomorrow," he quietly informed Jane. She responded with a silent nod, then hugged Rachel briefly before resolutely setting her away and moving to Micah's side. Lizzie wrapped her arms tightly about her older sister and whispered encouragingly, "Don't worry. It will turn out all right. You'll be home before you know it!" But even she could tell that her voice lacked conviction. She hadn't counted on Rachel having to live with Logan MacBride, and she was certain Rachel hadn't counted on it, either. What a fine mess they had made of things! What on earth was Rachel going to do now?

Much too soon thereafter, Rachel rode away again. This time, however, Logan kept his mount close beside hers. She would have been shocked to learn how very much the look of forlorn sadness on her face affected him.

Cursing himself for a sentimental fool, Logan nonetheless felt a twinge of guilt for his part in Rachel's distress. But his guilt was not so strong as to make him regret what had taken place that day. He had as yet to admit, even to himself, that marriage to Rachel was something he had wanted almost from the first moment he had set eyes upon her. The foremost thing in his mind as he stole another look at her valiantly tearless countenance was that she now belonged to him . . .

VIII

Rachel slid wearily from the saddle before Logan could dismount and move to assist her. The late afternoon sun beat relentlessly down upon her bare head as she miserably reflected that the day had without a doubt been the longest of her life. Grasping the saddlehorn for support when her legs threatened to give way beneath her, she felt as though her abused body, unaccustomed to enduring so many hours in the saddle, ached in places she had never before known to exist. She groaned inwardly as she put a hand to the small of her back and shook the dust from her skirts. But not even the intensity of her discomfort could prevent her from staring up at the two-storied building before her with appreciative awe in her widening opal gaze.

A large, rambling log structure built in the colonial style, the main house was the most impressive example of frontier architecture Rachel recalled ever having seen. Surrounded by numerous outbuildings—two barns, a stable, a blacksmith shop, several corrals, a cook shack, a long narrow bunkhouse and separate quarters for the foreman—the house had been designed and built more than seven years earlier by Logan's father, Dugan MacBride, and Dugan's three brothers. It boasted of six massive log columns in the front, as well as two opposite wings which had been added on at separate intervals throughout the years, and the entire sprawling edifice formed a giant E when viewed from the gentle rise in the land behind the house.

Situated near a wide, swift-flowing stream flanked by the ever-present plains cottonwood plus a few willow and ash trees, the ranchhouse had served as the original headquarters for the MacBride clan when they had left behind a flourishing cattle empire in the western part of the territory and ventured into the untamed, wide-open territory which they believed to promise even greater freedom and prosperity. In almost every way, their speculation had paid off—but none of the brothers had survived the transition long enough to see just how vast and prosperous the Circle M Ranch had become. It was now left to their many descendants to reap the benefits of what the four brothers from Scotland had worked so hard to build . . . and Dugan MacBride's son would see to it that the cherished traditions continued.

"Let's get on inside," murmured Logan, adroitly looping the reins of their mounts over the rough-hewn hitching post in front of the house. A sudden frown creased his handsome brow as he sauntered toward Rachel.

The woodsmoke-scented breeze tugged playfully at Rachel's thick golden tresses, which she had loosened from the restrictive pins during the course of the single rest stop Logan had allowed, and she reached up to instinctively smooth several gleaming locks from her face. It was then that she finally caught sight of the small group of men avidly watching her from their vantage point near one of the corrals across the yard. Dismayed to feel their eyes riveted upon her with such unabashed curiosity, she could not summon the strength to protest as Logan possessively took her arm and led her up the newly swept wooden steps of the porch. She found herself hanging back a bit, however, as he swung open the massive, polished oak door ornamented with an oval of etched glass, but he seemed not to notice her hesitancy, merely pulling her gently but firmly into the dim coolness of the entrance foyer.

"You look worn to the bone," Logan ungallantly observed once they were inside. Rachel jerked her arm free and directed a speaking glare up at him. She did not immediately vocalize her resentment—she had remained obstinately silent throughout the afternoon's journey—but the recipient of her animosity appeared totally unaffected by the venom in her gaze as he turned away and negligently tossed his hat to land in its proper place on the topmost peg of the hall tree beside the door. "Before you light into me with all the outraged femininity you've been saving up all day, I suggest you consider postponing the attack until you've rested up a bit," he lazily drawled, casting her a faint smile of wry amusement. Then, before she could even think of offering him a suitably scathing retort, Logan bent over her with lightning-quick speed and lifted her effortlessly in his strong arms.

"What do you think you're doing?" Rachel breathlessly demanded, initially too shocked to struggle. "Put me down at once!"

"The last thing I want on my hands is a swooning

female. And I figure you're too damned hardheaded to follow my orders and take yourself upstairs, so I'm going to oblige by personally 'escorting' you to your room," he proclaimed with a disturbingly purposeful light gleaming within his startlingly green eyes.

"No!" his unwilling burden gasped in rapidly escalating alarm. She began to squirm and kick, her hands pushing mightily against his chest, but to no avail. Logan easily held her captive and climbed the narrow, shadowed staircase to the bannistered landing above. "Let me go!" she cried, her voice rising on a shrill note as she felt a dismaying blend of light-headedness and enervation seizing her.

Heading toward a door at the farthest end of the hallway to his left, Logan kicked it open with one booted foot and strode inside, with Rachel still feebly pushing all the while and frantically wondering if she and Logan were all alone in the house and if it would do her any good to scream. She refused to acknowledge how, at the first touch of his hands upon her, she had trembled with something quite the opposite of either fear or disgust.

"I'll have a tray of food brought up in a few minutes. I'd suggest you have a bath and make use of the bed," he authoritatively ventured, finally setting her on her feet beside the huge, canopied four-poster bed he indicated with a curt nod of his head. He was bemused by his own good intentions, but all he could think of at the moment was that her face appeared unusually pale and strained, and that her well-being was now his responsibility. What was there about the beautiful but bedraggled young woman before him that stirred such feelings of tenderness and virtuous concern within him?

"You planned to bring me here all along, didn't you?"

Rachel hotly accused, rounding on him with a vengeance as she took a furious, slightly unsteady step backward and raised blazing eyes to his. "How very convenient that I was forced to come with you in order to convince my grandfather—"

"Not only to convince him, but everyone else as well," Logan broke in to calmly point out, his eyes surveying her closely. "Didn't it ever occur to you that you'd naturally have to live with your new husband if you expected anyone to believe our union was genuine?"

Rachel, flushing beneath his scrutiny, fell silent and uncomfortably shifted her gaze to the doorway as she bit at her lower lip. In truth, she hadn't wanted to think about it at all. She had purposefully refrained from pondering anything beyond the elopement, foolishly believing that everything would work itself out afterward. Mentally upbraiding herself for the folly of not discussing every detail of her agreement with him beforehand, she was now forced to concede that there was no other way. She would have to live under the same roof with Logan MacBride. She would have to play the role of his loving bride, no matter how desperately she wanted to run back to Micah and forget she had ever been insane enough to take part in such an outrageous scheme!

"I . . . once again, I have no choice but to agree," she cheerlessly allowed. She regained a portion of her usual spirit, however, as she raised her head proudly and feelingly asserted, "But everything else shall be exactly as we previously agreed!" She was nonplussed by the slow, mocking smile which spread across his rakish, sun-bronzed countenance.

"Tell me, *Mrs. MacBride,* are you afraid of me—or

yourself?" he asked in a low, resonant tone that contained an unmistakable challenge. Rachel, her eyes suddenly appearing quite enormous within the delicate oval of her face, inhaled upon a soft gasp and found herself unable to reply. Logan's smoldering gaze bored into hers for several long, tension-charged moments before he unexpectedly spun about on his booted heel and strode from the room. His movements were abrupt, almost angry, and Rachel stared after him with a helplessly dazed expression on her travel-smudged face.

Sinking numbly down onto the quilted coverlet atop the bed a moment later, she took a shuddering breath and choked back a self-pitying sob. Nothing had turned out the way she had planned! But that was the problem—she had done a woefully insufficient amount of planning. She had forgotten Micah's oft-repeated advice to "think things through till there's no more thinking to be done." And now here she was, forced to leave the security of her beloved family and offer a convincing semblance of happiness as the wife of Logan MacBride, the one man in the entire world who possessed the inexplicable power to make her behave so shamefully unlike herself!

You're a fool, Rachel Parker! You jumped at the chance to sacrifice yourself, but you underestimated the enormity of the sacrifice! a voice at the back of her mind took great pleasure in taunting. Rachel frowned and jumped up from the bed. Pacing restlessly about the well-decorated room, though she had as yet to take note of its finery, she released a heavy sigh and reluctantly came to a decision.

"What's done is done," she murmured aloud. She would have to try and make the best of things until such time that she would be free to return home and resume her normal life with her family. She would summon every ounce of patience and courage, and she would not give Logan MacBride the pleasure of believing that he had scored any sort of victory over her!

Although she was loath to follow Logan's bidding, she could not deny that soaking in a hot, soothing bath would be heavenly after all she had gone through that day. A look of characteristic determination crossed her lovely young face as she swept across the room to fling open what she correctly surmised to be the door to the bathroom. She did not pause to marvel at the luxuriously appointed surroundings in which she found herself, instead quickly shedding her dust-cloaked garments and turning the ornate handles above the gleaming porcelain tub situated in one corner of the sunlit room.

It wasn't until nearly half an hour later, after Rachel had vigorously scrubbed every inch of her rosily glowing body, as well as the mass of silken, honey-colored hair streaming damply about her shoulders, that a most perplexing realization dawned on her. Other than the things which lay in a discarded heap on the white-tiled floor beside the tub, she hadn't a stitch of clothing to put on. She had been too distraught upon leaving her family to think of taking a least a few personal articles with her.

"Now what?" she sighed. Eyeing her travel-soiled ensemble with feminine revulsion, she stood and reached for a thick towel which lay neatly folded on a shelf above the bathtub. She draped it around her and slowly eased open the door. Peering cautiously into the bedroom, her heart pounded in her chest as she thought of the possibility of her "husband" returning just as she left the sanctuary of the bathroom. A disturbing image of Logan turning those gleaming, sea-green eyes upon her virtually unprotected form sent an involuntary shiver running up her spine . . .

"You may as well come out. Mr. MacBride sent me up with these," Rachel was startled to hear a woman's voice proclaiming. Her bright head emerging from the bathroom, she found herself facing a large, fiftyish female who wore what could best be described as an expression of mingled suspicion and disapproval. The brown-haired woman was holding a tray laden with several dishes, which she set down with a loud clatter upon a small carved table beside the bed.

"Forgive me, but I . . . I'm not quite—" began Rachel, modestly hanging back in the doorway as she glanced down in embarrassment at her lack of attire.

"It matters none to me if you're naked as the day you were born. Mr. Logan said I was to bring you the food and see that you ate it!" A good head taller than Rachel, the woman's surprisingly well-muscled frame was encased in a severe gown of dark green cotton, and a starched white apron was tied about her ample waist. She folded her arms across her buxom chest with obvious impatience and announced in rather clipped tones, "I have other things to do, *Mrs. MacBride*. If you're going to eat, then you'd best be coming out and have done with it!"

Rachel, once again startled at hearing herself addressed as Logan's wife, particularly with such disparaging emphasis, was more than a little bemused at the woman's undeniably hostile attitude. Inwardly reflecting that she couldn't possibly have offended someone who was a perfect stranger, she finally emerged from the bathroom and pulled the towel more snugly about her nakedness.

"Who are you?" she evenly demanded.

"The name's Mrs. Smith. I've been cook and nursemaid and housekeeper to the MacBrides for nigh on to twenty years!" the older woman revealed with more than a touch of defensiveness.

"Well then, Mrs. Smith, perhaps you can help me." Rachel padded across the carpeted wooden floor to smile appealingly up at the other woman. "I'm afraid I've nothing clean to wear. You see, I've been on horseback for most of the day, and—"

"Mr. Logan said you'd be wanting something. I'm to get you some of Miss Moira's things as soon as you've eaten."

"Miss Moira?" echoed Rachel in puzzlement.

"Unless you're wanting to catch your death of cold, you'd best set about eating the food I brought you!" the woman snapped. Rachel was tempted to tell Mrs. Smith that she could very well remove the blasted tray of food and tell her employer that his "wife" would rather starve, but she took a deep, steadying breath and forced herself to utter politely, "I'll be more than happy to eat every bite if you will be so kind as to fetch me something to wear without further delay. I . . . I certainly wouldn't want my . . . my husband to return and find me so improperly attired." She smiled a bit nervously this time, but Mrs. Smith merely fixed her with a narrow, decidedly censorious look and remarked with disobliging bluntness, "Why not? I'll wager it's not the first time he's seen you 'improperly attired'!" Then, as if realizing that she'd allowed her intense displeasure with Logan's shocking news to drive her too far, the stern-faced housekeeper drew herself up stiffly and muttered, "I'll get you the clothes." She took herself off without another word, leaving both Rachel's thoughts and emotions in an even greater turmoil than before.

Suddenly recalling the fact that she had not eaten anything that day, save for the hard, almost tasteless piece of beef jerky Logan had pressed upon her during their brief rest stop, Rachel momentarily forgot her troubles and set about assuaging the gnawing hunger in her stomach. When the formidable Mrs. Smith returned bearing a nightgown and wrapper across one arm, she discovered that her new mistress had already downed more than half the contents of the tray.

"Thank you, Mrs. Smith." Rachel spoke with sincere gratitude as the woman carefully spread the borrowed garments upon the bed. She straightened and cast Rachel another critical look from her gray eyes before commenting with begrudging approval, "Mr. Logan admires a good appetite in a woman. His ma was a tiny little thing, but she could put away more food than most of the hands." Apparently feeling that she had spared enough kind words for the young woman she viewed as a scheming intruder, the housekeeper wheeled about and marched from the room, tossing over her shoulder, "I'll be back for the tray after I've served Mr. Logan his supper!"

Idly wondering just how many other servants and MacBrides inhabited the sprawling log mansion, Rachel mused that she was at least thankful for the fact that Logan was affording her such welcome solitude. She was too physically exhausted and emotionally drained to face anyone else that evening.

Logan. It was just beginning to sink in that she was now legally wed to him. In fact, this was their wedding night. And in spite of his assurances that theirs would be a marriage in name only, she felt trapped, a debilitating sense of panic hovering just beneath the veneer of composure she had erected about herself.

After hastily donning the soft cotton nightgown and red velvet wrapper, both of which provided an amazingly good fit and prompted her to wonder once again who Miss Moira was, Rachel finished a satisfying meal of baked chicken, potatoes, and fresh snap beans from the garden Mrs. Smith so lovingly tended in the early summer months. Feeling a warm languor stealing over her as a result of both the supper and the bath, she stifled a yawn and started to recline upon the inviting softness of the quilt-covered bed. At a sudden thought, however, she scurried across to the bedroom door and turned the key in the lock. Only then did she allow herself the luxury of drifting off into a deep, soul-refreshing sleep . . .

Logan stole quietly into the bedroom. Twilight had long since settled upon the prairie, chasing the shadows from the sun-warmed earth and bathing the room where Rachel slept in near total darkness. The breathtaking panorama of the endless Montana sky was blanketed by a thickening cover of nighttime clouds, effectively dimming the illuminating brilliance of a full moon. Logan, however, did not once stumble as he noiselessly approached the bed. He was well familiar with the particulars of the room—Rachel had spared only a passing glance at the connecting door of the bathroom, a door she had neglected to lock and one she did not realize led directly to her new husband's chambers—for it had once been his mother's.

His deep green eyes, already accustomed to the darkness, softened when they fell upon the slumbering form of his bride. Having convinced himself that he had come only to make certain Rachel was resting peacefully, he was once again surprised at the powerful surge of tenderness and protectiveness rising within him as he paused beside the bed and peered down at the only woman who had ever managed to touch his well-guarded heart.

Her beautiful face appeared even more youthful, more vulnerable, relaxed as it was in sleep, and Logan suddenly found himself unable to resist reaching out and gently smoothing a wayward golden curl from her silken brow. His gaze was drawn irrevocably lower, kindling with fire as it searched out the sweet curve of her breasts beneath the borrowed nightgown and wrapper, the satiny smoothness of one slender limb revealed against the multi-colored squares of the quilt as she lay partially upon her side with one arm draped across the velvet sash at her waist. Her magnificent hair was spilled across the snowy whiteness of a pillow, the ruby softness of her lips slightly parted and issuing an alluring challenge that Logan, his passion flaring to a dangerous level of intensity, could find neither the strength nor the inclination to resist meeting.

Battling the fierce desire threatening to overwhelm him, he bent over her and tenderly brushed her lips with his. The sleeping beauty stirred, but remained blissfully ensconced in the dreamy, hazy world existing between sleep and wakefulness. A soft sigh escaped her lips as Logan reluctantly drew away, and she frowned slightly, her head tossing slowly, restlessly upon the pillow as if she were protesting the loss of the beguilingly gentle caress of his warm mouth upon hers.

"Logan," Rachel murmured in a voice so soft that it was scarcely even a whisper. His name had quite naturally risen to her lips, for he had forcefully controlled her dreams—secret, wicked dreams she always staunchly denied upon awakening—since that first, tumultuous encounter between them in Billings. And now, when he had kissed her, her sleep-numbed mind told her it was nothing more than a startlingly real culmination of all the secret, previously unfamiliar yearnings which had been building to a fever pitch within her since a certain, green-eyed rogue had gazed upon her trembling nakedness.

Several conflicting emotions played across the rugged perfection of Logan's face as he thought he heard Rachel call his name in her sleep. Finally acknowledging to himself what his pride had not wanted him to admit—that he had never intended to honor the "in name only" aspect of his marriage to her—he now realized that he had never set aside his unwavering intention to make her his own in every way. He may have succeeded in deceiving the innocently seductive beauty whose delectable curves had driven him to distraction for weeks now, but he couldn't deceive himself. Being a man of honor, even though his sense of right and wrong might not conform to Rachel's exacting standards, he experienced a sharp twinge of guilt for the undeniable fact that he had made a promise he never intended to keep.

"Logan," breathed Rachel once more, then moaned softly and raised a faintly trembling hand to where her breasts rose and fell just below the rounded, lace-edged neckline of the delicate white nightgown. The criss-crossing edges of the velvet wrapper gaped as she turned more fully upon her back, allowing a strangely grim-faced Logan a glimpse of the tantalizing darkness of one rosy nipple straining against the thin, clinging gauze of the borrowed nightdress.

This time, there was no doubt that it was his name which had issued forth from her tempting lips. She was beckoning him with her heart as well as her body, and Logan felt the self-mastery over his volatile passion ebbing, felt the iron grip he'd so determinedly schooled himself to keep upon his smoldering desire slipping away . . .

Rachel moaned in satisfaction as she felt the longed-for pressure of Logan's mouth upon hers once more. Gone, however, was the former gentleness he had displayed, and in its stead was a dizzying fierceness. His lips were hot and demanding, almost savage, as they claimed hers, and his powerful arms tightened about her pliant softness with such turbulent possessiveness that she found herself gasping for breath. Her eyelids fluttered open, and total consciousness finally seized her.

This was no dream! Rachel's spinning mind cried out to her. Logan MacBride's impassioned embrace was all too real!

"N—no!" she choked out as she frantically tore her lips from his. Her face burned in the darkness, and she wasted no further time before beginning her frenzied struggles to escape. "Damn you, let me go!" she breathlessly shrieked, pushing violently against him and then gasping as her hands came into contact with the bare, muscular hardness of his chest. Clad in nothing more than a pair of trousers, his sun-streaked brown hair still damp from the bath he had taken shortly before entering his bride's room, Logan appeared more dangerously masculine than ever before to Rachel's sparkling opal eyes as they widened in shock and quickly accustomed themselves to the tension-charged darkness.

"You're mine, Rachel!" Logan ground out, his hands

gripping her arms with almost bruising force as he stood beside the canopied bed and drew her to her knees upon the quilted coverlet. She inhaled sharply and stared mutely up at him, her gaze filling with profound alarm as she viewed the look of near savage intent on his handsome, tight-lipped countenance. His glowing eyes narrowed and raked swiftly over her before he once again declared in a vibrant tone edged with passion's fury, "You're mine!"

"No! You . . . you promised! You agreed—"

"Our agreement be damned! You knew as well as I did that this was inevitable!" She opened her mouth to vehemently deny it, but it was too late . . .

He bore her relentlessly backward upon the bed, his weight pressing her into the mattress as he most effectively imprisoned her beneath his lean hardness, his lips masterfully silencing the belated scream which welled up deep in her throat. His hands released her arms and swept boldly up and down her outraged form, performing an intimate exploration of the soft curves beneath the velvet and gauze while her arms flailed at the bronzed smoothness of his back in helpless desperation.

A feeling of stunned disbelief assailed Rachel as she told herself that it couldn't be happening. She didn't want to face the truth—that her dreams had finally become flesh-and-blood reality. There was no escaping the Logan who held her captive, the Logan whose tongue forcibly plundered the softness of her mouth, the Logan whose long, nimble fingers had already untied the sash at her waist and was impatiently yanking apart the edges of the wrapper. He tugged the scooped neckline of the nightgown downward, tearing it in his haste to gain even greater access to the womanly treasure he sought to claim.

Rachel, gasping against his mouth as the delicate fabric gave way and a rush of cool air swept across her bared flesh, was shocked to feel the wild stirring of her blood at the first touch of his warm hands upon her naked breasts. His fingers hungrily yet tenderly cupped and stroked the satiny, rose-tipped peaks while Rachel was certain she would be driven mindless with the intensity of her own answering hunger, a hunger that prompted her to moan and arch her back instinctively upward, and then gasp anew as she felt the hard-muscled, softly furred warmth of his bare chest brushing against her sensitive nipples.

She was further shocked to realize that she had begun returning Logan's kisses with a rapidly increasing fire of her own, and it wasn't long before she actually demanded, by actions rather than words, the moist caress of his lips upon her quivering breasts. His mouth trailed a searing path across the pale, silken globes before capturing the pert, tingling rosiness crowning one entrancing sphere and saluting it with a deliciously tormenting swirl of his tongue. His lips gently suckled at first one breast, then the other, while his hands moved to draw the hemline of her nightgown upward.

Rachel's fingers curled almost convulsively within the damp, soap-scented thickness of Logan's dark hair as her pulses raced alarmingly, and she feverishly clutched him even closer while unknowingly urging him onward with her soft moans and sharp, reflexive intakes of breath. She was hardly aware of the fact that he was baring her lower body, but she was startled into acute consciousness of the success of his actions when his hand began smoothing purposefully upward along the soft flesh of her inner thigh . . .

"Oh!" she gasped, her eyes flying open in astonishment as his fingers lightly brushed the silken triangle of honey-colored down concealing the very center of her femininity. She blushed to the roots of her hair and weakly pushed against him, attempting to close her slender limbs and thereby spare herself the disturbingly volatile sensations he had elicited within her at the mere touch of his hand between her thighs.

Logan, however, would not be denied. He positioned a knee between both of hers, the roughness of his denim trousers slightly chafing the unprotected tenderness of her bare legs. The halfhearted, inarticulate protest rising to her lips was silenced by the returning pressure of his mouth upon hers as his oh-so-skillful fingers evocatively conquered the soft, secret flesh of her womanhood.

Rachel, her awakened desires careening irrestrainably upward, soon became almost totally incapable of coherent thought as her magnificently proficient husband employed the most sensuous persuasion known to man—and woman. Lost in a world inhabited only by herself and the man whose burning embrace she could no longer resist, she gave herself up to the wild abandon calling her, her hands roaming appreciatively across the sinewy hardness of Logan's back and shoulders while his gentle yet tempestuous wooing bore her heavenward.

Finally, Logan could prolong the delicious agony no longer, for his own inflamed passions were dangerously near the outermost limits of human tolerance. He reached down with one hand and swiftly unfastened his trousers, his mouth never relinquishing its possession of Rachel's as his other hand continued its rapturous assault upon her entrancing softness. She gasped anew when she felt his masculine hardness probing at her velvety treasure, and she was plagued by one last sobering intrusion of maidenly apprehension.

"Please, no! No!" she gasped, tearing her lips from his and squirming in a futile attempt to escape what Logan had quite accurately designated as inevitable. Unaware of the fact that her innocently arousing movements only served to increase his already raging desire, she was startled to hear his voice huskily decreeing close to her ear, "Damn, but you're sweet! My sweet, sweet love!" Any further objections she might have raised were forever banished from the turbulence of her mind as he sheathed himself within her moist, feminine warmth. Rachel cried out softly at the exquisite invasion of his manhood, the brief, sharp pain quickly replaced by the most acute pleasure she had ever before experienced. Logan's hands tightly clasped her buttocks, tutoring her to match the erotically undulating rhythm of his hips. The motion of his thrusts quickly intensified as the final, tempestuous blending of their bodies sent them both soaring higher and higher.

Rachel's fingers clenched upon his broad shoulders, and she instinctively arched against him, her eyes sweeping closed so that she could not see the way his piercing gaze fastened upon her beautiful, passion-flushed face. Stifling a scream when the bursting fulfillment came, she was totally unprepared for the breathtaking explosion of body and soul, was so overwhelmed by the surge of ecstasy coursing like liquid fire through her veins that she was perilously close to losing consciousness.

Their wildly impassioned union had also provided Logan with the most intense satisfaction he had ever known. His entire body tensed for several long moments before he relaxed atop Rachel, a wonderfully pleasurable languor stealing over him as he rolled to his back on the bed and pulled her against the hard length of him. Neither of them spoke, their breathing mutually irregular and their minds equally filled with a sense of wonderment and awe over what had just occurred between them.

Rachel lay passively within the gently cradling circle of Logan's arms. Never had she felt so warm and safe and secure . . . and so wickedly contented. Reason slowly began to return as numbness wore off and she became aware of the fact that one of Logan's hands was resting possessively upon her naked hip, the other upon the silken flesh of her arm, his fingers tracing light, repetitive circles close beside the soft curve of her breast.

A floodtide of humiliation suddenly washed over her as she recalled, with painful clarity, the way she had gloried beneath the hot, rapturous onslaught of his hands and mouth upon that same breast. Dear Lord, how could she have done such a thing? How could she have behaved so shamelessly, so . . . so downright wantonly? She would never be able to forgive herself!

In the next instant, however, her agonizing self-reproachment turned to vengeful fury and became directed at the devastatingly handsome seducer who held her with what she now perceived to be smugly triumphant complacency. Oh yes, she mused with rapidly increasing indignation—fueled by her own guilt as well as the realization that Logan had waited no time at all before breaking their agreement—the mighty conqueror was no doubt congratulating himself on his successful deception and victory! He had willfully broken his promise to her, and she had been foolish enough to believe him honorable!

Logan frowned in puzzled surprise when Rachel suddenly came bolt upright in the bed. Her long hair fanned about her inexplicably stormy face as she jerked the edges of her velvet wrapper together and yanked the hemline of her torn nightgown down over her exposed limbs.

"What's the matter?" he queried in a low tone, leisurely rolling to his side and propping himself up on one elbow.

"Get out of my bed!" hissed Rachel. She rounded on him like a veritable tigress, her blue eyes flashing and her beautiful features suffused with a bright, angry color. Before he could demand an explanation, she twisted angrily about and slid from the bed.

"Damn it, Rachel, what is it?" A note of rising displeasure crept into his voice now, and his frown deepened as she lit the lamp beside the bed and held it aloft as if it were a weapon. She fixed him with a venomous glare, then blushed fierily as her gaze fell upon the evidence of his manhood still visible within the gaping edges of his unfastened trousers. "What the devil's the matter with you?" Logan demanded once more, the bronzed smoothness of his lithely muscled upper body glistening beneath the soft golden glow of the lamplight.

"Leave my room at once, you . . . you—" She broke off and took a fearful step backward as he suddenly sprang from the bed and stood towering ominously above her, but she swallowed hard and forced herself to confront him as she bravely accused, "You lied to me!

You gave me your word that you would honor our agreement!"

"What difference does it make now? I think we both knew all along it would come to this. If you're honest with yourself, you won't deny that you've wanted it just as much as I have!"

"That's not true! You . . . you forced yourself on me, Logan MacBride! You crept in here while I was sleeping and took advantage of me!"

"Took advantage of you?" he echoed in disbelief, then gave a short, humorless laugh. His eyes gleamed mockingly as he took a step closer and folded his arms across his bare chest with studied nonchalance. "It might interest you to know, *Mrs. MacBride,* that you called for me in your sleep. You *asked* for what happened, and you got exactly what you wanted!"

"Why, that . . . that's a despicable lie!" she hotly dissented, yet could not prevent the telltale color from staining her cheeks. It was all too horribly true—she *had* been dreaming of him! But never would she admit to him that she had subconsciously beckoned him, that she had practically begged for his lovemaking! Lifting her head proudly, she furiously challenged, "You never had any intention of honoring the terms of our agreement, did you? You planned all along to—" She inhaled sharply as his strong hands closed upon her shoulders and administered a firm shake.

"Damn it, Rachel, stop behaving like a child!" There was a faintly menacing set to his jaw, and a fierce light in his darkening sea-green gaze warned of his own gathering ire. "Nothing you do or say is going to change the fact that you're mine now. It isn't as if I've stolen your virtue and left you dishonored—hell, woman, there's nothing wrong with a husband and wife making love on their own blasted wedding night!"

"Take your hands off me!" cried Rachel, still clutching the lamp in one hand and holding the edges of her wrapper closed with the other. Tears sparkled upon her lashes as she emotionally declared, "I'll never forgive you, Logan MacBride! And if you ever so much as touch me again, I'll—"

"I'm not asking for your forgiveness!" Logan ruthlessly ground out, dropping his hands from her shoulders as if the contact suddenly burned him.

"Of course not!" she retorted with biting sarcasm, driven to rashness as a result of his total lack of remorse for his part in what had happened. "After all, you're a MacBride, aren't you? And the MacBrides take what they want without bothering to consider anything beyond their own selfish desires! You're no better than your cousin Vance! And for all I know, the two of you schemed together to force me into this marriage!" She ignored the savage gleam in Logan's eyes as a sudden, awful thought occurred to her. A look of dawning horror crossed her face, and she took another step backward and lifted the lamp higher, her own eyes very wide and full of something suspiciously like pain. "It's true, isn't it? You tricked me into marriage so that you could regain control of my grandfather's land, didn't you?"

"You don't know what the hell you're talking about!" Logan bit out, an expression of barely controlled violence tightening upon his handsome visage.

"Last night, when you arrived just in time to prevent Micah's hanging—that was in actuality a carefully planned drama, wasn't it? And that night at the

Macqueen House, when you . . . you were unsuccessful in 'compromising' me—you were willing to employ any method to force me to wed you, weren't you?" She choked back a sob, and her heart twisted at the thought that he had viewed her only as a means to an end. How could she have been so blind? And why in heaven's name did it feel as if her entire world had come crashing down about her?

She wanted to lash out at him, to hurt him as he had hurt her. Her fingers curled tightly within the folds of the red velvet wrapper, and her other hand shook as she lowered the lamp with measured unhaste and met the hooded gaze of a dangerously grim-faced Logan with deceptive equanimity.

"I hate you, Logan MacBride. I don't think I've ever detested anyone as much as I do you. What happened between us tonight will be a source of everlasting shame to me. You can rest assured, however, that I will honor my part of our bargain as long as my family is allowed to live in peace on their land. In a few months' time, just as we previously agreed, we will go our separate ways and I will seek a divorce. Until then, I will remain here and play the part of your 'wife' in order to spare my grandfather further pain." She paused here and drew a deep, ragged breath. "But, let us understand one another. No matter what happened this night, we will return to our original agreement that ours be a marriage in name only. And never again will you set foot in this room!"

Logan, who had remained strangely silent throughout her unpleasantly amazing discourse, lost the battle with his damnable temper at this point. His hand shot out and wrenched the lamp from Rachel's startled grasp, slamming it down upon the bedside table and sending a narrow crack snaking up one side of the glass protecting the oil-fed flame. Rachel gasped loudly and backed away in growing alarm.

"You shrewish little hypocrite!" he growled, advancing upon her with slow and deadly intent, his handsome face a mask of explosive fury. "I'd deny those insultingly ludicrous charges you just made, but it's obvious you've already convinced yourself of my betrayal! You were shocked to discover the fiery, passionate woman in yourself, and now you're trying to assuage your own feelings of outraged morality by striking out at me!" She whirled to take flight, but it was too late. A tiny shriek escaped her lips when his hands shot out and yanked her close, and she fought against him in helpless frustration as he lifted her in his arms.

"I hate you! I hate you, Logan MacBride!" she tearfully reiterated, panicking at the thought that he meant to take her by force.

"Be that as it may, you belong to me now, and I'll be damned if I'm going to let you run roughshod over me! I'll come into this blasted room any time I damn well please, and I'll lay hands on my own wife whenever it suits me!"

"No! I will not allow—"

"I won't be asking your permission!" With that, he lowered his head and forcefully claimed her lips in a hard, demanding kiss that left her dizzy and gasping for breath once more. Her arms were just beginning to steal up about his neck of their own accord when he suddenly tossed her unceremoniously atop the rumpled coverlet on the bed. Then, without so much as a backward glance, he spun about and stalked from the room. The bathroom door slammed with resounding force after him.

Rachel, feeling both dazed and acutely disappointed, sat up and stared after him for several long moments before collapsing upon the pillow and bursting into a violent storm of weeping. Her body quaked with uncontrollable sobs, and she was certain her heart was breaking in two . . .

IX

"Coward!" murmured Rachel with a self-deprecating frown. Heaving a sigh, she reluctantly conceded to herself that she could procrastinate no longer. It was scarcely past six o'clock in the morning, but she had been awake for what seemed like hours. She had been startled to find another set of clothing neatly arranged upon the brass-edged trunk at the foot of the bed when she awoke from a restless and troubled sleep, and her face had flamed anew at the thought that it might have been Logan himself who put the blue silk dress and fine linen undergarments—no doubt belonging to the mysterious Miss Moira—there for her to find.

The high-necked gown was only a trifle loose, particularly about the waist and hips, but Rachel was too preoccupied to notice. There were faint shadows beneath her eyes, and the unusual pallor of her face was accentuated by the way she had drawn her honey-colored tresses into a severe style at the nape of her neck. Her beauty, however, could not be denied, though she spared only a passing glance at her reflection in the cheval mirror situated near the doorway to the bathroom, whose *both* doors she had earlier remembered to lock before performing her morning toilette.

Squaring her shoulders and holding her head high, Rachel opened the main door and swept from the bedroom. She could not help gazing curiously about her as she walked along the upper landing and down the stairway, and she was now suitably impressed by the tasteful furnishings she had failed to notice the day before. The floral wall coverings were bright and cheerful, the western-theme paintings admirably selected, and the wood paneling and bannisters were polished to gleaming perfection. The entire effect was one of casual elegance, and she found her curiosity aroused in spite of her solemn vow to take no more than a very mild interest in the household where she was in essence being forced to live.

Her steps finally led her across the darkened entrance foyer and toward the masculine voices she heard drifting outward from a room to her immediate right. It was no easy accomplishment for her to push aside her anxiety and enter the brightly lit confines of what she discovered to be the dining room, but she had already staunchly decided that she would not behave as a prisoner in Logan MacBride's house. She would not give him the satisfaction of believing her defeated! She would summon every ounce of courage she possessed, would never allow her pride to be vanquished as her traitorous flesh had been . . .

"Ah, the blushing bride herself!" the oldest of the three men seated at the far end of a long, linen-covered table genially proclaimed as he caught sight of her in the doorway. A tall, rather heavyset man with thick gray hair, he immediately stood, tossed his napkin beside his half-empty plate of ham and eggs, and hurried to greet Rachel with a beaming smile of genuine warmth. She was dismayed to feel her face coloring as her own gaze was drawn like a magnet to Logan's. Bristling as he rose from his seat and performed a faint, mocking inclination of his head in her direction, she could have sworn his imperceptibly narrowing eyes issued her a silent challenge, as if he were daring her to display the fiery side of her nature he had taken such pleasure in encouraging the night before.

But then, he had also taken great pleasure in displaying the predominantly wild and untamed facet of his own nature! reminded that persistent, uncomfortably honest voice in the back of her mind.

Inwardly quite distressed by the sudden pounding of her heart and weakening of her knees, Rachel gave no indication of her disquiet as she turned a thoroughly beguiling smile upon the older man, impeccably attired in a dark suit instead of in denim and boots as were Brodie and Logan, who took her hand affectionately between both of his. His kindly, dark blue eyes twinkled down at her.

"I'm Robert Pearson, my dear—your new uncle! Logan's just been telling us about your whirlwind courtship and elopement. My only regret is that I didn't get a chance to do my Christian duty and warn you away from the young rapscallion before it was too late!" he teased with irrepressible good humor.

"I'm very pleased to make your acquaintance, Mr. Pearson," Rachel responded with another smile, liking him almost against her will. She stubbornly refused to so much as glance at Logan again, though she could feel his piercing gaze upon her.

"Uncle Robert," the dapper gentleman amiably insisted. He winked before finally releasing her hand, at which time the third man in the room came forward and said a bit shyly, "I don't know whether or not you'll remember me, ma'am, but I'm Brodie MacBride." Rachel immediately recognized him as the same young man who had rescued Lizzie the night of the attempted lynching. "Welcome to the Circle M."

"Thank you. And of course I remember you," she warmly affirmed, her opal eyes shining with renewed gratitude for his assistance. In the next instant, however, it occurred to her that his part in that night's drama must have been a calculated piece of dissimulation as well. Her gaze became veiled with coolness, and she swept regally past him to take a place at the table. She purposefully sank down upon the velvet-cushioned chair at the opposite end of the table from Logan. Robert wasted no time in gallantly presenting her with a cup of hot, aromatic coffee while both Brodie and Logan resumed their seats.

As if on cue, Mrs. Smith suddenly emerged through the swinging door which connected the dining room with the kitchen. She made one swift, chilling assessment of Rachel's appearance before remarking with no pretense of friendliness in her tone, "As you can see, I've already prepared breakfast. But I suppose you'll be wanting me to fire up the stove again and—"

"Bring Mrs. MacBride some eggs and biscuits, Cora," Logan diplomatically intervened, the merest hint of a smile tugging at the corners of his finely chiseled lips.

"I'm not hungry!" Rachel declared a bit too hastily, then flushed at the curious looks Robert and Brodie turned upon her. She quickly composed herself enough to meet Cora Smith's icy stare and politely explained, "I . . . I'm afraid I overindulged myself with the delicious meal you brought me yesterday afternoon."

"Is that so?" muttered the stern-faced older woman in obvious disbelief. But she refrained from further comment as she whirled abruptly about and disappeared into the kitchen once more.

"Cora's not quite the terror she seems to be once you get to know her," Brodie offered by way of comfort, his gold-flecked blue eyes glistening with noticeable humor. "We always knew it would be quite a blow to her when Logan married," he added with a low chuckle, shooting his older cousin a good-naturedly teasing look. "One of the reasons is because she still thinks of this big buffalo as her 'baby', seeing as she helped his mother raise him. And the other—"

"That's enough." Logan cut him off with quiet sharpness. Rachel could not prevent her eyes from straying toward him, and she was immediately struck by the physical resemblance between the two men whose gazes were now briefly locked in silent understanding. Brodie was a few inches shorter and more youthfully slender, but his rugged, hard-muscled features were very similar to Logan's, she mentally concluded, then found herself musing that Logan was without a doubt the more handsome of the two. There was an aura of such sheer, forceful masculinity about him . . . it made her pulses quicken and her entire body tremble at the unbidden recollection of his bronzed, virile hardness moving over her soft curves to tenderly caress and masterfully conquer . . .

Rachel tightly closed her eyes against the disturbing,

breathtaking image. When they swept open again a scant moment later, it was only to encounter Logan's intense, unwavering counterparts. The expression on his face was inscrutable, but she glimpsed the taunting amusement lurking within those glowing, sea-green orbs. She inhaled upon a soft gasp, telling herself that it was almost as if he possessed the ability to read her thoughts, as if he were aware of the humiliating fact that she could not erase the previous night's madness from her mind.

"How about it, my dear?" asked Robert. Rachel suddenly realized that he was speaking to her, and she flushed guiltily before confessing, "I'm sorry, Mr. Pearson, but I . . . I didn't quite hear you."

"Uncle Robert," he gently admonished, then laughed softly and cast a knowing glance at Logan. "It's perfectly understandable that your mind would not be inclined to concern itself with such mundane matters when it's so full of enchantment. Not that I fully comprehend such happiness—I'm a confirmed old bachelor myself—but I can well imagine how it must be for two young people as much in love as you and my nephew obviously are!"

Thunderation! Rachel mentally exclaimed, quickly averting her eyes so that Robert would not see the way they were virtually shooting sparks. How could she possibly continue with this distasteful little charade a moment longer? And this is only the first day! she thought with an inward groan.

"But I'll still repeat my admittedly selfish offer—will you allow me to show you around the ranch after breakfast?" the older man queried, turning back to her with an expectant smile.

"I'm afraid you'll have to cool your heels until another time, Uncle Robert," Logan unexpectedly decreed at this point. Draining the last of the black coffee from his cup, he stood and leisurely eased his hat down over the sun-streaked thickness of his dark brown hair. "Rachel's coming with me."

"I most certainly am not!" she blurted out, earning herself another mildly astonished look from Brodie and Robert. It was as if Logan had never heard her. Reaching the opposite end of the table in a few long, easy strides, the crown of his wide-brimmed Stetson level with the sparkling crystal chandelier suspended from the beamed ceiling above, he reached down with one hand and took hold of the arm of an indignant and embarrassed Rachel, then drew her to her feet beside him.

"We've got a few things to talk about," he evenly stated, disregarding the near murderous glare she shot him when her face was momentarily blocked from the others' view.

"I don't blame you for being so possessive of your beautiful wife, Logan, my boy, but keep in mind a piece of marital advice which I've been told on good authority is quite sound," ventured Uncle Robert, exchanging a quick glance of shared, masculine amusement with Brodie as the two of them stood and watched Logan escort his stiffly erect but wisely unresistant bride from the room. "Too much togetherness outside of the bedroom can lead to *sleepful* nights!"

If Logan took note of his uncle's roguishly jocular bit of counsel, he gave no indication of such. Rachel, on the other hand, felt her embarrassment increasing tenfold as the true meaning of the older man's remark sank in. She was fairly quaking with the force of her outraged dignity by the time she and Logan stepped onto the front porch of the house. He finally released her arm, and she spun about to confront him with a clenched fist on either side of her hips, her eyes ablaze with blue fire as she tilted her chin upward so that she could face him squarely.

"How dare you treat me that way in front of those men!" she resentfully fumed.

"Like what? Like a wife? That's what you are, you know. A wife. *My* wife," countered Logan, crossing his arms against the broad, flannel-covered expanse of his chest with deceptive nonchalance. Inwardly, he was steeling himself for the battle he knew to be forthcoming. He had spent the better part of the night pondering the situation, and he had come to several very startling conclusions, conclusions he realized would only serve to further infuriate the beautiful, golden-haired wildcat before him. But his mind was made up, and not even Rachel's professed hatred would sway him . . .

"And I suppose that makes me little better than your horse or your dog or . . . or one of your prized bulls—"

"All of which are of the wrong gender to make an accurate comparison."

"Oh!" Rachel uttered with a contemptuous look that bespoke her extreme ingratitude for his sardonic levity. She was amazed at the explosiveness of her seldom-exercised temper, and the realization that her emotions had suddenly become so fierce and ungovernable only added more fuel to her anger. "You, Logan MacBride, are even more of an insufferable, unprincipled, arrogant scoundrel than I ever believed possible!"

"And you, 'Clover', are even more of a woman than I ever believed possible!" Before Rachel could demand to know exactly what he meant by such a perplexingly enigmatic comment, she found herself being seized by the hand and tugged insistently down the front steps after her new husband.

"What do you think you're doing? Let go of me!" She was practically forced to run to keep pace with him, her silken skirts flying about her trim ankles as he tugged her across the deserted yard toward one of the barns.

"First, we're going to have that little talk I mentioned. Then, I'm going to take you on a tour of *our* ranch, after which we'll present the new Mrs. MacBride to some of the hands. And the new Mrs. MacBride had damn sure better act like she's glad to meet them!" he warned, the tone of his voice promising dire consequences if she did not play her role to perfection. She was out of breath by the time he swung open the huge wooden door and pulled her inside the smaller of the two barns. It was empty, save for the sweet-smelling hay piled high in the loft and scattered about the hard-packed dirt floor.

Rachel's eyes widened in alarm as she watched Logan close the door and lower the crossbar into place, thereby ensuring their privacy within the fragrant, semidark interior of the barn. She shivered, but it had nothing to do with the last, lingering chill of the fading night. Neither combatant took the time to appreciate the beauty of the dawn, which sent soft golden rays filtering through the many cracks in the logs as well as through the narrow windows cut high near the rafters along the rear and side walls.

"To begin with," said Logan, slowly turning to face her, "I want to know if you see things any differently this morning than you did last night." He took off his hat and sent it flying to land with a quiet rustle upon the hay. His handsome countenance appeared quite solemn, prompting Rachel to swallow a sudden lump in her throat before dauntlessly replying, "If what you're asking me is if I still desire our marriage to be on a strictly impersonal basis, then the answer is yes—I mean no—I mean, I most definitely do *not* see things any differently this morning!"

"And what about the other little matter between us? Do you honestly believe I conspired with Vance to trick you into this?" he demanded, his deep voice filling the barn with its resonance.

"I . . . I don't know what else to believe!" she answered in a rush, then wheeled away in noticeable agitation. Moving across to the ladder which provided the only access to the loft, she raised an unsteady hand to one of the splintered wooden rungs. Her troubled gaze became fixed somewhere about the middle of Logan's chest as she turned back to him and somberly declared, "I don't know anything about you. You may have succeeded in turning my life upside-down, but you're little more than a stranger to me still. How can I possibly know what you're capable of doing in the pursuit of . . . of something you want?"

"And just what is it I'm accused of wanting?" he queried, the ghost of a smile tugging briefly at his lips. Rachel's softly iridescent eyes, flashing as their owner detected the note of mockery in Logan's voice, flew upward to encounter his at last.

"My grandfather's land, of course!"

"What makes you so certain my 'betrayal' wasn't prompted by something else entirely?" he challenged in a low voice, moving toward her now with disturbing unhaste. Unable to tear her eyes away from his powerfully muscled form, Rachel was dismayed to suddenly find herself musing with bold appreciation that his every movement bespoke an innate masculine grace, an undeniable virility of which she had been made all too humiliatingly—and thrillingly—aware the night before!

There was a faint, telltale gleam of purposefulness in the darkening green gaze he fastened upon her wide-eyed, increasingly alarmed features as he drew closer. Rachel despised herself for the sudden lack of courage which made her take an instinctive step backward. She endeavored to conceal her discomfiting apprehension by responding with a great deal more bravado than she felt, "Because I know how very determined the MacBrides were to regain control of Micah's property, property which belonged to a convicted murderer bearing the same name as your own! I know that you were every bit as determined as the others to convince us to leave!"

"For someone who professes to know nothing about me, you're sure as hell laying claim to a lot of information," Logan noted wryly, halting mere inches away and leisurely bracing a hand against the ladder as he stared down into her softly flushed countenance. Rachel felt more than a trifle intimidated as a result of his superior height and dangerously inscrutable visage, and she was thrown into a state of further confusion by the sharp feeling of mingled excitement and expectation rising within her. She was vividly aware of the male scent of soap and leather hanging about him, was acutely conscious of the sheer vibrancy emanating from the warmth of his hard body. An abrupt light-headedness assailed her, and the realization that she was perilously near to fleeing the barn in a panic impelled her to take defensive action.

"There's really no sense in prolonging this unpleasant little discussion," she asserted with outward poise, gathering up her skirts and favoring Logan with what she hoped was a cool stare. "As you've already pointed out, what's done is done. Whatever your motives in—" She broke off with a loud gasp when his powerful hands took her silk-clad arms in a firm grip.

"I'm only going to say this once, Rachel, so you'd damn well better listen!" he ground out, his fingers tightening almost painfully upon her soft flesh. The rugged planes and valleys of his handsome, sun-bronzed face were tightened in barely controlled anger, and his eyes blazed with a fierceness that sent an involuntary tremor of fear coursing through his momentarily speechless captive. "I did *not* have anything to do with what happened to your grandfather, nor did I seek to use his misfortune to my own advantage. Though I'm honest enough to admit that I wanted you, I did *not* marry you just to get you into my bed!" Rachel's cheeks flamed at his bluntness, but she lifted her chin higher and countered with biting sarcasm, "Oh, so your motives stemmed purely from a charitable desire to help my grandfather—a man with whom you are barely acquainted, the same man who arrested and hanged your kinsman?" Hot tears sprang to her eyes at the memory of the stark pain on Micah's face when it seemed she had chosen Logan over her family. It felt as if a knife twisted in her heart, but she refused to admit that her own pain had anything to do with Logan's deception. "I was a fool not to realize sooner that a man as powerful and ruthless as you would care nothing about one old lawman and three women. Your concern was only for the exalted name of MacBride, for keeping your empire intact without bringing further disgrace upon—"

"You bear the 'exalted' name of MacBride yourself now," he interrupted, his deep voice whipcord sharp, "so perhaps you should be concerned as well. And since you're going to bear it for the rest of your life, it might interest you to know that the MacBrides don't have the reputation of being cold-blooded murderers!"

"You'd have the reputation soon enough if your other methods of persuasion didn't—" Rachel lashed out, then inhaled sharply as the significance of his words sank in. "What do you mean by 'you're going to bear it for the rest of your life'?" she demanded in furious bewilderment.

"Exactly what I said. You're a MacBride now." His strong hands slid upward to close upon her shoulders, his fingers tightening as he proclaimed in a low, strangely emotion-charged tone, "You're my wife. No matter what your feelings toward me—even if I'm every inch the blackhearted son of a bitch you've accused me of being—you belong to me now. Last night proved that once and for all. After all that's happened between us, a divorce is out of the question." He unexpectedly pulled her toward him and brought his head lower, his face so close to hers that their lips were almost touching. His eyes were aglow with passionate intent as he vowed with deceptive softness, "You see, I hold what's mine." It was as much a threat as a promise, and Rachel felt a shiver run the length of her spine.

"No!" she cried in stunned disbelief, her thick, lustrous curls straining against their pins as she vigorously shook her head. "You . . . you can't mean that!" Twisting out of Logan's grasp, she began slowly backing away, her sparkling eyes wide and frightened and her hands clenching within the folds of her skirts. "You gave me your word! We agreed that I would seek a divorce—"

"That was before last night." A dark scowl creased the sun-kissed smoothness of his brow as he harshly demanded, "Damn it, Rachel, why don't you face the truth? Whatever blasted vagaries of fate brought us together, the fact is we *are* together! We're husband and wife in every sense of the word. Are you really foolish enough to believe I'd let you go? I don't know what sort of dimwitted bastards you've met before, but a man out here doesn't wed and bed a woman and then set her free!"

"Why not?" Rachel bitterly parried, her face coloring hotly at his indelicate references to her disgracefully wanton conduct. "Mere physical attraction is no basis for a marriage! Why should you want me as your wife when you care nothing about me and know I feel the same? People don't build a life together on nothing more than . . . than . . ." Her voice trailed away and her blush deepened.

"On nothing more than what?" Logan tauntingly challenged. A faint, meaningful smile played about his firm, chiseled lips as he began striding unhurriedly toward her again, his polished leather boots making noiseless contact with the hay-strewn dirt floor. "Than lust?" he quietly supplied, his smoldering, jade-green eyes catching and locking with Rachel's. Her luminescent eyes grew enormous when he stood towering above her once more, and she could feel her entire body tensing, could feel the riotous leaping of her pulse. "If that's all you think there is between us, then so be it," he concluded, a certain edge to his slightly husky voice. There was a grim set to his jaw now, and a tiny muscle twitched within the bronzed tightness of one clean-shaven cheek. "It's a start, Mrs. MacBride. It's a hell of a start."

"No it isn't!" Rachel exclaimed in breathless but quite vehement disaccord. She opened her mouth to say more, but impulsively decided to take flight instead. Driven by the desperate need to escape Logan MacBride's all too unnerving presence, she murmured something unintelligible and pushed abruptly past him, heading straightaway for the door and the sanctuary of the more public surroundings on the other side.

Logan easily overtook her before she reached the door. Her breath caught on a loud gasp as his arm shot out and clamped like a vise about her slender waist. He yanked her back against him with dizzying force, then muttered a savage curse when she unexpectedly jabbed an elbow into his midsection. His grip momentarily loosened, thereby enabling her to squirm free and beat a hasty retreat toward the door again.

Miraculously, however, he was there before her, quite effectively blocking what appeared to be her only avenue of escape. Rachel drew up short and glanced frantically about in growing desperation, her eyes finally raising toward the loft. Logan watched her with a satisfied smile as she spun about and raced for the ladder, scaling it with remarkable agility even though hampered by full, gathered skirts. She had not paused to consider what she would do upon reaching the top—her only thought was to prevent a repetition of the all-encompassing madness which seized her whenever Logan took her in his arms.

It occurred to her to pull the ladder up after her and thereby seal off Logan's route of pursuit, but the idea came too late. She had no sooner maneuvered herself from the uppermost rung to the fragrant assemblage of hay in the loft when the top of Logan's dark head appeared.

"I learned a long time ago never to hide in the hayloft," he lazily drawled, his countenance solemn but his green eyes alight with devilment as he climbed up before her. His movements were slow and deliberate as he transferred his booted feet from the ladder to the hay. "It was always the first place my father looked when he had it in mind to give me a hiding. And he had it in mind too damned often for my taste." He was advancing on her now, the faded denim of his trousers stretching tautly across his lean, powerful thighs as he stalked his prey with a pantherlike grace Rachel could not help noticing.

"No!" she cried, backing away and stretching out one arm in an eloquent but entirely futile gesture of defense. "Stay away from me!" It was difficult for her to maintain her balance as she tried in vain to find solid footing in the deep cushion of hay, the stiff, protruding blades of dried pasturage tugging at her skirts as she stumbled desperately backward. She toyed briefly with the idea of leaping down to the barn floor, but then bitterly mused that even if she survived the fall, Logan MacBride would in all likelihood have his way with her prone and battered body!

Suddenly, the heel of Rachel's high top boot caught upon the hemline of her gown, and a breathless cry of alarm escaped her lips as she tumbled downward to land squarely upon her backside. Her eyes, after shooting upward to encounter the gleam of triumph in Logan's as he began crossing the last few feet separating him from his quarry, fell upon a pitchfork leaning against the wall an arm's length away from her. Without sparing a moment to reconsider the wisdom of her actions, she seized it and aimed the pronged end of the long-handled fork at Logan.

"Stop right there! If you come any closer, I . . . I'll use this!" Rachel bravely threatened, her eyes appearing very round and luminous. Clambering hastily to her feet, her golden locks now streaming wildly about her rosily flushed face and her bosom heaving beneath the fitted silk bodice, she raised her chin in proud defiance and dramatically reiterated, "Not another step!" Her fingers tightened menacingly upon the smooth wooden handle of her chosen weapon.

"Do you really believe you've got what it takes to run me through with that thing?" challenged Logan, his gaze brimming with ironic amusement as he stopped and negligently folded his arms against his chest. A disarming grin tugged at his lips, and Rachel was shocked to feel her resistance temporarily melting away beneath his devastatingly irresistible charm. "Come on, Rachel, put it down," he idly commanded, the tone of his deep voice making it clear that he wasn't in the least bit uncertain of her compliance.

"No!" she willfully refused, her defiance strengthening again as a result of his obvious, maddening assurance that he held her completely within his power. She lifted the pitchfork a trifle higher and boldly directed, "Now get over there to the ladder!" All evidence of amusement disappeared from Logan's handsome face as he scowled and uttered in a low, tight voice, "I'm warning you, Rachel." He uncrossed his arms and took an intimidating step toward her. "Either you—"

"And *I'm* warning *you!*" she retorted with spirit, amazed at her own daring yet fiercely unwilling to back down. "You don't own me, Logan MacBride! I may be legally wed to you, but that does *not* give you the right to treat me as nothing more than a possession, as someone you can order about and . . . and assault at will!"

"Assault?" Logan tersely echoed, then astonished Rachel by throwing back his head and giving a loud, appreciative laugh. "I've never found it less necessary to 'assault' a woman in my life!" he proclaimed with a wicked grin.

"Why, you . . . you . . ." Rachel indignantly sputtered. She was so infuriated by his audaciously insulting remark that she could scarcely think straight. Provoked into rashness by the overwhelming force of her outrage, she suddenly retaliated by jabbing the pitchfork at Logan, the sharp metal prongs missing him by mere inches as she purposely held back. "You heard me—get over to the ladder!"

"Put that blasted thing down!" Once again, all traces of humor had been replaced by simmering fury. "This little game of yours has gone far enough!"

"I give you my word, Logan MacBride—I'll use this if you force me to!" she recklessly vowed. Then she made the mistake of trying to illustrate her point with another calculated jab. Logan's arm shot out with lightning-quick speed. Rachel, gasping sharply as he took hold of the pitchfork and easily wrenched it from her hands, turned to run just as he expertly tossed the implement to land pointed end first into a pile of hay below the loft.

In the next instant, she found herself being bodily tackled from behind. She shrieked in protest as she was sent sprawling into the hay, and she desperately tried to wriggle out of Logan's grasp. Disregarding her vehement struggles and highly vocal objections, he rolled her to her back and straddled her, his hands pinning her arms above her head and his long, lean-muscled legs holding the lower half of her furiously squirming body captive.

"Damn it, woman, I ought to wring your neck!" he ground out, his green eyes blazing. "Didn't that grandfather of yours teach you never to threaten a man unless you mean to carry through on it?"

"I would have carried through on it!" she wrathfully insisted, knowing good and well it was a bald-faced lie. "Now let go of me!" Her struggles intensified, her skirts and petticoats flying up about her shapely limbs as she kicked and twisted. "Take your hands off me, you . . . you bastard!"

"I think it's high time someone taught you better manners, 'Clover'—namely, that it isn't altogether proper for a wife to try to run her husband through with a pitchfork one minute and then insult his parentage the next." Though his voice was laced with mocking amusement, there was nothing in the least bit humorous about the way he suddenly moved off her and flipped her onto her stomach. With a swiftness that quite surprised her, he tossed up her skirts and yanked down her lacy, open-leg drawers. Rachel, shrieking again as she felt the rush of cool air on her bare flesh, made another desperate bid for freedom. She managed to scramble up to her hands and knees in the hay, but Logan, his eyes kindling with passionate intent as they took in the sight of her naked, delectably rounded derriere, lost no time in halting her flight.

His hand twisted within the folds of her petticoat and forcefully jerked, succeeding not only in upsetting her precarious balance so that she gasped and tumbled facedown in the hay, but also in effecting a sizable rent in the delicate linen undergarment. Before a momentarily stunned and speechless Rachel could prevent any further disrobing, Logan's nimble fingers moved to the row of mother-of-pearl buttons on the back of her bodice. Within seconds, he had liberated the buttons from their corresponding loops and was slipping the blue silk downward.

"No!" cried Rachel, shaking off the numbness as she felt the sleeves of her gown being swiftly tugged from her shoulders and then from the upper portion of her body entirely. She had no sooner struggled to her hands and knees once more when Logan, taking hold of both her dress and petticoat, pulled the garments down and off in one single, admirably dextrous motion. His shocked and outraged captive, now clad only in stockings, boots, and chemise, was sent sprawling back down into the hay as a result of his action.

Rachel, astounded to realize that she was now almost completely naked, became lost to all sense of decorum. Leveling a most unladylike curse at Logan's head, she began to fight like the wildcat he had once called her, rounding on him with a vengeance and pummeling his hard body with her fists in an effort to inflict as much bodily harm as possible. A deep chuckle rumbled up from Logan's chest as he caught her up against him.

"My wild little bride," he murmured wryly, imprisoning her arms behind her back. Her eyes were virtually shooting sparks at him, and he found himself appreciatively musing that her beauty was only heightened by her anger.

"Damn you! How dare you!" His warm mouth effectively silenced her furious remonstrations as it claimed the sweetness of her lips in a demandingly possessive but provocatively stimulating kiss. Rachel struggled and moaned in futile protest as his tongue masterfully plundered the softness of her mouth. He drew her even closer, the two of them kneeling together on the hay while he kept her arms safely restrained. In a disconcertingly short amount of time, however, she was returning his kiss with an answering fervor, her opposition to his embrace rapidly diminishing in the face of the rapturous enchantment that only he could create within her. The battle between them had only added fuel to their escalating passions, and her body soon strained instinctively upward against his.

Logan maneuvered so that he was rolling to his back on the hay, pulling Rachel along with him, their impassioned kiss deepening as his lips greedily refused to relinquish hers. He finally released her arms in order to untie her chemise, and she inhaled sharply as she felt the lace-edged undergarment being tugged from her trembling body with a benumbing urgency, but she could not find it in her power to stop him. She could no longer deny that his touch set her afire, and though she professed to despise him, she knew that it didn't matter. All that mattered was this wild, heart-stopping ecstasy that blazed higher and stronger with each passing moment, each burning caress. She might very well hate both Logan and herself afterward, but for now the feverish yearning to have him take her was so all-encompassing that it would easily have obliterated any objections her conscience impelled her to raise.

Reluctantly breaking the captivating spell of the kiss at last, Logan sat up and lifted Rachel in his arms, then lowered her to the protective cushion of discarded clothing atop the hay. Her creamy, voluptuous curves were finally exposed in all their womanly splendor to his searing gaze, and her initial reaction was to attempt to cover her nakedness, but her husband would not be denied. His hands pinned her arms above her head again so that she could not prevent his glowing, jade-green eyes from drinking their fill of her nakedness.

"You're even more beautiful than I remembered," he softly decreed, his voice hoarse with a passion raging almost out of control. Rachel could feel every inch of her exposed, satiny flesh blushing, but she could not tear her eyes away from the rugged perfection of Logan's face. His fiery admiration, his wholly masculine approval of her femininity sent an intoxicating thrill of satisfaction coursing through her veins. Never in her life had she been so acutely conscious of God's purpose for the fashioning of the female form—nor of man's appreciation for such.

Feeling as if lost in a dream, she watched in dazed and breathless fascination as Logan quickly divested himself of his own clothing and thus revealed the magnificence of his own body. Her pulse quickened when he knelt unashamed before her in all his masculine glory, and her eyes sparkled brightly as they scrutinized his unbelievably flawless physique. Below the bronzed smoothness of his broad shoulders and softly matted chest was a trim waist and flat, hard-muscled abdomen, which in turn tapered down into lean yet powerful thighs . . .

Hot color flooded Rachel's beautiful face when her gaze, seemingly with a will of its own, traveled to where his inarguably virile manhood sprang from a cluster of tight ebony curls. Experiencing a tantalizing combination of trepidation and excitement, she was aware of a sudden warmth stealing over her before Logan eased his naked body atop hers. Her breath caught upon a loud gasp when his bare flesh met hers, and she was given no further time to think of anything beyond sheer, tempestuous pleasure as his lips captured hers once more and his strong arms slid about her unresisting softness.

Their entwining bodies were bathed in the pale morning light streaming in through the narrow window above as they became lost in a world of sensual delight. Rachel's head tossed restlessly on the pillow of hay, her flowing tresses cascading riotously about her softly glowing face and shoulders while Logan's wonderfully skillful lips practiced their irresistible brand of enticement upon her full, rose-tipped breasts. Her fingers threaded within the gleaming thickness of his dark hair when his tongue flicked erotically across one pert nipple, and she arched against him, providing him with even greater access to the silken globe that ached for his caress. His mouth soon closed possessively upon the sensitive pink flesh of her other nipple, tenderly yet hungrily suckling while his hands stroked and explored her other feminine charms. Assailed by a thoroughly delicious weakness, Rachel gasped again and again, the yearning deep inside her prompting her to yield completely to the wild abandon calling her.

When Logan's warm lips returned to capture the alluring ripeness of hers a few moments later, Rachel grew emboldened and smoothed her hands across the magnificent broadness of his back, then down along the rock-hard leanness of his hips, her fingers curling briefly about the rounded tightness of his buttocks before moving to caress the very evidence of his desire. He moaned low in his throat and parted her trembling thighs with an ever-increasing impatience, and soon it was her turn to moan as his strong but gentle fingers demonstrated their eminently provocative comprehension of her womanly flesh and its purpose.

Soon, he was sheathing himself within her velvety passage, their bodies becoming one in the ultimate embrace. Rachel felt as if her very soul joined with Logan's, and she was startled by the fervency of her emotions as she clung to him, glorifying in her own femininity and Logan's exquisite mastery of it. Their shared fulfillment was fierce and complete, the afterglow of their loving sweet and harmonious. Then, the inevitable occurred . . .

"Well, Mrs. MacBride, I guess now you can understand why I'll never let you go," Logan remarked with a quiet chuckle, cradling Rachel against him. She frowned and raised up on one elbow to peer closely down into his handsome, faintly smiling countenance.

"What do you mean?"

"You're mine, Rachel. If there was ever any doubt about it, what just happened between us proves once and for all that—"

"What just happened between us proves nothing beyond the humiliating reality of our . . . our attraction for one another!" Pulling abruptly away from him, she hastily climbed to her feet and snatched up the torn petticoat, draping it across her body like a shield as she stood rigidly erect before him.

"Oh, so we're back to that, are we?" He merely crossed his arms beneath his head and smiled roguishly up at her, not at all perturbed by the fact that he was still entirely naked. "Hell, sweetheart, you ought to be grateful for the fact that I can't keep my hands off you. From what I've heard, there's many a bride with justifiable complaint about her husband's 'capabilities' and the frequency—"

"Why, that . . . that's disgusting!" Rachel indignantly exclaimed, her cheeks flaming.

"You wouldn't think so if you were among the neglected," he quipped, his green eyes twinkling.

Casting him a speaking glare of renewed hostility, though she could not say precisely *why* she felt such anger with him, she bent down and tugged insistently upon her other clothing, all of which lay beneath Logan's unabashedly bare form. He appeared not in the least bit inclined to move, and Rachel blushed again as her eyes fell on his manhood, now in repose. She purposefully averted her gaze and frostily demanded, "Would you be so kind as to let me get dressed?"

"What's your hurry? It's still early. None of the hands will be back from their morning rounds for another hour or so." He was already reaching for her, but Rachel avoided his grasp and clutched the torn undergarment even closer.

"Since I have every intention of leaving this barn without further delay, it might interest you to know that, if necessary, I will venture outside in nothing more than this petticoat! And I should think your pride would not relish the possibility of your wife's shameful lack of attire being witnessed by—"

"We both know you'd never do it," Logan sardonically retorted, nonetheless bending his tall, lithely muscled frame forward and rising to his feet as his gaze smoldered with a renewed surge of desire. He was sorely tempted to tumble her to the hay again, but he resisted the temptation, telling himself with an inward smile that there'd be plenty of time for further "wooing" of his reluctant bride later. Confident of his success in bringing her around to his way of thinking, he could afford to be patient, especially when his patience was rewarded with more of her delectable fire . . .

Rachel donned the last of her clothing and whirled away from Logan, who was just beginning to draw on his faded denim trousers. Before he could guess her intent, she climbed hurriedly down from the loft and sent the ladder crashing backward onto the barn floor.

"What the devil—" he muttered. Hastily pulling his pants upward and stalking to the edge of the hayloft, he scowled darkly as he observed the result of his wife's final act of defiance. "Damn it, Rachel, come back here!" She willfully ignored his thundering command and scampered to the doorway, blissfully unaware of the various methods of retribution already crossing his mind.

As he watched her sail complacently out the door, however, Logan shook his head in begrudging amusement. He finished dressing, musing that he sure as hell had to admire her spirit—she could use a bit of taming, but a woman with spirit was better than a spineless one any day! Holding that thought, he seized the length of rope hanging from a large pulley fastened to one of the rafters above and swung agilely down from the loft.

Rachel, meanwhile, sped from the barn and across the thankfully still-deserted yard, brushing the hay from her gown and twisting her hair into some semblance of order before entering the house. She had already begun to itch as a result of the fine layer of dust from the hay clinging to her skin, and she was none too pleased to encounter Mrs. Smith on her way up the stairs. The older woman subjected her to a frown of disapproval even more severe than before, and Rachel puzzled over it until facing herself in the mirror a short time later and noting the telltale blades of dried grass tangled within her thick mass of hair.

Mentally consigning Logan MacBride to the devil, she took herself off to wash the itch-provoking dust from her body . . . and to wash all traces of her green-eyed tormentor's burning embrace from her body as well.

X

More than an hour passed before Rachel gathered enough courage to venture downstairs again. Her skin was still pink and glowing from the vigorous scrubbing she had given it, and she had secured her freshly washed tresses at the nape of her neck with a black velvet ribbon, though several damp tendrils escaped to curl becomingly about her face.

The luxuriously unhurried bath had afforded her the opportunity to contemplate the many upheavals in her previously well-ordered life—all of which had been brought about, either directly or indirectly, by Logan MacBride. Within the course of a single day, she had found herself eloping with him, being forced to leave her family and travel to his home, and then, worst of all, becoming a shamelessly willing participant in his wildly rapturous lovemaking!

"Oh Rachel, how could you? Not once, but twice!" she chastised herself aloud, another fiery blush tinging the youthful beauty of her face. It was totally beyond her comprehension, the way she became transformed into a different woman—a passionate stranger with no sense of decency or propriety—every time Logan touched her. Was she now so lost to any sense of respectability and pride that she could no longer trust her own judgment? Unhappily, it seemed so.

You're mine, Rachel. I'll never let you go, Logan had vowed. What was she to do? It had never occurred to her that he would want the two of them to remain wed *forever!* Were his words merely an idle threat, or did he truly intend to keep her trapped in a marriage that was based on nothing more than a purely carnal gratification of the flesh?

Nothing more? her mind's inner voice pointedly challenged.

"Nothing more!" she feelingly asserted, disregarding the painful lurch of her heart at the recurring thought that Logan MacBride cared so little about her that he would use her in a scheme to regain control of her grandfather's land.

When her thoughts returned to the previous day and the heart-rendering scene with Jane and Micah, she found herself plagued by a sharp feeling of homesickness, and the almost desperate yearning to see her family lingered as she left the dubious sanctuary of her room and moved slowly down the staircase.

Without warning, the front door swung open. Rachel drew to an abrupt halt on the bottom step and caught her breath, certain that it was Logan finally seeking her out to avenge himself for her retaliatory bit of mischief with the ladder. She released a long sigh of relief in the next moment, however, when she saw that it was not Logan at all, but rather two women who were apparently well enough acquainted with the MacBrides to enter the house without first knocking.

"And I'm telling you, Aunt Tess, there was something terribly peculiar about the way Logan was behav—" the younger of the two was adamantly maintaining just as she stepped across the threshold and caught sight of Rachel. The brunette's pale green eyes first widened in shocked amazement, then swiftly narrowed in profound displeasure. "Who are you? And why are you wearing my dress?" she belligerently queried, a dull flush rising to her rather sharp-featured but nonetheless attractive face. Only a few years older than the golden-haired beauty she confronted, she possessed an undeniably haughty air to which Rachel immediately took exception. "Well? Out with it! Who the devil are you?"

"Moira, please!" gently admonished her companion, a slender and petite woman of perhaps forty-five. Her chestnut hair was neatly secured in a chignon beneath a small, feathered hat, and her countenance, though bearing a noticeable resemblance to the brunette's, was much more kindly. The two women were even dressed in a similar fashion—the one called Moira in a simple yet stylish gown of dark rose cotton, and the older one in an equally understated concoction of deep mauve silk.

Rachel endured their stares—one hostile and the other merely curious—with unflinching silence, her fingers tightening upon the polished smoothness of the bannister and her head lifting proudly. Suddenly, Logan's tall frame filled the open doorway.

"I see the three of you have already met," he noted with only the suggestion of a smile. His eyes immediately sought out Rachel, who inwardly bristled at the ironic humor she read within their gleaming virescent depths. What did he find so amusing about the situation? she resentfully wondered.

"Who is she, Logan?" Moira demanded tersely, rounding on him in obvious perturbation. "Who is she and what is she doing here?"

"Since it seems I was mistaken about the introductions, allow me." He spoke with mocking gallantry. Negligently sweeping the hat from his head, he nodded toward Rachel and evenly announced, "Cousin Moira, Aunt Tess, this is my wife—Rachel Parker MacBride."

"Your *what?*" gasped Moira, appearing thunderstruck.

"Oh Logan, how wonderful!" proclaimed Aunt Tess. She approached Rachel at last, smiling warmly as she declared, "I'm so happy for you, my dear! I won't say this isn't something of a surprise, but I'm quite delighted to welcome dear Logan's wife into the family!"

"Thank you," Rachel earnestly replied, her own features relaxing into a smile. The smile quickly faded when she looked back at Logan and glimpsed the familiar light of devilment in his eyes. Why, the arrogant scoundrel was enjoying himself at her expense!

"No," Moira whispered in stunned disbelief. Her face had taken on an ashen color, and her hand trembled as she raised it to dazedly tug the beribboned straw bonnet from her upswept raven curls. "No, it . . . it can't be!" she choked out, her horror-stricken gaze full of mute appeal as it fastened on Logan's handsome, inscrutable visage. "This is some sort of cruel jest, isn't it? You couldn't possibly have married her, not when you know how I—"

"We were married yesterday," he quietly confirmed, sparing her only a brief but significant look before shifting his gaze to Rachel again. "I've sent Brodie for your things." She had no time to respond before Moira, whose disbelief had turned into scornful fury, directed a scathingly malevolent glare at her and spitefully commanded, "Logan MacBride, tell that . . . that *woman* to take off my dress!"

"Nothing would give me greater pleasure," drawled Logan, his mouth twisting into a sardonic grin. Rachel was dismayed to feel herself blushing beneath the intimate boldness in his piercing gaze. "But, unfortunately, there are other matters requiring my attention at the moment." He donned his hat again and casually informed his wife, "I'm afraid your tour of the ranch will have to wait."

"That's *quite* all right!" she retorted in a tight voice, her beautiful eyes flashing their splendid opal fire.

"Go on about your business, Logan," Aunt Tess good-naturedly commanded with an airy wave of her hand. "Moira and I will be more than happy to entertain your charming bride!" She stepped up and linked her arm companionably through Rachel's. "Have you seen the house yet, my dear? If not, I'd love to show you about. It will give us the chance to get to know one another. I must confess that I'm almost unbearably curious to hear how you and my nephew met! You see, I had nearly abandoned all hope of seeing Logan settled down!"

Before a slightly bemused Rachel could decide what to say in response, the petite woman was leading her back up the stairs and chattering amiably all the while. Logan's mouth curved into a faint smile as he watched them go, then turned away to resume his work outside. He had just reached the edge of the porch when Moira's hand clenched the powerfully muscled hardness of his upper arm.

"Why did you do it?" she bitterly raged. "I go off for a

few days and return to find you shackled to some little bitch who couldn't possibly care for you as much as I do! Damn you, you heartless bastard, why did you suddenly take it into your head to do something like this?" Her eyes narrowed into mere slits of fury when he pried her fingers loose with deliberate ease and parried in a low tone completely devoid of warmth, "I owe you no explanation, Moira. I never lied to you." He caught her wrist in an iron grip when she muttered a particularly foul obscenity and raised a hand to strike him. His eyes glittered coldly down at her. "If there ever *was* anything between us, it was destroyed by you a long time ago." Abruptly releasing her as if scorched by the contact, he paused to grimly warn, "Mistreat Rachel in any way, dear cousin, and you'll answer to me. That, I promise." His lips tightened into a thin line and his hard gaze bored into hers for a long moment before he left her standing shaken and pale on the steps.

Moira glared at his retreating back until he disappeared into the stable across the yard. Her thoughts were already furiously churning to find an appropriate means of revenge, revenge for what she told herself was Logan's cruel and unprovoked betrayal of their love.

"He's mine," she proclaimed aloud. "He's always been mine. And whether it's with the aid of heaven or hell, he will be again!" Whirling purposefully about, she flew inside the house to find the woman who had been her faithful ally ever since she had come to live at the "big house" with Logan more than a year ago.

Rachel, meanwhile, was learning a good deal more about the MacBrides than she'd wanted to. Not that her curiosity wasn't aroused. But she had convinced herself that the less known about Logan MacBride and his family of rogues, the better! Aunt Tess, however, proved to be a veritable fountain of information, offering her inwardly ill-at-ease companion an endless number of anecdotes about the occupants, both past and present, of the various rooms she showed her. None of the remarkable woman's stories were malicious or improper—merely a bit more enlightening than Rachel would have wished.

For instance, she learned that Logan's parents—Dugan, a gruff Scotsman, and Anne, his adored, Boston-bred wife—had been married nearly four years before finally being blessed with children. Logan had been the firstborn, and then Anne had been delivered of a daughter, whom they had named Chloe, some five years later. Tragically, however, both mother and babe contracted influenza during a particularly harsh winter. Anne recovered, but the babe did not. Logan, as their only child, had been all the more cherished.

Which accounts for his arrogance! mused Rachel at that point, nonetheless experiencing more than a twinge of compassion at the thought of the terrible heartache his parents must have endured.

After that, she learned that Tess herself was the sister of Dugan MacBride, and the only daughter in a family of five sons. She had accompanied her brothers, all considerably older than herself, when they left Scotland and sailed for America more than forty years ago, their parents having been killed in an accident the month before. Although possessing little in the way of money or valuables, the young MacBrides had triumphed over their misfortune and made a new life for themselves, eventually settling in the wildly beautiful vastness of Montana. They had not only survived—they had founded two of the largest and most successful cattle ranches in all the West, first in the southwestern part of the territory, and then in the present location of the Circle M.

"Why did you leave—" Rachel started to ask, intrigued in spite of her resolve not to be.

"Leave behind what it had taken us so long to build?" supplied Aunt Tess, anticipating her question. She smiled softly and led the way back down the narrow hallway in the newest wing of the house. "Several years ago, Dugan prophesied that the time was coming when our ranges would become crowded and overgrazed. Unfortunately, he was proven right. There began to be so much competition for the land, especially when farmers and dairymen moved in to battle the ranchers for control. My other brothers finally listened to Dugan and agreed to move eastward." She sighed heavily and added, "In a way, it was the biggest mistake they'd ever made. The Circle M is every bit as successful as the other ranch was, perhaps even more so, but none of them are alive to appreciate it."

The two of them were now standing within the confines of a charming, sunlit room decorated in pastel shades of blue and gold. Rachel was surprised to see a shadow of pain cross the other woman's delicate features.

"This room has been mine alone for nearly three years, my dear. Before that, I shared it with my husband. William Anderson was his name, and he was the kindest, gentlest man I've ever known. He never quite fit in with my brothers, who were admittedly a bit rough, but he never complained. He was a bookkeeper by trade, so Dugan and the others were at least grateful for the fact that I married a man who could be of use," she finished with another faint smile that held just a hint of bitter irony.

"I . . . I'm sorry," murmured Rachel, not knowing what else to say as she detected the deep sadness Tess still felt. "Did you and your husband have any children?"

"None, I'm afraid. Which is why Logan has always been so dear to me." She linked her arm through Rachel's again and swept her from the room, declaring with a bright smile, "Enough about me and the rest of us old-timers! You've yet to tell me how you and my nephew came to be married!"

Rachel, after musing to herself with an inward smile that she hadn't been given the opportunity to say much of anything, searched for an explanation that would sound plausible and yet not too far from the truth. Thinking that she liked Logan's aunt very much, she realized that it was going to be extremely difficult to lie to the woman—and even more difficult to deceive her. She wisely sensed that Aunt Tess was not easily fooled . . .

"I scarcely know where to begin," she evasively answered, at the same time averting her eyes from the older woman's perceptive gaze. Having traveled back into the main part of the house, they now paused directly before the bedroom connecting to the one Logan had assigned his new wife.

"Let's start with the beginning," Aunt Tess suggested with a soft laugh. "Where did you happen to meet?"

"We met at . . . at the Macqueen House in Miles City. It was the night of the roundup dance." Rachel, dismayed to feel her face coloring as she uttered what was only partially a falsehood, hoped the other woman would believe her blush to be prompted by a bride's natural shyness.

"Only last week? Well, I had always expected that when Logan finally fell in love, there would be little time wasted! Moira and I would have been at the dance as well, but we were unfortunately called away at the last minute to attend the birth of the newest MacBride some distance away. In fact, we've just returned from there." Declining to add that Moira had resisted going and had complained quite loudly about the circumstances which had caused her to miss the dance, Tess merely smiled again and remarked with heartfelt sincerity, "I can't tell you how pleased I am that you and Logan found one another! And I still want to hear all about you—your family, how you came to be in Miles City, and so on—but I'm afraid I really must pay a visit to Mrs. Smith without further delay! The poor woman has no doubt been at her wits' end these past few days without Moira and me to assist her. As you've just seen, the house is quite large and requires all three of us to keep it running with anything resembling smoothness!"

"I would be more than happy to help," Rachel impulsively offered, then could have kicked herself. Though she would much rather work than sit idly about, she reflected that the last thing she needed was to become too involved with either Logan MacBride's family or his household! It would just make things all the more difficult when the time came for her to return home, she reflected, then was startled to experience a faint but very real sense of loss at the thought of leaving.

"Perhaps when you've had a bit more time to settle in," responded Aunt Tess with a gentle, knowing pat upon Rachel's shoulder. "After all, my dear, you've only just become a bride!" she went on to point out, as if the younger woman's newly altered marital status rendered her incapable of housework.

With an inner sigh of exasperation, Rachel watched

Aunt Tess move swiftly and gracefully down the staircase. Her hand closed upon the brass doorknob behind her as the other woman disappeared. The morning had certainly been full of surprises! she mused, then inhaled sharply when an embarrassingly vivid recollection of the first "surprise" returned to plague her. Thunderation! she swore in silence, so discomposed by the memory of Logan's enchanting mastery of her repeatedly traitorous body that she failed to notice she was opening the door to her husband's chambers instead of her own.

She stopped short as soon as she entered the room, her eyes widening in puzzled surprise. Unlike the delicately carved furniture and soft, muted tones of rose and cream adorning the bedroom in which she had slept, she found bold, undeniably masculine furnishings in shades of brown, rust, and beige. The bed itself was enormous—even larger than the canopied four-poster in her room—and was fashioned from deeper-hued oak, its posts twice the thickness of a man's arm and so tall they almost touched the beamed ceiling. The other furniture scattered about the room was of equally imposing stature, prompting Rachel to muse that it suited its owner well. It was just like Logan—bold and arrogant and damnably overbearing!

"What are you doing in here?" Moira's voice unexpectedly rang out in tones of obvious antagonism. Rachel started guiltily and spun about to face her, her face crimsoning at being caught in the intimacy of Logan's bedroom.

"I . . . I'm afraid I made an error—" she faltered, only to break off when it occurred to her that she didn't owe the woman any explanation whatsoever! After all, however disagreeable the fact might be, she was Logan MacBride's wife and therefore had every right to be in his bedroom. Lifting her chin in an unconscious gesture of defiance, she coolly amended, "Aunt Tess left me to complete my tour of the house alone."

"And did the house meet with your approval, *dear* Rachel?" Moira acidly inquired, her pale green eyes full of venom. She was a few inches taller than the beautiful young woman she interrogated, as well as several pounds heavier, and she possessed a certain, hardened look that prompted Rachel to absently muse that her life must not have been an easy one.

"It did." Rachel, not at all desirous of prolonging the confrontation, gathered up her skirts and prepared to leave. Moira, however, refused to vacate the doorway.

"How did you do it?" the brunette unexpectedly demanded. "How did you manage to trick Logan into marrying you?"

"I don't know what you're talking about," Rachel stiffly replied, her attempt to move past the woman once again meeting with failure. "Will you please get out of my way?" Her color was heightened by a growing anger now instead of discomfiture. Although perplexed by Moira's open hostility, she was nevertheless quite determined not to allow herself to be intimidated.

"There's no use denying it! Cora told me that Logan said last night when she asked him why he had suddenly taken it into his head to marry an outsider. 'I had no choice' was his answer. *I had no choice.* Just what the hell did he mean by that? Did you perhaps force him into it by telling him you're carrying his child? Did you play the whore and then—"

"How dare you!" Rachel indignantly charged, her eyes

flashing brilliantly up at her accuser. "How dare you subject me to such an insulting barrage of questions! For your information, I don't care what you or Mrs. Smith or anyone else thinks of my marriage to Logan—the fact remains that I *am* his wife and you have no right to pry into the personal details of our relationship!"

"I have every right!" Moira adamantly dissented, folding her arms tightly across her ample bosom. "Logan MacBride and I have been promised to one another since childhood! It's been understood for years that we would someday marry!" Her arms fell abruptly to her sides, her hands clenching into fists as she malignantly hissed, "And now you come along and spoil everything, you scheming little bitch! Logan is mine, do you hear? Mine!"

Rachel stared speechlessly up at her, wondering why the startling disclosure provoked such a wealth of emotion, not at all pleasant, within her breast. Her luminous eyes clouding with inexplicable pain, she raised a trembling hand to the vulnerable spot at the base of her throat where her pulse suddenly beat at such an alarming rate of speed.

"I . . . I didn't know," she murmured, then quickly regained her composure and added in a stronger voice, "Logan never told me of your engagement." Dear Lord, why did you allow me to go through with this disastrous charade? Why did Logan MacBride ever come into my life? she silently lamented.

"It was never officially announced," Moira reluctantly confessed, "but everyone knew of it! Logan's father and mine were the eldest MacBride cousins, and it was an established tradition within the clan that their children would marry! So perhaps now you can see why you'll never fit in. Go back where you belong, Rachel!

You're not wanted here and you never will be. No matter what form of trickery you used to make Logan marry you, you're a fool if you think he'll remain true to you. You're not the woman for him—*I* am! Ask him yourself if you don't believe me. Ask him—"

"Stop it!" cried Rachel, her head spinning and her eyes glistening with tears of mingled rage and anguish. Bewildered by the fact that she was so strongly affected by the spiteful young woman's remarks, she felt a powerful need to escape both Moira's presence and the overwhelming confines of Logan's room.

"What's the matter? Are you afraid to face the truth? Are you afraid to learn that your husband prefers another woman?" taunted the vengeful brunette. Her eyes gleamed with smug triumph when a noticeably distressed Rachel spun about and fled to the privacy of her own chambers by way of the connecting bathroom.

Logan's cousin laughed softly to herself before returning back downstairs to share the news of her success with the housekeeper. If all went as planned, they would soon be rid of the hated usurper, and she, Moira MacBride, would finally be able to take her rightful place as the wife of the clan's young patriarch. Possessed of an unwavering confidence that she could convince Logan to delay their union no longer, she smiled at the thought of the various methods of persuasion she could resort to if necessary. Why, the little blond ninny Logan had brought home couldn't possibly satisfy him as well as she herself had always known she could if given the chance! Yes, Moira told herself with another quiet, self-satisfied laugh as she reached the foot of the staircase and turned toward the kitchen, her forbearance and patience would soon be rewarded . . .

The present Mrs. MacBride was at that same moment pacing about her room in angry restiveness. Furious with herself for the uncharacteristic weakness that had made her retreat instead of standing her ground, Rachel heaved a confused sigh and paused beside one of the large, eastern-exposure windows. She distractedly fingered the chintz curtains as she peered down upon the stream flowing swiftly past the house and the cottonwoods which flanked the shimmering water, their leaves fluttering and branches swaying beneath the never-ending onslaught of the summer breeze.

I had no choice. Why had Logan chosen those particular words to explain their elopement? Why hadn't he told her about Moira and the "understanding" between them? And why hadn't he at least warned her about the inevitably explosive situation that would arise with Moira's return home? He had told her nothing, had left her completely at the mercy of his aunt's gentle prying and his cousin's malevolent accusations. The circumstances worsened with each passing hour of her regrettable marriage to the insolent rogue!

"Damn you!" muttered Rachel, shocked at the turbulence of her own feelings. Why should the discovery of his engagement to another woman cause her such disquiet? "Damn you, Logan MacBride!"

"If I'm to be damned, may I at least know for which transgression?" His deep voice, brimming with unmistakable amusement, startled her from her unpleasant reverie. She inhaled sharply and whirled to face him, her opaline gaze kindling with intense annoyance when she noted the familiar, mocking smile which touched the chiseled warmth of his lips.

"How *could* you? How could you bring me here

without at least having the decency to tell me about *her* first?" stormed Rachel. "To think that you were actually betrothed to another woman and that you violated your promise to her only to regain possession of a few insignificant acres of land—"

"I take it you're referring to Moira."

"You know very well who I'm referring to! I'm only now beginning to learn just how utterly ruthless and unscrupulous you are! What's worst of all is to realize that you were so lost to honor that you . . ." Her voice trailed away for a moment and she colored rosily before finishing. "You took advantage of me while still engaged to her!"

"I'm not engaged to her," Logan calmly denied, sauntering inside the room and closing the door behind him. "Until now, no woman's been able to lay claim to me," he added with a disarming grin as he leisurely crossed the distance between them. Rachel gasped inwardly at the sudden, disturbing flip-flop of her stomach.

"But she said—"

"I can well imagine what she said." Logan towered above her now, the expression on his handsome face becoming strangely solemn as he reached out to draw her slowly toward him. The beguiling, almost hypnotic glow in his magnificent, sea-green eyes prompted her momentary submission. "I don't give a damn what Moira told you. There may have been an understanding among the family, but it was none of my doing."

"Why should I believe you?" Rachel demanded a bit breathlessly, her eyes wide and sparkling as they searched for the truth in his.

"Why does it matter so much?" parried Logan. His

hands maintained a firm but gentle grip upon her arms as he bent his head closer to hers. "Could it possibly be that you don't hate me quite as much as you profess?" he challenged in a low, vibrant tone, his eyes darkening to a fiery jade. "Maybe you're beginning to realize that our getting married wasn't such a catastrophe after all."

Rachel felt herself swaying against him, felt the searingly intense current passing between them. But her grandfather's face suddenly swam before her eyes, immediately followed by unbidden images of Vance MacBride's cruelly taunting features and Moira's rancorous visage. No! her mind cried. She couldn't allow herself to be seduced into compliancy, couldn't meekly resign herself to an acceptance of the MacBrides and their villainous ways—not when there were still so many questions left unanswered, not when her heart and brain were constantly battling one another for supremacy!

"It was and still is a catastrophe!" she finally proclaimed in disaccord, twisting within his grasp. She was startled by the abruptness with which he released her, and she clutched at the windowsill behind her for support. There was a tiny glimmer of fear in the widening gaze she turned upon him, as if she half expected him to try and force her into an acknowledgment that her feelings for him were varied and conflicting, but that hate was definitely not among them.

"The only catastrophe is that you're too blasted stubborn to admit defeat, you little fool!" he ground out. His handsome, sun-bronzed features visibly tightened, and his eyes blazed with inordinate fury. Rachel, provoked to an answering indignation by his highly ungenerous remark, forgot her apprehension and countered with, "Defeat? I wasn't aware, Mr. MacBride, that we were playing a game!" Her silken voice was laced with biting sarcasm.

"Oh, but we are. There's a contest of wills taking place between us, Rachel, and as I've said before, I'll be damned if I'm going to let you run roughshod over me the rest of our lives!"

"There isn't going to be any 'rest of our lives'! Don't you understand? I will not allow this . . . this travesty of holy wedlock to continue beyond—" A loud gasp escaped her lips as his hands shot out and yanked her back against him.

"It may not be 'holy', sweet bride, but it's sure as hell 'wedlock' and that's what it's going to stay!" Rachel gasped again just before his hard lips descended upon hers with punishing force. His powerful arms enveloped her in a savagely possessive embrace, and she moaned in feeble protest at his impassioned siege, her senses reeling as she felt the hot invasion of his tongue within the soft, sensitive cavern of her mouth.

The "other Rachel," whose irrestrainable nature sprang to life only at Logan MacBride's touch, seized control and began returning his fiercely demanding kisses with tempestuous abandon, her supple curves pressing boldly, seductively against his taut, sinewy form and her arms entwining about the corded muscles of his neck as she arched her back to bring even more of her exquisitely feminine body into contact with the virile hardness of his.

Suddenly, a loud knock sounded at the bedroom door. Rachel crashed back to earth, her eyes flying open in reflexive alarm. It seemed at first as if Logan would pay the insistent rapping no heed, but he finally, begrudgingly released his ultimately willing captive, then swore roundly before spinning about on his booted heel and stalking to the door. He flung it open to reveal a noticeably agitated Mrs. Smith.

"Begging your pardon, Mr. Logan, but there's been some trouble up near the line camp at Crow Rock. One of the boys just rode in with the news. Said it looks for certain like the rustlers have struck again!" Her eyes narrowed as they moved past him to where Rachel had swiftly turned away to conceal her embarrassment and now stood facing the window as she made a valiant effort to regain her poise.

"Damn!" muttered Logan, a look of barely controlled violence crossing the rugged perfection of his face as he digested the unpalatable notification. "All right, Cora. I'll be right down." He didn't wait for a reply before returning to Rachel, his hands closing upon her shoulders and forcing her about to meet his sharp-edged gaze. He felt his heart constrict as he caught sight of the tears glistening upon her lashes, though he told himself he wasn't the least bit sorry for what had put them there. "We'll continue this 'discussion' when I get back," he grimly decreed.

"There's no need for a discussion," she declared woodenly, looking away and feigning cold indifference. In truth, her strained emotions were perilously near the breaking point! "You and I, Mr. MacBride, have nothing whatsoever to talk about."

"Confound it, woman! You are without a doubt the most infuriating, damnably exasperating female—" growled Logan, only to break off and breathe another harshly masculine oath. He subjected her to one last, smoldering perusal before flinging abruptly away and taking himself off. Rachel stared after him in cheerless preoccupation, feeling more confused and miserable with each passing second.

Although she would have believed it impossible, the situation had actually worsened throughout the morning! First Logan's shocking assertion that their marriage would not be a temporary one after all . . . followed by his humiliating conquest of her persistently disloyal body . . . then the astonishing, not at all pleasurable discovery that he was betrothed to another woman . . . and lastly, her own growing inadequacy to deal calmly and rationally with the many changes being wrought in her life with such dizzying concurrence!

I must get away, she thought, feeling a sudden and desperate need to be alone, to be free of Logan and his family and every blatant reminder of what a maelstrom her previously well-ordered life had become. If only for a brief time, she had to get away!

Feverishly telling herself that Logan's absence from the ranch provided the perfect opportunity to escape, Rachel was already scurrying across to the door when it occurred to her that she hadn't the vaguest notion of where to escape *to.* She certainly couldn't go home, no matter how much she longed to seek the comfort of her family. What would they think if she, a new bride supposedly much in love with her husband, suddenly appeared on their doorstep in such an obvious state of distress? Even if her marriage to Logan had not achieved the purpose she had originally intended, she realized that it would only make matters worse if she revealed the truth of the circumstances to Micah. Not only would it further break his heart to learn that she had sacrificed herself on his behalf, but she was well enough acquainted with her grandfather's sense of justice to know that he would seek revenge against the MacBrides.

"Then I'll just ride somewhere, *anywhere!*" she resolved aloud, her silken skirts rustling softly as she continued on her way. No sooner had she reached the doorway, however, when another sudden realization arrested her flight. She frowned impatiently down at her attire, reluctantly acknowledging the fact that it was inappropriate for riding—not that she would be consumed by remorse if Moira's dress were to be ruined! But it was entirely too constrictive for such activity, besides being too thin to provide any real protection against the sun and wind.

It took Rachel only an instant to hit upon a solution. Turning and racing through the bathroom into Logan's chambers again, she searched hastily through the drawers of the massive oak chest, her eyes sparkling in triumph when her search yielded a pair of denim trousers and a plaid cotton shirt. She quickly stripped off the borrowed silk gown and undergarments and drew on Logan's clothing, which appeared comically oversized on her much smaller frame. After rolling up the sleeves of the shirt and bending to form a deep cuff in the legs of the trousers, she snatched up the ribbon sash adorning Moira's dress and used it to tighten the waistband of Logan's pants. That done, she flung open the doors of the mirrored wardrobe near the bed and smiled to herself in satisfaction when she found a worn denim jacket therein. She tugged it down and started to turn away, when her eyes fell upon a gunbelt and holstered six-shooter hanging from a peg at the back of the wardrobe.

Remembering what Micah had told both her and Lizzie of the many dangers of the Montana prairie, including the still-prevalent threat of Indians who refused to adapt to the means and mores of reservation life, she impulsively took down the belt and buckled it about her hips. Then, almost as an afterthought, she grabbed one of Logan's hats from the wardrobe and tugged it low upon her head.

Emerging from the room at last, Rachel was quite determined not to allow anyone to sway her from her intent. She was vastly relieved, however, to encounter no one as she hurried down the stairs and out of the house. Correctly surmising that most of the ranch hands had ridden off with Logan, she reached the stable in a matter of seconds, where she was pleasantly surprised to find a horse already saddled and waiting in one of the stalls.

"Easy, boy, easy," she whispered soothingly, gathering up the reins and leading the gently snorting animal out into the sunshine. She experienced a brief twinge of guilt at the thought that she was confiscating someone else's mount, but any hesitancy disappeared when she detected the sound of voices, one male and the other female, nearby. Without another moment's delay, she swung up into the saddle and urged the horse forward with a light slap of the reins and accompanying nudge of her heels.

"What the—" muttered the owner of the male voice, rounding the corner of the stable just in time to observe someone galloping away on Miss Moira's horse. The startling thing was, he could have sworn the rider was the boss's new wife! "Hey, come back here!" he called out in growing alarm, but to no avail. The woman with him, though initially enraged to see that Rachel was making off with *her* mount, put a restraining hand on the man's arm.

"Let her go, Tommy," Moira commanded softly. Her

lips curved upward into a slow, catlike smile, her glowing, pale green eyes appearing equally feline.

"But the boss will have my head for sure if anything happens to his wife!" vigorously protested the lanky young cowpuncher.

"He won't be able to hold you responsible if you didn't see her leave."

"If I didn't see her leave?" echoed Tommy, frowning in bewilderment. "Miss Moira, what are you—"

"I'm merely trying to point out that Logan's wife obviously wants to be alone, and I don't think she'd take too kindly to any interference on your part. So why not do everyone a favor and just pretend you never saw her?" the attractive brunette smoothly recommended, favoring the slender, fair-haired man beside her with a most persuasive smile. Like nearly every other man at the Circle M, he was hopelessly enamored of the only young, unmarried female for miles around. He felt his better judgment giving way to the wild leaping of his pulse.

"All right, Miss Moira," Tommy reluctantly agreed, coloring faintly and swallowing a sudden lump in his throat as her smile deepened. "I'll forget I ever saw her. I just hope nothing happens to make me regret my bad memory," he added with a sigh.

"Don't worry. Nothing will happen," Moira reassured him, her hand tightening on his arm with enticing familiarity before she left the stable and began strolling leisurely back toward the house. With any luck, she told herself, something *would* happen and they would be rid of the intruder even sooner than she'd hoped.

Yes, she mused as she warmed to the subject, perhaps Rachel would meet with an accident, or would have the ill fortune to encounter a band of renegade Cheyennes, or even the rustlers Logan was so determined to hunt down. At the very least, the new Mrs. MacBride would without a doubt be the recipient of the full measure of her husband's wrath for her foolishness in riding off alone. She herself was well aware of just how fearsome Logan MacBride's temper could be. Her mouth curving into another smile of pure malevolence at the thought of that explosive fury being turned upon Rachel, Moira entered the house with a lightened step and glanced up at the elegantly carved clock ticking away on one papered wall of the entrance foyer.

Three or four hours, she told herself. That's how long she would wait before doing her "Christian duty" and sending Tommy out to look for the errant bride. Maybe by then, there would no longer be any need for her to worry about the blond witch and her mysterious hold on Logan . . .

XI

Rachel lost all track of time as she rode. The warmth of the sun's rays intensified as the brilliant fireball moved across the cloudless sky, but the wind was sharp and stinging, making her grateful for the protection of Logan's jacket. Having secured his broad-brimmed hat upon her head with a bright red kerchief she'd pulled from the pocket of his trousers, she frequently found it necessary to tilt the too-large headgear backward in order to clear her line of vision. In spite of any discomfort or inconvenience, she reveled in the sense of freedom she felt as the animal beneath her cantered northward across the sagebrush-mantled plains. Momentarily forgotten were all her recent trials and tribulations—there was only the awesome beauty of the earth and heavens, only herself and nature's wonderfully nonhuman creatures for company.

The sun was almost directly overhead when Rachel finally pulled the wearying animal beneath her to a halt. Having spied a small, particularly inviting grove of cottonwoods beside a narrow stream winding its way across the vast prairie, she dismounted and led the grateful horse to the vibrant patch of green at the water's edge. A lone meadowlark, disturbed from its resting place in the trees above, thrust out its bright yellow chest and emitted a sonorous protest before bursting from the cover of leaves and soaring upward to glide away upon the invisible, erratically shifting currents of air.

Rachel looped the reins over a low-lying branch and sank down into the thick carpet of grass. The horse grazed peacefully beside her as she drew her denim-clad knees up toward her chest and rested her folded arms atop them. She tugged off Logan's hat and stared down into the sparkling, crystal-clear water trickling unhurriedly over moss-slicked pebbles and powdery silt, her thoughts drifting with a will of their own to the events of the past twenty-four hours.

Why did it still pain her so to think of Logan betraying her in order to reclaim her grandfather's land? And why did it feel as if a knife twisted in her heart when she thought of Logan speaking words of love to Moira, of him holding Moira and kissing Moira and—

"No!" The strangled cry broke from her lips as she tightly closed her eyes against the revolting image of Logan doing the same things to Moira that he had done to her. Though she couldn't explain why, the thought of him sharing such intimacy with Moira, with *any* woman other than herself, provoked one of the most intense feelings of anguish she had ever experienced. But why? she asked herself in confusion. Why should it matter to her at all if Logan MacBride had loved, or still loved, another woman? Was it merely because of the vows he had exchanged with her, vows that were supposed to have been meaningless?

Thoroughly disgusted with herself, and suddenly feeling quite exhausted, Rachel released a ragged sigh and leaned back against the rough bark of the tree. She snatched up Logan's hat again to settle it forward upon her pinned-up locks so that its wide brim covered the upper portion of her face, then stretched out her shapely limbs and crossed her arms against the firm mounds of feminine flesh concealed by the loose-fitting plaid shirt. More than anything, she needed to give her mind . . . her emotions . . . and her body a rest . . .

Rachel awoke with a start, her eyelids quickly fluttering open in reflexive alarm, only to find that her horse was insistently nudging her leg and whinnying softly. Her mind still drugged from sleep, she blinked in an effort to focus more clearly on the animal now pawing with inexplicable disquiet at the ground beside her.

"What is it, boy?" she murmured a bit groggily, sitting upright and then wincing at the unexpected stiffness of her muscles. She climbed slowly to her feet and peered upward through the rustling leaves, astonished to see that the sun hung so low in the western sky. Why, she must have been asleep for hours!

The horse snorted and nudged her again, prompting her to glide a soothing hand along his sleek, whisky-colored neck. Wondering why the animal appeared so skittish all of a sudden, Rachel quickly scanned the surrounding countryside, her opal eyes narrowing against the bright sunlight as they swept across the landscape's magnificently untamed contrasts of plains, hills, and tree-flanked waterways. Catching sight of the reason for her mount's unrest, her eyes widened and her entire body tensed. There, on the horizon and thundering in her direction, were three horsemen.

"Logan," breathed Rachel, naturally assuming that he had returned from his morning's ride to discover her gone and had come to find her. Mentally cursing the fact that an involuntary tremor of fear coursed the length of her spine, she was further dismayed to feel herself coloring hotly at the thought of his certain disapproval of her immodest attire.

As the horsemen neared, however, she was startled to discover that the lead rider was not Logan at all, but rather the one MacBride she feared more than her husband. Realizing that she was all alone in the middle of nowhere with Vance MacBride bearing down on her, Rachel felt terror seize her in its grip. Her first impulse was to swing up into the saddle and try to outdistance him, but she frantically told herself that such action would avail her nothing, that she could never hope to escape all three riders. No, she would have to stand her ground, would have to pray that, because of her marriage to his cousin, Vance wouldn't even think of doing her harm.

He and the other men slowed their mounts to a walk as they approached the spot where Rachel, her right hand lowering to the holster and tightening in defensive readiness upon the handle of Logan's six-shooter, stood waiting beneath the trees. Vance, as it turned out, had been equally astounded to find that not only was it a female in masculine clothing who faced him with such a staunchly courageous demeanor, but that the female was none other than the beautiful, high-and-mighty granddaughter of Micah Parker.

"Now just what the devil are you doing out here all by your lonesome, Miss Parker, ma'am?" he mockingly queried, leaning an arm negligently atop his saddlehorn as he and his companions reined to a halt a few feet away. He smiled in derisive amusement while his hawk's eyes swept insolently up and down her rigid form. The other men boldly leered at her as well, their lustful gazes raking appreciatively over her shapely hips and legs, so well revealed in the denim trousers she wore.

Rachel drew the gun, her hand only slightly unsteady as she raised the gleaming, pearl-handled weapon and pointed it directly at Vance. With a nervousness she could not quite conceal, her eyes darted to the faces of the men flanking him before fastening upon his darkly malevolent countenance.

"Leave me be, Vance MacBride," she commanded with all the bravado she could muster. "I'll not hesitate to shoot if you force me into it!" Her alarm increased when he merely laughed softly in response.

"I've got to hand it to you, Rachel, honey—you're full of fire. Yes sir, you're a regular little spitfire. But I don't think you're using your brains. If you shoot me, then what's to stop my men from having their way with you?" challenged Vance, tipping his hat back upon his head with studied unconcern. His golden eyes danced with malicious humor. "You see, Miss Parker, ma'am, if I'm not around to hold them in check, they're liable to get a bit carried away and do all kinds of 'unpleasant' things—"

"I'm warning you!" Rachel bravely reiterated, raising the gun a trifle higher and desperately trying to ignore the fierce pounding of her heart. Dear Lord, what would she do if Vance refused to back down? "In spite of the fact that you and Logan are fellow conspirators in this whole contemptible affair involving my family and myself, I don't think your cousin is the sort of man who would allow one of his 'possessions' to be mistreated!" All traces of humor suddenly vanished from her adversary's hawkish features.

"What the hell are you talking about?" he bit out, abruptly straightening in the saddle and tightening his grip on the reins.

"Why do you pretend ignorance?" Rachel bitterly countered, her fear of him momentarily forgotten. "But in the event that the 'glad tidings' haven't reached your ears yet, you'll be pleased to learn that your evil plan worked! Much to my everlasting shame, Logan and I were married yesterday."

"You're lying!" snarled Vance, his face twisting into a mask of virulent misdoubt. "Damn you, you little bitch, you're lying!"

"Why should I lie about it? And why this ludicrous act of surprise on your part? If it's for my benefit, I can assure you—" Before she could complete the sentence, Vance flung off his horse and lunged for her. Rachel, taken completely off guard by his swift, unanticipated action, had no time to ponder the consequences or take careful aim before she pulled the trigger. Vance deflected her arm just as the sound of the gunshot split the air, its loud, echoing report carried away on the ceaseless wind. The bullet had whizzed harmlessly past the head of its intended victim, leaving Rachel defenseless as the gun was wrested from her grasp.

"I ought to kill you for that!" Vance growled, a fierce light of baneful intent in his fury-narrowed eyes. She turned to run, but his hand tangled within her thick mass of hair and jerked her back toward him. Rachel stifled a cry as she was spun about to face him, but she was unable to suppress a low moan of pain as his hands tightened cruelly upon her wrists and imprisoned her arms behind her back. Hot tears filled her eyes when he yanked her up hard against him. "Now, *Miss Parker*, I mean to show you what we do to women out here who traipse about pretending to be men!"

"I wasn't pretending to be a man!" she futilely protested, then gasped and bit at her lower lip when he pulled her arms even further backward.

"Come on, Vance, let's have a look at what's under them man's duds she's got on!" sneered one of his companions, a pug-nosed fellow of medium height with stringy brown hair and bloodshot gray eyes. He shifted in the saddle, the leather softly creaking beneath his weight.

"Yeah, get on with it, boss!" chimed in the youngest of the sinister trio, sweeping the hat from his head to reveal thin, greasy blond hair. His close-set blue eyes glittered with an almost maniacal light as he, too, shifted in the saddle with anxious expectation. Rachel, blanching at the lustful, predatory look she glimpsed on the faces of all three men, struggled wildly to escape.

"No! You . . . you can't do this! Logan will—" she feverishly protested, her words ending on an involuntary scream as Vance jerked her wrists pitilessly upward. His lips curled into a slow, sadistic smile as he lowered his face close to hers.

"Logan will do nothing, for the simple reason that you're not going to tell him! If you do, I'll take that sister of yours and—"

"Dear God, no!" Rachel breathed in horror. "She's only a child!"

"She won't be when I get through with her," he threatened with another sneer. Then, apparently feeling that he had wasted enough time on talk, he released one of her wrists and quickly drew a knife from a scabbard attached to his tooled leather belt. Rachel uttered a strangled cry as he brought the blade slashing upward, its razor-sharp edge cutting effortlessly through the silken sash tied about the waistband of her trousers.

"The shirt, boss! Start with the shirt!" gleefully urged the blond-haired horseman.

"Sims is right—first things first! Since we gotta make certain that ain't no man you got there, why not start at the top and work your way down?" his cohort suggested, chortling in unrighteous merriment.

"Suits me fine," Vance assented with a wolfish grin. Rachel twisted violently within his grasp as he jerked her other arm from behind her back and raised the knife toward her again. He was unprepared when she suddenly bent her head and sank her teeth into the fleshy part of the hand gripping her wrist. Vance yelped in pain, then cursed and pressed the tip of the blade against her throat. "Try that again, spitfire, and I'll carve my name on your lily-white ass!" he vowed menacingly, his eyes gleaming in triumph when he viewed the naked fright in her sparkling opal gaze. He had just moved the point of the knife to the top button of her plaid shirt when the man known as Sims announced, "Hey, boss, someone's comin'!"

Logan! Rachel cried inwardly. Whereas before she had dreaded her husband's arrival, she now fervently prayed for it. Please God, let it be him!

"Damn it, one rider or more?" Vance tersely demanded, maintaining a firm hold on his secretly hopeful captive.

"More! Looks to be six, maybe seven!" Sims licked his lips nervously and shifted his gaze back to Vance.

"Maybe we ought to get going!"

"He's right. Let's get the hell out of here, Vance!" the other man exhorted, his own anxiety quite obvious.

"Damn it, there's no need to turn tail and run!" their leader harshly proclaimed. Another evil smile touched his lips as he pressed the tip of the blade to Rachel's throat again. "The little spitfire here's not going to say one blessed word, are you, honey? No matter who it is, you're going to keep your pretty mouth shut, understand?"

Rachel hesitated only a moment before nodding mutely up at him, but her mind raced to think of a way to alert the approaching riders to her predicament. She drew in her breath upon a gasp when Vance suddenly positioned himself behind her and prodded her back with the knife, its point thankfully dulled by the denim jacket and heavy cotton shirt she wore.

"Not one word, or I'll make good on that threat about your sister," he whispered close to her ear, causing her to shudder uncontrollably. In the next instant, he returned the knife to its scabbard and draped an arm about her shoulders in a pretense of affection. Though she inwardly shrank from the contact, she was unable to do anything more than stand rigidly erect and wait.

The riders, closing in at near breakneck speed, were led by a tall, grim-faced man whose identity, when it became discernible mere seconds later, caused Vance to stiffen and mutter a blistering oath. Rachel nearly fainted with relief when she saw that her prayers had been answered, and she wasted no time in jerking away from Vance at last. Her eyes immediately sought Logan's as he reined to an abrupt halt, his men drawing up in a semicircle behind him, but her joy at seeing him was short-lived. His handsome face was a hard mask of raging fury, and his gaze smoldered with barely concealed savagery as it raked over her. His anger, more intense than she had ever seen, frightened her more than she cared to admit.

"Are you all right?" he questioned her, his voice dangerously low and resonant. Painfully aware of the fact that several pairs of eyes were fastened on her, she swallowed hard and managed to reply, "Yes. Yes, I'm all right." She could feel the hot color washing over her, and she quickly averted her gaze. The lingering image of her sister's face prevented her from telling him what Vance had done.

"Of course she's all right," Vance drawled with deceptive nonchalance. "We've been taking real good care of Miss Parker, haven't we, ma'am?" he smoothly challenged Rachel, snaking out an arm and pulling her back against him. Her eyes grew quite round as they flew to her husband's face. "As a matter of fact, cousin," remarked Vance, turning back to Logan, "we don't much appreciate this interruption. So why don't you and—"

"Take your hands off my wife," Logan commanded with deadly calm. His eyes, darkening to a fiery jade, narrowed imperceptibly as they fastened on the other man with piercing steadiness.

"Your wife?" Vance gruffly echoed, his teeth clenching when he realized that Rachel had apparently spoken the truth. His men visibly paled and exchanged quick looks of growing apprehension while Rachel held her breath and stared up at Logan in wide-eyed anticipation.

"You heard me."

"Well then, this is quite a surprise," Vance mockingly intoned, effectively concealing his extreme displeasure at the news. He hugged a startled Rachel even closer as he met Logan's hard, intense gaze with a smirk of unmistakable defiance. "Yes sir, it's a mighty nice surprise to find out you've brought such a beauty into the family. But tell me, cousin—how is it no one knew you and Micah Parker's granddaughter were so well acquainted with one another?"

"Because that's the way we wanted it. Now, for the last time, Vance—let go of her," directed Logan. His fingers gripped the reins so tightly that his knuckles turned white, but his handsome face remained dangerously inscrutable.

"Not until I kiss the bride. That *is* the custom, isn't it? And seeing as how the bride and I are now what you could call 'kissing cousins'—"

Rachel gasped as Vance suddenly wrapped both arms about her and brought his mouth grinding down upon hers. Forgetting all else, she obeyed her innermost impulses and pushed frantically against him, a scream forming deep in her throat. Before she quite knew what was happening, she found herself released and stumbling backward to grasp at a tree for support. She was stunned to see Vance crashing to the ground at her feet an instant later, dispatched to unconsciousness with a single, well-placed blow from Logan's fist.

Logan, who had also chosen impulsive action over cautious restraint, spared only a passing glance for the prone form of his cousin as he seized Rachel's hand and pulled her none too gently toward him. His searing gaze flickered briefly over her flushed and noticeably dazed features before he turned to Vance's men and curtly ordered, "Get him on his horse." Since they were both fully cognizant of the fact that they were woefully outnumbered, neither Sims nor his companion hesitated to follow his directive. They hurriedly retrieved their employer's limp body and deposited it facedown across the back of his mount.

"Take him home," Logan commanded as they mounted up again. "When he comes around, give him this message—tell him I consider Micah Parker to be a member of the family now, and whoever raises a hand against Parker raises a hand against me, and against the other MacBrides as well." After nodding once in unison, the men were gone, riding away at a carefully measured pace so that Vance would not have cause to rail at them later for bruises suffered as as result of their negligent haste.

Rachel was dismayed to feel her courage fleeing when Logan favored her with another brief, burning look. She could literally feel the explosive fury emanating from him, and it was with a rapidly increasing tenseness that she waited for him to administer the tongue-lashing she knew to be forthcoming. She didn't know whether to be relieved or not when he somberly proclaimed to his own men, "I'll bring Mrs. MacBride home myself." Without a word, they reined about and headed back to the ranch, leaving Logan and Rachel alone with only the two horses providing an audience for their inevitable confrontation.

"Why did you do it?" Logan began by demanding in a voice that was whipcord sharp. He towered ominously above her, his hands closing upon her shoulders with a controlled violence as a dark, menacing scowl marred the rugged perfection of his face. "Why, Rachel? Why did you ride away without telling anyone? And what the devil are you doing dressed in that ridiculous get-up?"

She took a deep, steadying breath before answering as evenly as possible, "I had to . . . to get away. I needed to be alone."

"That may well be," he tightly allowed, his scowl deepening and his eyes glowing fierily, "but I would have thought you had a hell of a lot more sense than to go gallivanting across the open range in some harebrained quest for privacy!" He abruptly released her shoulders, flung away, and swore roundly before confronting her again. "Do you have any idea at all what I've endured because of you?"

"What *you've* endured?" she repeated in furious indignation, her own eyes flashing.

"Yes, damn it! It so happens I've been through hell these past several hours!" he ground out.

"You dare to speak to me of what you've been through after all the humiliation and the . . . the outright degradation I've suffered ever since you forced me to leave my family—humiliation and degradation you yourself have obviously taken great delight in heaping upon me?" She fought back the hot tears stinging her eyelids and tilted her chin upward in a gesture of dauntless pride and unconquerable spirit. "It matters not to me if you approve of either my attire or my behavior! As I've found it necessary to remind you before, Logan MacBride—you do not own me!"

"The question of my 'ownership' is not the issue here! Damn it, woman, I want to know why you took off like that and what the hell you were doing out here with Vance!" His temper flared to a particularly treacherous level when she turned away and evasively murmured, "Vance and his men happened upon me quite by accident." She inhaled sharply as she was spun about to face him once more. His fingers tightened about her arms and he shook her a bit for emphasis.

"What happened, Rachel? Either you tell me the truth, or I swear I'll—"

"What will you do?" she rashly taunted, provoked beyond all reason now. It had been one of the most thoroughly distressing days of her life, and his selfish, insensitive attitude made it all the worse! "Will you belabor me with all the swear words contained within your no-doubt-considerable vocabulary of such? Or perhaps beat me like the *un*dutiful and *un*meek chattel you obviously perceive me to be?"

"Don't tempt me!" he parried in a low, vibrant tone, his eyes aglow with an alarming intensity. "I've always admired your spirit, Rachel, but I'll be damned if I'll let you endanger yourself just to prove your independence! Didn't your grandfather ever caution you against riding out alone in this country? What if something had happened and—"

"The only things that 'happened' to me were a few hours of peace and quiet and a most welcome respite from *your* presence!" she retorted. A telltale blush stained her cheeks as it immediately dawned on her that her wrathful statement was not completely true. She couldn't tell him about Vance, couldn't tell him of the humiliation she had very nearly suffered at his cousin's hands. Not only did she have to protect Lizzie, but there was no way of knowing what his reaction would be. He had been enraged over the kiss Vance had forced on her—but why? Was it simply because she belonged to him, because he felt the need to defend his "property" in front of so many witnesses? Or was it for another reason entirely, one that had nothing to do with mere pride or an emotionally uninvolved sense of honor? Was it because he truly cared? It amazed her to realize how desperately she wanted it to be the latter.

Once again, he released her and angrily spun away. He was making an obvious and valiant effort to control his temper, but Rachel was in no mood to admire his restraint. Never had her emotions been in such a turmoil, and never had she felt so utterly at a loss as to her next course of action. Her dilemma was solved a few short moments later by Logan, whose own emotions were in total and uncharacteristic anarchy. He raked the hat from his head and braced a hand against a tree, then favored his beautiful but recalcitrant wife with a forebodingly solemn look.

"Let's get something straight, Rachel," he decreed with deceptive equanimity, his eyes kindling with a volatile spark of intent. "Like it or not, you're my wife now. And as my wife, you're going to have to obey me—especially where your welfare is concerned. You don't know this country like I do, so you'll simply have to trust my judgment when I tell you it's too dangerous for you to ride out alone. And you'll also have to trust my judgment when it comes to the company you keep and the clothes you wear. For starters, you know as well as I do that any association with Vance could be risky," he stated with a visible tightening of his sun-bronzed features. He paused briefly as he subjected her appearance to a condemnatory assessment. "And the consensus in these parts is that only the sort of woman looking to earn her keep on her back would be caught wearing pants." The bluntness of his observation provoked another fiery blush to tinge the delicate smoothness of Rachel's face.

"How dare you compare me to . . . to—" she indignantly sputtered.

"To a whore?" willingly supplied Logan. A faint, mocking smile touched his lips before he remarked, "You may have the right equipment for such a profession, sweet bride, but I know there's only one man who can set your blood afire and release all those wild, passionate impulses you've kept bottled up for so long. What's more, you know it too."

"I don't know anything of the sort!" Rachel vehemently denied, her brilliant opalescent eyes narrowing and blazing with inordinate fury. "And for your information, Mr. MacBride, I happen to have a brain—one which I fully intend to put to good use in spite of your detestably overbearing manner! I may have promised to love and obey you, but I did so with the belief that neither of us ever intended to honor our vows!"

Reflecting that she'd been forced to endure more than her fair share of Logan MacBride and his insolence for one day, she bent and snatched her borrowed hat up from where it had fallen during her nap, jerked it on over her disheveled golden locks, and began marching rigidly toward her horse. Logan, moving to detain her, reached out a hand to catch the loosely sagging waistband on the back of her too-large trousers. Forcing her to an unceremonious halt, he quietly dictated, "Hold it right there, 'Clover'. You're not going anywhere till we get this settled."

"Let go of me!" She twisted furiously about and attempted to tug the denim from his iron grasp, her efforts only succeeding in allowing him a tantalizing glimpse of silken, rounded flesh as the front of her oversized plaid shirt gaped strategically.

"Not until you agree to do as I say," he responded with maddening aplomb, holding fast and apparently unconcerned by her frenetic struggles. Rachel drew in her breath upon a gasp as he gave a sudden yank on the waistband and brought her up hard against him, the curve of her denim-clad buttocks colliding intimately with his hard, denim-clad thighs.

"What do you think you're doing?" she breathlessly demanded, unable to escape before his sinewy arm clamped about her waist.

"There will be only one master in our household, Mrs. MacBride, and you can damn sure bet it won't be you!"

"I don't want to be in *your* household at all!" No sooner had the words left her mouth when she felt her feet leaving the ground. "Put me down!" Logan's arms tightened about her as he lifted her even higher.

"With pleasure." He carried his kicking, squirming, furiously protesting bride a short distance away to an even more secluded patch of green at the water's edge. Rachel was set briefly on her feet again, only to be spun about and forced down to the ground an instant later. A loud gasp escaped her lips when she landed hard on her backside, and she raised narrowed, reproachfully flashing eyes to Logan as he stood towering over her.

"How dare you! I've had quite enough of your manhandling, you—" she seethed, only to break off when he suddenly began unbuttoning his shirt. Her eyes now grew round as saucers as her heart began pounding quite erratically. "Wha . . . what are you doing?"

"Exactly what it looks like," he quipped, a strange smile playing about his firm, chiseled lips. "It's time I reminded you of certain things, Rachel—most particularly, the fact that you're a wife now and have to answer to your husband. I have no desire to break your spirit. I'll give you all the slack I think you need, but not until you learn to trust and obey me."

"I'll never do either!" She tried to move, but her legs would not heed the frantic impulses from her brain. It was as if her body had a will of its own, as if—heaven forbid!—her silken flesh actually yearned to be teased and tormented by Logan, as if her womanly curves longed to be conquered by his virile hardness. Her involuntarily fascinated gaze was drawn to the nimble movements of his fingers as he liberated the last two buttons.

"Yes you will," he calmly asserted, drawing off his shirt to reveal the magnificent, bronzed planes of his chest and granite-hard smoothness of his equally tanned arms. His eyes filled with a fierce yet unfathomable light as he tossed the shirt aside and quietly avowed, "There will come a day when you finally acknowledge the truth, Rachel." Trying in vain to ignore the fire coursing through her veins, she challenged in a far weaker voice than she would have liked, "And just what *is* the truth?"

"You've belonged to me since the first time we met. You were mine even then, though we both did our best to deny it. But nothing will ever change what was meant to be—you know it and I know it. You can make things a hell of a lot easier on the both of us if you'll forget all about your feminine outrage at the turn of events and concentrate on the more pleasurable aspects of your 'situation'," he concluded, the corners of his mouth turning up into another faint yet disturbing smile. The expression on his handsome face became purposefully grim in the next instant. "But, before we take full advantage of our 'connubial bliss', we've got to clear up a few pressing matters between us."

Rachel, sensing the renewal of his intense annoyance with her, grew more than a little frightened. Finally tearing her gaze away from his powerfully muscled form, she hastily scrambled to her knees. Before she could take flight, however, Logan was on the ground behind her. Disregarding her struggles, he easily imprisoned her within the iron circle of his arms and pulled her back across his lap as he knelt on the grassy stream bank.

"Tell me what happened between you and Vance!" he demanded sharply.

"Why don't you ask *him?*" she retorted, tears of angry frustration filling her eyes as she thrashed wildly against him. The last of her hairpins lost the battle with her willfully tumbling hair, so that the thick, honey-colored tresses swirled about her face and shoulders in riotous abandon while she fought. She hated to admit it, even to herself, but she knew that she was fighting against her own impulses as well as Logan's.

"What did he threaten you with, Rachel? What did he say to ensure your silence?" Her struggles came to an abrupt halt at his perceptive inquiry.

"How . . . how did you know?"

"It wasn't difficult to guess," he remarked, only the ghost of a smile touching his lips. "I've known Vance all my life." He loosened his hold on her, and Rachel twisted about to face him.

"If you know him for the fiend he is, then why do you tolerate him? Why do you—"

"Because he's a MacBride" came the terse reply. His eyes glittered coldly, his mouth tightening into a thin line of displeasure.

"And I suppose that gives him the right to terrorize the entire countryside!" Rachel declared with bitter sarcasm, two bright spots of angry color tinging the smoothness of her cheeks. "I suppose it gives him the right to threaten an innocent girl, to—" she raged, only to break off. She had intended to say "assault his own cousin's wife," but had quickly decided against it. Logan would probably only blame her for the loathsome incident, would more than likely claim that she had brought it upon herself by riding out alone and wearing such scandalously inappropriate clothing besides! She twisted back around and futilely attempted to rise.

"What else did he do?" When his harsh question was met with obstinate silence on her part, he ground out a curse and said, "Damn it, Rachel, if he hurt you in any way—"

"And what if he did? Why should it matter to you? The two of you are in league with one another, aren't you?" she recklessly dared. "Tell me—do the MacBrides believe in sharing *everything?* If so, then perhaps it may interest you to know that I have no intention of being further humiliated by either you or your kinsman! As a matter of fact, I have no intention of continuing this distasteful charade of ours any longer!" She dashed impatiently at the tears spilling over from her lashes and renewed her efforts to escape. "Let go of me! I want nothing more to do with you, Logan MacBride! I want nothing more than to forget I ever heard the name 'MacBride'!"

"You couldn't forget, Rachel," Logan murmured close to her ear, his deep voice sending shivers down her spine in spite of her present state of emotional distress. "No matter how hard you tried, you'd never succeed in putting *me* from your mind!" To prove his point, he roughly forced her about and brought his lips crashing down upon hers. She moaned in protest and pushed against the bronzed hardness of his chest, but he possessively cradled her in his lap, one strong arm moving beneath her knees while the other wrapped about her shoulders and relentlessly crushed the upper half of her trembling softness to him.

Rachel despised herself for the now familiar weakness that prompted her to moan—with something far removed from objection to Logan's masterful embrace—again a few moments later. Her arms came up to entwine quite ardently about his neck, and she strained instinctively against him, atremble at the blaze of desire shooting through her when the sensitive peaks of her flannel-covered breasts pressed boldly against his bare, softly furred chest.

Her surrender was stormy and complete, her lips parting to allow his provocatively searching tongue access to the sweet nectar of her mouth. Her fingers trailed downward from his neck, gliding appreciatively, hungrily across his powerful shoulders and back. It was little surprise to her when he impatiently tore at the buttons on her shirt and claimed the satiny, rose-tipped globes of her breasts with first his hands, then his mouth. She cried out softly as his hot tongue flicked erotically across the pink, delicate flesh of each nipple in turn, his lips demanding a response as they suckled as greedily as any babe's.

Soon thereafter, he deftly stripped the jacket and shirt from her body and bore her backward to the green-carpeted earth. Rachel shivered anew when her naked back came into contact with the cool, fragrant grass, but Logan quickly rolled so that she was atop him, his lips capturing hers in a fierce, volatile kiss that made her very toes curl. Reveling in the feel of his naked flesh against hers, her splendidly formed breasts tingling as they made contact with the soft, curling mat of hair on his chest, she returned his kiss with all the impassioned fervor he had unleashed in her. The warm afternoon breeze swept across them, the gently rustling leaves formed a protective canopy above, but they were oblivious to all else save one another as they sought the most fulfilling enchantment two vibrantly alive souls such as themselves could experience.

Rachel inhaled sharply when Logan's strong, urgently questing fingers suddenly insinuated themselves beneath the loose waistband of her trousers and moved to close boldly about the firm, delectable roundness of her buttocks. Although a bit shocked to find herself giving silent thanks for the fact that she wore nothing beneath the borrowed pants, she spent only a brief moment on such demure introspection before giving herself up to the wonderfully captivating persuasion of Logan's lovemaking. She did not feel in the least compelled to offer a protest when he slipped her trousers downward over her hips and thighs, thereby baring her almost completely to his burning caresses as he stroked and explored the most sensitive places of her woman's body with oh-so-arousing skillfulness.

When Logan's own smoldering desire flared to within the outermost limits of masculine tolerance, he rolled so that Rachel was beneath him again. Reluctantly drawing away, he left her just long enough to shed the rest of his clothing and tug off her boots and trousers, after which he returned to his amorous task with even more impassioned zeal than before. Rachel moaned and gasped softly as he caressed the budding flower of femininity concealed within the silken triangle of hair between her thighs. His warm lips branded her satiny skin as they followed an imaginary path from her mouth to her breasts. With her senses reeling and her passions careening wildly heavenward, she was almost beyond coherent thought when she found herself atop him again a few moments later. He gently pushed her upward into a sitting position, and her luminous opal eyes clouded momentarily with puzzlement.

Her unspoken question was answered in a highly satisfactory manner when he firmly gripped her about the waist and lifted her slightly, then brought her slowly downward. A soft cry broke from her lips when she felt his manhood sheathing within her velvety warmth, and she fell forward a bit, her fingers clutching almost convulsively at his shoulders as his hands closed about her hips and tutored her into the evocatively undulating motion of his.

"Oh! Oh, Logan!" she gasped out, scarcely aware that she had spoken aloud. Her knees tightened about his gloriously masculine torso, her hair streaming like a shimmering golden curtain about her beautiful, passion-flushed countenance as her eyes swept closed and she moaned again at the intensifying, white-hot flame deep within her.

"Rachel. My beautiful, beautiful Rachel," murmured Logan, his voice little more than a hoarse whisper. His eyes glowed like two deep-hued emeralds as they fastened unwaveringly upon his bride's rosy visage, and his devastatingly handsome face tightened as he became lost in the throes of a passion more forceful than any he had ever known. His strong fingers relinquished their hold on Rachel's adorable bottom and transferred their ecstasy-inducing attentions to the other pleasure points of her delicious flesh, one hand dedicating itself to the highly stimulating worship of her breasts while the other returned to perform its exquisite torment on the soft, womanly treasure at the juncture of her slender white thighs.

Rachel bit at her lower lip to stifle a scream when she reached the very pinnacle of rapturous fulfillment, but she could not prevent a soft, unintelligible cry from escaping her lips as she collapsed weakly atop Logan. His final pleasure followed quickly after hers, leaving him equally languorous and short of breath, but feeling wondrously peaceful and contented. He gently pulled her down beside him, his arm pillowing her head and his lips tenderly brushing against her temple.

"My little wildcat," he remarked in a quiet, husky tone as a faint smile of irony played about his lips. "Hell, Mrs. MacBride, I hope we always resolve our differences in such a gratifying manner!" He gave a low, appreciative chuckle at the thought, his bare chest quaking ever so slightly beneath Rachel's softly flushed cheek.

She said nothing in response, for the simple reason that she could think of nothing to say. What had just passed between herself and Logan had only served to toss her into further confusion. She was stunned by the profound feelings of tenderness and affection she was experiencing—affection for the same handsome, green-eyed rogue who had taunted her, humiliated her, and very likely betrayed her. How could she possibly be feeling so generous toward him all of a sudden? Was it simply because of the fact that he was an attentive and accomplished lover, because he had initiated her into the wonders of her own femininity with such marvelous patience and dexterity?

No, she mentally concluded as she heaved an inward

sigh, it was more than that. She knew that her heart was involved as well. Although she had been guarding against it from the first moment she encountered Logan MacBride, she could no longer deny the fact that he had found a place in her heart. To what extent, she had not yet discerned. But, like it or not, he was now an integral part of her life . . .

"Much as I'd like to remain here with my wife's naked body against mine for the rest of my life, I'm afraid we're both going to require nourishment and shelter by the time night falls," teased Logan, flashing her a brief, disarming grin as he hugged her close. "It's getting late. We don't want to be caught out here once the sun goes down." Summoning all his strength of will, he set her away from him and stood to begin dressing. He was puzzled by her continued silence, but he attributed it to the belief that she was more than a little taken aback by the explosive intimacy the two of them had just shared. He knew her well enough to realize that she was still bewildered, and a bit horrified, by her own passionate responses to his lovemaking. On the whole, however, things were progressing much better than he might have hoped. Although he was still furious with her for riding out alone, he was both delighted and encouraged by what had followed. Soon, he told himself as he fastened his trousers, soon she would acknowledge what he already knew . . .

Rachel was dismayed to feel her whole body coloring rosily as Logan turned a closely scrutinizing look upon her. Still maintaining her silence, she hastily climbed to her feet and bent to retrieve her shirt. She clutched the flannel garment to her bosom and straightened with a loud gasp in the next instant, thoroughly shocked to feel her husband's lips paying tribute to the small birthmark on her right hip. Rounding on him as he leisurely drew himself up to his full height again, she blushed to the roots of her honey-colored hair and indignantly sputtered, "Why, how . . . how dare you!"

"I've been wanting to do that ever since I set eyes on that damnably alluring little clover of yours," confessed Logan, noticeably unrepentant as his green eyes twinkled with devilish amusement. He laughed softly when she shot him a withering glare before whirling about to jerk on the flannel shirt.

Once the two of them were finally riding homeward, Rachel permitted herself a surreptitious glance at the tall, wholly masculine man astride the magnificent black stallion beside her. He had not mentioned Vance again, had not questioned her any further regarding the distasteful incident his arrival had thankfully interrupted. He had, however, cautioned her quite severely against leaving the ranch unescorted ever again, promising dire consequences if she dared to disobey him.

Logan turned his head and met Rachel's troubled look. What he did next was quite unexpected . . . and quite alarming, due to the floodtide of emotions it provoked within her breast.

Leaning over to take control of her reins, he forced her mount to a halt while Vulcan, obediently following the single command issued by his master's voice, slowed to a halt as well. Before a breathless Rachel could ask what had prompted his sudden action, Logan leaned across the short distance separating them and pressed a kiss of agonizing sweetness upon her startled lips. Then, favoring her only with a slow, enigmatic smile, he administered a light slap of his hand to her horse's rump.

Rachel grabbed hold of the saddlehorn as her mount surged forward again, with Logan's following immediately afterward.

In an amazingly short amount of time, they were back at the Circle M and drawing rein before the stable. She did not protest when he reached up to assist her down from the saddle, and she raised wide, shining eyes to his face when her feet met the ground and he did not release her, his hands lingering upon her until a familiar voice broke the spell.

Rachel jerked guiltily away from Logan, an expression of stunned disbelief on her beautiful countenance as she spun about to take note of the young woman, calico skirts flying immodestly and coppery braids streaming wildly behind, racing toward her.

"Lizzie!" she breathed.

XII

"Rachel! Jumping Jehoshaphat, Rachel, where have you been?" demanded the petite redhead as she launched herself at her sister and enveloped her in a rib-cracking bear hug.

"Lizzie, what are you doing here?" Rachel dazedly questioned, embracing the girl warmly before drawing away to peer anxiously down into her lightly freckled visage. "Oh, Lizzie, is something wrong? Micah, Grandmother, are they—"

"They're fine," the vivacious adolescent hastened to assure her. "I simply came to pay you a visit." Before Rachel could ask how she had ever managed to convince Micah to allow such a thing, Lizzie's youthful brow creased into a frown, her brown eyes flashing as she once again demanded, "Where have you been? Brodie and I got here nearly an hour ago! Everyone was talking about how you suddenly up and disappeared, and how that she-wolf's precious horse was missing, and how that husband of yours and most of the hands lit out to look for you just as soon as they got back from Crow Rock, and how they found you with Vance MacBride and—" Here she paused to mistrustfully eye the tall man behind her sister whose green eyes twinkled disarmingly across at her. "And how *he* said he'd bring you home! Confound it, Rachel, I was worried sick about you!" she finished with a reproachful look at her older sister.

"I . . . I'm sorry," Rachel murmured weakly, hastily averting her gaze as a vivid recollection of the reason for her tardiness in returning to the ranch flashed into her mind. Her cheeks flamed, and she was acutely conscious of the fact that Lizzie was fairly bursting with curiosity. Wondering how in the world she was going to explain the unbelievable, tempestuous events of the past twenty-four hours to her sister, she was drawn from her turbulent reverie when Logan finally uttered in a negligent tone that nonetheless made his words more of a command than a suggestion, "The two of you go on inside. You'll no doubt be wanting to rest up a bit before supper. Cora serves it promptly at seven, and anyone who dares to be late pays the price with a cold meal in the kitchen." Rachel turned to face him, only to find herself thoroughly nonplussed when he winked roguishly at her before leading the horses into the stable.

"Thunderation, Rachel, what's going on around here?" queried Lizzie in a strident whisper as Logan disappeared inside the log structure. "And what the devil are you doing dressed like that?"

Rachel sighed heavily and replied, "I'll try and explain once we're inside." Her perplexity was quite evident as she drew the girl's arm through hers and began crossing the yard toward the house. She was painfully aware of the inquisitive stares directed at them by the men who stood talking to one another near the bunkhouse and corral, and her discomfort only increased when she spied Moira standing on the front porch. The brunette's pale green eyes glittered viperously, and her full lips curled upward in a gesture of malicious amusement as she braced a hand on one of the porch columns with studied nonchalance and told Rachel, "I knew they'd find you sooner or later. I just wasn't sure whether you'd be alive or dead."

"I hope you're not too terribly disappointed with the outcome," Rachel couldn't resist parrying in a tone laced with sarcasm. She resolutely ignored Moira after that and climbed the steps with Lizzie, who momentarily hung back to shoot a murderous glare at the woman she had immediately recognized as an adversary. Moira's soft, scornful laugh followed them as they stepped inside the house.

"Rachel!" Aunt Tess's voice rang out in obvious relief as the two sisters crossed the threshold. Poised in the center of the staircase with Robert Pearson close behind, she immediately quickened her descent in order to embrace her new niece with genuine affection. "Oh my dear, we were so distressed over your disappearance! Thank heavens you are safely home again!" She could not prevent her gaze from flickering briefly over Rachel's trouser-clad form when she drew away, but she politely refrained from offering any comment on the younger woman's startling attire.

"Young lady, you gave us quite a scare," Uncle Robert declared in mock reproof, then smiled broadly as he reached the foot of the staircase and moved to put an arm about the shoulders of both sisters. "I must say, things are certainly starting to get lively around here—it's about time, too. Why, it's been nearly a month since I came West, and this day has been the most exciting yet!

And now we not only have the pleasure of welcoming Logan's bride, but her charming sister as well," he remarked with a quiet chuckle, his gaze shifting in turn to each of them.

"Come, Robert," Aunt Tess amiably insisted, her hand gently closing upon his arm and urging him in the direction of the parlor with her. "I'm quite certain these poor girls are exhausted! As you said, the day has been full of excitement. The least we can do is allow them some much-needed privacy and repose."

"Of course," Uncle Robert unhesitantly concurred, bestowing one last benevolent smile on them before gallantly escorting Tess toward the sunlit room to their left. Tess glanced back at Rachel, who sent her a look of warm gratitude, and said, "I'll see that your sister is made comfortable in a room of her own after supper, my dear."

Once the two older people had disappeared into the parlor, Rachel wasted no time in leading Lizzie up the stairs to her bedroom, where they immediately began a discussion of all that had occurred since Rachel's anguished departure from her family the previous day. The first thing Lizzie demanded to know was exactly where her sister had disappeared to that afternoon.

"I had to be alone, so I went for a ride," explained Rachel, sinking wearily down upon the bed and removing Logan's hat so that her bright curls spilled unrestrainedly down her back. Lizzie perched on the edge of the trunk and wrapped an arm about the bedpost.

"Only you forgot to tell anyone, didn't you?" the redhead sternly accused, as if she were the elder of the two. "Oh Rachel, no matter how much you despise Logan MacBride, you can't just go off whenever you please and leave everyone to wonder if you've been carried off by

Indians or—"

"Please, Lizzie, I . . . I don't need lectures from *you*, of all people!" Abruptly rising from the bed, she moved in noticeable agitation to the window. "You don't understand. Nothing has worked out quite the way I had anticipated."

"I'd say that's pretty obvious," Lizzie noted wryly. "How does that snake in the grass, Vance MacBride, fit into all this?" she then unexpectedly queried, closely scrutinizing her sister's reaction as Rachel spun about and began distractedly pacing beside the bed.

"All too prominently, I'm afraid! Too late, it occurred to me that he and Logan may have conspired together to trick me into this marriage, with the sole purpose of regaining control of Micah's property. Apparently, they weren't prepared to face a murder charge in the event of his death, so they formulated an alternate plan, one in which I so foolishly agreed to become a participant! Because of my marriage to Logan, the land remains a part of the precious MacBride empire. And because I can't bear the thought of Micah knowing the truth, I am a virtual prisoner in Logan MacBride's house!"

"You know," remarked Lizzie, frowning thoughtfully as she pondered all that her sister had revealed, "though I don't know much about him, Logan MacBride just doesn't strike me as the sort of man who would stoop to such tactics. He seems to be a pretty forthright sort of character, Rachel—not devious and underhanded like that cousin of his. Are you certain he and Vance are in league with one another on this?"

"Not entirely," confessed Rachel, startled to realize how very desperately she hoped her suspicions would be proven wrong. She suddenly recalled how Vance had purposely goaded Logan by forcing that kiss on her. It certainly hadn't looked as if the two MacBride cousins were on such friendly terms *then!* Another long sigh escaped her lips as she resumed her seat on the bed. "To tell the truth, I'm not certain about anything anymore!"

The two of them lapsed into pensive silence for several moments, Lizzie remaining balanced on the trunk while Rachel stood and quickly divested herself of Logan's jacket, shirt, and trousers. Wrinkling her nose in distaste, she reluctantly began to don Moira's velvet wrapper when her eyes caught sight of her recently delivered bags on the floor beside the mirrored wardrobe. She tossed the insulting garment aside and hastened to search through one of the leather valises for her own wrapper, which she luckily found among the clothing near the top of the bag. It wasn't until she was tying the sash about her waist that she finally remembered to ask her sister, "How on earth did you manage to persuade Micah to let you come?" A mischievous smile spread across Lizzie's attractive, round-cheeked features.

"He'll never own up to it, but he was every bit as worried about you as Grandmother and I were—though their anxiety was for entirely different reasons than mine, of course. Since I alone was aware of the fact that you had been forced to come here against your will, I knew you'd need me to provide moral support until we could think of a way to get you out of this mess."

"You've no idea how accurately that particular term describes my predicament," Rachel commented with a rueful little smile. Quite touched by her sister's concern, and experiencing another sharp twinge of homesickness, she battled a fresh onslaught of tears as she moved to place an arm about Lizzie's shoulders. "What exactly did you tell them?"

"Well, Grandmother and I were in the kitchen talking about you, and Micah didn't realize that I was well aware of the fact that he was eavesdropping on our conversation just outside the back door, which I'd purposely left open when I saw him coming out of the barn and heading toward the house. As soon as I told Grandmother how worried I was about you—being away from your loved ones for the first time in all these years and married to a man we still knew nothing about—she started crying again and told me she hadn't slept a wink all night and that she was certain Micah hadn't, either. She said she kept thinking about her 'darling girl' going off to 'God only knows what sort of place' with Logan MacBride, and that she'd never be able to rest easy until she knew you were all right. That's when Micah came barreling into the kitchen," Lizzie disclosed with a self-congratulatory grin.

"What did he do?" asked Rachel, her eyes growing very round.

"Exactly what I'd been counting on him doing. He acted angry as all get-out and said he figured that if we were ever going to 'have peace around the blasted place again,' he'd 'damned sure go and find out' how MacBride was treating you. And he would have, too, Rachel—he'd have come himself if I hadn't made the timely announcement of my own plans. I lied and told him you had begged me to come stay with you for a spell, and that you and I had already agreed that, with his permission, I would travel back to Logan's ranch with whoever came to collect your things." An endearingly crooked smile lit the youthful planes of her face as her gaze met her older sister's. "Micah loves you, you know. Grandmother wasn't fooled by his anger any more than I was. In the end, he had no choice but to agree to let me come."

Rachel swallowed a sudden lump in her throat and responded with a rather watery smile of her own before questioning, "But what about Brodie? What was his reaction when—"

"First off, I can't tell you how relieved I was to see that it *was* Brodie who came driving up in that wagon! I don't think Micah would have let me come at all if Logan's man hadn't turned out to be someone they knew and trusted. Since Brodie was the one who rescued me and Grandmother from Vance's henchmen the night Micah almost got hanged, I suppose they felt I'd be safe enough with him. Besides," she added with an irrepressible twinkle of her lively brown eyes, "Micah followed on horseback most of the way here. He didn't turn back until we were in sight of the Circle M."

"Oh, Lizzie," Rachel murmured with yet another sigh, her heart feeling quite heavy as she moved away and wandered aimlessly back to the window.

"Oh, and as for Brodie's reaction upon learning he would be transporting not only your bags but a passenger as well—he was admittedly a bit taken aback at first, but there really wasn't any way he could refuse!" Lizzie giggled softly at the recollection and observed, "You know, for a boy, Brodie MacBride isn't a half-bad sort, is he?"

"He isn't a boy, Lizzie," Rachel corrected with a deep frown. "He's a grown man. And hasn't it occurred to you yet that Brodie may not have been so heroic the night of Vance's attack upon Micah after all? What happened that night may have been nothing more than a well-calculated series of highly convincing theatrics!"

"That can't be true!" Lizzie adamantly disagreed, hot

color tinging her cheeks as she jumped to her feet and crossed her arms tightly against her still-blossoming breasts. "Brodie MacBride wouldn't take part in such a dastardly scheme! If you knew him like I do, you wouldn't think of accusing him of—"

"Please, Lizzie, let's not quarrel among ourselves," pleaded Rachel. Bewildered by her sister's spirited defense of a young man who was little more than a stranger, she nonetheless cast the stormy-faced redhead a conciliatory smile and said, "Now that you're here, things will be a lot easier to bear." Lizzie, immediately contrite over her outburst, hurried across the carpeted floor to hug Rachel close again.

"You know I'll help you any way I can. Since I've already had occasion to meet the others living here, I have a pretty good idea what you're up against!" Her face wore an expressive grimace when she drew away and remarked, "Uncle Robert and Aunt Tess seem nice enough, but Mrs. Smith is obviously something of an ogre, and that black-haired witch named Moira made it clear from the outset that she'd just as soon I went back home and took you with me. I'm looking forward to knocking her square off her high horse!" Rachel couldn't help smiling in response, and her spirits were considerably higher as she headed toward the bathroom.

"Would you care to bathe before supper, Lizzie?" she inquired over her shoulder.

"No thanks. You go ahead. I'll wait until after we eat." Lizzie followed close on her older sister's heels, leaning negligently against the door frame while Rachel bent over to turn the faucets above the tub. "I may as well share your bedroom. That way, we'll have plenty of time to put our heads together and formulate a plan to get you back home."

Rachel's hands froze on the ornate brass knobs. Dismayed to feel herself blushing crimson, she endeavored to hide her sudden discomfiture by declaring in an offhanded manner, "It would probably be for the best if you had your own quarters. I'm sure you'd be much more comfortable that way. This house is quite large, with half a dozen or more empty bedrooms, and Aunt Tess would no doubt be quite disappointed if you denied her the opportunity to make you welcome in one." How in heaven's name could she explain to her sister that Logan MacBride would most certainly not allow anyone to share his wife's room for the simple reason that he might feel inclined to pay his bride another nocturnal visit? Lizzie still believed her marriage to Logan to be in name only. How was she going to break the news of her body's humiliating betrayal to the innocent and impressionable fourteen-year-old who stood frowning at her in mild bemusement?

"Then she'll have to be disappointed, because I fully intend to remain close beside you at all times, sister dear. The two of us will show these confounded MacBrides that we Parkers have more than enough backbone to stand up to anyone who threatens us!"

Groaning inwardly, Rachel straightened and forced herself to meet Lizzie's bright gaze. She tried in vain to think of a delicate way to explain things, to spare herself as much embarrassment as possible, but she finally heaved a sigh of resignation and haltingly revealed, "I . . . I'm sorry, Lizzie, but, as I said, things haven't quite turned out the way I had planned. Unfortunately, my . . . my relationship with Logan took an unexpected turn." She could feel her face turning scarlet, and she hastily looked away. Lizzie, apparently not yet having grasped the meaning of her sister's disclosure, probed a bit impatiently, "What the Sam Hill are you talking about?"

"I'm trying to tell you that . . . that Logan and I . . . well, we're . . . we are truly man and wife!" Rachel finished in a mortified rush. Mentally consigning Logan MacBride to the devil for all the turmoil he had wrought in her life, she raised her eyes to Lizzie's visibly dumfounded countenance and explained in a manner which implored the petite redhead to try and understand, "Oh Lizzie, I'm so confused! My head has been spinning ever since Logan brought me here! It had never occurred to me that I would have to live with him, and I had certainly never counted on . . . on . . ."

"On falling in love with him?" Lizzie quietly finished for her. Rachel gasped and instantly denied it.

"How could you possibly think I would lose my heart to such a . . . a domineering, arrogant scoundrel?"

"Land's sakes, Rachel, why else would you let him—"

"I don't know!" she exclaimed, her color much heightened again and her voice rising on a shrill note. Whirling back around, she reached down and gave a furious tug on the faucet handles, sending a forceful stream of water pouring forth into the bathtub with a roar. "I honestly don't know!" she repeated, her fingers curling tightly about the top edge of the large porcelain tub.

Lizzie stared long and hard at the beautiful, noticeably distressed blonde before turning slowly about and leaving her to her bath. Still feeling a bit stunned by her sister's confession, she plopped down onto the bed and stretched out upon her back with her hands crossed beneath her head.

Rachel had certainly made a muddle of things! she mused in sisterly annoyance. Why, if left to her own resources, there was no telling what other "complications" she might interject into the already touchy situation! And just how the devil did Logan MacBride fit into the picture? Lizzie then wondered, her brow creasing into another reflective frown. Now that he had taken advantage of Rachel—she did not doubt for one second that it had been entirely his fault—would he still be willing to let his wife return home and seek a divorce? Would he perhaps consider allowing such a thing before the six months' time limit he and Rachel had agreed upon? And what would her grandparents say if Rachel deserted her husband after only a few short days of marriage?

"Hell's bells, it looks like I came none too soon!" she muttered aloud. She rolled onto her stomach and propped her chin up with her hands, her feet dangling off the edge of the canopied four-poster as she set about trying to think of a way to extricate Rachel from her present difficulty.

Supper that evening was quite an animated affair. Both Uncle Robert and Aunt Tess did an admirable job of preventing the conversation from lagging, Moira did her best to antagonize Rachel, Lizzie determinedly pursued a discussion of a ranch foreman's duties with a somewhat reluctant Brodie, Rachel paid scant attention to anyone but her husband as her eyes continually strayed in his direction, and Logan watched the proceedings with an expression of mild amusement on his ruggedly handsome face, his own unfathomable gaze traveling frequently to where Rachel sat at the opposite end of the long table.

Following the meal, everyone adhered to the time-honored tradition of gathering in the parlor for more conversation and, for the gentlemen, brandy and cigars. Only Uncle Robert chose to indulge in smoking, while Logan poured drinks for himself and the other two men. Aunt Tess drew Rachel and Lizzie down beside her on a chintz-covered settee as Moira drifted to take a pose near the massive stone fireplace, where a well-laid blaze emitted a comforting warmth and bathed the room in a soft golden glow.

"How did that business up at Crow Rock turn out?" Uncle Robert asked Logan, choosing a seat opposite the settee and watching as his nephew took the chair next to his.

"We found some evidence of brand blotting, but little else. Whoever these particular rustlers are, they're either a craftier bunch than we've had in these parts before or they've somehow managed to infiltrate several of the outfits around here." His intense gaze lit upon Rachel as he leisurely swirled the brandy around in the crystal snifter. She flushed and was forced to apologize to Aunt Tess for her inattention to the older woman's inquiries about her family.

"You mean you aren't able to keep someone from stealing your cattle?" questioned Lizzie in disbelief, much more interested in the masculine topics of conversation.

"With a herd numbering in the tens of thousands and a customary range covering literally millions of acres, it's no easy task to prevent our stock from being driven off or our brand from being altered," Brodie obligingly pointed out. He was rewarded for his trouble with a saucy grin from Lizzie, which so discomfited him that he hastily averted his gaze and cleared his throat.

"My grandfather said he'd heard the only way a man out here could keep possession of his range was to stock it to the limit. And I remember him mentioning something about 'grass pirates' and 'sooners.' What are those, Brodie?" persisted Lizzie, bound and determined to pay homage to his superior knowledge of the cattle business. The raven-haired young man gently cleared his throat again and explained with exaggerated patience, "A grass pirate is someone who comes along and shoves the stock that's already there off the range to make room for his own. A man's called a sooner when he rounds up his stock before anyone else, so he can gather up all the mavericks for himself and put his brand on them."

"Perhaps *dear* Miss Parker finds the subject of rustlers and the like so fascinating because her grandfather falls into that same general category," Moira startled everyone by commenting with smooth acidity. Logan turned a fierce scowl upon her, but Rachel was the first to react verbally.

"How dare you!" she uttered, her opal eyes flashing in righteous indignation as she abruptly stood in order to confront the spiteful brunette on an equal level. "My grandfather happens to be one of the finest, most honorable men who ever lived!"

"So honorable that he'd steal a ranch right out from under a man he hanged?" accused Moira. Aunt Tess gasped and raised a trembling hand to her throat, while Lizzie shot to her feet and furiously cried, "Why, you hag-faced witch, Micah Parker never stole a thing in his life!"

"No?" the other woman challenged with biting sarcasm. "I overheard some of the hands talking about what happened back in Wyoming, *dear* Miss Parker, and—"

"That's enough!" decreed Logan, his voice ringing out with authoritative clarity. He, too, had risen to his feet, and he wasted no more time before striding forward and seizing Moira's arm in a none too gentle grip. "I'm well aware of the fact that you've been doing your absolute best to ruin the evening, Moira. Now either you apologize to my wife and her sister, or you can damn well go to your room and stay there!"

"Apologize for *what?*" she sneered, jerking her arm from his grasp. "For daring to tell the truth? You may be able to intimidate everyone else on this ranch into keeping it a secret, but it's going to come out sooner or later! You've married into quite a family, Logan, a family of murderers, thieves, and scheming little strumpets—" Her words ended on a sharp intake of breath when he took hold of her arm again and forcibly escorted her from the room. Rachel and Lizzie sank back down onto the settee beside Aunt Tess, and no one spoke until the sound of a door slamming upstairs a few seconds later broke the expectant silence in the parlor.

"Moira is a bit high-strung, I'm afraid," sighed Aunt Tess, smiling rather lamely at Rachel.

"High-strung? I should think 'ungovernably rude and temperamental' would more aptly describe the young lady in question," casually opined Uncle Robert, puffing on his cigar and disregarding the sternly quelling look from Tess his candor earned him.

"I don't care *what* she is," asserted Lizzie, "she has no right to say those things about us! My grandfather was only acting in the line of duty when he arrested Tate MacBride for murder!"

"Lizzie, please!" Rachel admonished. She could feel Aunt Tess stiffening beside her, could see the way Uncle Robert shifted uncomfortably in his chair and the way the golden smoothness of Brodie's forehead creased into a deep frown.

"And how in tarnation was Micah to know when he bought the ranch that its previous owner would end up at the end of a rope?" Lizzie obstinately expounded.

"I don't think it's doing anyone any good to keep talking about it," Brodie declared in a low voice, his dark eyes narrowing ever so slightly as they fastened upon the young redhead. She bristled beneath what she perceived to be his unwarranted censure, but any defiant response she might have offered was prevented by Logan's return. His long, easy stride carried him toward the settee, where he paused before Lizzie. A brief smile crossed his handsome countenance as she stared mutely up at him.

"Sorry your first night here turned out to be so unpleasant, little sister," he told her, his sea-green eyes dancing with amusement when she rudely retorted, "I'm *not* your little sister!"

Aunt Tess appeared quite shocked by Lizzie's ill-mannered response to her host, while Rachel was torn between laughter and embarrassment. Her confusion only increased when Logan turned to her and lazily drawled, "There's certainly no mistaking the resemblance between the two of you, sweetheart." Both Uncle Robert and Brodie chuckled softly, and Aunt Tess finally relaxed and smiled once more. Rachel, dismayed to feel the color rising to her face as Logan's gaze swept intimately over her, was surprised when he moved to take her hand and draw her to her feet. Since she could not gracefully resist, she found herself standing perilously close before him, and it seemed that his gleaming eyes mocked her for the sudden irregularity of her breathing. "It's time for us to turn in, dear wife. We're going to make an early start of it in the morning."

"An early start of *what?*" Rachel demanded with forced politeness, trying unsuccessfully to free her hand from his.

"I know how anxious you are to see more of the ranch, so we're going to devote the better part of the morning to doing just that," he informed her, only the ghost of a smile playing about his lips.

"What time do *we* need to be ready?" asked Lizzie, jumping up and looping her arm through Rachel's. There was an impudently challenging expression on her youthful features, and her eyes silently dared Logan to deny her participation in the expedition he had just proposed. Deciding to charge ahead and take things a step further, she staunchly declared, "My sister and I still have a great deal to talk about, so it is indeed time we retired to *our* room."

"Oh, but my dear," Aunt Tess hastened to intervene after casting a solicitous look in her nephew's direction, "I have prepared a separate room for you only a short distance away in another wing." She smiled maternally up at Lizzie. "There will be ample time for you and your sister to visit in the—"

"A separate room? Why, I don't think I should like that at all!" protested Lizzie. Feigning distress, she asserted, "It's my first night here, and the house is still terribly unfamiliar to me, and I . . . I'm not at all accustomed to being away from home, and I'd really feel so much better if I could remain with my dear sister!" She inched even closer to Rachel for emphasis. Only a faint spark of humor in Logan's eyes betrayed his knowing appreciation of her tactics. Rachel, mentally applauding both her sister's ingenuity and tenacity, stole a surreptitious glance up at her husband and caught her breath upon a soft gasp when she discovered his penetrating gaze turned upon herself.

"But, my dear, you don't understand," Logan's aunt felt it her duty to point out. She smiled again and explained, "Your sister and her husband are but newly married, and—"

"It's all right, Aunt Tess," Logan finally decreed. He released Rachel's hand at last and schooled his features to remain perfectly solemn as he cautioned Lizzie, "Don't talk too far into the night, *little sister*, for we ride out at dawn." Turning back to a startled Rachel, he could not prevent a note of amusement from tinging the deep resonance of his voice when, lowering his head and gently taking hold of her arms, he murmured so softly that only she could hear, "A night's reprieve, wildcat—but only a night's." She did not have time to offer him a reply before he enveloped her in a possessive embrace, his warm lips claiming hers in a tender yet thoroughly stimulating kiss that sent an undeniable flame of desire coursing through her from top to toe. It took several long seconds after he released her for her to recall the fact that there were witnesses to this display of husbandly affection, and her opal eyes flashed with a combination of embarrassment, indignation . . . and a perplexing sense of disappointment. Covering her confusion with an attitude of rigid composure, she fixed Logan with a look that would freeze lesser men and uttered in a voice as totally devoid of warmth as her demeanor, "Good night, *Mr. MacBride.*" She managed to bid Aunt Tess, Uncle Robert, and Brodie a courteous good-night, then swept regally from the parlor with Lizzie in tow.

"You've a charming and beautiful wife, Logan, my boy," Uncle Robert proclaimed after the sisters had gone. He downed the last of his brandy, a broad grin spreading across his mature, aristocratic features as he added, "And I'm happy to see she isn't the sort who'll let you force your will on her at every turn. Yes sir, my boy, I always knew you needed a woman with spirit, one who would stand up to you and keep you from getting too damned cocky!" Brodie nearly choked on the mouthful of brandy he was in the process of swallowing. He coughed vigorously and wiped the back of his hand across his mouth.

"Hell, if either she or that sister of hers had any more spirit, the menfolk around here would end up with about as much power as a one-legged bull!" Although Robert laughed heartily at the remark, Logan was prompted to stifle the chuckle which rose in his throat when Aunt Tess frowned quite severely at the three and rose from the settee to offer a stern rebuke.

"Shame on all of you! That is *not* the manner in which you should be discussing those dear girls!"

"And why not?" challenged Robert with another unabashed grin, his gaze moving admiringly over Tess's attractive face and petite yet well-rounded figure. "We've done no more than make an observation about the newest members of the MacBride clan. But, as delightful as they are, they can't hold a candle to you, Tess Shelley." Appearing unaccountably flustered by the compliment, Tess hastily excused herself and left the room. Robert followed a short time afterward, leaving Logan and Brodie alone in the cozy, firelit parlor.

"What was that about riding out in the morning?" Brodie casually questioned his older cousin, taking a seat in the chair Robert had just vacated while Logan moved to take a stance before the fireplace. "I thought you'd planned on the two of us going on into town to set up another meeting of the Cattlemen's Association."

"I had. But the plans have changed." Logan stared deeply into the dancing, yellow-orange flames, his mind filled with images of Rachel as she had looked that afternoon when the two of them made love beneath the trees—every inch a woman, a woman of beauty and passion and courage. His woman.

"The plans aren't the only things changing around here," muttered Brodie, frowning in irritation at the recent turn of events. He was surprised to hear the other man's soft laugh.

"You'll acquire a perfect understanding of the reasons in a few more years. Because, like it or not, the first thing a woman does when she enters your life is change it. You can fight against it tooth and nail, Brodie, but it won't do you a damned bit of good. Not a damned bit of good." The fire cast intriguing shadows upon the planes of Logan's ruggedly handsome face, and his magnificent green eyes reflected the shower of sparks that signaled an abrupt shifting of the burning logs.

"Then I'll just have to make certain no woman gets the chance to try!" the younger man retorted. He was none too pleased when a faintly smiling Logan turned to him in the next moment and revealed, "By the way, you'll be riding out with us in the morning."

"Damn it, Logan, the last thing I want to do is play

nursemaid to that little—"

"I think I'll hit the hay, too. See you at breakfast." With that, he sauntered from the room. Brodie muttered a curse beneath his breath and marched swiftly out of the house to his quarters beside the bunkhouse, ignoring the group of cowpunchers waiting outside to tease him about having supper with so many attractive young females.

Upstairs in the main house, Lizzie was just finishing her bath. Rachel had already undressed and donned a fresh white nightgown, and her delicately arched eyebrows drew into a frown as she lay upon the canopied bed and thought of Logan.

Why had he given in so easily to Lizzie's demands regarding the sleeping arrangements that night? And why did the fact that he *had* agreed so readily sting both her pride and her heart?

Perhaps he didn't object because he was planning to seek consolation in the arms of another woman, an inner voice suddenly taunted. *Moira.*

"No!" Rachel emphatically rejected the suggestion.

"What was that?" called Lizzie. She strolled from the bathroom, still rubbing at her damp hair with a fluffy, oversized towel. "Did you say something?"

"No, I . . . I . . ." stammered Rachel, then firmly directed, "Come to bed, Lizzie. It's getting late!" She rolled to her side and pounded at the unresisting softness of her pillow.

Once she and her sister were settled in bed, Rachel did her best to clear her mind and relax into slumber, but sleep persistently eluded her. She tried changing positions a number of times, but to no avail. After listening to the sound of Lizzie's gentle breathing for what seemed like hours, she suddenly became aware of voices, two voices which were undeniably raised in anger, drifting outward from Logan's room. And one of the voices sounded suspiciously like Moira's . . .

Moira! Rachel came bolt upright in the bed. Moira was in Logan's bedroom! Why, Logan was alone with that she-devil . . . in the middle of the night . . . with his own wife in the very next room. The awful thought had become reality. A knot tightened in the pit of her stomach as a sharp, unbidden image of Logan and his attractive cousin in the midst of such an intimate setting insinuated itself into her mind. It certainly didn't require a great deal of imagination to guess what the two of them were very likely doing!

At the same time a deep pain settled in her heart, Rachel instinctively followed the overpowering impulse which seized her. Taking care not to awaken Lizzie, she eased from beneath the covers, slid off the mattress, and padded barefoot across the carpeted floor. She hurriedly opened the door to the bathroom, then pulled it to behind her. Creeping close to the opposite door, the one which led directly into Logan's chambers, she held her breath and waited for the occupants of the other room to exchange further heated comments such as the ones she had overheard but hadn't quite been able to make out . . .

"You're making a fool of yourself, Moira, and I'll be damned if I'll let you make a fool of me as well!" Logan ground out, his sea-green eyes blazing down at the half-dressed woman before him. "If you're going to continue living in this house, you're going to do as I say!"

"And what if I *don't?*" Moira impetuously dared, dropping her hands to her sides so that the unfastened front edges of her silk wrapper gaped strategically. She wore nothing underneath the clinging silk.

"Then you can pack your things and leave!" His smoldering gaze dropped to her revealed form for only the fraction of a second before his hands shot out to yank the wrapper closed and jerk the sash tight about her waist. "Now get out of my room!"

"You won't send me away! You'd never choose that pale little ninny over your own family!" She was nonplussed when the savage gleam in his eyes was replaced by a softer glow, his firm, chiseled lips curving into a faint smile as he proclaimed in a low, vibrant tone, "Rachel *is* my family now." Moira's throat constricted at the note of tenderness in Logan's voice when he spoke his wife's name. No! she frantically told herself. He couldn't love Rachel, he couldn't!

"You can't mean that! What about your own flesh and blood? You're a MacBride, aren't you? We MacBrides hold blood ties as sacred!"

"As Dugan MacBride's son, I'm an expert on the beliefs and traditions of our clan, Moira," drawled Logan, one dark eyebrow lifting mockingly. "Why else, other than to fulfill my responsibilities, would I have taken you in when you suddenly decided life with your father was intolerable?"

"Because you loved me! You've always loved me, Logan MacBride, and you always will!" In a desperate attempt to prove her point, she flung herself upon his chest, her arms coiling almost convulsively about his neck. "It doesn't matter about *her!* Make love to me, Logan! Make love to me and you'll see—" She broke off on a gasp when his strong hands reached up to seize her wrists in a bruising grip, his handsome features becoming a mask of barely suppressed fury. He forced her arms from about his neck and set her away from him as if the contact repulsed him.

"For the last time, Moira—either you treat my wife with respect, or you can damn well go back and live with your father. If it's true that he treated you so badly—and I have my doubts as to the severity of what you described—then maybe it was no better than you deserved!"

"You're still punishing me because of what happened between me and Vance, aren't you?" she charged, her pale green eyes narrowing into mere slits of vengeful rage. "That's why you married that little bitch, isn't it?"

"I don't give a damn who you choose to 'ensnare'—whether it's Vance or some other poor bastard—just as long as your conquests don't bring disgrace on this family. Your blasted selfishness almost tore the clan apart! If your father hadn't been so willing to take you back when Vance kicked you out—"

"He didn't kick me out!" Moira hotly denied. "I knew I'd made a mistake right from the beginning! I only ran off with him because you wouldn't listen to reason, because you acted so cruel! You hurt me terribly, and I . . . I didn't know what else to do!"

"Go to bed, Moira," Logan commanded in a quiet, dangerously calm tone, his eyes glittering coldly. "Go back to your room and make your decision." Moira searched his face for any evidence of yielding, but found none.

"Damn you!" she seethed. "Damn you, you heartless son of a bitch!" She lifted her hand to strike him, but his own hand moved with lightning-quick speed to prevent the blow. His fingers tightened painfully upon her wrist for only a moment before abruptly releasing it. Rubbing at her abused flesh, she shot him one last venomous glare before spinning about and storming from the room, slamming the door with resounding force behind her.

Rachel, meanwhile, turned numbly about and leaned back against the bathroom door for support. Stunned by what she had heard, she raised trembling fingers to her mouth and blinked slowly several times as if in a daze.

Logan had come to her defense, had clearly defined her position in his household. *Rachel is my family,* he had said, indicating that his wife was even more important than his own flesh and blood. Perhaps he had made such a statement purely for Moira's benefit, as some sort of retaliation for his cousin's disobedience. But, on the other hand, perhaps he had meant it . . . she was startled to feel the inexplicable soaring of her spirits at the thought.

Unbelievable as it seemed, he had resisted Moira's advances. But why? Why hadn't he taken advantage of what had been so blatantly offered? Was it indeed possible that he and Moira had never shared the same wondrous ecstasy he had shared with her?

Rachel was jolted from her silent reverie when the door upon which she leaned was suddenly thrown open from the other side. A soft, breathless cry escaped her lips as she fell backward. Two powerfully muscled arms caught her before she hit the floor, and she gasped to find herself being hauled unceremoniously upright before her husband.

"I wouldn't have believed you capable of such mischief, 'Clover'," he lazily drawled, favoring her with a sardonic grin. His green eyes were alight with roguish amusement.

"I . . . I was just . . ." she faltered, blushing fierily in embarrassment. Feeling much like a naughty schoolgirl, she pushed feebly at the hands which still clasped her about the waist, but he did not relinquish his hold. She was acutely conscious of the fact that she wore only a diaphanous cotton nightgown, for she could feel the heat of those strong fingers upon her thinly protected skin.

"You were just coming to kiss me good night, is that it?" supplied Logan, an affectionately teasing note in his deep voice. He had not known of her presence in the bathroom before opening the door. Though he wondered how much she had overheard of his confrontation with Moira, he did not broach the subject. The fact that she had obviously been drawn to eavesdrop pleased him, for he knew that she would not have done so if she did not care. The thought of her being jealous provoked a wealth of satisfaction within him!

"Of course not! Now, will you be so kind as to let me return to my bed?" she stiffly requested, doing her best to conceal the way her entire body quivered at his touch.

"Why not come to mine instead?" he softly parried, pulling her close with tantalizing unhaste. Rachel caught her breath when she glimpsed the undeniable passion in his darkening gaze. Her luminous eyes grew round as saucers in the delicate oval of her face. Heaven help her, but she *wanted* him to take her to that big bed of his and—

"No!" she virtually shouted, then colored anew and lowered her voice, "My . . . my sister . . ." she weakly protested, swallowing hard. "You promised!"

"I know I promised, damn it!" he growled with mock ferocity. An appealingly wicked grin tugged at the corners of his mouth as he remarked, "I'm a man who always keeps his promises. Unless someone releases me from them, that is. And if that were the case, I'd not feel in the least honor bound to remember what the devil I'd promised in the first place." Rachel inhaled sharply as her pliant curves were molded with intimate perfection against the length of his warm hardness. "You've only to say the word, sweet wildcat," he murmured, his voice nothing more than a husky whisper.

"But, Lizzie—" she gasped out, knowing that her inevitable surrender was only moments away.

"—will never suspect a thing. I'll have you tucked in beside her well before dawn," Logan assured her. Before she could say another word, he lifted her in his arms, closed the bathroom door with a negligent prod from his booted heel, and carried his beautiful young bride to the massive oak bed which dominated the room as completely as he himself dominated Rachel's thoughts and emotions, as completely as his virile, splendidly male body dominated her silken, passionately feminine flesh . . . and was dominated in return.

XIII

Daybreak had already deepened into a hot, windy morning before the four riders left the Circle M behind. Lizzie had insisted upon pausing to watch the activity at the corral as, following a hearty breakfast, Logan led his wife and sister-in-law from the house. Rachel had added her request for them to postpone their departure for a short time, her own gaze having been drawn in fascination to the exciting scene taking place beneath the lightening sky . . .

"How on earth does he manage to stay on?" marveled Lizzie, moving to stand beside Brodie, who had been waiting for them outside. The petite redhead's brown eyes were very wide as she watched one of the young cowpunchers hanging on for dear life atop a wildly twisting, fiercely plunging mass of horseflesh. There were more than a dozen other men lining the split log fence which formed the corral, all of them laughing boisterously and shouting encouragement to their comrade as they waited to see who would emerge the victor from the thrilling contest between man and beast.

"It's a matter of pride," Brodie told her with a quick, boyish grin. Tipping his hat further back upon his dark head, he rested his arms on the top rail of the corral and called out to the courageous fellow atop the bucking bronco, "Don't lose him, Waco!" Waco hit the ground a scant moment later. He hastily rolled to his feet and scrambled to the top of the fence to avoid being trampled by the outraged, furiously snorting animal who obviously had no intention of being broken. But another rider immediately volunteered to take Waco's place in the empty saddle.

"How can they endure such punishment?" Rachel asked Logan, glancing rather tentatively up at him as he casually leaned against the railing beside her. She could not erase the vivid memory of last night's fiery ecstasy from her mind, and she was stunned to realize that the perpetual resentment she had felt toward her husband since their very first encounter was now all but vanished. When had the startling transformation occurred? And, what was more important, what had caused it to come about? she dazedly wondered.

"Because they love doing it," Logan explained with a faint smile. "As Brodie said, it's a matter of pride to them. A man's horse is just about the most important thing in his life out here—no cowboy could do his work without a good mount beneath him." His glowing eyes roamed possessively over her soft loveliness as he, too, remembered what had passed between them in the night. Another half-smile briefly lit his handsome face when he disclosed, "You know, I've heard them make comparisons between their horses and their women. As a matter of fact, it's generally acknowledged that a woman takes just as much taming as an unbroken horse before she's gentled and knows her master."

"Then I suppose I should count myself fortunate that I haven't been saddled and ridden in the corral!" she sarcastically countered. She blushed to the roots of her honey-blond hair when he grinned wickedly and remarked in a low, vibrant tone, "As you well know, sweet wildcat, it doesn't require a saddle to ride a woman." Staunchly resolving that she wouldn't dignify such crudeness with a reply, Rachel lifted her chin and turned her full attention back to the rambunctious competition drawing to a close before her. The horse, a magnificent Appaloosa stallion with distinctive black markings on its left hindquarters, was obviously beginning to tire. Rachel felt a twinge of pity for the sweat-soaked animal as she watched it tossing its head in weary yet dauntless defiance. Although nearly collapsing with exhaustion it still refused to surrender to the inevitable.

Much like you have done with Logan—fought and resisted, defied and protested, but with no hope of victory over him . . . over your own deepest yearnings . . . over your own destiny, a whispered voice inside Rachel's mind proclaimed. She drew in her breath upon a gasp, breathlessly wondering why the thought of being Logan's wife for the rest of her life no longer brought a flash of opposition to her mind. What had happened to her?

"Come on," directed Logan, forcibly interrupting her thoughts as he took a firm but gentle hold on her arm and began moving toward the stable. Rachel's beautiful face wore a preoccupied frown as she allowed herself to be led along. Lizzie and Brodie followed close behind, the two of them arguing over whether it was Waco or his successor who had achieved the superior results with the Appaloosa now cantering obediently within the circular confines of the log corral . . .

Heading southward, they rode across the sun-drenched plains, the Montana "short grass" rolling like a vast sea beneath the warm summer breeze and the cloudless sky looking like a dome of brilliant blue stretched over the wildly beautiful countryside known for its extremes. Both Logan and Brodie related details about the range and the cattle they spotted along the way, as well as about the various landmarks they passed in the course of the group's explorations. Their voices were tinged with noticeable pride whenever they spoke of their work and the land, and the two young women with them listened quite avidly to their leisurely, never-boring narrative.

Rachel, flanked by her husband on one side and Lizzie on the other, gave silent thanks for the fact that she had chosen to wear a cool, open-necked cotton blouse with her split skirt of butter-soft cowhide, for the day was the warmest of the season so far. Taking note of the increasingly parched condition of the earth and the fading green of the prairie vegetation, she recalled the fact that there had been no sign of rain since the stormy night before her wedding. And she'd had no idea how appropriately prophetic the storms that night had been!

"Exactly how many MacBrides *are* there?" Lizzie questioned Logan after he mentioned something about another MacBride ranch being just a few miles beyond the horizon. Though attired much the same as her sister, the fourteen-year-old had chosen to wear her long hair in a single braid down her back instead of pinned up in a proper chignon like Rachel's.

"At last count, more than six dozen," he offhandedly disclosed, his green eyes full of amusement as he flashed her an indulgent grin. "Of course, that's just within a hundred-mile radius. Some of the family chose to remain back in the western part of the territory, while still others drifted to the East and gave up on this way of life altogether."

"But how can there be so many of you? It was my understanding that you were the oldest of the cousins," said Rachel, acutely conscious of his nearness as he rode beside her. There was something about him today, something that made him seem vastly different from the man who had deceived and humiliated her at every turn. "And I . . . well, it was also my understanding that you were the leader—"

"Only by virtue of the fact that I'm Dugan MacBride's son. He was the traditional patriarch of the clan—the dubious honor passed to me when he died," Logan explained with a faint smile of irony. "Actually, his brothers got a head start on their families, so there are quite a number of MacBrides older than me." He favored her with a strangely intense look, prompting Rachel to hastily avert her gaze.

"What about Tate MacBride? And Vance? Do any of their brothers or sisters live around here?" Lizzie persisted. She failed to glimpse the sudden shadow of pain crossing Brodie's attractive young visage, but Rachel caught sight of it and was puzzled as to why the subject caused the raven-haired young man such obvious distress.

"Tate's mother packed up and went back East to her

family more than ten years ago, taking her two girls with her" was all Logan told her, omitting any reference to Vance. Lizzie had no time to question him again before his green eyes narrowed a bit and he announced, "We'll stop for a while over there beside the river."

A short time later, while the horses grazed contentedly beneath the trees, Lizzie and Brodie wandered off together along the riverbank. Rachel was uncomfortably aware of the way Logan's penetrating gaze never wandered from her face as the two of them stood beside the swiftly coursing water. Feeling unaccountably awkward and shy, she bent and picked up a small, translucent stone which bore unique markings of orange, yellow, brown, and white.

"How beautiful," she murmured, cradling the stone in her open palm.

"It's agate," Logan casually observed, his sun-bronzed features relaxing into a soft smile as he noted the sparkle of almost childlike wonderment in her opal eyes. "The Indians used it to make jewelry. No two stones are alike." Placing his hand beneath hers, he slowly closed his strong fingers over hers, the piece of agate disappearing within her closed palm. "Just as no two people are alike." He appeared unusually solemn all of a sudden, and the note of vibrancy in his deep voice struck a responsive chord in Rachel's heart. Raising wide, luminous eyes to his, she found it quite difficult to control her erratic breathing as their gazes met and locked.

The truth hit her like a bolt of lightning. Completely unprepared for the staggering realization which chose that particular, inexplicable moment in time to make itself known to her, she could only stare helplessly up at the devastatingly handsome rogue towering above her, her parted lips forming a silent O as she felt her head spinning.

She loved him! Dear God, she loved Logan MacBride!

"Take you and me, for instance," Rachel was only dimly aware of him saying. She now peered dazedly up at him as his virescent gaze kindled with affectionately mocking humor. "Despite the fact that our life together got off to a rocky start, I'm convinced we were brought together by a force more powerful than either of us. You, on the other hand, seem determined to deny the possibility that our marriage may just have been made in heaven instead of hell." A slow, seductive smile tugged at his chiseled lips as he stepped even closer and remarked in a resonant voice that was scarcely above a whisper, "However, I don't believe even *you* would try and deny that what happened between us last night was anything but heavenly."

Heavenly, Rachel's benumbed mind repeated. It had been that . . . and more. And now, she understood why she had never been able to resist his embrace, why his every touch set her on fire. She loved him! She didn't know precisely how or when the miracle had occurred, but such things didn't matter. She loved him with all her heart and soul, and she knew that she would love him forever. Even if he were indeed guilty of tricking her into marriage, of conspiring with Vance to betray her . . . even if he did not love her in return.

Her heart twisting painfully at the thought, she blinked back the sudden tears stinging against her eyelids and abruptly pulled her hand away from Logan's. She sought to regain her composure as she spun about and walked a bit unsteadily to the water's edge. Feeling as if caught up in a whirlwind, she wondered again why the truth had dawned on her *now*, then wondered how in the world she was going to get through the rest of the day without falling apart . . .

"Rachel?" Logan called out quietly, his brow creasing into a frown as he watched her move away. Swiftly crossing the distance between them, he had done no more than raise his hands to her shoulders when Brodie, dragging Lizzie behind, suddenly came racing back along the riverbank.

"Someone's got a fire going just west of here," a grim-faced Brodie told Logan. Rachel immediately moved to a breathless Lizzie's side as Brodie added, "Looks like the smoke's coming from the base of Panther Butte." Logan muttered a curse, his eyes darkening in profound displeasure at the news. After sparing only a brief instant to ponder the significance of the younger man's words and formulate a course of action, he gripped Rachel's arm and tersely commanded, "You and Lizzie stay here." He strode to where the horses were tied and withdrew his rifle from its scabbard, then returned to thrust the weapon at a thoroughly bewildered Rachel. "Take this. If Brodie and I aren't back within half an hour, head on back to the Circle M without us."

"But what is it? Where are you going?" she demanded anxiously, her fingers curling obediently about the sun-warmed metal of the gun barrel.

"To find out who the hell's trespassing on our range!" he ground out. Rachel and Lizzie could only stand and watch as the two men lithely swung up into their saddles and thundered away across the sagebrush-mantled plains.

The four particularly bold rustlers gathered about the fire they had built in the shadow of Panther Butte were warned of the riders' approach by the sound of hoofbeats. Hastily tossing aside the brands they were using to blot the Circle M mark on the hides of a number of MacBride cattle, they cursed their ill fortune and scrambled toward their mounts. The youngest and least experienced of the motley group, his heart pounding in fear as he leapt to his feet and spotted the two horsemen closing in fast, made the mistake of darting too close to the fire. The well-worn toe of his boot caught the jagged edge of one of the burning logs and sent it skidding across the ground. It came to a stop in the midst of a thick clump of grass a short distance away. The flames took hold of the yellowing pasturage and intensified with remarkable speed, sending a dense cloud of black smoke billowing downwind to envelop Logan and Brodie as they drew their guns to give chase.

"Damn!" Logan jerked on the reins, forcing Vulcan to a grinding halt as Brodie's mount reared in panic at the smell of destruction. There was no time to waste—there was already a low wall of flames sweeping forward and widening its front all the while. "Get on back to the ranch and bring all the men you can find! I'll take the women and head on over to Stuart's!" Almost before the words were out of Logan's mouth, Brodie was on his way.

Rachel shaded her eyes with her hand, her entire body tensing as she viewed the black smoke heaving in the wind and spreading to curtain the western horizon. The smoke was getting thicker by the second.

"What in the—?" murmured Lizzie, frowning quizzically as she, too, focused her gaze on the obscuring blackness.

"Prairie fire!" Rachel breathed in growing horror. She had witnessed such a blaze once before, back in Wyoming, and she recalled, with terrifying vividness, how it had raged out of control for days, sweeping faster and faster across the perilously dry landscape just as the present conflagration was doing. In the end, there had been nothing but mile upon mile of ashes, the hooves of the cattlemen's surviving stock stirring up a fog of weightless, sooty dust until the air was choked with it.

Logan! Dear God, Logan was out there!

"There's someone coming!" exclaimed Lizzie. Rachel forced herself to raise the gun in defensive readiness, then nearly fainted with relief when she saw that it was Logan. He was safe!

"Mount up!" he commanded sharply, his handsome face a mask of grim purposefulness as he reined to an abrupt halt before them. Tossing a quick look over his shoulder at the encroaching, ever-swiftening wall of flames in the near distance, he ground out an oath and flung off his horse to bodily pitch first Rachel, then Lizzie up into their saddles before they could move to obey his command. "Follow me, and ride like your life depends on it!" he directed, swinging his tall, powerful frame onto Vulcan's back again and spurring the impatiently snorting stallion into a gallop. Both Rachel and Lizzie took Logan's words to heart, for they rode as they had never ridden before, following close behind him as he led the way to the ranch which lay only two miles to the east.

Stuart MacBride, a burly, brown-haired man of forty, was giving orders to several of his men near the corral when his ears detected the sound of approaching hoofbeats. Swiftly glancing up to see that it was his younger cousin and two unknown women who were riding toward him with disturbing haste, he whipped the hat from his head and raced to meet them.

"Fire near Panther Butte!" said Logan. Stuart needed to hear no more before springing into action. Within a matter of seconds, more than a dozen men were saddling their mounts and hitching up a wagon containing an old plow reserved for just such a disaster. Logan pulled his wife and sister-in-law from their saddles and gave them into the care of the noticeably pregnant, apple-cheeked woman who came scurrying out of the house to see what all the commotion was about.

"Logan! What is—" Stuart's fair-haired wife started to question in bewilderment, only to be brusquely cut off by Logan.

"There's a fire on the range, Eva. Look after these two for me!" Turning to Rachel, his gaze momentarily softened, and his mouth briefly curved into an encouraging smile as he told her, "You and Lizzie stay here. I'll be back as soon as I can." Rachel, feeling numb, blinked back the gathering tears as he spun about and mounted up again. There were so many things she wanted to say to him, but she could not find the words. She could only stand beside Lizzie and Eva and watch as the man she loved rode off into certain danger, Stuart and the others following his lead. The hooves of their horses left a thin layer of dust to settle upon the three women who now stood alone in front of the two-storied log ranch house.

"What are they going to do?" Lizzie asked the older woman who glanced at the sisters in open but affable curiosity. Like nearly everyone else in the county, she'd already heard the remarkable news of Logan's marriage.

Ironically, she had been in the process of sewing a quilt to serve as a wedding gift for the newlyweds when the sound of Stuart's raised voice startled her a few minutes ago.

"Whatever they can," Eva replied simply. "Don't worry," she added, forcing a smile of optimism to her lips, "both Stuart and Logan know better than to take unnecessary risks." It was clear that she was trying to convince herself as well, for her blue eyes were clouded with discernible apprehension.

"We can't just sit around and do nothing while they're out there battling the fire!" exclaimed Rachel, shaking off the debilitating numbness at last. "They'll be needing plenty of water, and someone to tend to them in case they get hurt!" She turned to grip Eva's arm, her opal eyes flashing in determination as she hurriedly demanded, "Is there another wagon I can use? And something I can use to carry water in?"

"But, you . . . you can't be meaning to go out there!" Eva protested in stunned disbelief. "Why, Logan would never allow—"

"I don't give a damn what Logan would allow!" Rachel shocked her by declaring. "Please, Eva," she earnestly appealed, "there's not a moment to lose!"

Eva visibly wavered. There had been many times when she had wanted to be with Stuart, to be at his side and help him, but she had always been fearful of his anger should she disobey. Logan's wife, however, did not appear the least bit afraid of her husband's disapproval. And for that, she admired her . . . and envied her.

"All right," she finally acquiesced, musing that she would go herself if not for the unborn babe.

Minutes later, Rachel snapped the whip above the

horse's head, urging it to a breakneck pace as the buckboard bounced and jolted over the uneven ground. Lizzie held onto the back and side of the wagon seat, blinking rapidly as the drifting smoke burned her eyes.

"We'll head toward the river!" decreed Rachel, shouting to be heard above the roar of the nearby fire and creaking of the wooden buckboard.

"Just make certain you get us upwind!" cautioned Lizzie. Although she prided herself on being something of a free spirit, the sort who relished excitement and adventure, she was beginning to doubt the wisdom of her sister's plan. The wind was playing havoc with the course of the deadly blaze, sending great, billowing puffs of black smoke every which way across the plains.

Logan was fortunately unaware of his wife's close proximity to the fire as he supervised the reluctant but necessary slaughter of several steers rounded up by Stuart's men. Brodie had already returned with a crew of fifteen from the Circle M, and they fell in beside the others to clear a wide swath in the unburned grass downwind from the fire. The plow was used to furrow a deep trench in the earth, after which the punchers, their eyes aching from the smoke and baking heat and the lower half of their faces covered by their kerchiefs, set about digging with shovels and hands to widen the trench. It was grueling work, and there wasn't a single man whose heart didn't pound in alarm each time the wind sent the approaching flames shooting higher.

"Let's go!" yelled Logan, tightening the rope about his saddlehorn. The other end was secured about the neck of a steer's carcass, and Stuart's rope was looped about the animal's hind legs. With Logan on the burnt-over side of the blaze and Stuart on the as-yet-untouched grass directly in front of the blaze, they spurred their mounts, dragging the carcass across the fire between the two wildly galloping horses in an attempt to smother the flames. Brodie and one of Stuart's men did the same with another carcass immediately afterward, with yet another pair of riders following close behind with a third carcass. Although they succeeded in temporarily slowing the advancement of the blaze, they failed to achieve the hoped-for result of extinguishing it entirely.

Rachel, meanwhile, drew the horse to a halt beside the river, in much the same spot she and Logan had stood earlier . . . where the knowledge of her love had hit her with such traumatic forcefulness. Climbing down from the buckboard as Lizzie did the same, she frowned speculatively toward the all-too-visible fire less than a quarter of a mile away, her heart pounding as she caught sight of the men and horses outlined against the brilliant glow of the menacing but strangely beautiful wall of flames.

Dear Lord, please keep him safe! she fervently prayed in silence.

"How are we going to let them know we're here?" asked Lizzie, staring toward the blaze as well before peering overhead at the darkening sky. Her brown eyes grew very round, and she swallowed hard as she observed a bit nervously, "Rachel, it might just be my imagination, but it seems to me that an awful lot of smoke's starting to come this way all of a sudden." Rachel immediately raised her eyes toward the heavens, growing increasingly uneasy when she, too, noted the thickening blanket of smoke curling on the fire-warmed currents of air in their direction. "Maybe we should think about moving farther upwind," Lizzie suggested, darting another anxious glance back at the fire.

"I think you're right," murmured Rachel. "Besides, we need to let Logan know we've brought water and supplies." Motioning for her sister to resume her place on the wagon seat, she climbed back up on the buckboard and released the brake. Her fingers tightened about the handle of the driving whip as she raised her arm to snap the thin leather above the head of the shrilly whinnying horse.

Suddenly, a particularly dense fog of black smoke enveloped them. The terrified animal reared in panic, causing the hitch to crack and splinter. He reared again before breaking free of the buckboard, leaping forward and dragging the harness along the ground behind him as he instinctively sought to escape the fire. The wind cleared the smoke away just in time for Rachel to watch the horse heading back the way they had come.

Within seconds, however, another blinding wave of smoke swept across them, prompting them to cough and rub at their fiercely stinging eyes. Lizzie grabbed at her sister's arm as she cried, "Heaven help us, Rachel, the wind's turning!" It was all too true. The course of the fire was being altered with horrifying swiftness as the capricious summer breeze whipped the flames higher and sent them racing toward the river. The two young women were trapped; there was no hope of outrunning the fire and even less chance of survival if they dared to try.

"Get in the river!" shouted Rachel, jumping back down to the ground and waiting for Lizzie to join her before scrambling down the riverbank into the water.

They shivered at the cold, clinging to one another and desperately praying that the previously inconstant wind would turn yet again before the fire reached them . . .

Logan reined Vulcan sharply about, then loosened the rope from his saddlehorn and rode back to where Brodie and the others who had been toiling to create a firebreak were now mounting up with the intention of repositioning their operations as the wall of fire snaked in another direction.

"Stay clear, damn it!" yelled Logan. "Wait until it crosses the river!" He pulled up beside Brodie, his handsome face blackened by the smoke, his eyes bloodshot and red-rimmed from having ridden so near the flames.

"God in heaven, Logan—look!" Brodie uttered in stunned disbelief, pointing toward the river. Stuart rode up at that precise moment, his gaze moving along with Logan's as it followed the aim of Brodie's upraised arm.

There, scarcely visible through the heavy curtain of smoke, Logan glimpsed the sight of two young women—one golden-haired and the other a redhead—standing in the shallowness of the river just off the rocky bank. A buckboard rested beside the water that swirled about the women as they clung to one another in obvious terror.

"Rachel!" His voice was nothing more than a hoarse whisper, his senses reeling from the impact of seeing her *there*, directly in the path of the inferno which was bearing down upon the river with such unswerving, decimating haste.

Rachel! The fire! Dear God, he had to get Rachel away from the fire!

"Logan! Logan, come back! You'll never make it in

time!" yelled Brodie, watching as the cousin who was more like a brother to him took off like a demon out of hell.

"Damnation, Brodie, he'll kill himself!" Stuart ground out. Neither one of them wasted another moment before giving chase . . .

"I . . . I can hardly breathe!" gasped out Lizzie, her youthful countenance appearing increasingly panic-stricken as her fingers tightened upon her older sister's arms.

"Don't try to talk, Lizzie!" cautioned Rachel, striving to remain calm. "We've got to move farther out into the water!" The acrid smoke threatened to choke them, and they could feel the heat of the fire as it swept closer. Within the next few seconds, its yellow orange flames topped the trees lining the riverbank.

Please God, please help us! Rachel prayed again and again. Pulling Lizzie into the deeper waters, the swift current posing as real a threat to them as the fire, she thought of Logan . . .

It was too late, Logan's mind dully repeated. In spite of the realization, he would have ridden directly into the flames if not for Brodie's and Stuart's timely interference. No matter how desperately he had tried, he had been unable to make it to the river ahead of the blaze. Now, as his cousins succeeded in momentarily blocking his path to prevent his self-destruction, he watched the fire sweeping in an arc across the trees which flanked the river, the black smoke completely obliterating any sign of Rachel and Lizzie.

"Get out of my way, damn you!" thundered Logan, Vulcan pawing and swinging impatiently about beneath him. When neither Brodie nor Stuart showed any signs of obeying, he deceptively maneuvered his horse to the left of the pair, then skillfully guided the well-trained stallion to their right before they could turn their own mounts to block him again.

He reached the water's edge a scant instant after the fire leapt to the opposite bank. The wind provided a belated assistance by clearing the smoke so that Logan's frantically searching gaze could locate the two women. Their heads broke the surface of the water in the middle of the fast-flowing river, and their choking coughs and determined thrashings were quite audible as they battled the current to keep from being swept away. The buckboard Rachel had been driving was totally engulfed in flames.

Reflecting that he had never been so glad in his life to hear the sound of someone making a conscious effort not to drown, Logan flung off his horse and immediately headed out into the river. Brodie wasn't far behind, and he, too, hurriedly plunged into the cold water to help Logan get the women to safety.

It took a moment for an exhausted Rachel to realize that it was Logan who clamped an arm about her waist and tugged her to solid ground. She looked up to see Brodie pulling Lizzie from the river, and she nearly fainted with relief to see that her sister was still alive and virtually unharmed. Her eyes swept closed as she held tight to Logan. He knelt upon the riverbank and pulled her close, and she could not see the way his own eyes swept closed as he thanked God for sparing the life of the woman in his arms.

Lizzie and Brodie sat beside one another upon the

alkali-streaked bank a short distance away, neither of them speaking as they watched the fire moving away from the river. Stuart, having already ascertained from his vantage point just beyond the still-smoldering trees that his cousins and both the women were safe, headed across the river to supervise the next assault upon the blaze. The other riders had already crossed upstream.

"I've got to go," Logan told Rachel, only the merest hint of an edge to his low voice giving evidence of the fury simmering within him. Though full of admiration—and the most profound relief he had ever known—for the level-headed way she had reacted to the inescapable danger of the fire, he was so enraged that she had disobeyed him and placed herself and Lizzie in such peril that it was all he could do to keep from surrendering to the violent tendencies threatening to overwhelm him. If not for the iron control he was striving to maintain over his savagely flaring temper, he would forget about the fire still raging out of control across the river and give himself the satisfaction of turning his beautiful, damnably headstrong wife across his knee and beating her bottom until she begged for mercy.

Assuring himself one last time that she was all right, he firmly set her away and rose to his feet. She gazed wordlessly up at him as he stood ramrod straight and ordered in a tight voice, "Stay here, damn it!" It soon became apparent that he didn't trust her to obey, for he charged Brodie with the duty of remaining behind to keep an eye on the women. Brodie was noticeably reluctant to do so, but he clamped his mouth shut and swore inwardly as he watched his cousin mount up and expertly ford the river, then ride hell-bent-for-leather toward the telltale curtain of black smoke in the near distance.

Rachel raised trembling hands to sweep the wet, tangled mass of hair away from her face. Climbing unsteadily to her feet, she was only dimly aware of the popping and hissing of the lingering flames which consumed the buckboard just beyond the riverbank, was scarcely conscious of the blackened surroundings as her wide, opalescent gaze remained fastened on the lone rider who soon disappeared into the cloud of smoke.

Logan! her heart cried. Renewed fear for his safety brought a rush of hot tears to her already burning eyes, and she could not prevent a choking sob from escaping her lips. Lizzie was beside her in an instant, wrapping a comforting arm about Rachel's shoulders and remarking brightly, "Wait till Micah hears about this! He'll never believe the two of us actually made it through the smack-dab middle of a prairie fire!"

"He'll never believe you were harebrained enough to be out here in the first place!" Brodie ungenerously amended, scowling ferociously down at the sodden condition of his clothing and favorite pair of boots. He muttered a curse and flung his hopelessly bedraggled hat to the ground. His gold-flecked brown eyes kindled with undeniable ire as he rounded on Lizzie and growled, "Of all the stupid, witless, jackass female—"

"May I remind you, *Mr. MacBride,* that a jackass is a *male* animal!" retorted Lizzie, her own brown eyes flashing as she moved away from Rachel and stepped forward to confront the angry young man squarely. "And for your information, we came out here to bring fresh water and to offer our assistance in case any of you *jackass* cowpokes got hurt!"

"Lizzie, please!" Rachel wearily admonished.

"Well you did a hell of a job, *Miss Parker!*" Brodie lashed out at the petite, spirited redhead standing so defiantly before him. It was as if neither of them recalled Rachel's presence at all. "You damn near got Logan killed, and you and your sister came close to—"

"You wouldn't have been sorry at all if we had died, would you?" Lizzie childishly accused. For a moment, it appeared as if Brodie would strike her, but he wisely resisted the impulse and instead wheeled away with another muttered oath. Lizzie hurled invisible daggers at his back before whirling about and marching back to Rachel's side. The two sisters sank back down onto the bank and lapsed into mutual silence as they stared solemnly ahead to where Logan and the others still battled the deadly wall of fire.

Finally, the ordeal was over. The second firebreak, with the help of the mercifully consistent wind, succeeded in halting the blaze and causing it to burn itself out. The exhausted men, their muscles and joints aching and their exposed flesh cracked and burning with dryness, rode their equally fatigued mounts homeward.

Stuart, accompanying Logan back to the river after the two of them inspected the sight of the rustlers' illegal activity at the base of Panther Butte, silently mused that he sure as hell wouldn't want to be in the unenviable position of Logan's wife at the moment. Being Logan's cousin, and possessed of the intimidating MacBride temper himself, he was all too familiar with what could happen whenever anyone—be it man, woman, or beast—

dared to cross the tall, forebodingly grim-faced man riding beside him. Preparing to smugly congratulate himself on having chosen a more biddable woman, it suddenly occurred to him that the buckboard now being reduced to nothing more than a pile of ashes was *his,* and that, unbelievable as it seemed, Eva must have been the one to provide it.

"I'll send one of my men over to get the other horses later," Logan informed Stuart in a low, even tone as soon as they drew up to where Rachel, Lizzie, and Brodie waited. Stuart, only too happy to take his leave, nodded wordlessly at his younger cousins and the two women before reining about and galloping back to his ranch, anxious to question Eva about her role in the near disaster.

Rachel's breath caught in her throat when her gaze met Logan's. His eyes, darkened to a brilliant-hued jade, were literally ablaze with the force of his smoldering but admirably well-controlled rage. Swinging down from the saddle, he quietly instructed Brodie, "Take Lizzie up before you."

"No!" the young redhead adamantly protested. She stayed close to Rachel and raised her chin in proud defiance. "I'd prefer to ride with my sister!" Disregarding her objections, a noticeably impatient Brodie hastened to obey Logan. He strode forward and seized Lizzie's arm. She tried to jerk free of his none-too-gentle grasp, but he determinedly clamped an arm about her waist and bodily lifted her off the ground, carrying her swiftly to his horse and tossing her up to land with an uncomfortable jolt on the animal's back. Mounting up behind her while she sputtered indignantly at such uncivil treatment, he tightly gripped the reins and urged the horse away from the river.

Hot color washed over Rachel as Logan continued to stare intently across at her. She knew he was angry with her, knew of the struggle taking place within him. But it didn't matter. All she could think of was the fact that he was safe. Even if she had still been uncertain as to the extent of her feelings for him, the fire and the threat it posed to him would have clarified her emotions once and for all. She loved Logan MacBride!

"There are a great many things I'd like to say to you," he finally ground out. And *do* to you! he added mentally, fighting down another wave of explosive fury. "But they'll have to wait." He crossed the distance between them in two long strides and paused to tower ominously above her. A muscle twitched in the fire-blackened smoothness of his cheek, and his eyes narrowed imperceptibly as they raked over her damp, wildly streaming hair, her becomingly flushed face, and her wet, clinging garments.

"I . . . I don't suppose it will make any difference," offered Rachel, inwardly blanching at the savage gleam in his eyes in spite of her newly acknowledged love for him, "but Lizzie and I were merely trying to help."

"You're right. It makes no difference," he muttered tersely. She gasped as he bent and lifted her in his arms. Just as Brodie had done with Lizzie, Logan carried her to his waiting mount and unceremoniously tossed her into the saddle. One powerful arm tightened like a vise about her slender waist as he settled himself on Vulcan's sleek back behind her and gathered up the reins.

Riding swiftly away from the river and the starkly

visible path of destruction, they soon caught up with the younger couple. The sun hung directly overhead, its fiery rays beating down upon the untamed countryside with disputable benevolence, its warmth combining with the wind to chase the lingering dampness from the hair and clothing of the stormy-faced Lizzie and her apprehensive but dreamy-eyed sister.

XIV

Logan's handsome face remained inscrutable and unyielding as he reached up to pull his wife from the saddle. Rachel was both hurt and confused by his aloofness and at the way his hands released her with such abruptness. Lizzie, after stubbornly refusing Brodie's assistance in dismounting, swung down from the saddle and immediately went to her sister's aid. Casting her brother-in-law a resentful glare, she grabbed Rachel's hand and tugged her insistently toward the house.

Rachel hesitated, her luminous eyes full of mute appeal as they raised to encounter Logan's coldly glinting gaze. He turned away without a word, and in spite of the fact that she was still secretly marveling over the realization that she loved him with all her heart, she was more than a trifle annoyed by his unrelentingly dispassionate behavior.

"Come on, Rachel. It's plain to see we're not wanted around here!" Lizzie haughtily asserted, her brown eyes flashing as she watched the two men lead the tired, sweat-soaked horses into the stable.

Rachel's own gaze filled with growing indignation. Allowing to herself that Logan had a right to be a trifle vexed with her for what had happened, she was nonetheless quite certain he was carrying things too far. After all, she and Lizzie were safe. The prairie fire had been extinguished. Why should he still be so angry? Was it merely because she had dared to disobey him, because she had once again exhibited the unquenchable spirit he claimed to admire? Or did his anger stem from another reason entirely?

The questions ran together in the turbulence of her mind, and they remained unanswered as she finally trudged inside the house with Lizzie. She and her sister retired to their respective bedchambers to strip off their dust-cloaked attire and bathe. They were both relieved to reach the sanctuary of their rooms without being detected by any of the other inhabitants, and Rachel was also relieved that her bath was uninterrupted by Logan. In truth, however, her relief was tempered by more than a little disappointment as her eyes strayed continually to the opposite door of the bathroom.

"Oh, Logan!" she sighed a bit disconsolately. Now that she knew she was in love with her husband, the situation was even worse than before! It pained her more than ever to think of his betrayal, and it was almost unbearable to consider the possibility that he cared nothing for her—nothing beyond an inarguably volatile physical attraction, that is. Although she gloried in the ecstasy of his breathtakingly virile attentions, it wasn't enough. She desperately yearned for her love to be reciprocated. She wanted Logan MacBride to love her, to cherish and keep her just as he had vowed to do only—incredible as it seemed—two days ago. The vows had meant nothing to her at the time, but heaven help her, they meant everything to her now!

Tossing the bath sponge into the cooling water with a vengeance, she rose from the tub and hastened to dress. She found Lizzie, Aunt Tess, and Uncle Robert waiting for her in the dining room when she finally made an appearance downstairs. Moira's absence was noted and appreciated, but Rachel was not at all appreciative of the news Mrs. Smith imparted with her usual gruffness.

"Mr. Logan said to tell you he had business in town and won't be back till nightfall," she told Rachel, setting the platter of baked chicken and rice in the center of the linen-covered table. As Rachel frowned to herself and wondered why Logan had chosen to make such a long trip after spending the better part of the morning battling the fire, and why he hadn't come upstairs to bathe and change his smoke-ravaged clothing, the housekeeper went on to divulge with a decidedly triumphant gleam in her eyes, "And Miss Moira's gone with him." She sailed complacently back into the kitchen, leaving Tess to exchange a worried look with Robert before she gently explained to Rachel, "Moira had business of her own in Miles City, my dear."

"Did Brodie go with them?" asked Lizzie with feigned indifference, spooning a generous portion of the chicken and rice onto her plate.

"No," Aunt Tess reluctantly disclosed, her expression one of maternal compassion as she glimpsed the stricken look in Rachel's eyes. "But as Cora said, Logan is planning to return well before nightfall."

"I'm certain he's quite anxious to hurry back to his beautiful bride!" Uncle Robert asserted with a bolstering grin.

Rachel managed a weak smile in response, then turned her attention, outwardly at least, to the meal. Though she had lost her appetite, she forced herself to take several bites of the rice.

Logan and Moira. They were alone together for the entire day! No matter that Logan had resisted the spiteful brunette's advances the previous night—Rachel miserably reflected that Moira would no doubt seize the opportunity provided by the trip to use all her feminine wiles on Logan. Logan. Would he continue to resist? The possibility that he would not provoked a wealth of anguish and jealousy within her, but she concealed her disquietude as best she could. After all, she staunchly reasoned with herself, it would avail her nothing to dissolve into a storm of tears at the mere thought of Logan and Moira riding into town together. She could not allow herself to believe the worst, to agonize over something that would in all probability never come to pass!

Rachel held fast to that firm resolution throughout the day, wavering only whenever Logan's name came up during the course of her conversation with others, which was much more frequently than she would have liked. She and Lizzie spent the remainder of the afternoon outside, where Brodie, his anger over the morning's events apparently all but forgotten, was gracious enough to take them on a proper tour of the ranch buildings and introduce them to the hands who had drawn home duty instead of range work that day. After Brodie reluctantly announced that he had several chores to finish before dark, Rachel and Lizzie wandered about on their own, finally settling beside the creek that flowed a short distance behind the house. Uncle Robert joined them just as the sunlight began to fade, resting an arm across the foot he propped up on a large rock and smiling down at the two young women who sat on the soft, grassy earth with their full skirts spread about them.

"You know, there's an old saying about the West—'it's a great country for men and horses, but hell on women and cattle.' Perhaps I'm not much of an expert, since I've only recently ventured out here again for the first time in years, but I firmly believe it's you ladies who are responsible for taming the wilderness! You and the fellow members of your fair sex bring a special touch of refinement that would otherwise be sadly lacking." Rachel smiled faintly up at him, but her mind was increasingly preoccupied with thoughts of Logan's return. "In many ways, the women here are very much like their counterparts in the East," he added.

"Rachel and I have never been back East," Lizzie companionably remarked, bringing her knees upward so that she could wrap her arms about them. "We lived in San Francisco before our parents died and we went to live with our grandparents in Wyoming. But Montana's different. The people here are different." The corners of her mouth curved briefly downward, and her brown eyes clouded with momentary bemusement as a clear picture of Brodie MacBride's face drifted across her mind.

"Outwardly, perhaps," said Uncle Robert. "But I think people are basically the same everywhere. There are simply different codes of behavior, different priorities." He turned to Rachel, his eyes full of kindness as he queried, "What about you, my dear? What do you think of the people here?"

"I . . . I'm not quite sure," she murmured, flushing guiltily over the knowledge that she had been paying only half a mind to him. It was getting late. Where was Logan?

"I gather there's one fortunate resident in particular who stands apart from the other men you've known," he teased, making a commendable effort to help erase the rather forlorn expression that had been in evidence on her beautiful young face since the noon meal. Silently cursing his nephew for a fool, Robert Pearson was just about to introduce another topic of conversation when the petite form of Aunt Tess suddenly cast a shadow on the ground beside the trio.

"I'm afraid Cora is quite insistent upon serving our supper without further delay," she informed them with a quiet sigh of exasperation. Uncle Robert beamed down at her, his eyes twinkling and a certain lilt to his voice as he asked, "How long has it been since someone told you how utterly charming you look in the last golden glow of the sunset, Tess Shelley?" Silently berating herself for blushing like an innocent schoolgirl instead of the mature widow she was, Tess chose not to reply. Robert chuckled softly, then stepped forward to gallantly assist the two sisters to their feet.

The next hour passed pleasantly enough, but Rachel was acutely conscious of the fact that darkness was stealing over the range. There was still no sign of Logan and Moira, and their delay in returning brought all sorts of unpleasant images to her mind, supplying her fertile imagination with plenty of fuel and heightening her already intense trepidation.

Finally, evening gave way to night, a warm and breezy night filled with the sounds of the moonlit prairie—a coyote plaintively howling in the distance, branches clicking softly together as the cottonwoods swayed beneath the wind, the gentle roar of the life-giving stream as the water rushed over smooth, moss-coated rocks, and the occasional bawling of the cattle settling down for the night on a grassy slope near the house.

Midnight came and went. Rachel absently scrutinized the shadows on the papered wall as she lay beside a peacefully slumbering Lizzie. Her eyebrows pulled together into a troubled frown as she released a long, pent-up sigh and eased herself from the bed. Moving restlessly to the window, she clasped the curtains with one hand and drew them aside to peer distractedly outward upon the silver-tinged landscape below.

What was Logan doing at that moment? she wondered yet again, her opal eyes clouding with renewed disquiet. Was he safe? Was he purposely staying away from her? Where was he spending the night? And, what was more important, were he and Moira spending the night *together?*

Allowing the curtains to fall back into place, she wandered into the bathroom, her bare feet moving almost of their own accord. She opened the opposite door and stood gazing upon Logan's empty bed, its massive bulk silhouetted by the lunar glow filling the room. Sudden tears glistened upon her eyelashes as she reflected that being in love with someone was both a joy and a torment.

"Please, God," Rachel prayed aloud, her voice a soft yet fervent whisper, "please keep him safe." She couldn't refrain from adding, "And please don't let my love for him be betrayed!" She stared long and hard at Logan's bed, her heart aching as she remembered the impassioned splendor the two of them had shared the previous night. Forcing herself to turn away and resume her place beside Lizzie in her own bed, she finally drifted off into a sleep of physical and emotional exhaustion, her dreams haunted by visions of Moira's triumphantly smirking face as the haughty brunette entwined her arms possessively about Logan's neck, and of Moira's lips pressing boldly upon the unresisting firmness of Logan's mouth . . .

It was an hour past noon when the buckboard rolled to a halt in front of the house. Logan looped the reins over the brake and climbed down, ignoring Moira's smiling, confidently expectant features as he strode past without so much as a glance in her direction. Her pale green eyes narrowed wrathfully, and the smile on her face was quickly transformed into a vengeful scowl. In spite of the disastrous failure of her most recent scheme, she was still unwilling to admit defeat. Logan *would* be hers! she silently vowed. Angrily gathering up her skirts, she slapped away the hands of the cowpuncher who had hurried across the yard to assist her down. The hapless young man stepped back in astonished confusion as Moira sailed purposefully up the steps and into the house after Logan without a word.

Rachel was alone in the parlor. Tess and Robert had impulsively decided to take advantage of the continued good weather to go riding together after the noon meal, and Lizzie was outside happily watching Brodie and some of the other hands do some more halter-breaking of half-wild range horses in the corral. Mrs. Smith emerged from the kitchen long enough to pointedly inform her new young mistress that they would have to make do with cornbread instead of white bread for supper, as their supply of flour had dwindled to near nothingness and Mr.

Logan and Miss Moira, who had so generously agreed to secure a new bag in town, had not yet returned. The woman didn't appear in the least bit sorry about the circumstances, and she had no sooner left Rachel to her troubled thoughts again when the front door was suddenly thrown open. Rachel's breath caught in her throat as she looked up to find Logan's tall, powerfully muscled frame filling the parlor's doorway.

The sparkling opalescence of her gaze met the intense, gleaming jade of his. Rising hastily to her feet, she allowed the bit of mending in her lap to slip unheeded to the carpeted floor. Her heart initially leapt for joy at seeing her husband safe before her, but joy gave way to sorrow when she glimpsed the look of cold fury he turned upon her. It was obvious that he had not yet forgiven her for her disobedience.

"Logan, darling, what are you—" Moira's voice intruded. She appeared at Logan's side, her fingers closing familiarly about his arm as her cat's eyes lit upon Rachel. "Oh. It's you," she pronounced with rude simplicity. A slow smile spread across her scornfully triumphant features in the next moment, much the same as in Rachel's decidedly unpleasant dreams. "I'm afraid Logan and I were delayed in town. But we were able to make ourselves quite 'comfortable' at the Macqueen House last night. I only hope you and the others passed the time as 'agreeably' as we did," she remarked with a discernible glimmer of victory in her feline gaze, her body pressing boldly against a stony-faced Logan. There was no mistaking her meaning.

A surge of the most profound jealousy and rage she had ever known threatened to overwhelm Rachel. She had worried and fretted over Logan MacBride for nearly twenty-four hours, and here he came strolling unrepentantly into the house with his . . . his *paramour* virtually joined to him at the hip!

To make matters worse, he had as yet to utter a single word to her, to offer any sort of explanation or apology for his actions, or to deny Moira's not-so-subtle insinuations of intimacy with him. Rachel's eyes were full of silent entreaty, but he merely stood arrogantly erect, his piercing gaze raking dispassionately over her while she felt her heart breaking. It was the final straw. She loved him more than life itself, but she could not and would not stand by and watch him flaunt his relationship with Moira, or with any other woman!

"I shall be more than happy to leave the two of you to your 'agreeableness'! It seems that I have been suffering under a very naive misconception, one that involved decency and honor and . . . and . . ." Rachel's voice trailed away when the appropriate words eluded her, and she choked back a sob as she fled from the room and up the stairs. Logan hesitated only an instant, his handsome face wearing a dark, tight-lipped expression, before he muttered a curse and spun about to go after her.

"Leave her be!" directed Moira, her hand tightly clenching his arm in a futile effort to detain him. "If she's going to behave like a childish little idiot, then—"

"One more word, Moira, and I'll give myself the pleasure of throwing you on a horse and sending you home to your father!" he ground out, the savage glow in his eyes frightening her as he jerked his arm free. She took an instinctive step backward, watching helplessly while he scaled the staircase with rigid intent in Rachel's wake.

Rachel, having stormed into her room and bolted the door, was already flinging her things into a valise when Logan's voice rang out whipcord sharp, demanding entrance. Too distraught and angry to ponder the wisdom of disregarding his demands, she continued with her frenzied packing, tears streaming freely down the satiny smoothness of her brightly flushed cheeks.

Suddenly there was a loud crash, and Rachel jumped in alarm, inhaling upon a gasp as Logan burst into the room. The door frame had given way beneath the considerable force of his broad shoulder, the wood beneath the bolt splintering and thereby allowing him to send the barrier of the door smashing back against the floral-papered wall. He slammed the door closed immediately afterward, his mouth tightening into a thin line of barely controlled fury and his green eyes blazing as he caught sight of the open, overstuffed valise on the bed.

"What the devil do you think you're doing?" he demanded harshly. The bronzed, chiseled planes of his face appeared quite menacing, though Rachel could not prevent a flash of admiration for the rugged perfection of him. He wore a double-breasted shirt of sky-blue cotton, and his lean hips and taut thighs were, as usual, expertly molded by the snug denim of his trousers. To her eyes, he was the most magnificent, irresistible man in the world, and yet her mind, staunchly reminding her of his unpardonable betrayal, told her that he was a blackguard, that loving him would bring her nothing but further pain and humiliation.

"I'm setting you free, Mr. MacBride! I'm leaving you to your . . . your *pursuits* and going back where I belong!" she told him, dashing impatiently at her tears and forcing herself to turn away and resume her packing.

"You belong here with me, damn it!" he thundered, stalking forward to loom intimidatingly over her. She was startled when he yanked the valise off the bed and tossed it to the floor, its contents spilling everywhere.

"You can manhandle me or my possessions all you like, but I will *not* remain under the same roof with you another night! It's plain to see that you certainly won't be lonely! After all, you and Moira—"

"What about me and Moira?" he tersely challenged, his smoldering gaze boring down into hers.

"You said you'd be back before nightfall, Logan MacBride! Instead, you don't come home until the next day is already half gone, and you have the audacity to expect me to meekly accept the fact that you have spent the night with another woman!"

"So, it appears that I've already been tried and convicted. Once again, you've chosen to believe the worst!" He was tempted to offer her a belated explanation, to tell her how, upon passing the railroad station late yesterday afternoon, he had found himself being hailed by an important cattle buyer from Billings—the same cattle buyer he had been doing business with only a few short weeks ago when he and the then-unknown beauty who was now his wife had argued over a bath at the Headquarters Hotel.

Although Logan had cursed the fact that his dealings with the buyer would prevent him from returning to the Circle M before the next day, he had reluctantly stayed in Miles City for the night, with Moira only too eager to agree to the delay. She had done her best to entice him, even going so far as to brazenly suggest that the two of them share a room, but he had curtly declined, his thoughts wholly preoccupied by the headstrong, golden-haired wildcat who waited for him at home—the same wildcat whose disobedience and subsequent endangering of her life still provoked an explosive flaring of his damnable temper.

"What am I supposed to believe?" Rachel countered resentfully, her eyes flashing their brilliant opal fire. Her full breasts rose and fell rapidly beneath the tight, square-necked bodice of her lavender silk gown. "You haven't even made an attempt to deny it, have you? Tell me then, Mr. MacBride—why should I *not* believe the worst? Our marriage may very well be nothing more than a disagreeable farce, but you have no right to treat me with such blatant disrespect! Why should I allow myself to be . . . to be treated so shamefully another moment?" She could scarcely get the words out, her voice quivering with emotion as a new rush of tears assailed her. Sweeping past Logan, she knelt upon the floor at the foot of the bed and began repositioning her things in the valise.

"Stop it, you little fool!" growled Logan, drawing her none too gently up before him again. His strong fingers closed upon the trembling softness of her upper arms, and her eyes grew very round as he proclaimed in dangerously low, clipped tones, "I ought to give you the thrashing of your life! First you nearly get yourself and your sister killed, then you take it into your head to run away because of some absurdly obvious plot of Moira's to cause trouble between us!"

"The only thing 'absurdly obvious' about this whole distasteful episode is your guilt!" Rachel lashed out, too upset to give any measure of credence to his denial, however indirect it might be. "You're attempting to cover up your own transgressions by focusing on what happened at the river yesterday! As I've already told you, Lizzie and I were merely trying to help!"

"Confound it, woman, when are you going to get it through that thick skull of yours that it's not your place to either question or disregard my orders?" Rachel's beautiful eyes kindled with furious indignation, and her entire body quaked with the force of her own perilously rising temper as she demanded in a voice laced with biting sarcasm, "Pray, Mr. MacBride, would you mind telling me exactly what my place *is* in this so-called marriage? For you see, I'm terribly afraid I will continue to have difficulty in remembering it!" No longer able to stem the veritable flood of tears, she did not give Logan time to answer before twisting out of his grasp and rushing blindly toward the door.

"Rachel!" He seized her arm and pulled her relentlessly back against him before she had done more than put an unsteady hand on the brass doorknob.

"Let me go! Let me go, damn you!" she brokenly commanded, struggling to escape. "I hate you, Logan MacBride! I hate you and I never want to see you again!" she untruthfully cried, her hurt and jealousy driving her beyond reason. She gasped as he lifted her in his powerful arms and carried her, kicking and writhing in heartsore desperation, through the connecting bathroom to his wholly masculine bedchamber. He strode with his violently protesting burden to the bed and dropped her onto the quilt-covered mattress to land in an inglorious tumble of skirts and petticoats.

"Love or hate—it makes no difference to me, *Mrs. MacBride,*" he asserted with a mendacious ruthlessness of his own, his searing gaze flickering briefly over her outraged, disheveled features. "But you *will* be staying here as my wife, and you *will* learn to obey me!" With that, he spun about on his booted heel and strode back the way he had come. Rachel sat breathlessly upon the bed, her eyes wide and dazed as Logan closed the bathroom door and turned the key.

Scrambling off the bed when her ears detected the unmistakable sound of the lock clicking into place, she hesitated only a moment before racing to the door which led into the hallway. She discovered, much to her chagrin, that it had also been locked from the outside.

Rachel leaned against the door in stunned disbelief. Why, Logan had actually imprisoned her in his room!

It occurred to her that she could scream like a banshee and undoubtedly attract the attention of Mrs. Smith or Moira, but she was loath to make either of those women aware of the embarrassing predicament in which she found herself. Besides, she mused umbrageously, neither of them would spare any sympathy for the "hated usurper" they considered her to be!

Still fuming over Logan's refusal to deny or explain what had happened with Moira, Rachel's bright gaze swept the room and lit upon the window. She hurried to open it, intending to call for help. But, once again, she was forced to admit the truth—no one at the ranch would aid her in escaping. Even Aunt Tess and Uncle Robert, as dear and kind as they were, would never dare to go against Logan's wishes. And Lizzie, though there was little doubt as to her loyalty, would probably balk at the idea of the two of them running away, for she would in all likelihood insist that no Parker could turn tail and run like a coward!

"You *are* a coward," Rachel condemned herself aloud, sinking down upon the bed with a despondent sigh. She couldn't bear the thought of Logan's caring so little for her that he would succumb to Moira's wantonly proffered charms. And she now realized that she could not remain his wife if there was no hope of having her love returned. She was selfish enough to want her husband to love her just as much as she had come to love him. She desperately yearned for a marriage based on love and trust—indeed, she could settle for nothing less.

Unhappily reflecting that the man she had married was still a stranger to her, Rachel sighed heavily and lay back upon the quilt. Several conflicting thoughts raced through her mind as she stared up at the beamed ceiling, the foremost thought being that she was hopelessly trapped—not by locked doors, but by the perverseness of her own desires and emotions. She loved Logan and couldn't bear the possibility of leaving him, and yet she knew she could not endure a relationship filled with agonizing doubts and suspicions . . .

"Rachel."

Her eyeslids fluttered open at the sound of her name upon his lips. Startled to discover that she had fallen asleep in his bed, she came bolt upright and stared speechlessly up at him with wide, sparkling eyes. Her heart pounded erratically within her breast when she glimpsed the unguarded look of tenderness in his glowing, sea-green gaze, and she was profoundly disappointed when he suddenly frowned and turned away.

"You've been asleep almost two hours," Logan stated in a deep, perplexingly harsh tone.

"Two hours?" Rachel echoed breathlessly. Her gaze flew to the window, only to find that the sky was ablaze with the golden radiance of the afternoon. Sliding hastily off the bed, she smoothed her silken skirts and attempted to set her disarranged hair to rights. Logan took a stance at the window, his handsome features inscrutable as he gazed outward and quietly announced, "We'll be leaving for the reservation in the morning."

"Reservation?" she echoed again, totally bewildered. Staring at the broad, rigid planes of his back, she felt a new rush of tears welling up in her eyes. He was behaving every bit as hard and implacable as before, and the terrible ache deep in her heart was joined by a returning sense of righteous indignation. What right had *he* to be so angry when *she* was the one who had been wronged?

"The Crow reservation. Brodie's mother lives there. We take supplies every three months." He briefly inclined his head toward her and declared in a low voice edged with still smoldering fury, "I hadn't planned on taking you along, but you've given me no other choice." His words only served to bring another storm of wounded outrage flaring up within Rachel.

"I will not go with you!" she vehemently asserted, her opal eyes blazing. He wheeled about at that, his sun-bronzed features visibly tightening.

"You will do as I say, damn it!"

"No!"

"Rachel, I'm warning you!" Logan ground out, swiftly

crossing the distance between them. Employing every ounce of iron will he possessed, he managed to resist the temptation to throw her back down upon the bed and subdue her with the most effective, and desirable, means he knew. Her willingness to condemn him so readily hurt him more than he cared to admit, even to himself, and his anger was made even more intense by the realization that she still apparently believed him capable of committing any sort of treachery or betrayal to achieve whatever he desired.

"Why not take Moira with you? Your *dear cousin* is obviously quite adept at providing 'comfort and solace' whenever you are away from home!" charged Rachel.

In spite of his own anger, Logan found himself appreciatively musing that his wife's beauty was only heightened by her outrage. Her cheeks flamed rosily, and her eyes, virtually shooting sparks at him, appeared quite large and luminous within the delicate oval of her face. His penetrating gaze dropped lower, lingering with bold intimacy upon the full curve of her sweet breasts, well outlined beneath the fitted silk of her bodice. Rachel could not prevent a soft gasp from escaping her lips when she noted the direction of his gaze, and she was thoroughly dismayed to feel a disturbingly pleasant tingle run the length of her spine.

Dear Lord, how she loved and wanted him! No matter what he had done, no matter how unscrupulous and dishonorable he might be, she could not deny the fact that he was master of both her heart and her body! She could not deny it, and yet she was fiercely determined that he should not know. If he became aware of just how much power he held over her, then all would be lost.

"I will not go with you, Logan MacBride," she forced herself to reiterate with deceptive calmness. Looking quickly away from the beloved, green-eyed rogue towering above her, she proudly raised her head and proclaimed with only a trace of telltale unsteadiness, "My sister and I will return to our home in the morning. You need not concern yourself with me, or with my family, any longer. You may consider our brief, unfortunate marriage a thing of the past, just as I assure you I intend to do. As for my grandfather's land, we—"

Logan's control over his more violent impulses, already strained to the limit, slipped away. Without warning, he seized Rachel and flung her backward onto the bed. The weight of his hard, lithely muscled body as it came atop hers pressed her stunned softness into the quilt-covered mattress. His hands closed about her wrists in a near bruising grip and forced her arms above her head, and he brought his handsome, savagely scowling face close to her visibly frightened counterpart as he ground out, "You're mine, Rachel! For the last time, you're mine! You'll never be free of me, you little witch—never!" Before she could reply, his lips crashed down upon hers with punishing force. She moaned low in her throat, hating herself for the undeniable passion which coursed through her like wildfire. A sudden, detestable vision of Moira as the recipient of similar attentions swam before her eyes, compelling her to twist her head and thereby tear her lips away from his.

"I won't let you do this to me!" she defiantly raged, summoning all her strength as her body writhed futilely against the immovable hardness of his broad chest. "Not after you've been with *her!* Damn you, Logan MacBride, I will not allow you—"

"Shut up!" he roared, his eyes gleaming with a menacing light. She inhaled sharply, her struggles ceasing as abruptly as they had begun. Logan stared deeply into her sparkling eyes for several long moments before he muttered a curse and demanded in a strangely vibrant tone, "Are you really daft enough to believe I'd want any other woman when I've got you?"

Rachel's eyes grew round as saucers. What was he saying? she dazedly wondered. Was this his way of telling her that he had *not* succumbed to Moira's enticements? Or was it simply yet another tactic employed by him to beguile her into letting down her guard?

"Wha . . . what do you mean?" Her heart leapt for joy, her spirits soaring heavenward when he gruffly declared, "Only that you are without a doubt the most maddening, bullheaded, aggravating female I've ever known, and I'll be damned if I can make heads or tails of why I find no pleasure at the prospect of being with anyone other than a certain golden-haired shrew who will no doubt continue to make my life a misery!" His features relaxed into a faint, mocking smile as he confessed in a low, wonderfully resonant voice, "It seems that I'm a one-woman man, Rachel, though I never knew it until I met you. How the devil can I be tempted by any other woman, particularly Moira, when I've already got the most desirable little wildcat on earth for my wife?"

"Then you . . . you didn't—" she had to ask, needing to have all doubts cast aside. She did not pause to ask herself why, after accusing him of lying to her about so much, she now felt compelled to trust him. She only knew that she *would* believe him if he denied it.

"No. I didn't," Logan answered in a husky whisper, anticipating her question. "Hell, sweetheart, it's all I can do to keep up with your demands!" he then teased with a low chuckle, his green eyes glowing with the promise of never-ending passion as they locked with the iridescent depths of hers. She hesitated only a moment before raising his head and touching her lips to his in a gentle, eminently alluring gesture that proved quite successful in persuading him to forget about anything other than making long, leisurely love to the beautiful young woman who lay, with intoxicating compliancy, beneath him.

Consoling herself with the fact that, although he had not gone so far as to declare his love for her, Logan had at least made a commitment of faithfulness, Rachel surrendered wholeheartedly to the tempestuous abandon calling her. Soon, and with dizzying swiftness, she found herself completely naked, her satiny curves yielding to the mastery of her husband's affections. His bronzed flesh was revealed in all its gloriously masculine splendor a short time later as he shed the last of his clothing and resumed his unhurried exploration of the most sensitive places on his wife's enchantingly formed body.

Rachel trembled with delight when Logan's warm lips trailed a fiery path downward from the silken column of her neck to her breasts. Her fingers threading within the thickness of his dark hair, she moaned softly at the exquisite torment he inflicted upon the voluptuous, rose-tipped globes with his evocatively skillful mouth and tongue, and she could not prevent a sharp intake of breath when he moved lower still, his lips pressing a tantalizing succession of whisper-soft kisses across the quivering smoothness of her abdomen and slender suppleness of her shapely limbs . . .

Suddenly, she was being turned gently upon her stomach, and her eyes closed in ever-increasing ecstasy when Logan swept aside the loosened mass of honey-colored curls to kiss the graceful curve of her back and shoulder blades. He moved his captivating attentions lower once more, his mouth following an imaginary path down along her spine until choosing to linger at the delectable roundess of her derriere. Rachel squirmed and gasped anew as his lips playfully nipped and teased at the firm mounds of her bottom, making a point to pay special tribute to the inviting little clover marking her right hip, before caressing her pale, velvety thighs and the surprisingly sensitive flesh on the back of her knees.

"Logan?" she breathed in puzzlement when lips left her and his strong fingers curled purposefully about her hips. He tugged them upward and back toward him so that she was urged onto her knees in the bed, and the unspoken question in her mind was quickly forgotten as he demonstrated the entrancing proficiency of his skills. Rachel shivered at the potent sensations building to a fever pitch within her when he insinuated a hand beneath her hips and stroked the womanly treasure between her thighs. He pulled her even closer to him as he knelt on the bed behind her, his other hand returning to its highly agreeable endeavors upon her full breasts.

Finally, when neither of them could endure another moment of the wildly chaotic yearnings of their mutual passion, Logan pulled Rachel's delightfully shaped hips toward him one last time. She stifled a cry of sheer pleasure when his manhood sheathed expertly within the honeyed warmth of her feminine passage. Straining back against him, she instinctively matched the slow, erotic rhythm of his thrusts as he leaned back upon his heels and drew her with him. The final blending of their bodies quickly escalated in tempo, and it seemed as if their very souls were entwined when they ascended to the most satisfying level of contentment known to man . . . and woman.

"Logan!" His name was nothing more than a hoarse whisper breaking from Rachel's lips just as she collapsed weakly against him. She would have fallen if not for his arms about her. He tenderly lowered her to her back upon the quilt, then stretched out on his side, flinging an arm possessively across her naked, softly gasping form.

"If it ever becomes necessary to prove my fidelity on an hourly basis, sweet 'Clover'," remarked Logan with a low, affectionate chuckle, "it may damn well kill the both of us!" The rosy glow tinging Rachel's face deepened, and she laughed softly before retorting, "Keep that in mind the next time you are tempted to remain in town for the night with another woman!" Growing serious in the next moment, she turned to him with a look of silent entreaty in her eyes. "Why *did* you stay?"

"I didn't want to, but I happened to run into a friend."

"Was this 'friend' by any chance a female?" queried Rachel in mock suspicion. Logan chuckled again and smoothed his hand along her arm.

"No, thank God. He was a cattle buyer from Billings. We talked far into the night, after which I fell into my bed at the hotel and dreamed of my beautiful, exasperating bride."

"What about Moira?"

"I have no idea how Moira spent the night, nor do I

care." He raised himself up on one elbow and peered solemnly down into Rachel's face. "I'm sorry she's so blasted determined to cause trouble between us. She's had a rough life, which is the main reason we tolerate her. I won't pretend she hasn't entertained notions of our relationship becoming far more than 'cousinly', but I swear to you I've never touched her."

"Why did you take her to Miles City with you? And why did you leave without saying good-bye? After the fire and all that happened—" A delicious tremor ran the length of her spine when his repetitively trailing fingers brushed against her naked breast.

"I didn't trust myself to say good-bye to you, damn it! I was furious with you for disobeying me and placing yourself in such danger! As for Moira's going with me—it was her idea, not mine. She said she wanted to get a few things in town."

"Yes, and you were one of the 'things' she wanted!" She could feel herself coloring from head to toe as his gleaming, sea-green gaze moved leisurely over her exposed flesh. When his eyes met hers again, she could see that there was a light of devilment in them.

"Why did you get so blazing mad at the notion of my spending the night with Moira? Was it merely because of a sense of outraged propriety? Or could it possibly be that you were jealous?"

"Jealous?" she repeated, feigning innocence. Of course she had been jealous! She longed to tell him of her love, to tell him how very much she wanted to hear that she was loved in return. But was now the right time? she asked herself. How could she bear it if he refused the gift of her love, if he denied caring for her as she so desperately cared for him?

The solution to her dilemma presented itself in a most unlikely form. A light rap sounded at the bedroom door, followed closely by another, and yet another.

"Logan? Logan, my dear, it's Aunt Tess! I'm sorry to disturb you, but there is a gentleman waiting downstairs. He claims to be Rachel's grandfather, and he insists upon speaking with you at once!"

XV

Rachel impatiently jabbed the last hairpin into place and hurried down the stairs. Following the sound of two undeniably masculine voices, she found her husband and grandfather in the parlor. Micah stood proudly erect with his hat clenched tightly in his hands. Logan had just sauntered over to a table in the corner to pour them both a drink when his wife, her beautiful face softly flushed and her opal eyes aglow, appeared in the doorway.

"Micah!" Rachel battled fresh tears as she gazed upon his lined, weathered features, and she was warmed by the unguarded spark of affection evident in his flinty gaze. "Oh, Micah, I'm so glad to see you!" Hastening to embrace the man who was second only to Logan in her heart, she was nearly overcome with emotion when his arms came up to tighten about her so that she could scarcely breathe. She was vastly relieved that he had apparently forgiven her, and she choked back a sob as she buried her face against the same hard, capable chest that had withstood a good many of her tears throughout the past seven years.

"Your grandmother hasn't given me a moment's peace since you left. I figured it was about time I came and saw for myself how you were getting on," the tough old lawman explained with an all-too-human unsteadiness to his gruff voice. He cleared his throat and scowled darkly when he caught sight of the way Logan was grinning at them. Firmly setting Rachel away from him, he nonetheless maintained his grip upon her arms and peered closely down into her smiling, upturned face. "You're getting along all right, aren't you?" he sternly demanded, then shot a quick look toward Logan. "Is he treating you well? I want the truth of it, Rachel."

"I'm fine," she assured him with a rather tremulous smile. Acutely conscious of Logan's presence, and recalling with shocking clarity the sensuous splendor they had so recently shared, she felt a telltale blush staining her cheeks. "How is Grandmother?" she asked Micah in a rush, anxious to steer the conversation away from her relationship with the devilishly irresistible man whom she could have sworn was sending her a wicked message with those gleaming, sea-green orbs of his.

"Missing you and anxious to have Lizzie back," her grandfather solemnly revealed, then allowed the merest hint of a smile to touch the frequently unyielding line of his mouth as he remarked, "She'll be none too pleased when she finds out I rode on over without her."

"So you've come to take Lizzie back with you?" asked Logan, moving to Rachel's side and offering Micah a glass of brandy. The older man accepted it with a curt nod of thanks.

"I have," he quietly affirmed. While there was no warmth in his eyes whenever he looked at Logan, neither was there the raw hatred he had displayed toward him at their last meeting.

"Oh, Micah, please let her stay a few days longer," Rachel entreated. "It's been such a great comfort having her here. I don't know what I would have done without her." She regretted her choice of words when she took note of the sharp look he cast her. Trying to conceal her sudden discomposure, she linked her arm through his and suggested, "Why don't we sit down?" Micah held back, giving a slight shake of his head as he asserted, "I've got to be heading back. I left Jace and Culpepper repairing the corral, but your grandmother will no doubt have them washing dishes and hanging out the blasted laundry if I don't get myself back soon." He set the untouched glass of brandy on a table and settled his hat over his thinning gray hair. His slate gray eyes narrowed a bit as he turned to Logan and declared a trifle begrudgingly, "I'd be lying if I said I was glad she married you, MacBride, but I'm grateful to see she's not been mistreated." His eyes narrowed even more and his weathered features tightened as he grimly avowed, "I'm giving you fair warning. Should you ever take it in mind to hurt her in any way, I'll—" His unnecessary warning was left unfinished, for Lizzie suddenly came flying into the parlor.

"Micah! Brodie said he thought he'd seen you riding up, but I didn't believe him!" She launched herself at him, the youthful vigor of her welcome making it seem as if she had not seen him in weeks instead of days. When she drew away, it was only to frown severely and demand, "What in tarnation are you doing here, anyway?"

"I've come to fetch you home. Go upstairs and get your things," he directed with his customary sternness.

"No!" the petite redhead unexpectedly refused.

"Brodie told me they're going to the reservation tomorrow, and I want to go as well!" Rachel, who had until that moment forgotten about Logan's plans for her to accompany him on the trip, glanced up at him with an earnestly imploring look in her bright gaze. He bestowed a brief, disarming smile upon her before intervening.

"I think it would indeed be to my wife's advantage to have her sister along," he told a scowling, noticeably reluctant Micah. "If you'll grant your permission, I give you my word she'll come to no harm. It's not a particularly dangerous undertaking. And since the journey only requires two days of travel each way, we'd be able to bring her home by the end of the week."

"I'd like her company very much, Micah," Rachel softly appealed. The sparkling opalescence of her gaze met and locked with the seemingly impenetrable steeliness of his. As had so often been the case, a silent understanding passed between them.

"Please let me go!" pleaded Lizzie, her hands closing anxiously upon one of Micah's flannel-clad arms. "We've been in Montana for weeks now, and I've yet to see any real Indians! Unless you count Brodie, that is, but then he's only half Crow and he—"

"All right, damn it!" her besieged grandfather capitulated with an ill grace. Irascibly musing that he sure as hell couldn't let Jane know anything about it until the day Lizzie was due home—she'd only worry herself sick if she knew—Micah exacted a solemn promise from Logan to guard both young women with his life, then finally took his leave. Aunt Tess and Uncle Robert, who had been sitting together in the swing on the front porch, wandered into the parlor not long afterward.

"Robert and I were fortunate enough to speak to your

grandfather for a moment, my dears," announced Aunt Tess, favoring both Rachel and Lizzie with a genuinely affectionate smile. "He's every bit as charming as I expected him to be," she graciously opined.

"Charming? *Micah?*" Lizzie blurted out in comical disbelief. Rachel, after shooting her sister a quelling glance and resolutely ignoring the sparkle of amusement in Logan's eyes, answered the older woman's smile with one of her own.

"Micah Parker is a very special man, Aunt Tess." Although pleasantly surprised when Logan suddenly placed an arm about her shoulders and hugged her close against him, she was even more surprised when he laughed softly and remarked, "He must be. After all, he *is* partially responsible for the existence of the newest and most beautiful MacBride." Tess and Robert exchanged indulgent smiles at this display of husbandly pride and affection. Rachel raised wide, luminous eyes to Logan's face, her heart melting at the tenderness she glimpsed within his unwavering gaze.

"Come on, Rachel!" Lizzie unexpectedly piped up, taking hold of her sister's hand and tugging her insistently toward the doorway with her. "There's no time to waste if we're to have things ready for the trip tomorrow!"

Musing with an inward sigh that Lizzie sometimes chose the most inopportune moments to intervene, Rachel nonetheless accompanied the well-intentioned redhead from the room and up the stairs. She soon found herself being confronted with a barrage of questions regarding the damaged state of her bedroom door and the clothing scattered in puzzling disarray about the room itself. Unable to think of a plausible explanation that would spare her further embarrassment, she murmured something to Lizzie about there having been a bit of a disagreement between herself and Logan, but that the "insignificant trouble" had been settled to their mutual satisfaction.

Lizzie shot her sister a narrow, decidedly suspicious look, but did not press the matter further. Later that evening, however, she once again insisted upon sharing Rachel's chambers. And, since it was her last night at the Circle M, Logan generously allowed her to do so, though he made no pretense of being anything other than reluctant to spend yet another night away from his bride.

The journey began shortly after dawn the following morning. With Rachel beside Logan in one wagon and Lizzie happily ensconced beside Brodie in the other, the foursome headed south toward the Yellowstone River. Favored with both a cool breeze and slightly overcast skies, they were spared the discomfort of glaring sunlight and parching heat. Logan had earlier announced that it would require the first half of the day to reach one of the numerous, privately owned ferry stations situated along the mighty waterway.

The morning passed all too quickly for Rachel, who reveled in the new feeling of comradeship with her husband. He answered her many questions about the Crows and the reservation without once complaining, and he even proved willing to discuss Brodie with her—up to a point.

"Why do they call themselves the Absarokee? What does it mean?"

"Children of the Raven." Logan snapped the reins together above the horses' backs and tossed a quick glance over his shoulder at the wagon behind theirs, satisfied to see that Brodie and Lizzie were engaged in what looked to be a pleasant conversation of their own. "They've only recently moved the tribal headquarters to the Bighorn Valley. As a matter of fact, the Crow Agency is only a stone's throw from the site of the Battle of the Little Bighorn. The entire reservation was rearranged a few years ago—much of the original reserve was ceded to the railroad. So much for progress," he concluded with a faint smile of irony.

"Why does your aunt—Brodie's mother—not live at the Circle M?" Rachel then queried, shifting a bit on the hard wooden seat after the wagon wheels bounced over a deep rut in what passed for a road. "Surely, as a MacBride, she's entitled to—"

"Willow isn't a MacBride."

"Not a MacBride?" she echoed in puzzlement. "But Brodie bears the name. And he *is* your cousin, isn't he?"

"He is. My uncle was his father. He legally adopted Brodie a few years back, not long before he died."

"Then Brodie is . . . is . . ."

"A bastard?" supplied Logan, smiling faintly at the expression of embarrassment crossing her features. "There are some who would still call him that. But he's a MacBride the same as the rest of us."

"Then why is he working for you? Why doesn't he have a place of his own?" she persisted, wanting to know all she could about the young man who had so obviously drawn her sister's youthful interest.

Logan did not immediately respond, and when he did it was only to say that they were nearing the river and would be pausing to rest after ferrying across. Rachel wanted to press him further regarding Brodie's position in the MacBride clan, but she deemed it wisest to broach the subject again at a later time.

Since no bridges had as yet been constructed across the Yellowstone, the ferry boat operations provided the only means of crossing the swift-flowing waterway. The ferryman chained the wheels of the wagons to the deck of the wide, flat boat and unhooked the horses in the event of an accident or a sudden spooking of the animals. Rachel stood beside the others on the rough-hewn deck, grateful for the support of Logan's strong arm about her shoulders as the boat pitched and rolled while fighting to remain steady in the current.

Once safely across, they settled in for the "nooning" beneath the trees lining the riverbank. Mrs. Smith, following Logan's instructions, had packed a large woven hamper with a vast array of food and drink. Surprised at the magnitude of her own appetite, Rachel ate very nearly as much as her husband, though Brodie's rapid consumption of half a dozen pieces of chicken, three pieces of corn-on-the-cob, four enormous helpings of baked beans, and nearly an entire loaf of buttermilk bread surpassed them all.

"Jumping Jehoshaphat, Brodie MacBride!" exclaimed Lizzie, eyeing the young man beside her in disbelief as she finished off only her second piece of chicken. "How come you're so skinny? You ought to be big as a barn, the way you put away that food!"

"Guess I work it off," he replied with an unconcerned shrug. Downing the last of his coffee, he rose to his feet and suddenly grinned at the petite redhead who sat perched upon a large, flat-surfaced rock with her calico skirts spread in characteristic disarray about her. "A lot of it has to do with age, of course. Some of us are long past the stage of baby fat," he declared, a mischievous twinkle in his gold-flecked brown eyes as they swept meaningfully over her still developing, adolescent form.

"Baby fat?" she indignantly choked out. Her own brown eyes narrowed and blazed furiously up at him. "Why, you—"

"Lizzie," quietly intervened Rachel, casting her sister a look that appealed for restraint. She could hear Logan chuckling softly as he stood to help an unrepentant Brodie make certain the canvas tarp protecting each wagonload of supplies was securely tied down.

"Confound it, Rachel, he treats me like a child!" Lizzie complained once the two men had moved away.

"Which is precisely what he considers you to be," Rachel pointed out. She stood and gently shook the wrinkles from her dark blue cotton skirts, then drew the resentfully scowling girl up beside her. "Don't be in such a hurry to become a woman, dear Lizzie," she cautioned with a smile. She was about to say more when she suddenly became aware of a soft buzzing, whirring noise coming from the direction of the rock Lizzie had just vacated. She glanced down in curiosity, idly musing that the sound was much like the one a locust makes, but her eyes widened in terror when they lit upon the six-foot length of deadly reptile coiled in belligerent readiness mere inches away upon the rock.

"Rattlesnake!" breathed Rachel, her hands gripping Lizzie's arms in a silent command to remain still. Both young women literally held their breath, their fearful gazes never wavering from the tiny, glittering eyes and the forked tongue shooting out with menacing frequency from between the diamondback viper's fang-studded jaws.

Several thoughts raced through Rachel's mind, and

she frantically wondered if she should risk calling for help. The risk proved unnecessary, however, as Logan, his voice low and comfortingly steady, ordered from a short distance behind them, "Don't move." Clinging tightly to her sister, Rachel stifled a scream when the single gunshot shattered the air. She stared numbly down at the headless, writhing coils on the ground less than a foot from where she and Lizzie stood.

"Come on," murmured Logan, holstering his gun and moving to take hold of Rachel's trembling arm. "Let's get going."

"Hell's bells, you act as if Rachel and I nearly get bit by a rattlesnake every day!" accused Lizzie, appearing much affronted by his nonchalance over the matter. Brodie, who came up and roughly grabbed her hand, remarked with more than a touch of masculine exasperation, "Rattlers are nothing uncommon out here. And the only reason Logan had to shoot was because you couldn't be counted on not to do something entirely witless, like trying to hit at it or badgering it until it was provoked into striking!"

Lizzie, after being true to her nature and protesting Brodie's disobliging assessment of the situation, climbed up onto the wagon seat and sat rigidly erect, her lips pressed obstinately together. Rachel determinedly attempted to put the frightening episode from her mind as she took her place beside her husband, who smiled briefly at her before taking up the reins. Logan and Brodie were soon guiding the wagons away from the Yellowstone, and it wasn't long until they had succeeded in putting the river, and the unfortunate snake, far behind them.

The remainder of the day passed without incident. It was approaching sundown when Logan informed Rachel that they would be spending the night at one of the MacBride ranches a few miles ahead.

"Are they expecting us?" she casually inquired, glancing overhead and smiling to herself as she caught sight of a lone, red-tailed hawk soaring majestically across the darkening sky.

"No, but it doesn't matter. We'd not be turned away in any event. Even outlaws and killers can claim the sanctuary and privilege of another man's hospitality—it's a tradition honored by everyone, or nearly everyone," he amended with a faint smile.

"What would happen if someone chose not to honor this 'code of hospitality'?"

"He's likely to go outside the next morning and find that a well-known vigilante sign has been scrawled above his door. The sign, consisting of the numbers '3-7-77', refers to the dimensions of a grave. And if a man finds such a sign, then he'd do well to beat a hasty retreat from the territory, just as a certain rancher did only last year after making the mistake of turning away a particularly vengeful bunch of cowpunchers."

Rachel's eyes widened in amazement. She found it difficult to understand why such a relatively minor offense should draw such harsh retaliation. Logan, as if possessed of the ability to read her mind, went on to explain, "Getting caught on the range after nightfall is something folks out here try to avoid at all costs. Turning a man away with darkness approaching is the same as sentencing him to an almost certain death."

"Because of Indians?"

Logan merely nodded in response, and the two of them lapsed into silence once more as the wagon wheels rolled across the windswept plains. When they finally reached the ranch belonging to yet another of Logan's cousins—he had not mentioned the cousin's name—Rachel was surprised to see that the old log house was in obvious need of restoration. The corral was also in a pitiful state of disrepair, and only one of the two barns was still standing. There were no other buildings, as well as no immediate signs of life about the place.

Frowning thoughtfully, Rachel gathered up her skirts and waited for Logan to help her down. Once again, it was as if he had read her mind, for he disclosed in a low voice as his hands closed about her waist, "Joseph's lived alone for a year now. Brodie and I stop by every once in a while to see if he needs anything."

"Why does he live alone?"

"Because his daughter refuses to live with him. And he refuses to move in with anyone else." He was already leading her toward the house, which Rachel continued to eye somewhat dubiously. Lizzie chose to remain behind and help Brodie with the horses.

Suddenly, the front door swung open to reveal a gray-bearded man of indeterminate age, though Rachel judged him to be at least fifty. His features were rather coarse, his raw-boned body a bit stooped, and there was something about his eyes—narrow eyes of a strange, greenish-yellow hue—that seemed vaguely familiar to Rachel. Clad in a shapeless, dirty cotton shirt and almost colorless denim trousers, the man looked every bit like the hermit he was.

"Evening, Joseph," said Logan, climbing the splintered, lopsided steps with an ease of manner that made it seem as if his visits were an everyday occurrence. "This is my wife, Rachel," he announced, carefully drawing her up the unsteady blocks of wood beside him.

"Your wife?" Joseph rasped out, his eyes narrowing into mere slits as they swept critically up and down Rachel's form. Although inwardly bristling at such a rude inspection of her person, she forced a smile to her lips and politely declared, "I'm very pleased to make your acquaintance, Mr. MacBride."

"Thought you were going to marry that girl of mine," grumbled Joseph, disregarding Rachel's civility as he fixed Logan with a sharp, glowering look. "But then, I guess you wouldn't have been of a mind to go through with it after what happened, would you?" Without another word, he turned his back on them and disappeared within the darkened interior of the house. Logan, appearing not in the least bit offended, escorted a thoroughly bewildered Rachel inside.

Although he scarcely spoke to them all evening, Joseph *did* have the courtesy to offer them lodging and a hot meal for the night. Of course the two women were called upon to prepare the meal, but even Lizzie failed to offer more than a token complaint at finding herself volunteered to help her sister with the cooking.

It wasn't until they had retired for the night, in a dust-caked but otherwise habitable bedroom, that Rachel was finally afforded the opportunity to question Logan about his cousin. Lizzie was settled in a much smaller room next door, while Brodie had chosen to bed down on the floor of the kitchen near the fireplace.

"Joseph is Moira's father, isn't he?" asked Rachel, shivering slightly at the chill permeating the lamplit room as she stepped out of her dress and hurriedly drew her high-necked cotton nightgown on over her head. Her back was turned toward Logan, and she waited until her body was draped in the nightgown's generous folds before slipping off her chemise and drawers.

"Yes," Logan answered simply, smiling at his adorable bride's belated modesty. Displaying no such proclivity toward shyness himself, he boldly stripped off his clothing and stretched the length of his magnificent, hard-muscled frame out upon the bed. Rachel eased onto the lump-ridden mattress beside her husband and quickly drew the covers up over them both.

"It's easy to see where Moira gets her sour disposition!" she commented, shifting about in the bed in a futile attempt to locate a spot where the mattress feathers were not bunched together.

"I don't believe Joseph's as hardened as he would like people to believe. While it's true that he and Moira were never able to get along after the death of her mother, I think a great deal of their trouble was brought on by Moira herself." He wrapped one bronzed arm about her shoulders and pulled her close, anxious to forget all about Joseph and Moira and turn his attention to more pleasurable matters.

"What did he mean when he said you wouldn't have been of a mind to marry his daughter after what happened?" Rachel's wifely curiosity prompted her to inquire. Logan frowned and released a heavy sigh before reluctantly divulging, "He was referring to Moira's elopement with Vance."

"Moira and Vance are married?" she demanded in stunned disbelief, raising up on one elbow to peer closely down into his grim features.

"No. Vance refused to marry her. She stayed with him for several days before returning home. By that time, however, Joseph had foolishly involved the law, and it wasn't long before everyone in the county knew about it. What happened brought disgrace on the whole family," he finished with a fierce scowl of remembrance, his eyes aglow with a savage light. Rachel dared not tell him that she had heard part of the story once before, the night she had stood in the bathroom and listened at the door while Moira raged at him for his denial of what she claimed to be her love for him.

"Do you realize that this is the first time the two of us have slept in the same bed for an entire night?" she brightly observed in an effort to change the subject. Her cheeks crimsoned delightedly when Logan, abruptly pulling her atop him, uttered in a low, vibrant tone that sent a delicious tremor coursing down her spine, "What makes you think we're going to sleep?"

Logan, talking briefly with their host the following morning, was gruffly assured by Joseph that he was doing well enough, and that he would be willing to do his duty as a father and take Moira back if she should be of a mind to come home.

"She'll not be ill-treated if she does?" asked Logan. Though still not entirely convinced Moira had ever been as cruelly dealt with as she claimed, he felt compelled to exact such a promise from Joseph. One thing was for certain—Moira could no longer remain at the Circle M. She was obviously determined to continue her troublesome behavior, and he wanted to spare Rachel any further heartache caused by her vengeful mischief.

"She'll have to work hard and do as I say," the older man tersely declared. His gaze met Logan's squarely as he begrudgingly professed, "But I'll not raise a hand to her." Satisfied that Joseph would remain true to his word, Logan thanked him for his hospitality and joined the others outside.

They were soon on their way once more, heading out across the wild, ruggedly beautiful terrain between Rosebud Creek and the Bighorn River. The chosen route would lead them to within a few miles of the newly created Northern Cheyenne reservation, and Logan etimated that they would reach the land of the Absarokee by mid-afternoon.

The day had dawned considerably warmer than the previous one, but the sky remained blanketed by a dense cover of clouds. There was an unmistakable scent of rain in the morning air, prompting Rachel to wonder if they would soon find themselves drenched by a sudden downpour. There was nothing within her immediate line of vision which could provide shelter in the event of a storm.

As her gaze swept across the seemingly endless prairie, she caught sight of a large herd of pronghorn antelope in the near distance. They were grazing peacefully at the sagebrush, their white necks and rumps making them easily identifiable.

"There's an old Blackfoot legend that says the 'Old Man'—the Blackfoot god—first made a pronghorn out of dirt when he was in the mountains," related Logan, noting the direction of her interested gaze. "But when he turned his creation loose, it took off so fast that it tripped on the rocks. So he placed it on the prairie to see how it would fare. Old Man was pleased by the creature's grace and speed as it raced across the prairie, which is why—the Blackfeet say—the animals are so prevalent out here on the plains today."

"You know a great deal about this land and its legends, don't you?" Rachel queried with a captivating smile. She untied the ribbons of her straw sunhat and tugged it away from her thick, honey-blond tresses, then inhaled deeply of the fresh, rain-scented air.

"My father used to tell me I *was* the land," he disclosed, his lips curving into a thoroughly disarming grin as his green eyes twinkled with amusement. "Dugan MacBride was as ornery and opinionated as they come, but he never let me forget how much he loved his adopted homeland, nor how much he counted on me to preserve the traditions and values of my heritage."

"I suppose you'll want to pass them on to your children as well," ventured Rachel, her breath catching in her throat when she viewed the unfathomable but strangely exhilarating glow in his virescent gaze.

"*Our* children," Logan corrected softly. He stared at her for several long, emotion-charged seconds before turning his attention back to driving the wagon. Urging the horses along with another slapping together of the reins, he lapsed into silence, leaving Rachel feeling oddly restless and more than a little discontented.

Oh Logan, will you ever say you love me? she silently appealed, her opal eyes glistening with all the love in her heart as she stole a glance at him from beneath the velvety fringe of her eyelashes. Sighing inwardly, she folded her hands tightly together in her lap and settled back against the hard slats of the wagon seat.

They paused to rest and eat the last of their food just before noon. The wind had steadily increased in velocity throughout the morning, and the clouds grew darker and more menacing with each passing hour. Noting the conspicuously threatening, anvil-shaped thunderhead looming on the horizon, Brodie frowned and remarked to no one in particular, "Looks like we won't be able to outrun the storm after all." In the process of finishing off yet another loaf of bread, he leaned negligently against the wagon. Lizzie and Rachel, having already eaten, walked alongside a nearby gully in order to ease the stiffness from their legs.

"That's the least of our worries right now," Logan murmured in response to his cousin's observation. His own intense, narrowing gaze was fastened on a small flurry of movement in the opposite direction.

"What are you talking about?" questioned Brodie in puzzlement. He abruptly straightened and tossed the bread aside when he, too, caught sight of the approaching horsemen. "Cheyenne?" he surmised, nevertheless seeking the other man's confirmation. Logan nodded curtly.

"They're probably harmless, but we'd better not take any chances." He and Brodie were both aware of the fact that the Northern Cheyennes, like many of their counterparts, had not yet been successful in adjusting themselves to reservation life. Forever destroyed was their nomadic, hunting civilization—the kind of life into which they had been forced proved both difficult and degrading for the once-proud warriors. Those who still refused to adapt found themselves reduced to begging or stealing, perhaps rustling a few head of cattle now and then . . . or sometimes even murdering in order to survive.

"What is it? What's the matter?" demanded Lizzie. She and Rachel came hurrying back to the wagons at a shout from Brodie.

"Logan?" Rachel searched the grimly set planes of his handsome face as he pulled her close for a brief moment.

"You and Lizzie get out of sight between the wagons and stay there," he quietly commanded. "They've no doubt already seen you, but there's no sense in providing them with such a visible reminder of your presence."

"Who?" Lizzie asked in growing exasperation, her eyes making a quick sweep of the area and finding nothing. Brodie took her arm in a firm grip and personally escorted her to the narrow gap between the wagons.

"Cheyenne," he finally answered as Rachel moved to her sister's side. "Now both of you stay down!"

Tugging Lizzie insistently downward to kneel upon the ground beside her, Rachel peered through the spokes of the wagon wheel. She waited and watched anxiously as her husband and his cousin positioned themselves in front of the wagons.

The five riders, who soon drew their mounts to a halt a short distance away from where Logan and Brodie stood with their guns in purposely evident readiness, were a surprisingly ragged lot. The Indians' long, unbound hair hung lank and greasy about their shoulders, their tattered shirts and trousers appeared every bit like the cast-offs they were, and the tight, guarded expression on the faces of them all seemed to bespeak their desperation and lost sense of pride. They were all no more than a year or two older than Brodie, judged Rachel, but the hatred blazing within their dark gazes was ageless.

Logan nodded a silent greeting at the Cheyennes. His eyes narrowed imperceptibly, an instinctive wariness darkening them to jade. Brodie, facing traditional enemies of his mother's people, lifted his head proudly and tightened his hold upon the rifle in his hands.

"What do you carry in your wagons?" the self-appointed leader of the renegades demanded in a low, guttural voice.

"We are bringing gifts to the mother of my brother," Logan answered truthfully, for, among the Crows, a male cousin was considered the same as a brother.

"What are these gifts?" the Indian persisted. Neither he nor the four men flanking him had as yet made a move for their own guns, prompting Logan to wonder exactly what sort of maneuver they were plotting. He thought of Rachel and Lizzie, but he displayed no apprehension as he casually replied, "Nothing of great value. Some blankets, a few bags of flour. The gifts are of no importance to anyone but a Crow squaw." This last was spoken as a pointed reminder of the Cheyennes' reputation as fierce warriors, as well as a reminder of their belief that the Absarokee were an inferior tribe. Unfortunately, the leader would not be swayed by mere words.

"The Cheyenne have need of such gifts. We will take them." It was a supremely confident statement of intent. Logan, giving a slight shake of his head and leveling his gun at the horsemen while Brodie did the same, evenly dissented, "No. You will not." Wondering why the

Indians still made no attempt to draw their guns, he grew increasingly wary, his entire body tensing.

Suddenly, there was a commotion behind him. Two more Cheyenne braves, who had first ridden up from the opposite direction, then had stealthily crept closer to the wagons on foot, lunged forward to seize Rachel and Lizzie. The sisters cried out sharply and struggled against their assailants, but to no avail. They were forcibly dragged from between the wagons, their captors lifting them off the ground and swiftly moving to stand with the other Cheyennes, who had taken advantage of the momentary distraction to finally produce their own weapons.

Logan found himself gripped in the throes of a helpless rage as his savagely gleaming gaze met the terror-filled luminescence of Rachel's. She was held before her captor like a shield, the Cheyenne's arm clamped painfully about her waist and threatening to cut off her breath. Lizzie was suffering the same cruel treatment beside her.

"Tell your men to let them go," Logan forced himself to demand calmly as he raised his carefully inscrutable gaze to meet the haughtily triumphant one of the renegades' leader.

"We will trade you these women for the wagons and horses," the Indian avowed with a faint smile of contempt.

Logan's coldly glinting eyes lit briefly on Rachel once more. Although he read the fear in her wide gaze, there was an admirably defiant set to her shoulders, and her head was lifted in an unconscious gesture of dauntless spirit. His heart swelled with pride for the beautiful, courageous woman he had married.

Tearing his gaze away from Rachel, he was about to offer the Cheyennes the only response he could—that they were to take the wagons and horses and leave the women—when he caught sight of yet another group of horsemen in the distance. He knew that Brodie had seen them, too, for he felt the younger man stiffening beside him. The strengthening wind whipped across the rolling prairie, effectively obliterating all sound of the approaching riders' hoofbeats.

"There will be no trade," Logan told the Cheyenne.

Rachel gasped in stunned disbelief while her sister breathed a curse. The leader of the renegades, and his companions as well, stared in open-mouthed amazement at the tall, green-eyed man who suddenly faced them with such bewildering nonchalance. Amazement quickly turned to angry suspicion.

"What trick is this?" growled the Cheyenne, his dark eyes glittering fiercely.

"Take the women. I have no use for them." Logan schooled his features to remain impassive as the Indian subjected him to a long, narrow look.

"You would give up your women for blankets and flour?"

"I would," Logan stated simply. The Cheyenne, much taken aback at the unexpected turn of events, allowed his gaze to linger upon Brodie for the first time and demanded scornfully, "You are of the same mind as your white brother?"

"I am. The women are nothing but trouble. You are welcome to them, especially the little one with the flaming hair," he added with a nod in Lizzie's direction, mentally noting that the other riders were closing in fast behind the Cheyennes.

"Why, you yellow-livered son of a—" snarled the outraged redhead. Just as she was preparing to hurl a string of the foulest imprecations known to man at Brodie, a shot rang out.

Caught off guard, the Cheyennes jerked around to see that more than a dozen Crows were thundering down upon them. A blood-curdling yell split the air, then another and another. Rachel and Lizzie were knocked brutally to the ground as their captors flung themselves up behind two of their mounted companions. The Cheyennes, faced with almost certain death if they remained to fight the Crows, spurred their mounts into a gallop and raced away across the plains. With the women safely out of the way at last, Logan did not hesitate before ducking behind one of the wagons and firing at the fleeing band of renegades. He succeeded in wounding their leader at the same time that a bullet from one of the Cheyennes' stolen guns tore through Brodie's left shoulder.

"Brodie!" screamed Lizzie. Scrambling to her feet, she flew to his side as he fell to one knee and grabbed at his burning flesh. Rachel was there an instant later, her face paling when she viewed the gaping wound. She wasted no time, however, before tearing a strip from her fine lawn petticoat and forming a thick bandage to press firmly upon the young man's bleeding shoulder.

"You'll be fine, Brodie, just fine," she reassured him, smiling tremulously up into his stoic features. Logan ceased his firing and spun about to check on his cousin as the band of Crows took off after the Cheyennes with a vengeance.

"You blasted fool!" he muttered to Brodie, abruptly

shouldering Rachel aside as he made a quick inspection of the younger man's wound. "Why the devil didn't you take cover?" Brodie grinned sheepishly through his pain as he reluctantly admitted, "Because I was too damned set on getting even with those Cheyenne bastards, I guess." Logan's mouth curved into a begrudging smile, and he shook his head in wholly masculine admiration for his cousin's bravery.

"You . . . you were going to give us to those murdering savages!" Lizzie indignantly sputtered at Logan, suddenly remembering what she believed to be her brother-in-law's treachery. She shot him a venomous glare and drew herself up to her full height, which was little more than five feet. "If you had only given them the confounded wagons, Brodie wouldn't be sitting there with a bullet in him!" she charged.

"Shut up, you little idiot!" Brodie bit out. "You don't know what the hell you're talking about!"

"Yes I do! And you, Brodie MacBride—why, you practically *begged* them to take us!" she furiously recalled.

"Lizzie!" Rachel rose hastily to her feet and gripped her sister's shoulders, administering a slight shake as she said, "Don't you see? They were only stalling for time until help arrived!" She cast a look of mingled uncertainty and appeal at Logan as he stood beside her. "Weren't you?"

"Though I must confess it was quite tempting to get the two of you off my hands," he remarked with only the ghost of a mocking smile, "I sure as hell would have traded you for more than some blankets and a few bags of flour."

A somewhat mollified Lizzie sank back down onto the

ground beside Brodie, who scowled darkly at the way the headstrong girl fussed over him. Rachel was surprised to feel Logan's arm slipping about her waist, and she gazed expectantly up at him, her heart twisting at the thought that he had very nearly got himself killed.

"Damn it, woman, don't you know by now that I value you above anything or anyone else?" he murmured softly, his green eyes aglow with something she dared not name.

It was the closest he had ever come to a declaration of love. Rachel's eyes filled with tears, and she would have gladly cast herself upon his beloved chest and wept freely if not for the fact that the Crows, satisfied that they had sent the renegade Cheyennes hightailing it out of the county, came reining up at that moment.

"Many thanks, Gray-Bull," Logan told the young Crow brave who, following a disturbance earlier in the day along the narrow strip of land separating the two reservations, had been leading his band on a search for the renegades. Having met Gray-Bull several years earlier, and thereby familiar with the Crow's reputation as a fierce and relentless warrior, Logan mused to himself that the Cheyennes were fortunate indeed to have escaped with their lives.

With the Crows escorting them the rest of the way, Logan, Rachel, and Lizzie headed on toward the reservation. Although Brodie had vehemently protested, he had been lifted up onto horseback and taken to the reservation ahead of the others. One of the young Crows took his place in the wagon beside Lizzie, who made no secret of the fact that she would much rather have been allowed to go with Brodie and see to his injuries herself.

Rachel, hugging to herself the knowledge that Logan

cared deeply for her—whether he chose to call it "love" or not—held fast to the back and side of the wagon seat as the wheels bounced and jolted over the seldom-traveled road. A clap of thunder rang out, and the heavens opened up shortly thereafter, but not even the increasing discomfort of the last part of the journey could dampen her spirits.

XVI

Although their holdings had sharply dwindled throughout the past several years, the Absarokee were fortunate in that their reservation encompassed millions of acres that were rich in natural resources. With endless plains, crystal-clear streams, high mountains, and an abundance of timber lands, there was a wealth of all kinds of game, grass, roots, and berries. And with nearby Fort Custer to aid in protecting their lands, the Crows had made rapid progress. Log cabins were beginning to replace the traditional tipi, farming was gradually being accepted as the new way of life, and even the traditional hide clothing was giving way to calico and denim. Many of the old traditions, however, would never be completely abandoned.

Rachel lifted the canvas slicker covering her head, her gaze drawn in fascination to the rain-drenched sights about her as Logan drove the wagon past the buildings of the Crow Agency and on toward the tipi belonging to Brodie's mother. Willow-By-The-Water, as she was called by her people, had not as yet fully embraced the advancements of civilization, in spite of her son's encouragement for her to do so.

The storm showed no signs of letting up. Rachel was disappointed at not being able to view more of the surroundings, for Logan had told her a good deal more about the reservation as they had traveled closer to the northern boundaries of the Crow lands. She had wanted to watch the children playing at their games of stick dice and "magpie," or to perhaps watch the women painting on bark the starkly realistic battle scenes for which Logan had said they were so renowned.

"This is it," Logan suddenly announced. The rain streamed in rivulets off the broad brim of his hat as he drew the wagon to a halt before a large, conical shelter of canvas stretched over a frame of tall poles. When he led Rachel and Lizzie inside the tipi a few moments later, they were met by a tall, slightly plump Indian woman of no more than forty who was attired in a fringed, two-skin dress and moccasins. Speaking nearly flawless English, the once beautiful, and still attractive, Crow woman formally invited them to enter her home.

"Thank you, Willow," Logan solemnly replied, then introduced Rachel and Lizzie to Brodie's mother. She smiled warmly at the two young women and drew them farther inside the traditional lodge, where Brodie was lying on a pallet near the fire. His handsome young face was set in taut, determinedly impassive lines as his wound was dressed by a friend of his mother's—an ancient, white-haired woman who, it was generally believed, possessed mystical skills of healing and prophecy. Fortunately for Brodie, the bullet had been extracted without too much difficulty, and all that remained to be done was to bandage the wound and make certain it was kept clean and dry.

"She-Who-Knows has said my son's shoulder will heal quickly," Willow told Logan, her lips curving into a smile of maternal pride as she looked at Brodie. After inviting her guests to sit about the fire, she knelt beside her son and patiently awaited any further instruction from the old woman who tended him.

Logan watched with a faint smile of approval as Rachel and Lizzie sank down upon the ground and modestly drew their legs up under the concealing folds of their full skirts. They were unaware of the fact that they had followed a time-honored Crow tradition that permitted only men to sit with their feet and legs in full view.

Soon, the "healing woman" finished her work and, without a word to any of the visitors, left the tipi. Willow then hurried to offer food and drink to her guests, firmly declining Rachel's offer of assistance. Brodie, his bronzed features looking more than a little drawn and pale, leaned back upon the bed Willow had fashioned for him out of buffalo robes.

"My mother told me they're going to have the Goose Egg Dance tonight," he remarked to Logan. A boyish grin briefly lit his face as he added, "I don't know if she'll ever be able to forgive me for getting shot and missing out on the perfect opportunity to get myself a true Absarokee wife." Logan smiled and asserted, "You know as well as I do that you'd never have gone through with it even if you *hadn't* done such a good job of giving those Cheyennes target practice."

"What are you talking about?" Lizzie sharply demanded, her damp red curls plastered close to her head. She and Rachel had both been almost soaked to the skin by the unavoidable downpour, and they were both now grateful for the warmth of the fire.

"You can go and watch if you want to, but they don't allow *children* to take part," Brodie informed her. Lizzie would have offered him a suitably scathing retort, but Willow returned just then. Ducking back inside through the hide flap protecting the opening, she brought them a fresh supply of rain water, as well as a generous portion of newly smoked venison.

It was still raining when Logan and Rachel were escorted by Willow's young niece to a neighboring tipi much later that afternoon. The usual custom would have been for Lizzie to take up residence with her sister throughout their visit, but the petite redhead had stubbornly refused to stay anywhere but with Brodie and Willow.

"I'm afraid we've appropriated someone's home, haven't we?" Rachel murmured once she and Logan were alone in the roomy, firelit lodge. As in Willow's tipi, the canvas walls were adorned with vivid paintings of animals and scenery.

"It belongs to Willow's sister," confirmed Logan, bending down on one knee beside the fire and leisurely placing more wood on the dwindling blaze. "But these people consider it a great honor to give up their home to a guest—particularly if the guest is an adopted member of the family and has brought his new wife with him," he added with a low chuckle. The fire crackled and popped, sending a shower of smoke and sparks curling upward to the flap cut for ventilation at the top of the tipi where the poles converged.

Rachel, perhaps struck by the undeniable feeling of intimacy within the lodge, experienced a sudden shyness as she moved slowly toward the fire. Acutely conscious of

Logan's eyes upon her, she gently cleared her throat and asked, "Did . . . did Brodie spend his childhood here on the reservation?"

"Part of it. My uncle brought him to live at the Circle M more than ten years ago." With an easy, masculine grace of movement, he shifted about to sit cross-legged in typical Indian fashion. He lifted a hand to Rachel, and she hesitated only a moment before clasping it with one of her own and allowing him to pull her down beside him. Logan's eyes softened as they drank in the sight of the firelight playing across her beautiful countenance, and the way her unpinned tresses flowed like a shimmering, golden curtain all the way to her slender waist.

"Didn't Willow object to being separated from her son?" Rachel queried a trifle breathlessly, her luminous eyes widening as they raised to encounter the glowing intensity of his.

"I'm sure she was reluctant to give him up, but she believed a son should be guided into maturity by his father. So, when she felt the time was right, she sent Brodie to live at the ranch with us. By the time his father died, it was too late for him to return to his former way of life here."

"It was a bit like that for me and Lizzie, I suppose," she commented with a sigh, then smiled at the frown of bemusement creasing her husband's sun-kissed brow. "After spending all those years with Micah and Grandmother in Rock Creek, it would have been impossible for us to fit into San Francisco society any longer."

"Impossible for Lizzie, perhaps, but not for you," Logan quietly disagreed, slipping an arm about her shoulders and pulling her even closer. He gazed deeply into her splendid opal eyes, his head lowering so that his warm mouth was mere inches from hers. "You could fit in anywhere, Mrs. MacBride. You're every inch a lady—a feisty, hardheaded, temperamental one at times, but a lady nonetheless." An affectionately mocking smile played about his lips as he declared in a low voice brimming with amusement, "And I'm glad, damned glad, that you forgot to lock that bathroom door in Billings, sweet 'Clover'."

Coloring rosily, Rachel demanded in mock indignation, "*Must* you keep reminding me of—"

Silenced in a most gratifying manner, she moaned softly and entwined her arms about her devastatingly irresistible husband's neck. His lips swiftly grew more demanding as he tugged her onto his lap, and it was highly probable that the impassioned embrace that followed would have flared to an eminently desirable conclusion if not for the unexpected reappearance of Willow's niece at the tipi opening.

The girl, a bashful young maiden of thirteen, hastily bent to set the bundle of clothing in her arms on the ground just inside the lodge. Flushing in embarrassment at having interrupted what was obviously a tender moment of marital intimacy, she murmured something about her mother's sending the things for the Goose Egg Dance, and something else about Willow's family gathering for a meal of celebration at the present time. A nervous giggle escaped her lips before she whirled about and darted back out into the rain.

"It seems we're in for quite a festive evening," murmured Logan. He didn't sound particularly pleased about the matter as he set Rachel away from him and rose to his feet. Drawing her up beside him, he smiled what she could have sworn was a wolfish smile. "We'll continue this 'discussion' later, Mrs. MacBride," he vowed in a deep, resonant tone that sent a shiver—one that had nothing whatsoever to do with the cool turn of the weather—racing down her spine.

The Goose Egg Dance was to commence at sundown. Originally learned from the Hidatsa tribe, the closest relative to the Crow, the dance was performed primarily for amusement, but it also served the purpose of bringing many a young Absarokee couple together.

Rachel, her honey-colored tresses secured in two long braids, appreciatively smoothed a hand along her borrowed gown of soft deerskin. Extending from her chin to her feet, the gala dress was worn with knee-high leggings and decorated with a remarkable array of elk teeth. The leather clung to her supple curves like a second skin, prompting her to muse that it was no wonder so many young Crow women found themselves betrothed at the conclusion of the dance!

Although Logan had already described the proceedings to her, she still experienced more than a twinge of nervousness for what lay ahead. Their invitation to participate in the dance was considered quite an honor, for the event was primarily restricted to unmarried men and women.

"Well, Golden-Swan, are you ready?" a familiar voice drawled behind her. Rachel, feeling a bit self-conscious in her unfamiliar garb, blushed faintly as she turned to face the tall, green-eyed rogue who ducked inside the tipi. The welcoming smile on her face slowly faded, and her eyes grew very round when they fell on the arresting sight before her.

Clad in a fringed and tasseled buckskin suit that fit his powerfully built form to perfection, Logan looked every inch like the magnificently virile man he was. The soft leather shirt, stretched tautly across the hard muscled breadth of his chest, was trimmed with intricate beadwork down the front and at the cuffs. The leggings, which tightly encased the sinewy leanness of his lower torso, were beaded down the outside. A pair of moccasins, also beaded, adorned his feet. He was smiling across at her, the rugged perfection of his bronzed countenance appearing more irresistible than ever before.

"You look beautiful," he softly proclaimed, his smoldering gaze moving over her with intimate leisure.

"So do you," she responded in a voice scarcely above a whisper, unable to take her eyes off him.

"Golden-Swan and White-Hawk," Logan murmured with a low chuckle of appreciative irony. The fringes of his suit swayed gently to and fro as he sauntered forward. "We make quite a pair, don't we?" His eyes gleamed with a returning spark of passion as they caressed the loveliness of her upturned face.

"Why do you call me that?" asked Rachel, the familiar weakness at his close proximity causing her head to spin.

"That's the name you've been given by Brodie's family. To the Absarokee, you will now always be Golden-Swan, wife of White-Hawk." Reaching out to take her arm in a firm but gentle grip, he smiled softly once more and said, "It's time to join the others."

Rachel smiled in response and accompanied him from the lodge. The rains had finally ceased a short time earlier, leaving the brisk twilight air smelling clean and fresh. The lingering moisture of the storm coated the leaves on the trees and glistened in puddles on the ground. Logan led the way across the split-log planks that had been placed atop the soaked earth to prevent as much mud as possible from being tracked inside the huge community lodge situated in the center of the settlement.

They paused in the doorway to the lodge, and Logan spoke one last encouragement to Rachel before moving to take his place inside with the other men. A friendly young woman appeared beside Rachel and presented her with a beaded headband containing two eagle tail-feathers, as well as a blanket of red flannel. Speaking only halting English, she instructed Rachel to don the headband and wrap the blanket about her. Other young women formed a line behind them, all of them dressed in a similar manner.

Six male singers began chanting inside the lodge, their traditional songs accompanied by the pounding of drums. A herald waited in the center of a large ring of spectators, and it was he who gave the signal for the procession to begin. Rachel held tightly to the blanket, keeping pace with her newfound friend as the line of female participants filed two abreast inside the brightly lit, ceremonial tipi. They were led by two previously selected, chaste young women, and they immediately formed a circle about the men who stood in a smaller circle around the herald.

Rachel's nervousness increased when she saw the number of spectators. Her eyes searched for Logan, and she was disappointed to find that he was standing with his back turned toward her. Her gaze was drawn past him to the ring of onlookers, and she felt at least a small measure of comfort when she glimpsed a wide-eyed Lizzie sitting beside Willow.

Suddenly, the singing and pounding swelled to a crescendo. Although unfamiliar with the steps of the dance, Rachel was fortunately able to follow her friend's lead well enough as the young women began to glide and twirl about the circle of their male counterparts. The men, who were attired much the same as Logan, stood perfectly motionless while the women danced slowly about in a clockwise direction, their movements graceful and rhythmic and in perfect harmony with the music.

Logan did not return his wife's smile when she finally stood before him, but his eyes conveyed a silent message of reassurance to her. Rachel was reluctant to move away from him, for she was still acutely conscious of the appreciative crowd who watched her with such open curiosity, but she obediently executed the steps of the dance alongside the other young women. The Crow men who formed the circle of which Logan was a part betrayed absolutely no emotion as their future sweethearts and brides glided past them. At last, following several uninterrupted minutes of the dance, the music abruptly stopped and the herald announced in a booming voice, "Come, young men, find the one you like best and kiss her! Give her presents, and if your heart is greater so that you wish to marry her, give her a horse and take her away with you this night!" He spoke in the Crow language, and though Rachel was unable to understand his words, she understood his meaning perfectly—not only because of Logan's previous explanation, but also because of what followed.

The spectators laughed and cheered as the men in the circle finally came to life. Rachel watched as the young woman next to her was seized by a particularly handsome fellow and kissed soundly in front of everyone. There was much commotion as the women either accepted the embrace of a suitor, or, as in the case of some, rejected the man's attentions outright. Several men offered their chosen brides a stick representing a horse, while still others stepped up to the woman's family and made a public declaration of their intentions.

Fascinated by it all, Rachel was caught by surprise when she herself became the recipient of a kiss that was searingly passionate enough to curl her toes. When she was finally released several long moments later, her opal eyes danced with loving mischief, and her mouth curved into a beguilingly sweet smile as she told Logan, "Why, it *is* you, Mr. MacBride! I wasn't quite certain."

"What the devil do you mean you weren't certain?" he demanded in obvious displeasure, his eyes suddenly ablaze.

"It's just that there are so many—" she began to explain with a look of wide-eyed innocence, only to be cut off as she was rewarded for her wifely impertinence. Logan's strong arms enveloped her with possessive fierceness, and his warm lips crashed down upon hers in a kiss that proved even more breathtakingly provocative than the one preceding it.

There was a rumble of appreciative comments and laughter as White-Hawk lifted a blushing Golden-Swan in his arms and carried her from the ceremonial lodge. Minutes later, the two of them were alone within the privacy of their own tipi.

"You danced very well," Logan remarked as he set her on her feet beside the comforting blaze. There was an unmistakable note of pride in his deep voice, and Rachel found herself mesmerized by the fiery glow contained within the darkening, sea-green depths of his eyes.

"The steps were not as difficult as I had feared," she replied a bit breathlessly, her own eyes shining softly. Her hands trembled slightly as she reached up and carefully removed the beaded headband.

The golden firelight played across their faces, casting giant shadows on the opposite canvas wall of the shelter. They could hear the faint strains of renewed singing drifting on the night wind, could detect the sound of other lovers talking and laughing together as the newly betrothed couples made their way to secluded trysting places of their own.

Without another word, Logan unhurriedly bent his tall frame downward until he knelt beside the dancing flames. Rachel's breathing grew increasingly erratic as she watched him place more wood on the fire, and a becoming rosiness tinged the smoothness of her cheeks when he rose to his feet once more and stood gazing inscrutably down at her. Time held no meaning as a long, highly charged silence passed between them.

Rachel was the first to move. Inwardly marveling at her own boldness, and yet unable to resist the sudden, heartfelt impulses calling her, she tossed the headband to land upon the pile of buffalo robes on the other side of the fire. She then slowly raised her hands to begin freeing her shimmering blond hair from the restraining braids. Her eyes never wavered from her husband's as she ran her fingers through the loosened tresses and sent them spilling in glorious abandon across her shoulders and down her back.

The expression on Logan's handsome face remained unfathomable, but the glow in his intense, virescent gaze deepened until his eyes took on the appearance of two fiery-hued emeralds. Rachel experienced a brief hesitancy on her part, but she resolutely banished it. Though she could not explain why, even to herself, she felt an overpowering need to demonstrate her love for Logan, to give of herself completely and without constraint. She would endeavor to put aside all inhibitions and reserve, would think only of showing him—in the most convincing way she knew—how very much she loved him, and how very much she needed to be loved in return.

Drawing confidence from her love, she raised her chin in an unconscious gesture of determination and smiled softly before bending down in a single, graceful movement to unfasten her leggings and ease them off. When she straightened again, she was satisfied to glimpse the undeniable spark of rapidly escalating desire in Logan's green eyes. There was a noticeable tightness about his firmly chiseled lips, giving evidence of the fact that it was requiring every ounce of iron will he possessed to keep from crushing her to him without further delay. But he forced himself to wait, and he soon found himself well rewarded for his patience.

Rachel dispensed with the last barrier between Logan's smoldering gaze and her delectably curved nakedness when she untied the leather fastenings of her dress and allowed the soft deerskin garment to slide downward to land in a heap about her trim ankles. Much to her husband's delight, she stood still and unafraid before him, allowing his fiercely glowing eyes to drink their fill of the sight of her firelit loveliness.

Never had Rachel felt so certain of her love for Logan, nor of her body's God-given purpose to the man she loved. She could literally feel his searing gaze as it lingered in turn upon her full, rose-tipped breasts, the womanly flaring of her hips, and the beckoning triangle of honey-colored curls between her silken thighs. A warm flush stole over her, and she trembled with the force of her own spiraling passions. She yearned for Logan's touch as never before, and it was with another flash of boldness that she took a step forward and murmured in a teasing yet eminently seductive tone, "Are you content to merely stand there and look at me, Mr. MacBride, or will you perhaps be wanting to do more?"

"More," came the reply in a voice that was nothing more than a vibrant, husky whisper. "A hell of a lot more!" With a low groan of almost unbearable desire, Logan finally yanked her against him and claimed the sweetness of her lips with the demanding warmth of his. His hands swept up and down her naked curves with a provocative urgency that made her dizzy, and it wasn't long until he was lifting her in his powerful arms and carrying her to the bed of buffalo robes.

Rachel's skin tingled as it came into contact with the soft fur, but the mildly pleasant sensation was nothing compared to what she felt when Logan's naked hardness came atop hers a few moments later. His mouth descended upon hers with exhilarating vehemency once more, his fingers returning to their ecstasy-inducing labors upon her quivering, satiny flesh. While his tongue plundered the willing softness of her mouth, he moved so that one of his hands could pay stirring homage to her breasts. His strong fingers closed over first one voluptuous globe, then the other, tenderly caressing in a circular motion before teasing lightly at the sensitive pink nipples.

Rachel inhaled upon a sharp gasp when his lips, after

scorching a path downward and then hovering just above her breasts with loving mischievousness until she moaned in protest and arched her back to bring them invitingly closer to his mouth, finally possessed one of the rose-tipped peaks. Her head tossed restlessly upon the buffalo robes, and she cried out softly when his tongue flicked lightly, erotically across the nipple. Her fingers clutched almost convulsively at the bronzed smoothness of his shoulders, and she endured several more moments of the exquisite torment, her other breast receiving its fair share, before pushing Logan firmly aside and struggling into a sitting position.

"What are you doing?" he demanded, frowning in bemusement as she climbed to her knees beside him. Her mass of long, honey-blond hair swirled sensuously about her naked curves, and her sparkling opal eyes were alight with the sweet glow of passion. She answered him—not with words, but in a much more satisfying manner.

Bending over Logan so that her thick curls tumbled onto the softly matted expanse of his bare chest, Rachel first proceeded to press her lips upon his in a thoroughly bewitching kiss that caused him to lie back upon the buffalo robes and draw her down atop him. He was both surprised and enchanted when, several long moments later, she straddled his lean hips and began nibbling and teasing lightly at his hard, bronzed flesh. His fingers curled tightly about the slender indentation of her waist as her sweetly provocative lips traveled lower and lower, and he moaned low in his throat when she finally reached the place between his taut thighs where his manhood sprang forth from a tight cluster of dark curls.

"No more, you beautiful little wildcat!" Logan ground

out, abruptly tugging her back up so that her face was level with his. She colored hotly and stammered in embarrassment, "I . . . I'm sorry." She tried to avert her mortified gaze, but he gently cupped her chin with his hand and forced her to look at him. His face wore a smile of such incredible tenderness that Rachel found herself moved to tears.

"What for? You've done nothing wrong. My sweet love, I'm already burning with desire for you! And by damn," he then declared with mock ferocity as he hugged her close, "there's only so much a man can take!"

"You mean you . . . you don't think it unseemly of me to—"

"Unseemly?" he echoed with a frown. His brow cleared in the next instant, and he chuckled softly before affectionately nuzzling the silken column of her neck and murmuring wryly, "Hell, Mrs. MacBride, I hope our lovemaking continues to be 'unseemly' for the rest of our lives!"

A faint sigh of relief escaped Rachel's lips, and a soft gasp quickly followed, for Logan wasted no time in stoking the fires of passion once more. His hands skillfully searched out her most secret places, and his lips claimed hers with a vehemence that sent her innermost yearnings careening wildly upward. Rolling so that she was beneath him again, it was his turn to bestow deliciously "unseemly" caresses upon her alluring form, and she was soon rendered almost totally incapable of rational thought as she answered his passion with a freedom born of love.

By the time he positioned himself above her, Rachel dazedly mused that he had kissed and caressed nearly every square inch of her trembling flesh. She gloried in his body's possession of hers, her fingers stroking feverishly across his smooth, hard-muscled back as his manhood sheathed perfectly within her velvety warmth. Obeying the most basic of her feminine instincts, she wrapped her shapely limbs about the magnificent litheness of his hips and followed the mastery of his rhythm. Together, she and Logan soared heavenward, their emotions climbing ever upward until attaining the cherished goal of the most complete, earth-shattering fulfillment that was humanly possible.

The once-substantial blaze in the center of the tipi was nothing more than a pile of glowing embers when Logan finally stirred to nourish it with more wood. Rachel's eyes were shining with love and contentment as she watched him, her cheeks flaming slightly when she found herself admiring her virile husband's naked, splendidly masculine body. She snuggled happily against him when he resumed his place beside her and cradled her in his strong arms.

"Do you suppose the others who took part in the dance are as satisfied with the outcome as we are?" she asked with a soft laugh.

She felt Logan's broad chest quake with a low, answering chuckle. "I'm sure at least some of them are. If tradition didn't demand otherwise, they'd probably have the celebration with a great deal more frequency. And there'd probably be a great many more Absarokee who could trace their beginnings to the night of the Goose Egg Dance," he concluded with an endearingly crooked grin. Rachel smiled, her fingers tracing a repetitive pattern along the upper portion of his bronzed chest. A sudden, extremely pleasant thought occurred to her, and she took a deep breath before idly questioning,

"And what if there happens to be a future MacBride who can trace his—or her—beginnings to the night of the Goose Egg Dance?"

"His—or her—father would no doubt be called upon to relate the story many times in the years to come." Raising up so that she could closely scrutinize his beloved features, Rachel's eyes clouded with more than a touch of genuine concern as she asked more seriously, "Do you truly want children, Logan?"

"Of course I do," he unhesitantly assured her, a faint frown of bemusement creasing his handsome brow. "Why wouldn't I?"

"Well, I . . . I didn't know if you were the sort of man who considered children a nuisance, or even the sort who—"

"Damn it, woman, do you still know so little about me?" he demanded with a sigh of mild exasperation. "I would have thought that, by now, you'd be certain enough of my feelings for you to know that I want our love to—"

"Our *what?*" interrupted Rachel, her eyes growing very round. "Wha . . . what did you say?" Logan frowned again and looked at her as if she had suddenly taken leave of her senses.

"Only that you ought to know enough about me by now to realize I'm ready to settle down and—"

"Logan MacBride, are you by any chance saying that you love me?" she impatiently demanded, scrambling up on her knees beside him, her shimmering curtain of hair only partially concealing her womanly charms. He did not immediately answer, his green eyes darkening with renewed desire as they virtually devoured her exposed beauty. "Do you love me?" she finally gathered courage enough to bluntly demand.

"Of course I do," he responded once again. His hands were already closing about her bare arms to draw her back down to the buffalo robes, but she firmly resisted.

"Then why have you never said so? Why did you allow me to worry and fret about—"

"Because I wanted to be sure you felt the same way about me. I've loved you from the very first, Rachel," he now confessed, his eyes aglow with all the love in his heart and his handsome features suddenly appearing more vulnerable than ever before. He sighed heavily before solemnly revealing, "I think I always knew it, but it didn't become clear to me until the morning after we were married. I wanted to tell you then, but I knew you weren't ready to hear it—nor to believe it. I decided to bide my time, to do my best to make you realize you cared for me in return. My methods may not always have been to your liking," he recalled with a quick, disarming grin, "but I always believed you'd come to love me as I love you."

"Oh, Logan," whispered Rachel, feeling quite stunned by what she was hearing. "I *do* love you! Like you, I suppose I always knew it, but I . . . I didn't want to face the truth. And after we were married, there were so many things . . ."

"Such as your suspicions about me and Vance?" She nodded wordlessly, her blue eyes filling with remorse for ever having doubted him. He waited no longer before pulling her back down into his warm embrace, and another long sigh escaped his lips as he settled her body next to his. "You know, I tried my damnedest to convince myself that the only reason I offered to marry you was to prevent useless bloodshed. I wanted you more than I'd ever wanted any woman, and yet I was too blasted stubborn to admit that you'd somehow managed to get under my skin—and into my heart. No matter how hard I tried, I couldn't get you out of my system. When all that trouble between Vance and your grandfather came up, our getting married seemed like the natural course of action."

"But then you . . . you came to my room that first night at your ranch. Why?"

"Because you're a golden-haired vixen who sets me on fire," he retorted, a faint smile of irony tugging at his lips. His hand smoothed lovingly over the delectable roundess of her naked hip as he sighed again and admitted, "I suppose I never really intended to keep our bargain. Though I didn't come to your room with the purpose of making you mine, once I was there I couldn't force myself to leave. And you sure as hell didn't help matters any by calling for me in your sleep! You were enough of a temptation when awake—how could I possibly resist you when you were lying there all soft and alluring in that bed, with my name on those sweet lips of yours?"

"Perhaps I *was* secretly hoping you'd defy our agreement," Rachel allowed with another soft laugh, her eyes kindling with a spark of remembrance for what had passed between them on their wedding night. "When we married, I believed I was sacrificing myself on Micah's behalf. Little did I realize that a certain arrogant, maddening, decidedly overbearing rogue had already stolen my heart!" she teased.

"I may very well be all those things and more," said Logan, his voice wonderfully low and resonant, "but I love you nonetheless, and I'll never let you go. You're mine, Rachel—or Clover or Golden-Swan or whatever else suits you. You're my wife, my temptress, my own true love." To prove his point, he tugged her atop him again and claimed her lips in a kiss of such impassioned enchantment that it became a treasured memory, along with the others she would forever associate with the night of the Goose Egg Dance.

XVII

Logan, Rachel, and Lizzie bid a reluctant farewell to Brodie and Willow early the next morning. They were unable to delay their departure for the three or four days it would require for Brodie's shoulder to heal. Not only had Logan promised Micah to have Lizzie home by the end of the week, but he had also made plans to attend an important meeting of the Cattlemen's Association in Miles City on the way back from the reservation to the Circle M.

It was arranged that Brodie—with an escort of Crows—would drive the second wagon home when he was once again able to travel. Lizzie was noticeably crestfallen over the fact that he would not be accompanying them, and the handsome young half-breed looked none too pleased about the matter himself. But there was nothing for him to do but accept the situation and endure a volley of well wishes and advice from his three departing companions while he lay on the bed of buffalo robes in his mother's lodge. Lizzie's good-bye proved a trifle unsettling to Brodie—her brown eyes glistened with uncharacteristic tears as she knelt beside him and whispered something about seeing him at the Goose Egg Dance in a few years hence.

When they were on their way at last, both Rachel and Lizzie twisted about on the wagon seat to gaze southward upon the distant, snow-capped peaks of the Pryor Mountains. The countryside was ablaze with sunlight, and there was not even a single cloud dotting the brilliant blue of the sky. The parched earth had been gratefully replenished by the previous day's rain.

Rachel's excitement was rapidly increasing as they neared her grandparents' ranch later that same day. She had missed Micah and Jane a great deal, and she was particularly anxious to speak with her grandmother and assure the kindly, maternally protective woman that her marriage to Logan had indeed been made in heaven and not hell.

"Looks like Jace and Culpepper have given Micah his money's worth after all," observed Lizzie, nodding to indicate the new corral beside the barn just ahead.

"There's no doubt about it—Micah's putting a lot more care into the place than Tate ever did," Logan conceded. "But then Tate didn't exactly relish the idea of working hard to keep up the ranch when his father died. I think once the other MacBrides see what's been done, they'll not begrudge your grandfather the land."

Rachel merely smiled in response, her gaze sweeping across the ranch yard in search of her grandparents. It wasn't until Logan had slowed the horses to a halt in front of the house that Jane finally appeared, her face wreathed in smiles as she came bustling through the doorway and down the steps of the porch.

"Rachel! Lizzie!" Her brown eyes, so much like those

of her youngest granddaughter, filled with tears of joy at seeing them again. Once they had alighted from the wagon, she immediately hugged them to her ample bosom. Several long moments of the emotional reunion passed before she remembered her manners and greeted Logan. Hastily drying her tears, she turned to him and spoke with heartfelt sincerity, "Thank you for taking such good care of them, Mr. MacBride."

"It's 'Logan'," he insisted with a disarming grin, his green eyes twinkling irrepressibly down at her. Jane, musing to herself that it was easy to understand why Rachel had been charmed by the man, impulsively embraced him as well, then linked her arm through Rachel's and led the way inside the house.

"I'm afraid we won't be able to stay long, Grandmother," Rachel announced as they entered the kitchen. "We have to make it to Miles City before nightfall." She smiled at her husband as he set Lizzie's things on the floor, then took his leave to go in search of Micah outside. Lizzie followed in his wake, anxious to tell her grandfather all about her trip to the reservation, and also wanting to give Jane and Rachel an opportunity to talk alone.

"There's no need to ask if you're happy," remarked Jane, quickly setting a fresh pot of coffee on to boil. She took a seat at the table and beamed at Rachel as the younger woman sank down into a chair beside her. "It's plain to see whenever I look at your face, honey. You're very much in love with that husband of yours, aren't you?"

"Yes," Rachel answered with a gentle nod, her opalescent eyes glowing with the certainty that her love was reciprocated. "Now I know how you must have felt when you married Micah, and I can better understand why Father put Mother's wishes first and moved to San Francisco all those years ago."

"Even though it broke your grandfather's heart, I never blamed Ethan for loving your mother the way he did. It was only natural that he wanted to make his wife happy. But once you're older and have children of your own, you'll maybe be able to see Micah's side a bit more clearly as well." Jane paused and heaved a sigh, her gaze drifting toward the window. "Micah Parker's a proud man, Rachel, but there's none better."

"Is he contented here, Grandmother?" Rachel solicitously queried, leaning forward to take Jane's hand between both of hers. "Do you think he regrets leaving behind his old way of life?"

"At times, perhaps. But I think he's as determined as ever to stay here in Montana and raise cattle. He's even talking about adding a few head of sheep to his stock." She brought her other hand up and gave Rachel's arm an affectionate squeeze before rising to her feet. "On the whole, I'd say he's content. He still misses you something fierce, but I think he'll get over it, especially since you're within a few hours' ride. And he's going to have his hands full with Lizzie now that she's getting older!" She chuckled softly and moved to the stove.

Outside near the barn, Lizzie's narrative of her adventures was cut short when Jace and Culpepper came riding up with yet another report of rustlers making off with some of the stock in broad daylight.

"Damn it, why didn't you go after them?" Micah angrily demanded.

"We couldn't, Mr. Parker," Jace explained regretfully, his once fair skin now tanned to a light golden color. "There were more than a dozen of them!"

"Those no-account bastards are getting bolder all the time, that's for sure!" opined Culpepper, his usual, easygoing manner giving way to helpless fury. Suddenly recalling Lizzie's presence, he flushed uncomfortably and muttered by way of apology for his choice of words, "Begging your pardon, Miss Parker." Lizzie was about to tell him there was certainly no need to apologize for using the same designation she would have given the cattle thieves, when Logan solemnly asked Micah, "I take it this isn't the first time you've had them make off with some of your stock?" Micah shook his head, his flinty gaze narrowing as it met the other man's.

"This is the third time in a row now. We've had no other trouble since you and Rachel got married." His weathered features tightened into a harsh scowl. "It's crossed my mind more than once that Vance MacBride might be responsible for what's going on. Maybe he no longer has the guts to face me outright. Maybe he's set on breaking me bit by bit now."

"I might be inclined to have the same suspicions myself, if not for the fact that every rancher in the county's having the same trouble," declared Logan. "There's to be a meeting of the Cattlemen's Association in town tonight. Our first priority will be to draft measures for dealing with the rustlers. You're welcome to attend."

"What the hell good are meetings and talk?" growled Micah, whipping the hat from his head. He looked at Jace and Culpepper and nodded curtly toward the barn. Obeying his silent command, the two young men reluctantly led their horses away.

"Nothing else is doing any good, is it?" Lizzie

challenged her grandfather. "You can't be out on the range day and night!" She was not the least bit intimidated when he turned to glower down at her. "It certainly can't do any harm to go and listen to what the others have to say!"

"I've got work to do," he tersely decreed, "and I'll not leave my ranch." It was obvious that he considered the matter closed. Lizzie released a sigh of total exasperation as he began striding toward the house. Logan smiled to himself at the disgruntled expression on her freckled young face.

"You can't change a man's ways, little sister."

"It seems to me that Rachel's changed a lot of *your* ways, 'big brother'!" she retorted, her brown eyes flashing. He chuckled and casually draped an arm about her shoulders.

"Maybe so, but as you'll no doubt discover for yourself in the not too distant future, a wife's influence holds a lot more weight than a granddaughter's." His sea-green gaze was alight with amusement, and it wasn't long until the petite redhead's lips curved into a begrudging smile.

"You know, for a MacBride, you're not too bad a sort," she impishly pronounced.

"I take that as quite a compliment, coming from someone who will in all likelihood bear the name herself someday." With another low chuckle at the look of startlement on her face, he sauntered away and into the house.

Logan and Rachel soon thereafter took their leave of the Parkers. The afternoon was just beginning to fade into dusk when they reached Miles City. After leaving the team and wagon at one of the livery stables, they secured a room at the Macqueen House and went upstairs to bathe and change before having dinner in the hotel's restaurant.

"Why don't we save time and share a bath?" Logan suggested with a decidedly roguish grin as Rachel gathered up her things and moved to the doorway of their room.

"I doubt very seriously if it would save time at all!" she countered, a becoming flush rising to her cheeks. A smile tugged at the corners of her mouth, and her eyes sparkled delightedly as she ventured in a soft voice, "Perhaps another time, Mr. MacBride." She did not wait for a response before opening the door and scurrying down the narrow hallway to the bathroom.

Minutes later, she eased her tired body into the water's soothing warmth and relaxed against the high curved back of the tub. She released a long sigh, then reluctantly took up the cake of lavender-scented soap she had brought with her and began scrubbing at the silken smoothness of her skin. After soaping and rinsing every inch of her womanly form, she came up on her knees in the bathtub and bent forward to wash her hair.

Suddenly, Rachel became aware of the unmistakable pressure of a pair of warm, firmly chiseled lips upon the glistening, satiny roundess of her right hip, in the exact spot where the clover-shaped mark was so invitingly visible. Inhaling upon a sharp, highly audible gasp, she flung her bottom downward and her head upright. Her wet tresses streamed across her furiously blushing face, and she hastily parted the dripping mass of honey-colored hair so that she could gaze upon her bold assailant.

"Logan!" she breathed, torn between relief and outrage.

"Once again, sweet 'Clover', I couldn't resist," he lazily drawled, his green eyes dancing with unrepentant devilment. His splendidly masculine form was clad only in a pair of denim trousers—just as when Rachel had first set eyes on him in precisely the same environment in Billings.

"I distinctly remember locking that door!" she accusingly proclaimed.

"Your memory serves you correct. The Macqueen house boasts of many achievements, but foolproof locks are not among them," he explained with another unconcerned grin. Folding his arms across his bare chest, he leaned negligently back against the door and directed with husbandly arrogance, "Finish your bath, woman. Then you can stay and scrub my back for me."

"After scaring me half to death, Logan MacBride, you may very well scrub your own back!" she defiantly retorted. She eyed him mistrustfully when she bent back down to wash her hair again, but he merely watched her, his eyes gleaming with appreciation for her exposed shapeliness.

Once Rachel had stepped from the tub and wrapped a towel about herself, Logan wasted no time in stripping off the last of his clothes and plunging his bronzed, lithely muscled nakedness into the soapy water. He cursed at its coolness, then made all haste to wash the dust of the journey from his tall frame. His wife, meanwhile, had donned her undergarments and wrapper and was proceeding to the doorway with the obvious intention of leaving the room.

"Come back here," Logan masterfully commanded. A soft rosiness tinged Rachel's face as she turned back to the naked, devastatingly handsome man who splashed the last of the soap from his hard body.

"It's getting late. If we're to have dinner before your meeting, we'd—"

"Not until you scrub my back." He leisurely sat up and rested his arms atop his bent knees. "Hurry up. The water's getting colder by the minute." There was a strange smile playing about his lips, and Rachel was almost certain she glimpsed a spark of renewed, unholy mischief within his gaze.

Surrendering to the inevitable with a faint sigh of resignation, she set the bundle of discarded clothing in her arms atop a chair and moved to stand beside the tub. She took the bath sponge Logan offered her and gathered up the folds of her wrapper to kneel on the floor.

"Will you always be so autocratic and demanding?" she asked with mock discontent, dipping the sponge in the water and gliding it across the broad expanse of his naked back.

"Invariably. Then again, perhaps you can reform me," he quipped with a deep, pleasantly mellow laugh. Before she could guess his intent, he twisted about and yanked her down atop him in the bathtub. A tiny shriek escaped Rachel's lips as she hit the water, her undergarments and wrapper soaking up the soap-clouded liquid much like the sponge she still clasped in her hand.

"Logan! Logan, stop it!" she breathlessly protested, striving in vain to escape and climb from the tub. His strong arms easily held her against him.

"Stop thrashing about, sweetheart—you're getting water everywhere!" he chuckled, his legs wrapping about hers. Managing to free one of her arms, Rachel brought the bath sponge sloshing up into his wickedly grinning face.

"Why, you little—" sputtered Logan. Briskly shaking his head to clear the water from his eyes, he peered narrowly down into his wife's beautiful, smugly triumphant features.

"*Now* will you allow me to get up?" she challenged. A slow, meaningful smile spread across his wet, rugged face as he avowed in a slightly husky tone, "*Now* you've sealed your fate, my love." She gasped as his hands moved to the sash of her wrapper, his fingers deftly untying it before she could do more than push feebly against him and murmur a half-hearted protest. He swiftly peeled the drenched garment down and off, flinging it to land in a soggy heap on the floor and leaving Rachel only in her chemise and open-leg drawers, which were now almost totally transparent and clinging to her luscious curves in a highly revealing manner.

"Logan! Logan, what are you—" she started to question, only to break off with yet another gasp as he pulled her farther upward so that her firm, full breasts were more conveniently positioned for his purpose. He captured the thinly covered pertness of one rosy nipple with his mouth, while his hands closed about the alluring roundess of her derriere.

Rachel's eyes swept closed, her fingers curling tightly within Logan's thick, damp hair. The gentle but insistent pressure of his lips and tongue through the delicate layer of wet fabric at her breast sent her passions flaring almost out of control. She was scarcely conscious of the fact that she was lying atop her husband in a tub full of rapidly cooling water, for his artfully seductive attentions warmed her and succeeded in driving all else but their present, wonderfully spontaneous intimacy from her mind.

Soon transferring the moist caress of his lips from her breasts to her mouth, Logan kissed her with an all-encompassing intensity that prompted a floodtide of almost unbearable longing within her. She responded with a vehemence that thrilled him to the core, her lips parting so that her tongue could dance sinuously with his, and her hands roaming over his naked, hard-muscled body with rapturous abandon.

"Rachel, Rachel," Logan whispered hoarsely, his lips relinquishing hers several long moments later and hungrily exploring the silken planes and hollows of her face, throat, and shoulders. She moaned softly at his delectable assault upon her flesh, and her own emboldened maneuvers evoked a similar response in him.

She inhaled upon another gasp when his hand moved to the secret place between her thighs. Because of the convenient design of her undergarment, his efforts were happily unimpeded, his sensuously persuasive fingers searching out her velvety treasure and prompting a surge of near painful desire to course through Rachel's body like wildfire.

Glorifying in her tempestuous response, Logan slowly leaned forward and drew himself farther upright in the tub so that his wife's shapely, parted limbs were on either side of his lean hips. The cool water swirled about their nonetheless feverish bodies as he tasted of her lips once more, their mutual passions building to a fever pitch. A soft cry broke from Rachel's lips when the undeniably virile evidence of her husband's maleness eased within her well-placed feminine passage. She clung tightly to him, her buttocks settling upon his hard thighs as he loved her in a gently rocking motion that prolonged the delicious agony.

"Oh, Logan!" she gasped out, grateful for the support of his powerful arms about her trembling softness. Soon, his mouth was swallowing her breathless cry of fulfillment, and she collapsed weakly against him at the same time he leaned back against the cold porcelain of the bathtub with a heavy sigh.

"It seems we're destined to share particularly 'stirring' encounters in hotel bathrooms, my love," Logan mused aloud a short time later. Having already donned his trousers, he stood watching with a quizzical smile on his handsome face while Rachel drew on her travel-worn but thankfully dry gown.

"It will probably take all night for these things to dry," she pronounced with a sigh, turning to wring out her sodden wrapper and undergarments. In truth, she didn't mind in the least, for every fiber of her being was vibrantly alive. She returned her husband's smile with a special, captivating one of her own. Her heart sang as she accompanied him from the room and back down the hallway, and her opal eyes remained aglow throughout the evening.

Rachel wandered aimlessly toward the window again. The meeting taking place downstairs had been in progress for less than an hour, and yet she was feeling inexplicably restless. Logan had cautioned her to remain in the hotel room until he returned—Miles City, he had firmly asserted, was no place for a young woman to be wandering about alone at night. Although she had agreed to do as he bid and stay put, she was now contemplating the notion of doing precisely the opposite.

Surely it wouldn't do any harm to venture forth from

the Macqueen House for a brief time, she rationalized to herself. The night was pleasantly cool and moonlit, and there were street lamps situated along the boardwalk in either direction from the hotel. And, since Logan had informed her that the cattlemen's meetings usually became quite spirited and lasted until well after midnight, it would be several hours before she could even begin to anticipate his return.

Rachel made her decision and resolutely turned away from the window. After pausing to fling a lightweight, hand-crocheted shawl about her shoulders, she swept from the room and down the stairs.

The meeting of the Cattlemen's Association, meanwhile, had grown every bit as spirited as Logan had predicted. Quite a number of ranchers were advocating vigilante action to help curb some of the lawlessness, while another faction insisted upon controlling the pilferage of their stock by passing legislation against the cattle thieves, horse thieves, and other assorted desperadoes. Though putting a stop to the increased tide of rustling was of foremost concern, various members also initiated discussion of the flood of immigration, the deplorably large export of beef, and the growing problems of open grazing. It was obvious that not all those gathered in the hotel's dining room were in accord.

Before long, a shouting match erupted, and Logan was hard pressed to restore order to the proceedings. His deep voice rang out above the commotion, appealing for level heads to prevail. Thus occupied, he did not see the familiar, raven-haired man who slipped from the room, nor did he catch a glimpse of his wife sailing across the hotel lobby in a blatant disobedience of his orders.

Vance MacBride, however, *did* see her. He emerged

from the noisy, smoke-filled dining room just as Rachel was stepping through the main doorway and onto the boardwalk outside. His golden eyes narrowed and gleamed as they fell upon her well-remembered form, and his thin lips curled up into a predatory smile. Negligently tossing his cigarette to the lobby floor, he ground it beneath the heel of his boot and strode purposefully after the golden-haired young beauty who, he mused acrimoniously, had not only made the mistake of openly defying him, but had also underestimated his determination to exact revenge upon her grandfather.

Rachel inhaled deeply of the cool, fragrant air and impulsively turned her steps toward the row of saloons and dance halls at the opposite end of Main Street. She felt perfectly safe, for there were a number of men and women promenading together along the boardwalk on their way to one of the town's many restaurants. Straightening the pert velvet bonnet atop her honey-colored chignon, and taking care to lift the hem of her embroidered muslin skirts away from the dried mud caking the wooden planks, she strolled leisurely away from the hotel.

There were lively strains of music drifting on the night air, as well as the sound of boisterous, masculine laughter and the more high-pitched tones of mirth from the "loose" women who entertained the men. Rachel stared in wide-eyed fascination at the frilled, feather-bedecked saloon girls who paraded in front of the drinking and gaming establishments in an effort to lure even more customers inside. Aware of the fact that the boardwalk was becoming increasingly crowded as she neared the Cosmopolitan Theater, she glanced up to take note of a large, hand-lettered sign announcing that there was to be a special performance of an "All Female Orchestra and Dancers."

Rachel smiled to herself at the sign's meaning, then suffered a sharp pang of conscience when a vision of Logan's handsome face suddenly flashed across her mind. Releasing an audible sigh, she turned back to retrace her steps, only to find her path blocked by an all-too-familiar man with black hair and strange golden eyes.

"Vance!" gasped Rachel, her gaze clouding with instinctive terror.

"Evening, *Mrs. MacBride,*" he insolently drawled, his swarthy features wearing a covertly menacing smile. His smile broadened as he tipped his hat with unconvincing politeness. "Don't you know how dangerous it can be to go gallivanting around here alone at night?"

"I did not consider it in the least bit dangerous until now!" she retorted with spirit, her eyes flashing before making a quick, pointed sweep of the surrounding crowd. "And as you can well see, I am *not* alone!"

"Then where's Logan?" Vance challenged.

"My husband is . . . is waiting for me at the hotel," Rachel partially fabricated. "He is no doubt becoming quite impatient by now, so if you will allow me to pass—" She tried to do so, but he moved to intercept her, his fingers closing with rude firmness upon her arm. The people milling about on the boardwalk paid them no heed, for it was not apparent as yet that anything was amiss.

"You know, *cousin,* I've been meaning to congratulate you on keeping your pretty mouth shut about the other day. I know you didn't say anything to that hot-tempered husband of yours, or else he'd have paid me a call." His hawkish eyes kindled with a brutal light, and his mouth curved into a sneer as he spoke in a rasping undertone, "In spite of Logan's attempts to keep the truth from me, I've found out about Tate. Yes, sir, *cousin*, I know that your grandfather murdered him! And that old bastard's going to pay. I don't give a damn what Logan says—Micah Parker's going to pay!"

"Let go of me!" she demanded hotly, jerking her arm free. Several men turned toward them with a frown now, and Rachel was sorely tempted to call for assistance. But she knew Vance MacBride to be a very dangerous man, knew he was capable of vile treachery. She thought of Logan, of her grandparents, of Lizzie—if she antagonized Vance, there was no way of knowing exactly what he would do.

"I've business to settle with Logan as well," Vance muttered tersely, his words sounding very much like a veiled threat to Rachel's ears. Although he glared down at her, he made no move to touch her again. "And you—you've done nothing but cause trouble ever since you came here! You may have been able to fool Logan, but you sure as hell haven't fooled me. I see you for the conniving little bitch you are!"

"Get out of my way," Rachel bravely directed. Her beautiful countenance appeared proud and aloof, and her eyes betrayed none of the fear which formed a tight knot in her stomach. A contemptuous smile spread across Vance's darkly attractive features before he finally stepped aside. Rachel gathered up her skirts and fled, forcing her steps to remain steady and measured. She heard Vance's low, scornful laugh behind her.

"I'll be seeing you again real soon, *cousin*—real soon!" he called after her. A sharp quiver of alarm raced down her spine, but she did not pause or look back. When she reached the sanctuary of her hotel room once more, she closed the door and leaned breathlessly against it.

What was she going to tell Logan? How would he react if she told him of Vance's threats? She shuddered to think of what Vance might do if Logan confronted him.

"Dear Lord, what should I do?" Rachel prayed aloud in agonized uncertainty. Crossing to the bed, she sank wearily down upon the embroidered coverlet, her mind in a dizzying whirl and her emotions feeling raw and strained.

Logan bent over the slumbering form of his wife and awakened her with a tender kiss. He smiled down into her beautiful, sleep-drugged features as he announced in a low tone brimming with fond amusement, "Time to get up, my love."

Rachel's eyes flew to the window, where she was startled to see the bright sunlight filtering in through the curtains. She hastily drew herself upright in the bed, sweeping the thick blond tresses away from her face as she asked Logan in astonishment, "Good heavens, did the meeting last all night?"

"No," he answered with a soft, vibrant chuckle that sent a pleasurable tingle through her. "It broke up about two. You were sound asleep when I came in, and I thought it best not to disturb you." He smiled again before reluctantly straightening and heaving a sigh. "Much as I would like to climb back into bed beside you, I'm afraid we've got a full day ahead of us. I've got to visit with the commandant over at Fort Keogh this morning before we head on back to the ranch."

"Fort Keogh?" echoed Rachel with a puzzled frown.

She tossed back the covers and slid from the bed, the hem of her gauzy cotton nightgown slipping upward to reveal a goodly portion of her bare, shapely limbs. Logan groaned inwardly and forced himself to refrain from tumbling her backward onto the bed. A frown creased his sun-kissed brow as he mentally cursed the fact that he had to keep the appointment at the fort.

"In order to prevent certain members of our group from taking the law into their own hands—something that's going to happen soon if we can't find a solution—I agreed to try once more to procure the military's assistance in fighting the rustlers." A near painful surge of desire shot through him as he watched her shed the nightgown in order to don her lace-trimmed undergarments. His green eyes smoldered as they lingered upon her silken nakedness, and he envied her delicate white cotton chemise and drawers as they closely hugged her supple curves.

"Why would they refuse to help you?"

"Because they consider the matter out of their jurisdiction. However, I intend to place it *in* their jurisdiction without further delay."

"And how do you propose to do that?" Rachel questioned with genuine interest. Drawing on the same embroidered muslin gown she had worn the night before, she was suddenly reminded of her brief but highly unpleasant encounter with Vance. Her eyes clouded with renewed apprehension, and she was torn between the desire to seek comfort from Logan, and the fierce determination to protect her husband and her family from Vance's possible retaliation. Having reached the conclusion that Logan would of a certainty seek out his cousin if he knew of Vance's threats, she had made the decision not to tell him of last night's episode. She could only pray that she was doing the right thing.

"By informing them that not only are the rustlers making off with privately owned stock, but with government property as well," Logan explained. "We've all got contracts with the cavalry for several thousand head a year, to provide beef to the reservations as well as to the posts. It's hoped they'll agree to cooperate when they learn that some of the ranchers have every intention of listing their stolen cattle as among those already purchased by the military."

Rachel, her mind still plagued by thoughts of Vance, finished pinning up her long hair and forced a beguiling smile to her lips. Her eyes sparkled brightly as she stepped forward and linked her arm through her husband's.

"Is there time for breakfast before we leave?"

"Only if you don't persist in looking at me like that, woman!" Logan retorted with mock gruffness.

It was already mid-morning when they drove away from Miles City and headed toward the nearby military post, which was situated on the right bank of the Yellowstone some two miles above the mouth of the Tongue River. It was necessary for them to cross the Tongue in a flatboat ferry, after which they soon spotted the red-roofed buildings of the fort.

Established more than eight years earlier, and named in honor of a heroic captain who was killed at Little Big Horn along with Custer, Fort Keogh boasted of being one of the largest and finest cavalry posts in Montana. There were no walls and no stockade; the barracks, store houses, and officers' quarters faced upon a big quadrangle of grass-carpeted ground, in the center of which stood a tall flag staff.

Rachel, musing to herself that the fort resembled a small, neatly arranged town, smiled at the sight of the numerous wives and children who moved about the broad piazzas with the off-duty officers. There were blue uniforms everywhere as the usual bustle of activity brought the post to life.

"This is it," said Logan, drawing the team to a halt before the commandant's quarters. They were now at the west point of the diamond-shaped fort, where Rachel noted the row of two-story buildings with huge cottonwoods shading the front yard of each. "That's where the officers and their families are quartered. The enlisted men have to settle for the barracks," Logan explained with a faint smile. He secured the reins and climbed agilely down from the wagon, then reached up for her. "I don't expect this to take long. You can wait out here if you'd prefer."

"It would no doubt be best," she replied as his strong hands closed about her waist and effortlessly swung her down. "I certainly hope you and the military are able to come to terms."

"So do I," murmured Logan, his mouth tightening into a thin line for a brief moment. "Don't stray far. And don't let some young officer sweep you off your feet," he commanded with a playfully stern look. He brushed her cheek softly with his lips before striding up the steps and disappearing inside the building.

Rachel smiled after him, then began strolling leisurely past the line of officers' quarters. Her ears detected the faint strains of music coming from a building at the opposite end of the fort, prompting her to muse that the Fifth Infantry orchestra must be practicing for an upcoming dance or military parade. She recalled what Logan had told her—now that the Indian wars had ended, life at the post had turned to noncombat duties and training. Since he had also made mention of the fact that the enlisted men complained about the frequency of target practice, she wasn't surprised to hear the sound of distant gunfire mingling with the band's music.

"Miss Parker?" a vaguely familiar voice addressed her. Rachel turned to its owner with a mild frown of puzzlement, her silken brow clearing when she caught sight of the fair-haired young captain who had spilled punch on her at the Roundup Dance. Sweeping his hat from his head, he hurriedly descended the steps of one of the two-story buildings and approached her with a delighted smile on his boyishly attractive countenance. "Miss Parker, what a pleasant surprise!"

"Hello again, Captain—" Answering his smile with one of her own, her greeting ended on a note of inquiry, for she did not remember his name.

"Martin. Captain William Martin," he amiably supplied, a flush of pleasure rising to his face. He presented quite a dashing figure—the deep blue of his uniform was adorned with gold epaulettes and his gleaming leather boots were polished to perfection. "I certainly never expected to see you here at the fort, Miss Parker! If you don't mind my asking, what brings you here today?"

"I . . . I accompanied my husband, Captain Martin," she explained a bit hesitantly, for it was obvious that he hadn't heard of her marriage. "He had business with your commanding officer."

"Your husband?" echoed the young officer. An undeniably crestfallen expression crossed his face, and his blue eyes dulled as the meaning of her words sank in.

"Yes. Perhaps you've met him—his name is Logan MacBride," she told him with another smile.

He shook his head and stiffly declared, "The MacBride name is well known in the area, but I have never personally made your . . . your husband's acquaintance." He said nothing else, and Rachel grew uncomfortable beneath his unwavering stare. Several other young officers passed by her and her silent admirer, each of them tipping their hats to the post's beautiful visitor before flashing their comrade a broad, teasing grin.

"I suppose I should return—" Rachel ventured once the other men had gone.

"I would consider it an honor if you would allow me to show you about, Mrs. MacBride," Captain Martin unexpectedly broke in to proclaim. His eyes were now filled with a sort of hopeless, sorrowful resignation.

Rachel was thrown into a quandary at that point. She could not help but feel sorry for him—even though she did not believe he could have formed a lasting regard for her after only one night of dancing and conversation, she reflected that he had apparently been infatuated enough to suffer a very real disappointment. Although she knew that Logan expected her to be waiting close by, she could not bring herself to refuse the young captain's offer. Telling herself that a few minutes' stroll with him would do no harm, she politely accepted his escort.

"Very well, Captain Martin. But I must return to the commandant's quarters before too long."

"I'll have you back in plenty of time," he assured her, a small glimmer of satisfaction visible in his gaze. Rachel took his arm and allowed him to lead her toward the buildings at the opposite end of the post.

Half an hour later, Logan concluded his meeting with

the commandant. He returned outside with the intention of offering his wife a sincere apology for having kept her waiting so long. But there was no sign of her. His dark brows knitted together into a deep frown as his narrowed eyes once again scanned the surrounding area without success.

"Damn it, Rachel!" he muttered beneath his breath. Impatient to be off, he was none too pleased at the prospect of having to go in search of her. The meeting hadn't gone half as well as he'd hoped, and now his wife had disappeared! He sighed in husbandly exasperation and began striding across the grounds to find her.

At that same moment, Rachel was adamantly insisting to her gallant escort that she *must* return to the commandant's quarters without further delay. She and Captain Martin were standing in the midst of one of the store houses. When their conversation had earlier turned to a discussion of the Indians in eastern Montana and the Army's responsibility in controlling them, she had mentioned her recent visit to the Crow reservation. The young officer had then suggested a tour of the store houses, where the supplies destined for the various reservations were kept until orders came through for them to be delivered.

"I'm afraid, Captain, that I've been gone much too long already!" Rachel protested when he expressed a desire for them to visit yet another building. She was beginning to regret her decision to accompany him, for she was certain Logan's business would be finished soon. Disregarding Captain Martin's efforts to persuade her from doing otherwise, she gathered up her skirts and marched toward the doorway. "Thank you very much for showing me about. I think I can find my own way back."

"Miss . . . Mrs. MacBride, please wait!" he pleaded, desperate to prolong their time together. William Martin had never wanted a woman as much as he wanted the golden-haired beauty who had captivated him from the first moment he set eyes upon her. Still reeling from the news of her marriage, he mentally cursed the fortunate man who had claimed her for his bride.

"I'm sorry, but—" Rachel started to refuse for the last time, only to break off as her full skirts became snagged on a nail protruding from one of the many crates stacked on the floor of the store house. She tugged impatiently at the fabric, then released a long sigh when it stubbornly resisted her efforts to free it.

"Hold still," directed the young captain, bending down on one knee to try his hand at disentangling the embroidered muslin. Suddenly, he was seized by the overpowering impulse to take advantage of Rachel's temporary detainment. Although his conscience sternly reminded him of the fact that she was a married woman, that she was forever beyond his reach, he paid it no heed.

Surrendering to the momentary madness calling him, Captain Martin rose abruptly to his feet and wrapped his arms about an unsuspecting Rachel. Her eyes flew wide in startlement, and she could initially do nothing more than stand passively within the attractive officer's ardent embrace. At the first touch of his lips upon hers, however, she was finally moved to resistance. She twisted and squirmed quite vigorously, her hands pushing at his uniformed chest and her mouth jerking away from contact with his. Captain Martin released her and dazedly took a step backward, his gaze wide and full of shocked amazement at what he had done. Rachel was fairly quaking with the force of her indignation. Just as she was preparing to offer him a scathing assessment of his outrageous behavior, a deep voice sounded in the doorway, causing them both to spin about in guilty alarm.

"You were supposed to stay close to the wagon." Logan's handsome face was inscrutable, and his eyes gleamed with an equally unfathomable light as he casually stepped forward to take hold of a stunned and speechless Rachel's arm. "It's time we were leaving, my love." His piercing gaze moved to the young officer, whose features were tinged by a dull flush. "My thanks to you, whoever you are, for taking such good care of my wife," he uttered in a low, level voice that gave no clue whatsoever as to his true feelings. Captain Martin offered no response as he watched the tall, green-eyed man lead Rachel out of the store house.

A telltale blush stained her cheeks, and she frantically wondered if Logan had witnessed the way the captain had lost his head and grabbed her. But he *couldn't* have, she told herself, for he certainly wouldn't have treated the matter so lightly if he had seen another man kissing his wife—would he?

She stole a number of anxiously speculative glances up at his tight-lipped face as he led her along at a brisk pace. They had already traversed nearly half the distance back to where the team and wagon waited before she gathered courage enough to ask falteringly, "Logan, did you . . . how long were you—"

"If you're wanting to know if I saw exactly what happened between the two of you—the answer is no." His eyes glowed dangerously now, and a tiny muscle in one bronzed cheek twitched as if to signal a warning. "If you'd like to know whether or not I was able to discern that *something* occurred to make you both look guilty as hell—the answer is yes. And to satisfy your curiosity even further, I'll tell you that I'd have given myself the pleasure of beating your 'gallant escort' to a bloody pulp if not for the fact that I consider you just as much at fault—maybe even more so—for whatever the devil happened!"

"It was *not* my fault!" she vehemently denied, her opal eyes ablaze. Infuriated at his presumption, she tried to jerk her arm free, but he held fast. "How can you even suggest that I would . . . that I would—"

"Keep your voice down, damn it!" he growled. "Your first mistake was in disobeying my orders to stay close; your second was in being witless enough to go traipsing off alone with a poor fool who's obviously so enamored of you that he was willing to overlook the existence of your husband!"

"Witless?" she indignantly gasped, much affronted by what she perceived to be his unwarranted censure of her kind-hearted actions.

"Witless!" Logan confirmed in a low tone seething with mingled jealousy and anger. They had reached the wagon by now, and he wasted no time in seizing her about the waist and tossing her up to land with an unceremonious jolt upon the hard wooden seat. Rachel shot him a venomous glare, but he seemed oblivious to her outrage as he climbed swiftly up beside her and snapped the reins.

The silence was heavy and charged between them, but neither of them broke it until long after they had left Fort Keogh behind. By the time Logan spoke again, the sun hung directly overhead in the cloudless sky, bathing the wild prairie landscape in brilliant golden light.

"What the devil possessed you to go off with him like that?" he finally demanded, his manner one of deceptive calm.

"If you must know—I felt sorry for him!" Rachel answered resentfully. "And I did not consider it in the least bit 'improper' to allow him to show me about the post, not with a good hundred or more chaperones surrounding us at all times!"

"You weren't surrounded by any 'chaperones' when I came upon the two of you inside that blasted store house!"

"Confound it, Logan MacBride, he was merely—"

"I suppose the poor bastard can't help it. He's probably been burning for you ever since the night of the dance," he muttered crossly, his hands clenching upon the reins. He had immediately recognized the young officer as the same one who had monopolized Rachel's attentions at the Roundup Dance. A fierce scowl marred the rugged perfection of his face as he demanded with biting sarcasm, "Hell, there's no telling how many others were so charmed by you that they'd do just about anything to get you alone! I'll have to take care never to let you out of my sight, dear wife, or else I might find myself having to shoot or maim your admirers by the dozens!"

"Why, of all the . . . the despicable, ludicrous . . ." Rachel furiously sputtered, unable to continue when appropriately castigating terms failed her. The expression on her beautiful face growing quite stormy, she folded her arms tightly across her heaving bosom and twisted back around on the seat to face rigidly forward.

Logan swore and jerked on the reins. Snorting in protest, the horses slowed to a halt.

"Damn it, Rachel, you—" her husband started to try and reason with her. His words were cut off by the echoing report of a gunshot.

XVIII

"Get down!" roared Logan. Rachel, instinctively tossing a startled look over her shoulder as yet another gunshot rang out behind them, found herself being pushed roughly to the floorboard beneath the seat. A third shot split the air, and a bullet smashed through the wood at the rear of the empty wagonbed.

"Dear God!" breathed Rachel in horror when it dawned on her that someone was shooting at them. Hastily raising her wide, frantic gaze to Logan, she watched as he brought the reins slapping down upon the horses' sleek rumps with a vengeance. The frightened animals lurched forward, dragging the wagon wheels across the rutted track of the road at a breakneck pace. The breath was literally knocked from Rachel's lungs as she clutched at the side of the wagon for support, and she winced in pain as her knees made bruising contact with the floorboard. Her thoughts, however, were concerned only with her husband, for she was terrified that he would be struck by one of the bullets now being fired at them in rapid succession.

Urging the team relentlessly onward, Logan had no time to think of anything other than outdistancing the unknown assailants who were giving chase on horseback. His first reaction had been to take a stance and return their fire, but he had immediately abandoned the idea. Fearing that such a maneuver would only place Rachel in even more danger, for he had counted more than half a dozen riders, he had decided the best course of action would be to try and make it to the ranch less than a couple of miles farther ahead—a ranch belonging to yet another MacBride cousin.

"Logan!" cried Rachel above the din of gunfire and the clatter of the wildly careening wagon. Managing to twist about and raise one of her arms upward, she tugged frantically on the long sleeve of his shirt. "Logan, get down! They'll . . . they'll kill you!"

"Stay down!" he thundered, giving her a hard, insistent shove that sent her tumbling back down to the floorboard. She gasped as another bullet splintered the wood just above her head. A volley of shots followed.

Suddenly, one of the horses emitted a shrill, piercing scream. Logan cursed when he saw the blood streaming from the roan's neck, but he could waste no time on compassion for the poor animal, whose legs were already beginning to buckle. Seizing hold of Rachel's arm, he yanked her upright against him and yelled just as the wagon began pitching to its side beneath them, "Jump!"

She never had the opportunity to follow his directive. A sharp cry broke from her lips as she was forcefully hurled through the air and to the ground, where she landed with a breath-taking jolt and rolled over and over upon the hard, grassy earth. Dimly aware of the sound of the wagon crashing upside-down beside the road, and the loud protest of the uninjured horse as the harness snapped in two, she raised her head to look for her husband. Her vision was blurred, and her bruised body began to ache and throb as the initial shock wore off, but she whispered a heartfelt prayer of thanksgiving when she spied Logan staggering to his feet a short distance away.

"Rachel!" Her name was a hoarse cry upon his lips as he ran toward her with his pistol drawn, his wary gaze making a broad, hasty sweep in an effort to locate the mounted assailants. He spotted them on the horizon—for some inexplicable reason, they had reined about and were galloping away in the opposite direction.

"Logan, the . . . the men—" she gasped out, her eyes filling with renewed terror as her benumbed mind finally cleared. She attempted to rise, but collapsed weakly back upon the ground.

"They're gone," Logan hastened to assure her, dropping to his knees and holstering his gun. Gently turning her upon her back, he commanded softly, "Lie still, my love." With hands that were at once tender and capable, he quickly examined her for any broken bones, then expelled a heavy sigh of relief.

"I'm all right," Rachel tremulously declared. "A . . . a bit shaken, perhaps, but . . . oh, Logan, we could have been killed!" He pulled her into the loving security of his strong arms and uttered in a voice raw with emotion, "Dear God, Rachel, I was afraid I'd lost you!" His arms tightened almost painfully about her, but Rachel felt no inclination to complain. She closed her eyes and lay pliantly against him, her own heart rejoicing in the miracle of their survival. He held her for several long moments, after which he reluctantly set her away and stood to help her to her feet. "There's a ranch up ahead. We'll have to walk the rest of the way." He strode away to inspect the remains of the wagon, his handsome face shadowing with renewed fury as he gazed upon the destruction.

"Why do you suppose those men shot at us like that?" Rachel wondered aloud. Smoothing the tangled mass of golden hair away from her dirt-smudged face, she gathered up her hopelessly torn and stained muslin skirts and moved to her husband's side. "Why on earth should they want to kill us?"

"I'm not sure that was their intention," Logan grimly expounded, his eyes darkening. He muttered another curse as he turned away from the sight of the dead horse and mangled wagon. "They could have finished the job if they'd wanted to."

"Then why—"

"I don't know. But whatever their purpose, they were very nearly successful in eliminating any witnesses to their attack," he murmured, glancing one last time toward the spot where he'd seen the horsemen mysteriously retreating. There was no sign of them now.

An involuntary shiver ran the length of Rachel's spine, and she was grateful for the comforting presence of Logan's arm about her shoulders as he slowly led her away.

They soon reached Colin MacBride's ranch, where the owner himself ushered them anxiously inside the single-story log house. A tall, slender man who was only a year or two younger than Logan, Colin resembled his cousin a great deal. He was enraged upon learning what had happened, and he immediately offered to lead some of his men out on a search for the aggressors. Logan, however, wisely pointed out that there'd be no way of positively identifying the riders.

"But damn it, Logan, we can't let them get away with it!" protested Colin, his deep blue eyes ablaze with vengeful wrath. "Those are probably some of the same bastards who've been stealing or butchering our stock and taking potshots at our men!"

"That's very likely," Logan quietly allowed. He tossed the damp cloth he had been using to cleanse most of the dirt from his face back down beside the bowl of water on the kitchen table. "But you can't go around stringing up every suspicious-looking character in the county because of what's happening."

"We sure as hell didn't come up with any other solutions at the meeting last night, did we?" countered the younger, lighter-haired MacBride, irritably musing to himself that the stance taken by the opposing faction—the group favoring vigilante action—was making more sense all the time. Feeling guilty for such disloyal thoughts, he cleared his throat and earnestly declared, "All of us in the family will back you up, Logan, no matter what you decide to do. Even if you can't convince the military—"

"They won't help," Logan informed him. With a frown of remembrance, he related details of his unsuccessful conference with Fort Keogh's commandant.

"Damn!" muttered Colin once his cousin had finished. He paced restlessly back and forth in the rather close confines of the kitchen—a kitchen that obviously lacked a woman's touch—before concluding, "Then we've got no choice but to take matters into our own hands!"

"Maybe not. But allowing ourselves to turn into a

bloodthirsty mob will only result in the innocent as well as the guilty getting hurt. No, Colin," Logan asserted with another frown and a curt shake of his head, "we can't let this country be ruled by vigilantes. If we're ever to have any sort of law and order in this wilderness we call home, we'll have to work for it. And that means trying our damnedest to make certain *only* the guilty suffer for their misdeeds."

They lapsed into thoughtful silence after that. Rachel, having retired to another room and bathed as well as she could from a pitcher and washbowl, rejoined the men in the kitchen. She and Logan soon took their leave, the two of them riding homeward with an assurance from Colin that he would send one of the hands over the next day to retrieve the horses and bring whatever baggage was recovered from the wagon.

Arriving home without incident that same afternoon, Logan and Rachel were met with two surprising pieces of news—one pleasant and the other not. The pleasant news, at least to Rachel's ears, was that Moira had disappeared.

"I don't understand it!" Aunt Tess proclaimed again. "I just don't understand why she packed her things and left without telling a soul!" Robert and Logan stood near the fireplace in the parlor, while a freshly garbed Rachel sat beside Logan's aunt on the sofa. Darkness was stealing over the plains, but the moon's silvery glow joined the brilliant sparkle of the first evening stars in illuminating the country the Indians called "land of the big sky."

"You know as well as I do that Moira does most things on impulse," remarked Logan. A faint, ironic smile tugged at the corners of his mouth. "She's probably come to her senses and gone back to live with Joseph."

"It's certainly no secret that she was unhappy here at the Circle M," opined Uncle Robert, his gaze straying involuntarily in Rachel's direction. "But I can't honestly say I'm sorry she's gone. I rather prefer life a bit less 'dramatic'!"

"Robert Pearson, were you or were you *not* complaining just the other day that life had only recently become exciting enough for you?" Tess playfully challenged. He merely chuckled and flashed her an indulgent grin. Rachel smiled to herself, musing that the older couple's fondness for one another was becoming increasingly apparent.

"It doesn't sound like things were all that dull while we were gone," murmured Logan. He'd been none too pleased to learn of the most recent raid upon the stock—the rustlers had hit even closer to the ranch than before, and they'd stolen several horses as well as cattle.

"It appears this problem with the rustlers is getting quite out of hand," Robert commented with a heavy sigh. His eyes were full of genuine concern as he asked his nephew, "Were you and the other ranchers able to come up with anything at the meeting last night?"

"No. Or at least nothing of any real value. I tried my best to convince the military to join us in our efforts, but to no avail." The dancing flames of the fire were reflected in his green eyes, and the flickering light played across his handsome face as he turned to stare deeply into the golden blaze beneath the mantel.

"Do you suppose that reprehensible attack upon you today had anything to do with your efforts to put a stop to the thievery?" Aunt Tess wondered aloud. She squeezed Rachel's hand comfortingly, repeating a silent prayer that the two young people had emerged unscathed from the incident. "These men have so far confined themselves to attacks upon the stock—what if they're now bent on turning their attention on even worse treachery?" Recalling what Logan had said earlier, Rachel hastened to point out, "They could have killed us if murder had truly been their goal."

"But, my dear, they very nearly *did* kill you! Why, it's a miracle neither you nor Logan were at the very least seriously injured!" argued Tess in a burst of emotion. "To think that those . . . those cowardly villains—"

"Now, Tess, there's no use in upsetting yourself any further," Robert gently admonished. "Logan and Rachel are safe and sound at home now. The men who attacked them are no doubt boasting of it in some saloon somewhere, which might in fact be to our advantage yet. I fear it's going to take something mighty drastic for the military to get involved, and for the entire country to join together and press for adequate legislation—and protection—against these desperadoes."

"Let's just hope time doesn't run out first," Logan added grimly.

The next few days proved to be busy for everyone at the ranch. Rachel and Aunt Tess—who had finally consented to the younger woman's assistance in household matters—took advantage of the favorable weather and submitted each and every room to a thorough cleaning and airing-out. Mrs. Smith, more taciturn than ever now that Moira was gone, engaged in a veritable storm of baking toward the end of the week. When Rachel displayed a very natural curiosity about the reasons for such a noticeable increase in culinary output, the stern-faced cook muttered something about "Mr. Logan *liking* fresh baked pies and cakes."

Brodie returned home three days after Logan and Rachel. Declaring that his shoulder was "almost good as new," he and the other hands set to work with a vengeance. With a large number of young horses still to be halter-broken, hay to cut and stack, calves to be branded, stock to check on with as much frequency as possible, and various other chores to be tended to, there was little time for leisurely pursuits. Any man caught slacking off while still on duty was subject to severe punishment—denial of the privilege to visit Miles City one night a week.

Logan worked as hard as any of his men, but he had special compensations—when he returned home from a day spent almost completely in the saddle, he found Rachel waiting for him. The two of them would talk while he cleaned up, after which they would share supper with Robert, Tess, and Brodie, then retire to Logan's room for the night. Sometimes their lovemaking in the big oak bed was wildly impassioned, other times sweetly unhurried, and still other times they would simply lie in one another's arms and drift contentedly off to sleep.

It wasn't until the latter part of the week that Rachel discovered the reasons for all the housecleaning and baking. Aunt Tess, who surrendered to the temptation to reveal that she had intended to keep secret, prefaced her disclosure with a plea for Rachel to pretend surprise when the time came.

"Pretend surprise?" Rachel echoed in bewilderment.

"Yes. You see, my dear, everyone would be so disappointed if they knew you were aware of it already,"

Aunt Tess responded with a sigh.

"Aware of what?"

"Why, the party, of course! It's to be a family celebration in honor of your marriage to Logan. All of the MacBrides will be descending upon us this coming Sunday."

"*All* of them?" Recalling what Logan had once said about the size of the MacBride clan, Rachel felt a sudden knot of apprehension in the pit of her stomach. Tess nodded, and her mouth curved into a knowing, sympathetic smile.

"The more I thought about it, the more I became convinced it would be kinder to give you warning of it."

"Does Logan know about this . . . this celebration?" asked Rachel, musing that she would somehow make him pay if he had known all along and hadn't told her!

"To tell the truth, my dear, I'm not sure!" the older woman admitted with a soft laugh. "But you know how Logan is. If there's something brewing, my dear nephew has his own methods for discerning the truth."

"And I have *my* own methods as well!" Rachel murmured only half aloud, her opal eyes sparkling determinedly. Resuming her work in the parlor with Tess, she silently vowed to question Logan about the matter as soon as an opportunity presented itself.

Much later, Rachel cornered her husband in the bathroom, where he had just finished washing the day's grime from his magnificent, hard-muscled body.

"You know all about Sunday, don't you?" she flatly accused, her hands on her hips and her face becomingly flushed from the soap-scented warmth permeating the room.

"I know it's the day after Saturday," he retorted in a

lazy, mocking drawl. He stepped out of the bathtub and wrapped one of the thick, oversized towels about his lower body. His dark hair was damp and rakishly tousled, and his eyes gleamed with a mischievous light.

"Logan MacBride, you know about the celebration, don't you?" Rachel tried again, a note of wifely exasperation creeping into her voice.

"Everyone knows about it." Securing the towel at his waist, he sauntered complacently past her and through the doorway into his bedroom. She was close upon his bare heels.

"*I* don't! That is to say, I know about it *now*, but that's only because your aunt was—"

"I wondered how long it would take before Aunt Tess told you," he remarked with a low chuckle. He stood beside the bed now, and a roguish smile played about his firmly chiseled lips as he turned to gaze down into Rachel's beautiful, visibly annoyed features.

"You should have been the one to tell me!" she asserted, folding her arms tightly across her splendidly endowed chest. "I thought we had agreed there would be no more secrets between the two of us!"

"It wasn't a secret between us," he leisurely disagreed. "It was between you and Aunt Tess." His bronzed, sinewy arms were slowly enveloping her as his smile deepened.

"But you . . . you . . ." Her voice trailed away as she was pulled unresistingly against him. Growing increasingly breathless, she raised softly glowing eyes to his handsome, sun-kissed face.

"If we're going to argue about secrets, sweet wildcat, then suppose you tell me—exactly what *did* happen between you and that blasted captain at the fort the other day?" Logan demanded in a low, slightly husky tone, his smile temporarily replaced by a frown of lingering displeasure over the incident.

"Why, *everyone knows about it,*" she saucily parried, using his own words as a weapon against him. Smiling rather tauntingly up at him, her arms entwined about his neck as her luminous eyes issued him an undeniable challenge. A few brief moments of silence followed.

"You little witch," Logan finally muttered with a strange half-smile. Suddenly, without warning, he took a seat on the bed and yanked an unsuspecting Rachel facedown across his knees.

"Logan!" she gasped out, too stunned to do more than offer a token resistance. "Logan, what—" She broke off with another sharp intake of breath when he tossed her skirt and petticoat above her head. "Logan!" She began struggling in earnest now, but his arm was clamped like a band of steel across her back. "Logan, stop this at once!" His only response was to raise his other arm and deliver a stinging slap to her wriggling backside—protected only by the thin cotton of her drawers—with the palm of his hand. She shrieked in protest and doubled her efforts to escape, but his hand found its target a second time, and a third. The blows were only a trifle more forceful than love-smacks, and Logan merely chuckled at Rachel's highly vocal expressions of outrage. Turning her over in his arms, he was forced to subdue her again, which he did by flipping her back upon the bed and imprisoning her body with his.

"From here on out, Mrs. MacBride, you're to do as I say, understand?" he growled with mock ferocity, his face close to hers. The towel had fallen away, leaving his wholly masculine nakedness completely exposed. Rachel was acutely conscious of this fact, for she could feel the heat of his hard body even through the layers of clothing she wore. Her anger with him quickly evaporated.

"Is that in regard to my relationship with forward young officers, or in regard to what occurs in this bed?" she boldly retorted, her eyes alight with mingled passion and playfulness.

"Both!" he avowed in a deep, resonant voice, then proceeded to give her wickedly amorous instructions which she in turn followed with an enthusiasm and willingness that delighted him almost beyond endurance.

The newlyweds were late for supper for the second time that week, but if either Tess or Robert considered such tardiness peculiar, they never remarked upon it.

On Friday, Rachel was afforded the rare pleasure of having the house to herself. Mrs. Smith and Aunt Tess had previously announced their intentions of journeying to Miles City to purchase some last-minute necessities for the upcoming celebration, and Uncle Robert had insisted upon accompanying them. Because of the recent trouble, Logan had also sent two of the ranch hands along to provide an armed escort for the trio.

It was scarcely past ten o'clock in the morning when Rachel, having invaded Cora Smith's domain in order to prepare a meal for Logan with her own two hands, was surprised to see Brodie striding purposefully inside the kitchen. The grim set to his attractive young face told her something was wrong. Hastily setting aside the bread dough she had been kneading, she stepped forward to meet him and demanded anxiously, "What is it?"

"It's Eva. The baby's coming."

"The baby? But I thought it would be another month—"

"It should have been. But it seems there was an accident—Stuart's been hurt. One of his men rode off to try and find the doctor, but Eva needs help right away. Logan said to gather up anything you think you might need and meet him outside." Nodding mutely, Rachel hurried to wash the flour from her hands and do as her husband had bid. Logan was lifting her to the back of her horse a scant five minutes later. After swinging up into the saddle atop an impatiently prancing Vulcan, he reined about and rode swiftly toward Stuart MacBride's ranch, with Rachel close behind and urging her mount to keep pace.

When they arrived, it was only to find that Stuart had regained consciousness and was in a great deal of pain as a result of the injuries he had sustained. He had been thrown and trampled by one of the range horses he was attempting to break. Eva, who had often remonstrated with him about trying to do the same things he'd done years ago, had taken one look at her beloved husband's inert, bruised and bloody form being carried from the corral and had gone into premature labor.

"One of the hands knows a bit about doctoring, so he's up with the boss now," Stuart's young ranch foreman explained as the two newcomers hurried inside the house.

"What about Eva?" Logan questioned sharply, tugging off his hat and helping Rachel sort out the things she had brought.

"We put her in the room next to Mr. Stuart's. I've been staying up there with her myself, seeing as how I've got eight brothers and sisters and know something about birthing. But she's in a bad way. She keeps crying and asking for Mr. Stuart. I think the pains are starting to hit her pretty hard now."

"I'm going to need a great deal of hot water," pronounced Rachel. The young foreman scurried about the kitchen, setting pots and pans full of water on to boil, while Logan took Rachel's arm and led her up the narrow staircase. It was no difficult task to locate the room where Eva lay, for her pitiful cries could be heard all over the house.

"Eva. Eva, it's Logan. Rachel and I have come to help," Logan murmured in a low, soothing voice, bending over the poor woman whose features were contorted with pain.

"Oh Logan, Stuart . . . Stuart!" she choked out in anguish, her fair, perspiration-soaked head tossing on the pillow. She was still clad in her dress of blue calico, and her body was trembling violently from head to toe. Rachel sank down upon the bed and firmly clasped one of Eva's hands with both of hers.

"Your husband will be fine," she spoke reassuringly, smiling down at the older woman. "Right now, you've got to think of yourself and the baby."

"You know that's what Stuart would want," Logan added with a warm smile of his own. He was pleased to see Eva's fear-clouded blue gaze clear somewhat. "Rachel's going to stay with you until the doctor comes. I'll be in the next room with Stuart, and I give you my word that you'll be the first to know if there's any change." His eyes met Rachel's in a look of silent understanding before he left the two women alone.

After getting Eva undressed and into a fresh white nightgown, Rachel opened the door and called down for more water, which was delivered with remarkable speed by the attentive young ranch foreman. Another pain wracked Eva's body, leaving her weak and gasping for breath.

"I . . . I'm glad you . . . you're here," she told Rachel as she collapsed back against the pillow. "I wanted another . . . woman with me when the time came. Stuart's the one who . . . who always insisted on having the doctor out." A fresh surge of tears glistened in her eyes as she revealed in a voice scarcely above a whisper, "We . . . we had three babies before this one, but they were all . . . stillborn."

"Well, this baby is going to be fine!" decreed Rachel, fighting back tears of her own. She perched on the edge of the bed again and applied a cool, wet cloth to Eva's feverish brow.

"Have you ever attended a . . . a birthing before?"

"Only once, but I remember it well. My grandfather was a lawman in Wyoming before we came to Montana. There was a robbery at one of the stores in town one day, and the culprits were arrested almost immediately afterward. One of them had a young wife who was going to have a baby. She had no money and no place to go, so Micah, my grandfather, brought her home and placed her in my grandmother's care. Her son was born the very next day. There had been no time to send for the doctor, so Grandmother and I were the ones who delivered the baby."

"What happened to the woman after that?" Eva asked, then inhaled sharply as another pain started.

"Micah arranged for her to go back to her family in Texas. We received a letter from her a year later, telling us that her husband had joined them following his release from prison, and expressing her gratitude for all we had done on her behalf. We never heard from her again." Eva's hands gripped hers so tightly that she winced involuntarily, but she did not draw away.

The next two hours passed with agonizing slowness. Rachel did her best to keep Eva's spirits up, encouraging her to talk about her childhood and her marriage to Stuart, and telling Eva more about her own life. The pains neither worsened nor slackened during this period of time, but their longevity drained the woman's strength. Rachel's thoughts frequently turned to Logan and Stuart, for she was certain they could hear Eva's cries and moans in the next room. Not only did she wonder about Stuart's physical condition, but she was also concerned about his reaction to the unmistakable evidence of his wife's suffering.

Finally, Eva's labor intensified. She clung to Rachel as if she were drowning, her breath coming in short, panting gasps. The entrance of the baby into the world was an alarmingly silent one. Even after several attempts to force a cry from the tiny, perfectly formed girl, she still made no sound. Eva had slipped into unconsciousness, mercifully unaware of her child's heartbreaking silence.

After calling frantically for Logan, Rachel suddenly remembered something her grandmother had done all those years ago at the other baby's birth. She whirled about and plunged Eva's new little daughter into the basin of warm water beside the bed. Praying in desperation, she nearly collapsed with mingled joy and relief when the baby finally sputtered and coughed. Logan was at her side as she lifted the healthy, indignantly wailing baby from the water and swaddled her in clean toweling.

"You can tell Stuart he's the father of a beautiful little girl," Rachel tremulously directed, the tears streaming freely down her face as she smiled up at her husband. She cradled the tiny bit of humanity lovingly in her arms before handing her to Logan and turning back to attend to the baby's mother. A tender smile lit the ruggedly handsome planes of Logan's face as he peered down at the newest MacBride, whose crying had miraculously ceased at the first touch of his strong, capable hands.

When Eva awakened and held her daughter in her arms for the first time, she was overcome with emotion. She reached up to take Rachel's hand, her shining blue eyes full of unspoken gratitude.

"If . . . if it's all right with Stuart, I'd like to call her 'Rachel'," she announced once she found voice enough to speak again.

"You don't have to do that," Rachel gently protested, her own eyes glistening with renewed tears at the gesture.

"I know, but I want to. This family could use two 'Rachel MacBrides'!" she insisted with a soft, watery laugh, then grew solemn and earnestly declared, "I'll never forget what you did for me, Rachel. Never." Rachel leaned over and hugged her, and the two of them knew that a special bond of friendship had been forged between them that day, a bond that would never be broken.

The doctor arrived later that same afternoon. After assuring himself that mother and child were doing well, he set to work on Stuart, whose own spirits had been considerably lifted upon hearing the news of his daughter's birth. The doctor, gruffly proclaiming that his patient was lucky to be alive, bandaged his broken ribs, stitched up the gash on his forehead, and informed him that he would be confined to bed for at least a couple of weeks. Pausing to add that Stuart would have to take it easy for a good month after that, he took his leave, anxious to get back to town and spend some time with his own family.

"Damnation! How the hell am I supposed to take it easy when my wife's just had a baby and I've got a blasted herd to—" growled Stuart, grimacing at the soreness in his head and ribcage.

"Your men will take care of the herd. As for Eva and the baby—knowing Aunt Tess, she wouldn't hear of anyone else coming to help out," Logan remarked with a wry grin down at his cousin. "I expect her to show up before nightfall. Once she gets back from town and finds out why Rachel and I aren't there, nothing will keep her away."

"Lord help us," muttered the other man. He loved Aunt Tess dearly, but she was such a managing sort of female!

Proving Logan's prediction quite accurate, Tess and Robert arrived at Stuart's ranch just as the sun began to sink below the line of clouds hovering along the western horizon. Rachel and Eva bid one another an emotional farewell, after which Logan took his weary bride up before him on Vulcan's back for the ride homeward.

"Oh, Logan," sighed Rachel, relaxing back against him as he slowed the black stallion to a walk. "I'm so glad everything turned out as it did."

"So am I," he replied, a mellow smile curving his lips as his arms tightened about her. "I'm very proud of the way you handled yourself today, Mrs. MacBride. Damn, but you're something!" he pronounced with a soft, vibrant chuckle that sent a pleasurable tremor coursing through her tired body. "Not only are you a bewitching tigress in bed and a proper lady out of it, but you've got enough backbone to endure whatever comes along without falling apart. Eva needed you, and you came through. That's not something she and Stuart will take lightly."

"Naming their daughter after me was the most profoundly moving token of gratitude I could ever receive." She released a long sigh and settled herself more comfortably before him. They rode in silence for a while, each lost in their own thoughts. The buildings of the Circle M were already visible in the twilight-mantled distance when Logan spoke again.

"I don't want you suffering the way Eva did, Rachel. After listening to what she went through—" He broke off, his mouth compressing into a tight, thin line and his eyes gleaming dully before he continued. "God knows I wanted sons and daughters to continue the family line, but you mean more to me. I couldn't bear losing you."

"You won't lose me!" She tilted her chin back so that she could meet his gaze. "I want to have your children, Logan—*our* children. I'm not afraid, even after witnessing Eva's pain. Seeing the love and tenderness reflected in her eyes as she held her daughter for the first time . . ." Rachel's own eyes glistened with tears of remembrance as she smiled up into his somber features. "We can't deny ourselves the most natural fulfillment of our love, my darling." Her smile grew affectionately teasing as she declared, "I fully intend to have at least a dozen babies, Mr. MacBride, so you may as well accustom yourself to that particular fact!"

"Unless I'm sadly mistaken, such a feat will require my cooperation as well," he drawled with a faint smile of irony.

"Not necessarily!" quipped Rachel, her light blue eyes sparkling with loving mischief. She was rewarded for her impertinence with a hard, familiar smack upon the curve of her backside and the promise of a good many more if she ever dared to so much as look at another man.

That night, Logan and Rachel lay together in his massive, four-poster bed, their bodies entwined as their passions met in a glorious blaze of love's ecstasy. In the soft afterglow of their fiery union, they talked of many things, foremost of which was Rachel's insistence that her family be invited to attend the MacBride get-together on Sunday.

"I'm afraid it would only be asking for trouble," murmured Logan. His warm fingers traced a light, tantalizing pattern across the silken smoothness of her naked back as she snuggled against him beneath the covers.

"But if they're ever to have your family's complete acceptance, you've got to make a public stand. You once told Vance that you considered Micah part of the MacBride clan because of our marriage—Sunday's celebration will be the perfect opportunity to demonstrate it to everyone." She suddenly recalled her last encounter with Vance, and she flushed guiltily when she also recalled that she had never told Logan of it.

"I doubt if that pigheaded grandfather of yours would even accept the invitation."

"He'll accept."

"Just what the devil makes you so certain of it?"

"Because I know Micah Parker. He won't back down. And to his way of thinking, that's exactly what he would be doing if he didn't show up," she smugly asserted. "So you've simply got to invite him." Logan's green eyes twinkled indulgently down at her as he growled in mock exasperation, "If I'd had any notion what an impudent, bossy, demanding female I'd be stuck with, I'd have gotten myself the hell out of that bathroom in Billings while I had the chance!"

"Would you truly?" she challenged softly, her beautiful face aglow with the certainty of his answer as she smiled beguilingly up into his handsome, scowling features.

"Damn right!" he muttered, then proceeded to make a liar out of himself.

Rachel gasped in delight as he abruptly shifted about so that his mouth could capture the delectable, rose-tipped fullness of her naked breast. The moist warmth of his tongue flicked erotically about the nipple while his possessive lips drew hungrily upon the satiny peak. His knowing hands sought the tempting swell of her hips before moving to the delicate, velvety flesh between her thighs.

"Oh! Oh, Logan!" breathed Rachel, her eyes sweeping closed as she strained instinctively upward for his caress. He was only too happy to oblige, his hands gently parting her pale, trembling thighs so that his fingers could pay wonderfully slow and highly sensual tribute to the budding flower of womanhood concealed by the triangle of honey-colored curls. She gasped again and again, her silken limbs stretching even wider as Logan's hard, muscular body slid downward, his lips scorching a trail from her well-attended breast to the inviting perfection of her navel, then back up to her other breast.

Passion's fire was quickly rekindled, and by the time Logan's mouth finally claimed hers once more, an increasingly emboldened Rachel had done her fair share of stroking, exploring, kissing, and tasting. With the final blending of their bodies, it seemed as if their very souls became joined as one, their hearts soaring to those wild, dizzying heights of rapture such as only the truest and most devoted of lovers can find.

XIX

Entire wagonloads of MacBrides began arriving by mid-morning on Sunday. Aunt Tess, after reluctantly agreeing to be relieved by Eva's younger sister for the day, had been fetched home at first light by Brodie and Uncle Robert so that she could oversee the final preparations for the celebration. She and Mrs. Smith were much like two generals, issuing orders to the ranch hands as to the placement of chairs and quilts and various tables of refreshments outside in the yard.

Even though Rachel had been forewarned about the vast numbers of family members she would be meeting, she was nonetheless more than a trifle awed by the seemingly endless stream of arrivals. Men, women, and children of all ages were gathering beneath the cloudless blue sky, and Logan took what Rachel could have sworn was perverse pleasure in introducing her to each and every one of them.

She had dressed with particular care that morning, choosing to wear a pretty, ruffled and flounced gown of cream-colored foulard, its fitted bodice trimmed with pale pink lace and blue ribbon. The day promised to be a warm one, making her glad she had chosen a dress with short puffed sleeves and a low, rounded neckline. Logan had at first complimented her on her selection, his wickedly gleaming gaze lingering upon the properly displayed hint of her bosom. His wolfish grin, however, had turned into a scowl when it suddenly occurred to him that his male cousins would no doubt be just as appreciative of his wife's charms. Although he had demanded that Rachel choose something a great deal more modest, she had laughingly defied him, declaring that the gown was her most becoming and that she naturally wished to make a good impression. Conceding defeat, Logan had muttered an oath, seized her arm with something less than gentleness, and ushered her outside into the welcoming sunshine.

Soon there were children laughing and dashing everywhere, babies crying, women trading gossip and advice as they took a seat on the chairs and quilts spread beneath the trees, dogs barking, men clustered about in small groups to discuss the price of cattle and the ongoing threat of rustlers, and Aunt Tess bustling about in the midst of it all as she and Mrs. Smith made certain there was always plenty to eat and drink.

Rachel lost count of how many MacBrides she met, though she did remember certain individuals. She was glad to see Colin again and to meet his pretty young wife, who had been away the day of the wagon "accident," and she especially liked Eva's older sister, who was married to another of the MacBride cousins. Nearly everyone was quite gracious and friendly, and it was quite apparent that Logan was both well liked and well respected by his family.

It was almost noon before Micah, Jane, and Lizzie arrived. A smile of mingled pleasure and relief lit Rachel's face when she caught sight of them. Politely excusing herself from a conversation with several of the older women in attendance, she gathered up her skirts and hurried across the yard to greet her family. Micah drew the team to a halt beside the stables, then turned to help Jane and Lizzie down.

"I'm so glad you've come!" Rachel exclaimed, warmly embracing each of them in turn.

"I was afraid there for a while that Micah would back out!" disclosed Lizzie, her lively, expressive gaze already scanning the crowd for one MacBride in particular. "Grandmother and I practically had to drag him here!" It was obvious that she had taken special pains in choosing her own attire, for she looked quite lovely in a fitted gown of peacock blue twill. Her bouncy red curls were restrained in what she hoped was a mature-looking chignon, and she had even gone so far as to "borrow" some of her grandmother's powder and rouge. Micah had let her know in no uncertain terms that he disapproved of the alteration in her appearance, but she had stubbornly disregarded his opinion.

"Merciful heavens, Rachel, there are so many of them!" Jane murmured in wonderment as she eyed the assembly. "And the place is . . . is so much grander than I expected!" She hastily retied the ribbons of her best straw bonnet and smoothed down the generous folds of her dark blue calico dress. "Why, I had no idea Logan's family was so large. There must be well over a hundred people here!"

"I know, and I do believe I've been introduced to some of them three or four times!" laughed Rachel. Smiling up at her stern-faced grandfather, she linked her arm through his and remarked, "Well, Micah, I see you decided to show these MacBrides once more that we Parkers never back down from a fight."

"I didn't know I was coming to fight," he grumbled, then relented enough to give her a faint, begrudging smile. She paused to hug him again before leading her family forward to where her husband stood talking to Brodie and Colin on the front porch. Looking quite handsome in fitted denim trousers and a double-breasted shirt of dark red cotton, he hooked his thumbs through the front belt loops of his Levi's and leaned negligently back against one of the posts.

Logan immediately straightened when his eyes fell on the approaching Parkers. Stepping down from the porch with a disarming smile on his face, he greeted both Jane and Lizzie with genuine affection, then extended a hand of welcome to Micah. The former lawman hesitated only an instant before accepting it.

"You know, MacBride, I figured you had us come for a reason," Micah commented shrewdly as he met the younger man's sea-green gaze. He briefly turned to take note of the many curious stares being directed their way before facing Logan again. "It doesn't require a hell of a lot of thinking to guess just what that reason was." The hard line of his mouth curved into a faint smile that bespoke his growing approval of his granddaughter's husband.

"Actually, it was Rachel's idea," Logan confided with a wry grin, reaching out to draw her closer. "And seeing as how she used the most damnably effective blackmail on me, there was no possible way I could refuse!" Crimsoning in embarrassment as her grandfather startled her by chuckling appreciatively, Rachel directed a sharp, wifely jab to her husband's ribs.

When Logan took a stance upon the top porch step a few moments later and lifted his arm in a silent command, an obedient hush fell over the majority of the crowd. He raised his deep voice to be heard above the lingering din of babies, animals, and the ceaseless blowing of the Montana wind.

"There are some new members of the clan I'd like to introduce." The expression on his sun-bronzed countenace was quite solemn as he placed a hand on the shoulder of the flinty-eyed man standing proudly erect on the step below him. "This is my wife's grandfather, Micah Parker. And this is Micah's wife, Jane," he announced, placing a hand on her shoulder as well. "Rachel's sister, Lizzie, is beside Brodie there," he added with a curt nod in the petite redhead's direction. "As I said, they're new members of the clan and should be treated as such. By now, I'm sure you're all aware of the circumstances surrounding Tate's death and Micah Parker's acquisition of his ranch." He paused here, his piercing gaze sweeping over the sea of MacBride faces as a quiet murmur rose upward. His voice grew even more commanding as he decreed, "What's past is past. The Parkers are here to stay. They have a right to that property. And since they're now part of *my* family, I want it known that any insult offered them is offered to me as well—the same holds true for friendship and neighborliness." In conclusion, he smiled broadly and proclaimed, "Now that we've cleared the air, let's get down to some serious celebrating!"

His words were met with enthusiastic approval from the crowd as they began making straightaway for the tables of food and drink set up in front of the house. A side of beef had been roasting over a fire near the corral since before dawn. Added to the substantial feast Mrs. Smith had prepared were the covered dishes brought by the other women, so that there was an abundance of fried chicken, baked beans, boiled potatoes, fresh bread and biscuits, and a dazzling array of cakes and pies. By way of liquid refreshment, there was sassafras tea, coffee, milk, and the perennial bowls of "spiked" and "unspiked" fruit punch.

The afternoon passed in a leisurely, highly enjoyable fashion for everyone. In no time at all, Jane found herself included in a circle of women discussing the joys and tribulations of child-rearing, while Micah was drawn out of his usual reticence by a group of MacBride ranchers who were once again cursing the necessity to place extra patrols out on the range. None of them were immune to the increasing wave of stock thievery, and Micah soon learned that, though they had all sworn loyalty to the patriarch of the clan, they were almost evenly divided on the issue of vigilante action against the rustlers.

As was usually the custom at such gatherings, the men and women did not socialize with one another—the women seemed perfectly content to spend time with members of their own sex, while the men would have been shocked if one of their wives or daughters dared to intrude upon "men talk." Rachel, although taking pleasure in the company of the other women, was inwardly bristling over the fact that she was provided with no alternative to conversation centered entirely around domestic matters. Her gaze frequently drifted across the yard to Logan, who was obviously caught up in a spirited discussion near the corral.

Finally wandering away from the spot where Jane, Aunt Tess, and other more matronly women were happily whiling away the hours beneath the trees, she went in search of her sister, whom she had seen disappearing around the far corner of the house a short time earlier. She rounded that same corner herself, then drew up short at the astonishing sight of Lizzie perched on a rock beside the stream, the redhead's features looking quite animated as she flirted and laughed with the five young men—none of whom were much older than Lizzie—surrounding her.

"It's a good thing we don't have one of these confounded things more than a couple of times a year," a familiar voice murmured behind Rachel. She whirled to face its owner.

"Oh, Brodie, you startled me!" she told him with a breathless laugh. Quickly sobering when she viewed the unmistakably stormy look on his handsome young visage, she followed the direction of his smoldering brown gaze. He was staring at Lizzie. "She's always possessed the ability to make friends quickly," Rachel stated by way of explanation. Although wondering why her sister's popularity should cause Brodie displeasure, for she had received the distinct impression that he considered Lizzie nothing more than a child, she smiled warmly across at him and remarked, "I suppose you're well accustomed to these reunions of the MacBride clan by now."

"To tell the truth, I try my best to avoid them," he admitted a bit sheepishly as he finally tore his gaze away from the group beside the stream. "I usually arrange to be out at one of the line camps."

"I can't say that I blame you," she replied, the corners

of her mouth turning up into a quizzical little smile. Suddenly, Rachel's ears caught the sound of music, and she frowned slightly in bemusement.

"Colin and Jack have broken out their fiddles," Brodie supplied with a grin, "which means everyone will finally be stirring themselves to dance." Shooting one last narrow, speaking look at Lizzie and her youthful admirers, he gallantly offered Rachel his arm. "Would you care to have this dance, Rachel MacBride?"

"I'd love to, Brodie MacBride," she accepted with another soft laugh. She took his arm and strolled back around to the front of the house, where several couples had already "stirred themselves" and were promenading about in time to the fast-paced fiddle music.

Rachel and Brodie had done no more than take a turn about the area of the yard designated for such activity when Logan cut in. Brodie graciously agreed to relinquish his partner to her husband, leaving Rachel to be clasped possessively in Logan's arms as he maneuvered the steps of the reel with such skill and agility that she was quite duly impressed.

"Do you realize this is the first time the two of us have ever danced together?" she pointed out to him, her opalescent eyes sparkling and her face becomingly flushed by her efforts.

"Is it? Then we've a lot of wasted time to make up for, haven't we?" She was thoroughly captivated by the smile he bestowed upon her, and she soon forgot about all else but the sheer pleasure of being whirled round and round in his strong arms.

The dancing continued well into the warm summer evening, for most of the MacBrides had made plans to stay the night—many would sleep in their wagons, while others would either share quarters in the house or one of the barns.

Just as the sun's radiant glow began to give way to the shadows of the dusk, three riders unexpectedly approached the ranch, bringing with them news that proved unwelcome to some and a blessing in disguise for others—the vigilantes had organized and were planning to launch an attack on the rustlers at their newly discovered hideout.

"Where are they headed?" Logan questioned sharply. The three young cowpunchers, all of whom worked for Stuart MacBride, had gone into Miles City for their usual Saturday night revelry. While there, they had heard about the planned attack and had ridden like the devil to get home and tell their boss, who had in turn sent them on over to the Circle M to inform Logan.

"It's a place up in the badlands, called Bates Point," one of them eagerly answered. "From what we heard tell, there's a whole outfit of them bastards holin' up there." His eyes made a hasty sweep of the crowd gathering about him before he continued. "Yes sir, there's nigh on to forty or fifty of them thievin' varmints—"

"What the hell happened to finally set the vigilantes off?" demanded Colin. His wife stepped closer to him, and he put out an arm and drew her comfortingly against him.

"Mr. Latham got himself shot by one of the rustlers today." This startling bit of information came from the oldest of the trio. "He's alive, but I guess it was the last straw. Anyways, his men captured one of the gang who shot him. Seems the man told 'em everything they wanted to know before they hung him—told 'em about the hideout and how many head of cattle they got up there right now."

"And that ain't all!" the first puncher declared, his eyes alight with excitement. "Before they went and stretched his neck, he named the son of a bitch who's the boss man of the whole outfit." After pausing for effect, during which time he was satisfied that he had everyone's complete and undivided attention, the young man took a deep breath and steadily revealed, "It's Vance MacBride." His disclosure was followed by a highly charged silence.

"You're lying!" Colin finally snarled, his face contorted with fury as he took a menacing step forward. "Damn it, no MacBride would—"

"It wasn't me that said it, Mr. MacBride!" the visibly frightened cowboy, barely out of his teens, hastened to point out. "I . . . I'm just telling you what that rustler said!"

"It's the truth, Mr. MacBride," the third puncher finally spoke up, his voice scarcely audible above the increasing murmur of the crowd. Vance's name was on everyone's lips, and the face of every MacBride present displayed mingled shock and outrage. "The bastard they hung was one of Vance MacBride's men. I seen him in town with Mr. Vance just the other day." He looked to Logan, his eyes falling before the intensity of the other man's gaze. "I'm sorry, Mr. MacBride, but it's true."

"Then we've no time to waste," Logan tersely decreed. He faced the crowd, his deep voice ringing out in the cool evening air. "If a MacBride's involved, then we're all involved. And that means we'll have to do what we can to make sure justice is done." His gaze met Brodie's. "We'll try to reach Bates Point ahead of the vigilantes."

There was a great flurry of activity as the men bid their families good-bye and saddled their horses. Logan searched for Rachel about the yard, but she was nowhere to be found. Suddenly recalling that he had last seen her talking with Mrs. Smith at the foot of the porch steps, he hurried toward the house.

Micah, insistent upon riding out with the MacBrides in spite of his wife's pleas for him to remain, was taking his leave of Jane and Lizzie when he saw Logan striding their way.

"You looking for Rachel?" he asked the younger man. A frown of growing perplexity creased Logan's brow as he nodded wordlessly.

"I saw her going inside the house with that crabby housekeeper of yours a few minutes ago," supplied Lizzie. She ignored the sternly quelling glance Jane shot her. "I heard that Smith woman say something about needing Rachel's advice in the kitchen."

"Thanks, little sister," Logan murmured with a faint smile. He soon disappeared inside the house as well, anxious to see Rachel and hold her one last time before commencing with the night's distasteful—and dangerous—work.

Reaching the dining room, he pushed on the connecting door to the kitchen, only to find that it had been locked from the other side. He frowned in puzzlement at the discovery, but he wasted no time before striding back outside and around to the rear entrance. The nagging feeling that something was wrong increased tenfold when he saw that the kitchen's outer door was slightly ajar.

"Rachel!" he called out sharply as he burst inside the semidarkness of the kitchen. His eyes made a hasty search of the room, but there was no sign of Rachel. As he turned to leave, his steps were arrested by the sound of a low moan. His gaze was drawn downward when he heard another moan. There, on the floor beneath the table, lay the crumpled form of Cora Smith.

Muttering an oath, Logan fell to his knees and carefully eased the awakening housekeeper out from under the table. He raised her head and pillowed it with his arm, and he scowled fiercely at what the fading light revealed—a large, swollen bruise on the left side of her face.

"Cora! Cora, it's Logan!" He shook her with gentle insistence. "Cora, what happened? Where's Rachel?" Regaining consciousness at last, Mrs. Smith opened her eyes and met Logan's penetrating gaze.

"It . . . it was Mr. Vance. He and Miss Moira . . . they took her. They took your wife! I tried to stop them, but he . . . he hit me. As God is my witness, Mr. Logan, I tried to stop them!" she cried, the tears spilling forth at the awful memory of what had happened.

Logan, seized by a murderous rage at the news, mentally cursed himself a thousand times over for underestimating both Vance and Moira. *Dear God, not Rachel!* He'd kill them with his bare hands for this!

"Do you know where they're headed?" he asked Cora with deadly calm.

"I heard him tell Miss Moira they were going to join the others at the point, but I . . . I don't know what he meant by that."

"I do," Logan ground out, his green eyes filling with a savagely foreboding light.

Rachel winced involuntarily at the sharp pain. Vance

had fastened the gag about her mouth with cruel snugness, and his arm was now threatening to cut off her breath as he held her before him on the wildly galloping horse. Moira rode beside them, her rancorous gaze frequently straying to Rachel's pale, tear-streaked face. The encroaching darkness would soon chase the last of the shadows from the prairie, but Vance betrayed no concern for the dangers of nightfall. His golden, hawkish eyes were suffused with an almost maniacal glow, and Rachel blanched inwardly at the look of treacherous intent on his swarthy face.

Frantically wondering where her abductors were taking her, she thought of Logan again. Had he discovered her disappearance by now? Would he know where to search for her? Had Mrs. Smith been able to tell him anything at all?

Her thoughts returned to the terrifying incident which had taken place only a short time ago. Mrs. Smith had appeared outside and curtly informed Rachel that her assistance was required in the kitchen. When the younger woman had visibly hesitated, the housekeeper had declared with even more firmness that her advice was needed right away and would only take a moment.

Upon entering the kitchen, Rachel had been quite startled to discover that it was none other than Moira who had sent Cora Smith to lure her away from the festivities. The spiteful brunette's eyes had glittered with triumph as she locked the door . . .

"Moira! What are you doing here? We thought you'd—" began Rachel, only to be rudely cut off by the sound of Moira's scornful laughter.

"Why shouldn't I be here? After all, *I* am a true MacBride!" Her expression grew undeniably rancorous as she hissed, "Now we'll see who's to be mistress of the Circle M! I'm going to take my rightful place at Logan's side!" Rachel's eyes widened in confusion and alarm, but she had no time to offer a response before the outer door swung open to reveal Moira's partner—Vance MacBride. His hard, malignantly glinting gaze flickered over Rachel as she gasped loudly, but his words were for Moira.

"Come on, damn it! We've got to get out of here before someone else shows up!" Rachel opened her mouth to scream when he lunged for her, but it was too late. Clamping his hand brutally across the lower half of her face, Vance yanked her back against him. She struggled furiously, but he easily restrained her and instructed Moira to gag her. The brunette swiftly did as he ordered, but Vance was dissatisfied with the results and jerked the strip of cloth even tighter, bringing tears of pain to Rachel's eyes. She looked in silent desperation to Mrs. Smith, who now hastened to intervene.

"What are you doing that for, Mr. Vance?" When he did not answer her, Cora turned to his accomplice and demanded, "Miss Moira, what's going on? You told me all you wanted to do was talk to her and shake her up a bit. You never said anything about taking her away!"

"Oh, Cora, don't you see? This is the only way!" asserted Moira. She quickly stuffed some provisions into a bag and moved toward the doorway as Vance positioned a bound and gagged Rachel over his shoulder.

"I won't let you do this!" Mrs. Smith defiantly proclaimed. There was a wounded expression in her eyes as she appealed to Moira once more. "Don't betray my trust! You can't do this, Miss Moira, you just can't!"

"Shut up!" snarled Vance. Cora made the mistake of gripping his arm.

Rachel watched in horror as Vance spun about and struck the older woman in the face with sadistic force. The unconscious housekeeper fell heavily to the floor. There was a flash of pity in Moira's eyes, but it disappeared as Vance ordered her to hide the woman's body as best she could. Bending down, Moira employed all her strength to shove her former ally underneath the table, then rose to her feet again and followed Vance outside.

The music swelled to a crescendo as they crossed the stream and made their way unobserved up the hill behind the house. Mounting the horses they had left tied on the other side, they triumphantly rode off with their captive. It had been a bold and risky scheme, but it had worked . . .

It was impossible for Rachel to prevent the revolting contact with Vance's body as the animal beneath them thundered over the darkening plains. She soon lost all track of time—there was only the cool wind stinging against her face, only the mournful howl of the coyotes and the vast, moonlight-bathed wilderness. Her heart cried out for Logan as she slumped in exhaustion before her evil captor, and her mind repeated a desperate prayer for her beloved husband to find her.

Rachel knew nothing about their destination. Although vaguely familiar with the term "badlands," she was unaware of the fact that the area which bore the name was a lonely, unearthly realm—a magnificent, untamed country where isolated hills and cliffs rose unexpectedly from the canyon floor. Consisting of hundreds of thousands of almost completely uninhabited acres, the Mississippi River badlands had recently gained notoriety as a favorite hideout of the rustlers. There was certainly an abundance of places to hide, for thick groves of spruce, cedar, and scrub pine trees dotted the purple-shadowed coulees and the sudden rises in the land. Apart from those who were on the wrong side of the law, few white men ventured into this magnificent yet hostile wilderness.

The isolated camp of Bates Point, situated on the Missouri some fifteen miles east of the mouth of the Musselshell River, had been chosen by Vance MacBride as the headquarters for his own criminal activities. He and his men—nearly fifty in all—had encountered no significant resistance in driving the stolen cattle and horses toward the northwest once they left behind the environs of Miles City.

Rachel was afforded her first glimpse of the hideout camp later that same night. Illuminated by the moon's silvery glow and several torches burning outside, Bates Point consisted of nothing more than one single-story cabin, a large log barn, a pole corral connecting the cabin and the barn, a couple of ramshackle outhouses, and—approximately a hundred yards from the cabin—a wall tent constructed of poles and tarpaulins.

There seemed to be men and horses everywhere, and Rachel was almost certain she had seen some of the men before. When Vance dismounted in front of the cabin and roughly pulled her down, her eyes fell on another rider who was drawing his mount to a halt nearby, and she gasped inwardly. The horse, a beautiful Appaloosa stallion with distinctive black markings on his left hindquarters, was without a doubt the same one she had watched being halter-broken in the corral the day of the prairie fire. He had been among those stolen while she and Logan were at the reservation.

"Go on!" Vance ground out, giving her a hard push toward the cabin. The other men who were gathered about in the torchlight, their gazes full of either curiosity or lust, or even what appeared to be pity, made no move to help her. Although her legs threatened to buckle beneath her, Rachel walked the short distance to the cabin, her head at a proudly defiant angle in spite of the fact that her hands were still bound before her and a dirty strip of cloth was still tied across her mouth. Vance impatiently shoved her through the open doorway, then stepped inside after her and slammed the door behind them.

"Come now, cousin," Moira admonished sarcastically, "such rough treatment for the wife of the most powerful rancher in the county?" She stood near the blackened stone fireplace, her malevolently smiling features silhouetted against the roaring blaze. Vance forcefully propelled his captive across the dirty, foul-smelling room and into a chair near the fire. Chortling banefully, he leered down at Rachel and proclaimed, "Logan won't act so powerful once he finds out we've got his little whore! The almighty leader of the MacBrides is finally going to topple from his self-erected throne!"

Rachel's widened eyes flew upward to his face. So that was the reason he had abducted her! She was to serve as the means of revenge against Logan, not Micah. But why? What was there between the two MacBride cousins that had driven Vance to take such drastic measures?

"Damn it, Vance, you promised not to hurt Logan!" Moira angrily reminded him. Stalking forward, she seized his arm and forced him about to face her. "Our agreement was that you would take the money and leave him be!"

"Why should I?" Vance countered with disturbing nonchalance. His eyes gleamed with sinister amusement as a slow, meaningful smile spread across his swarthy countenance. "Did you honestly believe I'd be satisfied with money alone?"

"Wha . . . what are you saying?"

"Only that things aren't going to turn out quite as you'd planned. You see, *partner,* I'm going to be master of the Circle M before I'm through, and your beloved Logan is going to be dead."

A muffled scream of protest sounded low in Rachel's throat as her eyes filled with terror. *Logan!* Leaping to her feet, she raced frantically toward the doorway, so desperate to prevent Logan's death that she gave little thought to her own safety. Vance easily caught her, and he yanked her back against him as he gave a cruel laugh and murmured close to her ear, "You'll be a widow before dawn, *Mrs. MacBride.* I've already sent a message to that husband of yours. He thinks he'll be riding to save you, but he'll be riding to his own death!" Screaming beneath her gag once more, Rachel struggled violently in his brutal grip. Vance laughed again before he spun her about and brought the back of his hand crashing against the unprotected smoothness of her cheek. Reeling beneath the blow, she was only half conscious as she fell to the hard wooden floor.

"You said you were going to hold her for ransom! You said you'd take her away with you once Logan paid you the money!" cried Moira, sparing only a brief, merciless glance down at the other woman. Her face displayed a sort of horrified disbelief as realization began to sink in. Vance shot her a look of pure contempt.

"You're as much of an idiot as ever, Moira.

Remember—*you* came to *me.* I don't give a damn about all your plans! Once Logan signs over control of the Circle M to me, he's going to get what's coming to him!" He strode to the fireplace and stared deeply into the flames, the light of the fire mingling with the feral glow in his strange golden eyes. "I've waited a long time for this. I've endured years of scorn from the other MacBrides, from everyone in the county, and all because of Logan! He and Dugan—that heartless old bastard—they turned my own father against me. They took in that worthless half-breed, they chose him over me! Nothing was the same after that—nothing!" His gaze hardened when he recalled how his mother, betrayed and full of shame, had fled back East to her family and died soon thereafter. His father had shown no remorse. Declaring that she had never loved him and made his life a misery, he had paid less and less attention to their only son . . .

"That wasn't Logan's fault!" Moira adamantly disagreed. She moved to his side, her hands clutching at his arm. "Blame Dugan if you must, but not Logan!" Jerking his arm away, Vance snarled with an accusing glare down at her, "You always took his side, didn't you? Even when you begged me to marry you, I knew it was really Logan you wanted! But it doesn't matter now. After tonight, there won't be any more Logan MacBride!"

"No, damn you, no!" Moira shrieked in growing hysteria.

"It will give me a great deal of pleasure to see you beg again—only this time, it will be for your life!" he ground out, his hands closing painfully upon her arms. Moira cried out sharply before his mouth descended upon hers with punishing force. She tasted her own blood when he finally released her, and she stumbled weakly back against the stone fireplace as he turned his attention back to his captive.

Rachel was just staggering to her feet when Vance rounded on her again. Clamping an arm about her waist, he dragged her back to the chair and flung her down into it. The pain in her head was almost blinding, but her mind still worked feverishly to try and think of a way to escape and warn Logan before it was too late. Although the situation appeared hopeless, she refused to give up. *Dear God, please! There had to be a way!*

"No doubt you're wondering about your own future," sneered Vance. A malignantly taunting look played across his face while his hawkish eyes raked over her with deliberate unhaste. "Once Logan is dead and the Circle M is mine, I intend to finish what should never have been interrupted—Micah Parker's going to swing at the end of a rope, while you're going to find out what it means to be truly 'humbled' by Vance MacBride!" One of his hands shot out to delve into the tangled thickness of her golden hair, while the other closed ruthlessly about the fullness of her silk-covered breast.

Her eyes flew wide in mingled shock and disgust, and she instinctively brought her hands—bound tightly together with rope—slashing upward in an attempt to protect her body from such loathsome violation. Chuckling in fiendish enjoyment of her defiance, Vance took advantage of her defensive action. He seized the rope binding her wrists and yanked backward, forcing another scream to well up deep in Rachel's throat as he sent her sprawling onto the floor again. Vance straddled her before she could get up.

"You need to be taught a lesson, honey!" he said with another derisive laugh. Rachel sent a silent, desperate plea for help in Moira's direction, then kicked and twisted in growing panic when she felt Vance tugging up her skirt and petticoat.

Moira, telling herself that now was her chance to save Logan, flew across the room and snatched one of Vance's six-shooters from the holster fastened low upon his hips. Although her hands were shaking uncontrollably, she managed to cock the gun and aim it at her cousin's dark head before he jerked about to face her.

"What the—" he muttered, forgetting all about Rachel as he rose abruptly to his feet and glowered murderously across at Moira. "Put that down, damn it!"

"I'm sorry, Vance, but I can't let you do it! I can't let you kill Logan! You were right—even when I tried to make you marry me, Logan was the one I really wanted. And I mean to have him!"

"Shoot me, you stupid bitch, and my men will tear you to pieces!" he warned. He edged closer to her. "Put the gun down, Moira! Put it down and—"

"No!"

Rachel watched in breathless anticipation as Moira, her finger trembling upon the trigger, pointed the barrel of the pearl-handled gun at Vance's chest. The brunette's pale green eyes narrowed imperceptibly as she began squeezing the trigger . . .

Suddenly, gunfire erupted outside. Men's voice rang out in the night air, their shouts and curses followed by more shots.

Moira, taken off guard by the commotion, wavered in her intent for only a brief instant, but it was time enough for Vance to hurl himself forward and wrest the pistol from her grasp. She screamed for mercy as he turned the gun on her, but he did not hesitate before pulling the trigger. Her lifeless form collapsed into the dust caking the splintered wooden floor.

Horrified by what she had just seen, Rachel choked back a sob and averted her gaze from the ghastly sight of Moira's body. One of Vance's men burst inside the cabin at that point, his coarse young features betraying his fear.

"Hell, Vance, we're under attack! There must be more than a hundred of them firing on us! Men are dropping like flies out there!" Giving no evidence of his own fear, Vance swore and directed, "Get back outside! Tell the men to hold their positions and return the fire!"

"But, Vance, there's too many—"

"Do as I say, damn it!"

The frightened young rustler wheeled about to follow Vance's orders—or at least half of them. He'd get back outside all right, but he'd be damned if he'd hang around for any longer than it took to find himself a horse and ride hellbent for leather away from there! A great many other members of the band had also chosen flight over an honorable death, so that the camp was a mass of noise and confusion as the gunfire continued to split the air with terrifying regularity.

A bullet smashed through one of the front windows just as Vance seized Rachel's arm and yanked her upright. She held back, but he dragged her forcibly across the room to the rear door of the cabin. When she still resisted, he brought his fist smashing up against her chin, thereby rendering her unconscious. He hoisted her to his shoulder, then fled with his burden across the moonlit grounds of the hideout camp to where a string of horses was staked near the tent.

Bullets whizzed all about them, while the screams and

moans of the wounded on both sides of the rapidly intensifying confrontation filled the air. Vance spared no compassion for the fallen as he quickly flung Rachel on the back of a horse and mounted up behind her. Jerking cruelly on the animal's reins, he rode away from the battle raging at Bates Point. And when he realized that no one was giving chase, he smiled to himself in malevolent satisfaction. All was not yet lost.

XX

Logan's heart twisted in alarm as he heard the sound of distant gunfire. *Rachel!* Cursing the fact that he and the other MacBrides had apparently arrived too late to prevent the vigilantes from launching their attack, he raised his arm in a silent command for the riders behind him, then thundered headlong toward the camp which lay just beyond the next hill. He thought of the danger Rachel was in at that very moment—in the midst of the gun battle, she could easily get hit—and his handsome, sun-bronzed features hardened into a mask of savage fury. Vance would pay with his life for what he had done, Logan vowed to himself, his narrowed eyes glowing like two fiery-hued emeralds.

The assault upon the hideout—successful because the vigilantes had been able to take the thieves by surprise—was already drawing to a close by the time the MacBrides rode into Bates Point to confront the men who had chosen to take the law into their own hands. Most of the rustlers were either dead or wounded. Several had made a desperate bid for freedom by concealing themselves in the shadowed coulees, and a few had even managed to escape downriver, only to be caught and hanged by the same revenge-hungry men whose stock they had been pilfering for months.

With a single-minded purposefulness that made him oblivious to the danger such action posed, Logan charged straightaway into the middle of the camp. There were still shots being fired from all directions, but he was like a man possessed, his only thought to save Rachel. Following his instincts, he flung himself off Vulcan's back and burst inside the bullet-ridden cabin. His smoldering gaze was met by the sight of Moira lying on the floor near the fireplace. The bullet from Vance's gun had entered her body just above her left breast, sending a dark red stain spreading across the bodice of her yellow gown.

"Moira!" He was beside her in an instant, dropping to one knee and slipping an arm beneath her shoulders. Miraculously, she was still alive. "Moira! Moira, it's Logan!" He gave a silent prayer of thanksgiving—for more than one reason—when her eyelids fluttered open.

"Logan?" she murmured weakly, her gaze focusing with noticeable difficulty on the familiar face bending over hers. "Oh, Logan, Vance—" She broke off as a paroxysm of almost unbearable pain seized her. Gasping for breath, she clutched at her chest, her eyes clouding with shocked disbelief when she abruptly drew her hand away and saw that it was covered with blood. "He . . . he shot me! Dear God, Logan, I was only trying to save *you!* He was going to kill you! I couldn't let him, I couldn't—"

"Moira, where is Rachel? Where did Vance take her?" demanded Logan. Although he suffered more than a twinge of pity for the gravely injured woman in his arms, his compassion for Moira was nothing compared with his love for Rachel. She meant more than life itself to him, and the only thing that mattered to him at the moment was finding her. "Please, Moira, tell me where he took her!" Another spasm of pain crossed her face, but it was more from the final realization that she would never have Logan's love . . .

"To Lewistown, I think." Her voice was scarcely above a whisper, and she drew a deep, ragged breath before revealing, "Vance said if anything went wrong with . . . with our plans, he'd go to Lewistown and make contact with a man there who bought most of the horses . . ."

"Where can I find him?"

"At the . . . the Gold King Saloon. The man owns the place," she finished. A sudden, violent tremor gripped her pain-ravaged body, and her fingers tightened convulsively upon Logan's arm.

"Dear God, Logan, wha—" exclaimed Brodie as he stood framed in the cabin doorway. Micah impatiently shouldered him out of the way. His slate gray eyes reflected little emotion as he swiftly moved to where Logan still knelt beside Moira.

"Where's my granddaughter?"

"Vance took her to Lewistown. I'm on my way there now," disclosed Logan, his features tightening as he carefully lowered Moira back to the floor. "Brodie, see to her," he tersely ordered, then stood and began striding outside.

"No." Shaking his head, Brodie continued to block the doorway. His uncharacteristic defiance provoked a sudden narrowing of his older cousin's green eyes. "I'm coming with you." For a moment, it seemed as if Logan would repeat the command, but he finally nodded curtly and stepped outside into the cool, torchlit air. Micah was close behind, and it was obvious that he intended to ride with them to Lewistown. Colin and a few of the other MacBrides were just drawing to a halt before the cabin, and Logan paused only to announce his destination and to charge Colin with Moira's care before swinging up into the saddle and urging Vulcan away from the camp. Brodie and Micah spurred their own mounts to keep pace.

Lewistown, situated in the exact center of the territory amidst beautiful, green-carpeted hills and valleys, was a burgeoning cowtown in its own right. Replete with a hotel, a blacksmith shop, and an impressive array of saloons, it was a popular place for many a lonely young puncher—and, unfortunately, for men like Vance MacBride.

Although it was well past midnight, the revelry filling the Gold King Saloon was just reaching its peak. Men crowded about the poker and roulette tables, and along the high, polished wooden bar spanning most of one wall. The saloon girls, their painted faces wearing smiles that never quite reached their eyes, flirted with the patrons who bought them drinks and spoke wistfully of home. Boisterous laughter, a heavy fog of smoke, and the pungent odor that was a combination of whiskey and sweat permeated the room. A large, gilt-edged mirror hanging behind the bar reflected the almost frenetic bustle inside the frontier saloon, while the dust-caked chandeliers hanging above cast a somewhat unearthly glow upon the entire proceedings.

Logan, Micah, and Brodie drew their weary mounts to a halt and swung down from their saddles. Silently motioning the other two to stay put, Logan moved stealthily to the swinging half-doors of the Gold King. His wary gaze quickly scanned the crowd for any sign of Vance before he turned back to Micah and Brodie.

"He may be in Webster's office, in which case Rachel is either in there with him or in one of the rooms upstairs," he told them in an undertone. He was familiar with Zach Webster and with the Gold King Saloon, for he'd had a run-in with the man there some months back. He was still convinced Webster had cheated one of the younger MacBrides.

"Is there a back stairway?" asked Micah, already drawing his gun. Logan nodded.

"If you find Rachel, get her away from here as fast as you can." Without another word, Micah disappeared around the corner of the saloon. Logan then told Brodie, "I'll head back to the roulette table. Webster's office is just under the stairs. You come in after me and guard the front." Their eyes met, and a look of silent understanding passed between them. "He's gone too far this time, Brodie," Logan grimly decreed.

"I know." Brodie's youthful countenance displayed a certain resignation for what was to come. Logan briefly lifted a hand to his cousin's shoulder, then strode through the swinging doors of the saloon with deceptive nonchalance.

Rachel strained feverishly against the ropes which bound her to the iron bedstead. Her mouth was bruised and aching from the gag, and she was beginning to feel increasingly light-headed from the lack of food and water. But she gave little thought to her discomfort at the moment, her attention focused solely on escape. Vance would soon be returning to the darkened room where he had left her, and she knew that her only hope lay in working her hands free of their bonds.

Hot tears started to her eyes as yet another image of Logan's beloved face drifted across her mind with taunting clarity. Where was he now? she wondered as a sob welled up in her throat. *Dear God, please keep him safe! And please, Lord, please let him find me!*

Suddenly, Rachel heard what sounded like someone slowly turning the doorknob. Believing it to be Vance, she caught her breath and fought against the rising tide of panic which threatened to overwhelm her.

A widening shaft of light fell across the bed and illuminated Rachel's beautiful, terror-stricken face as the door, its hinges creaking softly, was eased open by a man holding a gun in defensive readiness. His dark form was finally outlined in the doorway, and it took only an instant longer for Rachel's shining eyes, well accustomed to the darkness by this time, to fill with recognition.

"Rachel!" Her name was a hoarse whisper on Micah's lips as he hastily closed the door behind him and flew to her side. He quickly lit the lamp beside the bed, then withdrew a knife from his belt to cut the gag and the ropes binding her. Nearly fainting with relief, Rachel clung weakly to her grandfather as his arms tightened about her for a brief moment.

"Oh, Micah! I . . . I thought it was Vance! He said he was going downstairs and would be back—"

"Logan and Brodie are down there now," he quietly informed her, giving silent thanks for the fact that she was alive and unharmed. Rachel's eyes clouded with renewed horror as she abruptly pulled away from him.

"Vance will kill them! Dear God, Micah, we've got to stop him!" Sliding from the bed, she would have collapsed if not for the timely support of Micah's arms. He pushed her firmly back upon the mattress.

"You're going to stay here." Pressing his gun into her hand, he commanded in a low tone, "Don't hesitate to use this if the need arises. I'll be back for you soon." He moved swiftly toward the door again, prompting Rachel to anxiously demand, "What are you going to do?"

"I figure that husband of yours can use a little help." After pausing to send her a faint, bolstering smile, he was gone. Rachel perched on the edge of the bed in breathless anticipation, her fingers tightening about the pearl handle of Micah's revolver as her wide, opalescent gaze fastened unwaveringly upon the door. Mentally repeating the same heartfelt prayer over and over again—that the lives of Logan, Micah, and Brodie would be spared—she leaned over and blew out the lamp.

Logan's smoldering green gaze shifted to the door beneath the stairs as it was suddenly flung open. Every muscle in his tall frame imperceptibly tensed when he caught sight of Vance moving out into the main room. Zach Webster, a rather short, flaxen-haired man of middle age, chewed leisurely on his cigar as he walked beside his frequent business associate. He and Vance had just completed yet another transaction, but he was unaware of the fact that he had been deceived into offering payment for horses which would never be delivered—which were, in fact, now in the custody of the ranchers who had launched the successful attack upon the camp at Bates Point.

"You've turned out to be one hell of a deal-maker, MacBride," Zach Webster remarked with a begrudgingly appreciative chuckle as he and Vance reached the foot of the staircase.

"Maybe that's because I was lucky enough to find a man who didn't—" Vance's mocking reply was cut short when his strange golden eyes fell on the fury-hardened visage of Logan, who stood a few feet away in the midst of the crowded room with his gun aimed directly at Vance's cowardly heart.

"Hold it right there!" Logan ground out, his gaze suffused with the most intense rage he had ever experienced.

A slightly inebriated woman, unaware of what was happening in the noisy, smoke-filled saloon, chose that inopportune moment to cast herself gleefully upon Vance's chest. A cry of startlement broke from her lips as she suddenly found herself seized in Vance's cruel grip and jerked around to shield his body.

"Drop your gun or I'll blow her head off!" he threatened, pressing the barrel of his own gun against the poor woman's temple. Paralyzed with fear, she neither struggled nor screamed, but her bloodshot eyes flew in desperate, mute appeal to Logan's face.

"What have you done with Rachel?" Logan demanded, his gun still trained on the other man. Zach Webster stood stock-still a short distance away, his ruthless features wearing only the ghost of a contemptuous smile as he declined to help Vance. Most of the men inside the saloon were oblivious to the confrontation, while those who did notice it wisely refrained from intervening. Such occurrences were commonplace in Lewistown, so why get themselves shot trying to help someone who in all likelihood deserved killing?

"She's upstairs, patiently awaiting my 'attentions'!" sneered Vance. "Now drop your gun!" he reiterated, his swarthy features growing particularly ugly as he jammed the gun even closer against his captive's trembling head.

Logan, praying that Micah had found Rachel and was now spiriting her away, hesitated only an instant longer before beginning to lower his gun. By no means willing to admit defeat, he was mentally weighing his chances. He knew there would be a split-second when Vance was off his guard, and it was then that he would make his move. Catching sight of Brodie out of the corner of his eye, he allowed his gun to slip to the dust-caked floor.

"If I can't have the Circle M, I'll at least have the revenge I've waited so long for!" Vance triumphantly snarled. "You and old Dugan always considered yourselves a notch above me, didn't you? You treated me like scum, while you treated that half-breed cur like a true MacBride!"

"Brodie *is* a MacBride," Logan insisted in a low, level tone, his penetrating gaze never leaving Vance's face. "Like it or not, he's your brother. Your father's blood runs through his veins." He could see the way Brodie was cautiously making his way toward them, concealing himself in the crowd while edging closer.

"He's no brother of mine, damn you!"

"None of that matters now, Vance. You know you'll never get away with this. Why don't you let the girl go and—"

"No!" A smile of pure malevolence spread across Vance's hawkish features, and his dark eyes glowed with a murderous light. "I've finally got you right where I want you, *cousin,* and I'm going to make you pay!"

"You'll never get the Circle M if you kill me," Logan calmly pointed out.

"Maybe not, but I'll have the satisfaction of knowing you're dead, and I'll have *your wife!"* With that, he aimed the six-shooter at Logan, his finger twitching on the trigger. "Say your prayers, *cousin!"* His golden eyes narrowed as he smiled again and prepared to kill the man he held largely responsible for his unhappy lot in life.

"That's it, MacBride!" a voice rang out from the landing above just as Brodie broke free from the crowd. Logan's eyes traveled hastily upward to where Rachel's grandfather stood at the top of the stairs. "Put down your gun, Vance," Micah instructed in a gruff, authoritative tone.

Vance MacBride's hate-filled gaze was irresistibly drawn to the young, raven-haired man who looked so much like their father. Mere inches of space separated the half brothers, and it seemed for a moment as if time stood still. Then, Vance's lips curled into another sneer as he made his choice.

He shoved the saloon girl away and spun about to fire at Micah. With lightning-quick speed, Logan bent and retrieved his gun. Brodie had just instinctively raised his own weapon when the sharp, echoing report of a gunshot split the smoke-fogged air of the saloon.

Several of the women screamed as Vance toppled over, his darkly attractive features frozen in death. Rachel, no longer able to wait patiently in the room when she heard the shot, flew across the landing to her grandfather's side. Micah's gun was still smoking as he holstered it. Slipping an arm about Rachel's shoulders, the grim-faced old lawman led her down the stairs.

"Logan!" He caught her up against him before she reached the bottom step, his strong arms holding her as if he would never let her go. She wept tears of relief and joy, burying her face against the familiar, cherished security of his hard chest.

"Rachel, Rachel!" murmured Logan, his deep voice raw with emotion. "Oh my love, I was afraid I'd lost you forever!"

"And I . . . I was afraid Vance would kill you!" she confessed with an involuntary shudder as her gaze fell on the man lying at the foot of the staircase. Brodie knelt beside Vance's body, his youthful countenance betraying only a hint of his inner turmoil as he gazed upon the brother who had unfairly blamed him for the loss of their father's love.

"It's over with," Logan reassured his wife. Lifting her in his arms, he pressed a tender kiss to her bruised lips. "And God help any man who ever tries to part us again," he vowed in a low, vibrant tone, his sea-green eyes aglow with a fierce light. Rachel leaned her head upon his broad shoulder, her long, honey-colored tresses spilling about them both as he carried her from the saloon and into the welcoming coolness of the moonlit night.

EPILOGUE

Brodie MacBride and Elizabeth Parker joined hands beneath a clear, brilliantly blue Montana sky and repeated the vows which would forever unite them in marriage. Rachel stood proudly beside her sister, while Logan appeared more ruggedly handsome than ever as he performed the duties of best man for Brodie. The ceremony taking place on the front steps of the house at the Circle M was well attended by the MacBrides. The yard was brimming with kinfolk of all ages, just as it had been nearly three years earlier during the celebration for Rachel and Logan.

Rachel's luminous gaze swept across the faces of those gathered for the happy occasion, and she heaved an inward sigh. The familiarity of the assembly prompted her thoughts to drift back over the events of the past three years . . .

The assault of the vigilantes upon the rustlers at Bates Point brought far-reaching repercussions. Not only were their actions for the most part condemned by the general public, but it became more difficult than ever for the

Cattlemen's Association to get important legislation passed. None of the vigilantes were prosecuted, but the majority of them bore a sense of shame the rest of their lives for their part in the slaughter. Many of the rustlers had been less than twenty years of age.

Moira's recovery was long and painful. Although her character had not undergone a complete transformation, she did express remorse for her part in Vance's treachery. Joseph welcomed his daughter back and lovingly cared for her. Once she was well enough to travel, he took Moira to live with her mother's family back East. Surprisingly, Joseph remained there with her.

Brodie grieved for the brother he had never really known. As the only other child of their father, he inherited Vance's ranch, but he chose to continue working for Logan until nearly a year following Vance's death. Lizzie was a frequent visitor to the Circle M during that time.

Uncle Robert and Aunt Tess were married less than a month after Logan brought Rachel home from Lewistown. Robert, declaring that he could no longer return to his "sedate" life in the East, became a successful attorney in Miles City. Tess, after spending most of her life out on the range, was now perfectly content to live in the city that was becoming more civilized with each passing year.

Because of the winter of 1886–1887, cattle ranching in Montana would never be the same. Known as the "Great Die-Up," the winter had followed a severe drought and brought with it relentless blizzards and unusually bitter cold. Thousands of cattle died, and many ranchers plowed what little money they had left into sheep and horses. Other far-sighted ranchers forsook the open range and actually purchased the land, then set about fencing it. The MacBrides, who had certainly not been exempt from the hard times, chose to do just that. Vast numbers of their own stock had perished, but they were determined to return the MacBride spread to its former prosperity. The challenge was something Logan and the others relished—their fathers had carved a cattle empire from the wilderness, and now the second generation would begin anew . . .

Rachel's thoughts were drawn back to the present when she heard the justice of the peace, Sam Lexington, pronouncing the young couple husband and wife. Tears sprang to her eyes, and she smiled tremulously as she watched Brodie take Lizzie—who had blossomed into almost as much of a beauty as her sister—in his arms and bestow upon her the traditional kiss. Her shining gaze traveled upward to meet Logan's, and her heart did a sudden flip-flop when she saw the love reflected in his gleaming, sea-green orbs. The child growing within her stirred as if to offer its blessings, prompting her to raise a hand to the gentle swell of her belly and cast Logan a look of such tenderness that he was forced to swallow a lump in his own throat.

At the height of the merrymaking following the ceremony, Logan seized Rachel's hand and pulled her insistently away from where she was talking with her grandparents.

"I'm borrowing my wife for a few minutes," he proclaimed with a disarming grin.

"I guess that's your right," drawled Micah, an answering twinkle in his gray eyes. "I just hope you and Brodie don't plan to return them to me on a permanent basis, seeing as how I intend to enjoy the peace and quiet after all these years of being surrounded by females."

"Micah Parker, you know as well as I do that you wouldn't have traded these past ten years for anything!" retorted Jane, giving her husband a playful slap on the arm. Micah chuckled softly as Logan led Rachel away.

"Where are we going?" she laughingly queried, then sobered at a sudden recollection. "Oh, Logan, I told Cora I'd be inside at six to feed the baby his supper and put him to bed!"

"Dugan is two years old and no longer a baby, and Cora will be glad to perform the honors herself. I think she spoils the little scamp even more than she did me when I was his age," he remarked with an endearingly crooked grin.

Rachel cast an apologetic smile at Stuart, Eva, and Little Rachel as Logan hurried her past them on the way to the barn. A smaller corral had recently been constructed on the far side of the building, and it was filled with a dozen calves who all started bawling loudly when they caught sight of the approaching humans.

"You wanted to show me these?" Rachel asked in mild bemusement, eyeing the sturdy little creatures dubiously. The fragrance of the summer wildflowers scented the warm afternoon breeze which tugged at her upswept, honey-colored tresses and sent the full skirts of her blue silk gown sailing up about her trim ankles.

"Look at the brand," instructed Logan. His handsome, sun-bronzed features remained impassive, but his eyes were alight with loving mischief. A slight frown creased Rachel's silken brow as she leaned over to peer through the log railings. Her eyes grew very round when they fastened on the mark burned in one of the animals' tough hide.

There, nestled below the familiar "Circle M," was a tiny four-leafed clover.

"Logan!" breathed Rachel, blushing fierily as she straightened and whirled to face him. He was grinning unrepentantly.

"You can imagine all the explaining I had to do when the word got out that I'd changed the brand."

"And just exactly what sort of explanation did you offer?" she demanded with wifely severity, the rosiness tinging her beautiful face deepening with embarrassment at the thought of everyone knowing such intimate details about her person.

"I merely said that the clover was my lucky charm—and my wife's as well." She did not protest when his strong arms came about her and pulled her close. "Someday, when our children are older, we'll have to tell them the truth," he declared with another roguish grin. His gaze was already darkening with the fierce desire she always aroused in him, and Rachel caught her breath at the familiar weakness stealing over her.

"Not all of it," she insisted, a secretive little smile playing about her lips as her luminous, opalescent eyes issued an unmistakable invitation to passion.

"Not all of it," Logan murmured in perfect accord, his arms tightening about Rachel's pliant softness with the same typically masterful intensity he had displayed toward her from the very beginning. Her last coherent thought, before their lips met in a kiss of rapturous enchantment that transported them to a special world all their own, was that she would always be glad a certain tall, green-eyed rogue had possessed the audacity to intrude upon her bath and refuse to leave . . .